HOBO-ING AMERICA

By

RICHARD EDWARD NOBLE

Copyright (c) 2008 by Richard Edward Noble

All rights reserved. No part of this book may be reproduced in any form or by any electronic or mechanical means, including information storage or retrieval systems without permission from the publisher.

Revised Edition

ISBN 978-0-9798085-1-7

Published in the United States of America by Noble Publishing, 889 C. C. Land Rd., Eastpoint, Fl. 32328.

All characters in this book are based on real people, some characters are composites, and are not meant to represent any actual person living or dead.

Cover and layout designed by Carol Noble

Table of Contents

Introduction 5

Chapter 1: Topping Onions in Southern California 7

Chapter 2: Gravenstein Apples in Sebastopol 22

Chapter 3: Peaches in Mena, Arkansas 29

Chapter 4: The Chicken Factory 38

Chapter 5: Oranges in Altoona 49

Chapter 6: Peaches in Michigan 63

Chapter 7: Michigan Apples 74

Chapter 8: The Teachuum Farm 90

Chapter 9: The Orange Grove Strike 98

Chapter 10: Foster and the Padidiot 105

Chapter 11: Bill and His Dog, Larry 110

Chapter 12: Orange Juice in Umatilla 119

Chapter 13: The Carrot Factory 132

Chapter 14: Cherries and The Old Mission 147

Chapter 15: Celery Packing 162

Chapter 16: Canada, Fishing 166

Chapter 17: Butchering Meat, in Miami 177

Chapter 18: Back to the Land, in Arkansas 192

Chapter 19: Oysters in the Florida Panhandle 213

Chapter 20: Troubles in Paradise 227

Chapter 21: Oyster Farming 237

Chapter 22: Restaurant Work 244

Chapter 23: Hobo's Ice Cream Parlor 255

Introduction

What is the big deal about seeing the U.S.A. anyway? Ten million Americans go off to see the U.S. every day. How many trite descriptions of the Grand Canyon does one need in his library? Well, to put it mildly, I think that seeing America clinging to the elbow of Carol and Dick, will be an awakening for most Americans no matter how many times they have toured the U.S.A.

If you toured America by way of Ramada Inns across the country, you would undoubtedly consider the U.S. to be a country full of well dressed salesmen. If you went by way of McDonald's franchises you would, more than likely, consider acne to be a major medical epidemic in the States. If you drove one of those big trucks, America will be an interstate highway, gas stations, bathrooms, and a never ending chain of sleepy eyes, cigarettes, blue jeans, giant belt buckles, and little girls knocking on your sleeper window saying ... Can you spare fifty dollars for a cup of coffee, Sir?

If you toured with Charles Kuralt, a fine adventure indeed, you will nevertheless see America as a country full of semi-retired, middle-aged folks or better, all of whom can knit, sew, weave on a handloom, whittle a Louisville Slugger from an old scrub oak tree, or construct a Stradivarius in their barn using nothing but popsicle sticks and a rusty, old, double-edged razorblade.

Come along with Carol and Dick and live in the places where Charles Kuralt was afraid to park his bus ... even for an overnight stay. Meet, and tour the homes of the ninety-eight percent of America that will not be televised on the lives of the rich and famous. Come with us and grovel in the dust, dirt, and sweat ... feel the pain, joy and anger. Shake the calloused hands that make America what it is. We'll tip it all upside-down and see America bottom side up.

Stay with us in the fields, groves, orchards, under equipment shelters and county bridges. Meet the homeless, the helpless, the bent over, the rich, the poor and the ugly.

See America in its glory and its shame. See it from the highways, the sidewalks, and the gutters.

Meet Asians, Indians, Jamaicans, Haitians, Mexicans. Meet most of them in one chicken factory in central Arkansas on the third shift.

Find out the answer to the question that has plagued most of America for three decades ... Why don't tomatoes taste like they did when I was a kid? ... At the same time, find out why you can jump up and down on the top of a bag of peaches and barely bruise the skin.

Find out why you can hardly tell the difference between an apple and a banana if you eat them both with your eyes closed.

Learn the author's, not yet famous and soon to be forgotten, apple theory of value.

Find out why it makes no difference whether you eat a tree ripened sweet cherry, or a chocolate bar.

Find out why you should eat up the box and throw the corn flakes away.

Find the answer to all of these burning questions and many, many more. See America from the bottom of the cracker-barrel. Come along with Carol and Dick. Talk to the "Crackers", and fill the barrels. See our America.

I don't know if following Dick and Carol up the furrows and down the assembly lines of this land will change your lives as it has changed ours, but I can guarantee that you will see America as you have never seen it before.

1 Topping Onions in Southern California

Our first job was in Santa Rosa, California. He called it topping onions - he, being the man at the Farm Labor Bureau. Believe it or not, nearly every government employment office in the country has a Farm Labor Bureau or Department. He got quite a kick out of us. Obviously two middle-class, white Americans who were going to find out, for the first time in their lazy, privileged lives what real work was all about. He was actually laughing by the time we left his office.

"Here's two people," he announced to the room full of desk personnel surrounding him, "who are going to show the folks how to top onions."

I suppose that he had good reason to be amused. I guess that we were asking a lot of non-migrant type questions. How much does one make an hour topping onions seemed like a reasonable enough question to me.

"Well, that depends on you." He hesitated and then by way of explanation added. "The pay is according to how much you do; it's piece work."

"Well how much on the average does a person earn doing this type of work?" He smiled, leaned back in his swivel chair and laughed. "Well, can a person make a living topping onions?" I said, regrouping.

"Lots of people do," he said matter-of-factly.

"Do you know any people who perform this type work?"

"Sure, plenty."

"Well okay," I said. He paused, still smiling, and staring at me curiously.

"Ah, okay what?" he questioned.

"Okay, how do we get the job?"

He started laughing again. It didn't seem that he was laughing at us. It was more like he was amused by my face or maybe by the way I was answering his questions. In any case, we laughed with him. Then seeing that we were quite serious he started scrambling around his desk.

"Now let me just fill out a couple of these cards and you'll have these, ah ... jobs." He said the word "job" as if he had never heard it applied to this type work before. He laughed a little more as he busied himself with his clerical work.

Moments later we were off in our van with our hand drawn map to the onion field. When we arrived, we parked under an equipment shelter. We were really eager to go to work. We weren't exactly in the position of Richard Henry Dana Jr. and his historical, *Two Years before the Mast*. Neither Carol nor I would be returning to our studies at Harvard or Yale. We were working folk. All of the pennies that were in our savings account or pockets were the product of many anxious moments struggling with the minute hand of a punch clock or boiling chicken necks and gizzards as opposed to slicing T-bones and fillet mignon. But, by our way of thinking, we had found the perfect way to make a living while on the road. Carol and I could both work together and at the same job. We didn't have to lie to anybody about living in our van or how long we intended to stay in the area. We weren't forced to get an apartment or a telephone, or pay electric bills, or shell out money for security deposits. All that we had to do was find out where and what they were harvesting and go there.

If, by chance, you don't know what an onion field looks like, I'll try to explain.

One, there are no shade trees in an onion field; no pine trees and no weeping willows. There are no Coke machines in an onion field. In most onion fields there are millions of onions and hundreds of Mexicans. This particular field was about twenty or thirty acres; twenty to thirty football fields lined up in a row. No grass, though. No artificial turf, either; just long, long rows of mounded up dirt; dry clumpy dirt - dry, dusty and hot, a mini desert, if you will.

Most of the football fields were devoid of people, but the first one was very busy. The majority of the people were on about the fifty yard line. They were all bent over at the waist, straddling a row of onions. They looked very busy, except for one man. He was sitting on a pail in the limited shade provided by an old tractor. I immediately presumed that he was the boss. He was wearing a large sombrero. It was obvious that he saw us standing there off in the distance, waving. It was also quite clear that he had no intention of rising from his comfortable position to come over to greet us into his labor force. But why should he make a move to welcome us? He had a job. We were the ones who were unemployed.

We proceeded to march across this burning desert to confront our prospective boss at the fifty yard line.

"Hi, ah, we were told that you had some positions available?" The patriarch spread his knees apart; put his right thumb to his right nostril and blew heartily in an attempt to clear the left of dust, debris or whatever. He was successful, and nearly cleared my stomach in the process. He looked up at us and smiled. His upper, front teeth were probably tucked away safely in his shirt pocket. He didn't say anything, but bobbed his head interrogatively. I determined from this gesture that he didn't comprehend my inquiry. I decided to rephrase. "We heard that you needed some onion toppers. The guy at the unemployment office sent us out." I exhibited our little unemployment information cards.

"Oh? You wanna work?"

"Yes, we're looking for a job. We don't exactly know how to top onions, but ..."

"No problem," he said, as he got up from his five gallon pail and proceeded to stroll off. Carol and I were both left there talking to ourselves, as our friend casually wandered off into the distance.

"Should we follow him, do you suppose?" Carol asked, as we both stood there staring at the gentleman's gradually disappearing back. I wasn't one hundred percent positive but it did seem like the right thing to do.

Momentarily we were off trotting eagerly behind our man. He seemed to be heading for an inactive tractor that had old sacks and plastic buckets strewn about it. His pace was rather slow and leisurely and Carol and I were shuffling and stumbling trying not to walk up and over his rear end. I suppose we were somewhat eager. I mean, here we were, Carol and Dick and the *Grapes of Wrath*, in the middle of an onion field, in *The Fertile Valley*.

He picked up a couple of buckets and then marched us all the way back to where we were in the first place. Then he stopped, turned and pointed across the field. The field was, of course, furrowed. Rippling mounds, of dusty, dry, clumpy dirt seemed to stretch forever into the distance.

"Okay, you start here. You take a four row - two for you y two for su esposa," he said and then he started to walk away.

"Hey, wait a minute, wait a minute!"

"Si'?"

"This is our first experience at onion topping. I don't think that we will need four rows." The rows appeared endless and they stretched for miles. Four rows would undoubtedly take us the rest of our lives.

"You wanna dos linas, take a two." He started to walk off again. I was rapidly getting the impression that this fellow didn't think that we were going to be around too long. Two rows or four rows, what did it matter? These gringos will be into their motor home before they pick one sack.

"Ah sir? Sir?"

"Si'?"

I stepped up closer. I was a little embarrassed. Although I had eaten many onions in my lifetime, I hadn't the slightest idea of what topping an onion entailed. Sounded like a very intricate process. I can honestly say that in my neighborhood of origin, I had never actually seen an onion in the act of growing. I observed some other workers in the distance. I could see that they were picking up the onions and doing something to them with their hands or with some kind of mechanical implement. They then tossed the finished product into a five gallon pail. What were they doing to them and what about the tools? I was rather apprehensive. The Boss man didn't seem very interested in us.

We wanted this job. This job and others like it could very well be the solution to all of our problems and the means for fulfilling our dream. We had organized our traveling to the point where a few dollars was enough capital to fund a week on the road. This minimum amount of money bought the groceries and paid for the gasoline for our vehicle. That was it. Gasoline and groceries were our only expenditures. We had long since learned how to avoid paying rent. We had no cable TV, telephone, electric bills, property taxes etc. A few bucks covered the basics. Then again, if our van camper collapsed, weeks would have to be deducted from our new found freedom on the highways of America.

As for health insurance, neither of us had ever had a job that provided such a benefit anyway. One day's work even at minimum wage would pay for one week's freedom in our new lifestyle. Seven day's work could equal seven weeks of fishing off some ocean pier or camping by some pristine lake. One month of work would mean over one half year of playtime. Now that is more in tune with the way my God designed the world. My God liked people. He wanted them to have fun and enjoy life. This was it! Topping onions was God's way of saying; "Okay kids, ENJOY!"

So, as you can imagine, I didn't want to offend my new boss. I approached him cautiously and respectfully.

"You see, sir," I said softly, not wanting everyone within listening distance to be made aware of the fact that we were novices at topping onions, "as I tried to tell you when we first arrived, my wife and I have never done this before. In fact, we know very little about farm work." He stared, blankly. That look analyzed in terms of dollars and cents, registered "no sale". "The problem put simply is unfortunately we don't know how to top an onion. What does one have to do to an onion to have it in a satisfactorily topped condition?" The confused stare remained, but it was now enhanced by the addition of a gaping jaw. "In other words, if I could impose on you for just one moment; if you would take just one moment of your time and demonstrate to my wife and I the process involved, I am absolutely sure that in a matter of minutes we will have this onion topping under control. You may have to waste a minute of your time demonstrating, but I will assure you that we will definitely make it worth your while."

Obviously he had never met a pair like us. It was virtually unimaginable to him that there were people alive and functioning on this planet who needed to be instructed on how to top an onion. He remained immobilized. That was strike two. "Listen, just show us how to top one onion, and you can go on your way, O.K.?"

"Okay."

I was never so relieved. I was beginning to think that we had to be experienced toppers, or have a job training completion card from an Onion Picking University or something.

He squatted down into a furrow. Coming out of the mound of dirt next to the furrow were a number of sprigs or straw-like protuberances. He dug with his hands around one of these sprigs and behold, there was an onion. He pulled this big, fat, softball sized onion out of the ground. The onion, now in his hand, had these withered sprigs coming out the top and a bunch of scraggly roots dangling from the bottom. Holding the onion in one hand, he pinched the sprigs with the other and then twisted them until they were severed from the onion. Then he flipped the onion around and twisted the roots off in a similar fashion. After completing this process, he held the finished product up to Carol and me who scrutinized the result with smiles of enlightenment.

"That's it?"

"Dat's eeat, amigo."

"You can be on your way my friend," I encouraged eagerly. "This job is under control; no problem."

"You fill two of these," he said tossing a five gallon pail at my foot. "Put eem in da sacks." Numerous burlap sacks were tossed about in the furrows.

"Ah right - two five gallon pails make one sack and we get paid how much a sack?"

"You get paid at the end of the week at dee hotel een town."

"No no, I mean, how much do we get paid for each sack?"

"Thirty cent a sack."

"Thirty cents a sack! Beautiful! No problem. We just fill up the sacks and leave them right there in the row, right?"

"In your row, man. You two leave deem in dis row here. Dis row." He pointed to the furrow in which we had recently been squatting.

"No problem. We got it."

Suddenly giving instructions on how to top onions seemed intriguing to the man. Probably never before in his life had he been required to give instructions to anyone on how to do this job. Though at first he didn't think that he would, now he liked it. He bent down into the furrow again and scooped up another onion. "Like a dis." He twisted the scraggly appendages off both ends of the onion again. "You see, like a dis." He tossed the completed onion into the five gallon pail. He then dug out another onion. He kept repeating the process and displaying the completed onion to Carol and me before tossing it into the five gallon pail.

"No problem. I got it. Do you see how he did that Carol?"

"Yes, I see how he did that. I think I can do that."

"Well, okay. We understand sir. We'll take it over from here."

"Like a dis, you see? Push a dirt, like a dis. Get a onion. Twist a here. Twist a dare; into the bucket. You got it?"

"We got it. Thanks a bunch, I really appreciate you taking this time with us. You won't be sorry."

"Okay, and the bucket; dump a in the sack. You got it?"

"Right! Yes sir."

"And da sack go over a here, in da middle of da row. You got it?"

"Si', yes sir, no problem."

He got up and smiled. Then he grabbed a burlap sack up off the ground.

"No putta da sack over here." He demonstrated by putting the sack in the next furrow. "No good over here. Like a dis here. Only dis row; you got it?"

"We got it. Most definitely, we got it!"

"You putta over here es no dinero. Over here," he shuffled the burlap sack into the wrong furrow, "nudder hombre gets dee money." He laughed. "You get it?"

"Right! I've got to make sure that I put the sack in my row. If I put it over here, no money for me. I've got to put it right here in the middle of my rows." I smiled at him and nodded my head affirmatively.

"Okay you got it." He walked away, turning back every now and then to give us a semi-toothless smile.

As he walked away Carol and I looked at the millions of sacks that were scattered about the rows that had already been picked. If there weren't millions of sacks, then certainly there were thousands. Definitely a lot of full sacks - a lot of thirty cents-es.

"Carol this could be it. I am definitely serious. There are enough onions in this field to keep us in petrol and beans for the next three years. I mean, how long does it take to pick a sack? Look here." I grabbed the five gallon pail that our boss man had been tossing his demonstration onions into. "He nearly filled this pail already."

I could see by the look in Carol's eyes that she was excited. We were on the verge of breaking new ground. Maybe not as exhilarating as landing on the moon, but certainly of equal importance! A life in which two months of, admittedly, hard labor would set us up for ten months of folly and frolic; ten months of living like the big shots; ten months of touring and observing; ten months of scoffing at all of the suckers who broke their butts for fifty weeks, to get two weeks off. Can you believe it? Work fifty weeks to get two off? Here we would work eight weeks, and then take forty off! Could it be possible? Could this be eureka, the electric light of freedom!

Thoreau said that man did not have to live by the sweat of his brow - simplify; simplify my friends! Wasn't that just what we were doing? Our little van camper replacing that one hundred seventy-five thousand, three bedroom, two bath. Who needs it if you have to work every minute of every waking day to get it? Who needs a telephone? Freedom - work a little - then vacation a lot. That's the way it should be.

Carol and I didn't have to speak. We had talked enough. Our minds were one when it came to this topic. We hit the dirt - bing, bang, boom. We had our first sack full. "Look! A sack full already. How long do you think that took us Carol, a minute?"

"Oh, I think it took more than a minute."

"Okay, so it took two minutes - two minutes a sack! That's thirty sacks an hour. Thirty times thirty cents equals? That's nine dollars an hour, Carol. Nine dollars times eight hours - that's seventy-two bucks a day. My God! We can work one month and make enough money for eleven months off. We're just learning how to do this. Holy cow, wait until we get used to it and learn a few of the little tricks of the trade.

"Look at all of these people out here." She looked around the field. "All of these people might be simple, but they ain't stupid. They're out here making seventy bucks a day. They have five in the family - five times seventy? One family makes three hundred and fifty bucks a day. Can you believe it? They take that money. They go back to Mexico. They're millionaires!

"These people work over here one year, and that's it. They're home free. They take the five kids back to Mexico, buy a villa, hire a bunch of poor Mexicans as servants, and it's the good life from then on.

"I knew it had to be something like this. The days of the *Grapes of Wrath* are over. This is modern America. No one has to work anymore, if they don't want to. These people are out here because there is money to be made. There's no poverty in this country anymore. There are only people who want to work, and people who are too damn lazy to do anything. I mean look at this; Mexican people - all here from a foreign country. These people just aren't afraid of a little hard work. They're over here getting rich. You mean to tell me some of the people on welfare in the Big City couldn't do this? Of course they could. Anybody can do this. It doesn't take any education. You don't have to be anything special. All that you have to do is get off your butt and dig in."

"Well Richard, that's not entirely true. I mean, we do have that camper. Some of those people in the Big City don't even have a car. If they don't even have a job, where would they get the money to buy a van like ours? First they have to be able to get here. If the State had to pay to get all of the unemployed workers here; then set them up in housing; then day care centers for the children - and what would they eat? How would they get to the grocery store? What about medical care?"

"All right, all right, all right - I give, I give! The heck with all the poor people in the Big City. Let's just dig in and get ourselves rich. Once we're rich we'll send two poor people to Mexico. They can sneak back over the border; find their own onion field; just like we've done, and make themselves rich. Then they can finance two of their poor relatives and they can do the same thing.

"We'll start a chain. Instead of a chain letter, it will be a chain worker program. Pretty soon there will be so many wealthy, ex-onion toppers living in villas in Mexico, that middle-class southern Californians will be sneaking across the Mexican border in hopes of finding good jobs working as high paid domestics for these ex-poor people"

"What part of Mexico are you people from?" A huge man, with hands that appeared to be the size of baseball gloves, loomed up behind us from out of nowhere. Carol and I both stopped our frantic furrowing, and looked up.

It was clear to the man behind us, that he had startled us both. He smiled, apologetically, and quickly squatted down next to our furrow. He was wearing a plaid Scottish tam, and plaid suspenders. While he waited for a response, he busied himself, shyly, digging up onions, topping them, and then flipping them into our pail. I was still a little groggy from my daydreaming.

"We're not from Mexico," I offered dumbly. He smiled and kept topping onions. Then, after a moment, he added with a big grin.

"I guessed that." He topped two or three more onions without a word, and then added. "What are you guys - working your way around the country?"

It was funny that he would put it that way. I really hadn't thought of it in that context. I, myself, was actually on a personal search for the Holy Grail. I was looking for the New World. I was discovering. I was finding myself - along with truth, justice, and the American way. I was in the process of encountering the lost world of Atlantis. I was on the route 66 to immortality. I was living a dream. I was traveling down the road less traveled. I had stopped by the wood side on a cold, snowy night and exclaimed with a yelp - the hell with this! I'm outta here! But, at this moment, passing a stranger in this wilderness, I suppose that it did look as if we were - how had he put it - working our way around the country. I guess that is the way a steady, reliable, earthy man, like this simple farmhand would put it. I was about to elaborate, when Carol popped in.

"Yes!" she piped, enthusiastically. "That's exactly what we are doing. We're working our way around the country." She spoke these words as if she had just realized that working our way around the country was actually what we were doing.

"And who are you?" I asked. I wanted to divert this conversation before Carol expounded on the intimate details of our personal lives to this total stranger who had just gotten off a tractor, probably to simply say hello or possibly to politely inform us that we were in the wrong furrow or topping onions backwards.

"Oh?" he said, rather humbly. "These are my onions you're topping."

These were his onions! He was - the farmer! We were talking to our first real, live farmer! And he looked like a farmer! He was big and strong looking. He appeared to be slow moving and thoughtful. He squatted down on his hams, just like the farmers in "The Grapes of Wrath". He didn't scratch any pictures in the dirt though. Instead, he kept himself busy topping onions and tossing them into our pail. I kind of felt like it was a good idea to talk to him. For one thing, he was the man who owned these onions, and for another thing - he was filling up my pail.

"These are really beautiful onions," I said, awkwardly. "They're the biggest onions that I've ever seen." And they were. Each onion was about the size of a softball. But as the farmer sat there on his hams, his face slowly lost its grin and twisted up into a grimace.

"Yup, they are mighty pretty." He took one of the huge onions up into his hand, and then rubbed it between his mitts like a major league pitcher rubs a baseball. When he was done, most of the light, flaky, rust-colored skin was gone, and the moist, white flesh was exposed. He then brought the onion up to his mouth and bit into it. He took a bite out of it as if it were an apple or a peach! God, I thought, this guy really is a farmer! He eats onions like apples! He crouched there chewing on his onion. Then said; "It's as sweet as sugar."

I didn't question his word. I had never seen anybody just eat an onion like an apple - and his eyes weren't tearing or his nose running. I didn't know how sweet an onion could be, but that one was either mighty sweet or this guy's taste buds had been totally destroyed from swallowing dust and dirt for the last thirty years.

Wasn't that just the way a farmer should do it? Wow, chomping down on a raw onion! Next he would probably pick up a handful of dirt, toss it into his mouth like a piece of rock candy, swish it around, then after a thoughtful moment announce; "A little low on potassium, a touch heavy on the magnesium - nitrogen seems good though. Guess I'll have to plant sweet corn here next year."

I LOVED IT! This was the real thing: "Life on the Back Forty" - no no -"The Death of a Farmer" - no no - "The Dark Side of a Dusty Furrow" - no, no - "Dirt, American Style."

"I've always wanted to work my way around the country," he said. "I thought I'd just go here and there, doing farm work. Just make enough money to get to the next farm, or the next harvest." His eyes were starting to sparkle as he talked about it. It was plain that he was serious. He had thought about it, and maybe quite often. "Is that your camper?" He nodded over to our brown van, sporting its new fiberglass top.

I suppose that it did kind of look like a camper now, but no one had ever called it a camper before. It was just a van. But now with that fiberglass top, it did look kind of spiffy. I hoped that he wouldn't ask to look at the inside. Looking at its exterior now, one could mistake it for one of those expensive jobs, complete with shower stall, stainless steel sinks, furnace, air-conditioning, hot water tank, waterbed - the works.

But, in reality, the interior was more - traditional dumpster. In fact, most of the wood cabinets, we had made ourselves from scrap wood and discarded wooden packing crates. To this day, in fact, it is difficult for me to drive past a piece of stray plywood, or a partially broken chunk of two by four. My wife will see that look in my eye and say. "Just leave it Richard. There will be more laying on the side of the road, when we need it."

There always has been.

"I've always thought I'd have a pickup truck with a camper on the bed, but yours looks mighty nice. That's all two people would really need - isn't it?

"Well, it gets us there."

"Yes," he paused. He didn't appear to be a very talkative fellow. It seemed as though talking, more or less, interrupted his solitude. He only did it when it was absolutely necessary, and then sparingly. "Guess I'd better get back to loosening up these onions before you folks catch up to me."

I hated to see him leave. He seemed like a kindred soul as well as a man who was interested in people - at least us people anyway. Besides, he had topped nearly a pail full of onions while he was squatted there - each pail grossing another fifteen cents, as you'll remember.

We scurried along until about three o'clock. It was really hot. We had anticipated working until dark but we noticed that the crew had been gradually dissipating, and now the workers were walking from the field in clumps.

"Looks to me like we have come to the end of a perfect day, Carol." She sat up in her furrow, and flopped back onto her calves. We were both sporting grand smiles. It was a hot, hard day's work, but - we did it.

We turned and took a gander down our row. The burlap sacks seemed to stretch endlessly nipping up at the horizon. We had marched to more than half the distance across the football field. In point of fact, we seemed rather close, or at least closer, to the finish line. I stood up. Everything hurt - my back, my legs, even my toes. I knew that Carol had to be suffering.

"What do you say? Shall we total up our sacks?"

With my arm over her shoulder, and hers wrapped about my waist, we walked slowly, gently supporting one another, as we both counted aloud. One; ... (walk awhile); two ... (walk a while); three - and on we went until we hit the last sack. "Thirty!"

"THIRTY? That can't be right!" I marched back down the row, but this time it was no leisurely stroll. Carol double-stepped right behind, verifying my count. "Twenty-eight; twenty-nine; thirty," I stopped and waited for Carol. "How many did you get?"

"Thirty."

"THIRTY SACKS! I can't believe that! How much money is that?" My mind just wouldn't perform the necessary mathematics, as if it were unwilling to do that much work for such a small amount of money. I forced myself orally. "That's ... ah ... three times three equals nine. What the hell is that, ninety dollars, right?"

"I don't think so. Thirty times thirty is nine hundred, with two decimal places, that's nine dollars."

"Nine dollars? That's totally impossible. That can not be right. No one in America works for nine dollars a day. What am I talking about? We didn't make nine dollars. There's two of us. That's four dollars and fifty cents each - per day! That's not $4.50 per hour. That's $4.50 PER DAY. This is insane. Somebody has got to be kidding here!"

The field was now empty. All the Mexicans had left. Their trucks and cars were rattling down the dirt road with a cloud of dust, and the high pitched ringing of accordions and marimbas blasting from their radios. We hiked the football field one more time. This time counting the sacks of the old man who worked next to us. He had twenty three sacks. We made two dollars and ten cents more than he did today. We really couldn't believe it. No wonder everyone was looking at us. They were asking themselves why two healthy looking, white people, who should, most definitely, have their green cards, would be out here in this onion field.

After our initial outrage, there was a profound silence. The setting was now much subdued; no music playing; no people in the fields - no tractor puffing and huffing. It was quiet. We were now the only humans left in the field. The field was filled with hundreds and hundreds of burlap sacks bulging with onions.

I felt very low. No, low is too pacific a term. I felt cheated, used, and abused - not to mention, bewildered. I imagined that Carol was having similar thoughts as we drudged our way back to the equipment shelter where our van was parked. It was hard to believe that people, any people, living in this country, would be out here working for this kind of money. I don't care if they did live ten in a room; they still had to pay money for a loaf of bread, a bag of flour, and a gallon of milk - even a pound of rice cost something. They had to put gas into their vehicles. They didn't walk here. Even with four or five in a car, it had to cost each of them a dollar or two for gasoline. This farm was way out in the country, here. What is this? And who was making all the money? Just look at all the sacks of onions, hundreds - possibly thousands. I couldn't really tell. Judging from our thirty sacks it must have been more in the hundred category. Regardless, how much does a sack of onions sell for - a bushel of these big, pretty, Spanish onions?

There were onions laying everywhere, like so much trash. I picked one up. One that already had the skin rubbed off it, and I bit into it - almost out of spite. I couldn't believe it. That farmer wasn't joking. It was as sweet as sugar. I had never tasted an onion like that in my life.

It was a long, quiet walk back to our van. I didn't want to face the reality that our dream was biting the dust - onion field dust. All that we needed was a lousy few bucks a day - not a bunch of money. The thought of going into town and getting a real job seemed like a major defeat.

You know, we could get a job washing dishes or something for a month to pay our fare around the country. It just didn't have the flare. It wasn't very glamorous - not very exciting; not to mention, not very much fun either. Imagine; "How to get a job at the day labor center"- "Washing your way around the country"; "How to manage your life on minimum wage employment". Who would be interested in that? Besides, thanks to the Repubocrats much of America already knows how to live on minimum wage.

It was a long walk. Indeed; a quiet walk - and a very, very, very depressing walk.

We had topped onions for one week, grossing forty one dollars which, as I later learned, might have been more than our farmer friend earned - that year!

2 Gravenstein Apples in Sebastopol

At next sighting we find Carol and Dick, balancing precariously, atop three legged ladders in a Gravenstein apple patch in the remotest parts of a primitive American village, named Sebastopol by the local, California aborigines.
 A three legged ladder is the giraffe of the ladder species. At first inspection any self-respecting city boy would exclaim. "Holy cow! They forgot a damn leg on this contraption. Find me a real ladder before I kill myself, will you please?" Lucky for me, my bride had once been out to Uncle Merton's farm, and was exposed in her childhood to such a twelve foot, three-legged monstrosity as the one brought to us by Mr. Donaldson, the apple farm manager. We found Mr. Donaldson, again, through the farm labor advisor at the Sebastopol employment office.
 Upon arriving at the apple farm we had our first challenge getting past the little old, widowed lady who owned the farm. Believe it or not I literally had to beg her for the opportunity to work our butts off in her apple patch. She kept telling me that she didn't need any help. I kept telling her that, despite that fact, I was completely convinced that we were an absolute necessity to the eventual success of her enterprise.
 "Sonny," she said. "I have been operating this "apple farm" successfully, by myself, for the last twenty-two years. For the thirty years before that, I had my husband's help. He had three generations of experienced "apple farm" instructors in the form of grandparents and great grandparents to inch him along. I appreciate your offer, but I think that I'll just struggle along here by myself."
 Wouldn't you know, our first apple picking experience and I have to meet the Katherine Hepburn of apple farming. She had already closed the door, and was sliding the laced curtain

across the window opening in the door when I desperately hit her with my last trump.

"Of course, it goes without saying, that my wife and I are both experienced workers in the business of harvesting farm products. We have just completed a stay at the Harkin Farm, just down the road here a piece, "topping onions." I emphasized the word topping, John Steinbeckly. I was just about to squat down onto my hams, when she reopened the door.

"You folks have been topping onions?" she said exhibiting a very cynical disbelief. Without saying a word, Carol and I both popped our hands out towards her, all four palms up for her inspection. She looked down at our numerous, newly formed, immature calluses, and our tenderly red, still swollen, misshapen fingers. She then looked up into our faces and smiled ever so slightly. In a moment she was off and down the steps motioning us to follow. "Mr. Donaldson, Mr. Donaldson!" she screamed to this man who was bouncing along on the unpadded, metal seat of an old, red and roaring Ferguson tractor. "These two young farm laborers would like to pick our Gravenstein apple crop for us this year. Get them some ladders and a bin and get them started would you please." She then turned slightly towards us and winked. At the time, I thought that she was winking at us, but looking back on the experience, I think her wink was truly intended for Mr. Donaldson who had burst into a huge grin.

That next day with the help of our three-legged ladders, we picked three bins (20 bushels each) of shiny, green Gravenstein apples at a pay of eight dollars a bin - twenty four big ones. By the next morning, our bodies were so stiff and sore it took us that whole day to pick but one bin. Over the next two weeks we managed two bins per day. That was sixteen bucks, eight dollars apiece - slightly less than one dollar per hour. Obviously Gravenstein apples were not bricks along the road to the land of milk and honey. When Mr. Donaldson informed us that we had picked his last ancient, overgrown, giant of a Gravenstein apple tree, we were almost, within the instant, re-established in the downtown parking lot of the Sebastopol employment office.

The nice lady at the employment office didn't want to give us a job either. On this occasion we skipped the farm labor management advisor and went right to the real job department. John Steinbeck was right, and his book *The Grapes of Wrath* was still a valid description of the perils of migrant farm workers as far as we were concerned. We would try our hand at a conventional temporary job, if we could find one.

"Don't you know that there is a recession going on?" the lady at the real job section of the employment office informed us after our initial two hours of form filling. "Where are you people from, anyway? You mean you had good jobs and quit them? You've both been to college? Are you children crazy? My God!"

We lived in the parking lot of the Sebastopol employment office for three days, before anyone else employed there would speak to us again.

"I'm afraid you folks can't live here in the employment office parking lot," a very nice, well dressed, employed, man from inside the Sebastopol employment office informed us.

"But we need a job and we figured that this would be the best place to find one."

"Have you tried the apple cannery?"

"What apple cannery?"

"There's a big apple cannery just on the outskirts of town. They should be starting up production any day now."

Within the hour Carol and I were again self-respecting, employed, tax paying, union dues paying citizens. We were told to report that next morning. Carol was going to the apple peeling plant, and I was assigned to the third shift, hose everything down, scruba dub dub, clean up crew.

Carol had one of two jobs. Either she was sorting bad apples from good ones as they were being transported in a water trough conveyor system that floated them from place to place; or she was busy laying acceptable apples on the receiving pedestals of automatic coring and peeling machines.

The apple would be placed on the tiny, stainless-steel, receiving platform. Almost instantly an apparatus would come down from above, core and peel the apple, re-immerse it into another watery conveying trough to be transported to its next destination. There it would be sliced into donut shaped portions and dumped into a huge dehydration chamber.

I worked for about a week in my slicker suit hosing and cleaning. I was then transferred to the second shift juicing department. It was my job to pour rice hulls and sawdust (wood fiber, product of Weyerhaeuser) into this huge stainless steel juicing screw.

Before we get to this, it is interesting to note how the apples got to me.

The machine that I helped manage was located up on the second floor of the plant. The apples came into the plant on the backs of heavy duty dump trucks. They were dumped into a concrete, Olympic-sized, swimming pool vat. The vat was on the ground floor. From there they were sucked up to my station, water and all, by way of this metal culvert type looking pipe or tube. Before the apples were dumped onto a conveyor belt sorting station, the transporting water had somehow vanished. I presume that the water was recycled back to the concrete swimming pool. The apples, sticks, pipes, beer cans, rubber balls, hats, gloves, M-D 20-20 bottles, hypodermic needles and other necessary paraphernalia used in the daily plying of the harvesting craft by us skilled migrant farm workers, then tumbled onto the sorting conveyor belt which was manned by two or three women. The women were usually wearing bandannas, plastic aprons and gloves.

Why was I dumping rice hulls and sawdust into the juicing end of this gigantic piece of machinery, you ask? Good question.

Well, as I learned, if you simply dump raw apples into the juicing screw, a large part of the juice contained in the apple does not get captured. Consequently, you end up with more of a sauce than a juice. The rice hulls and sawdust add body to the chopped apples. Obviously, the rice hulls and sawdust absorb juice escaping from the chopped, mangled apples so that all of the juice is carried along to the press. The press then squeezes the juice out of the apple pulp and the absorbent rice hulls and sawdust. I was told that by doing this they were able to obtain over ninety percent of all the juices contained in the apple.

The only problem I observed with this process was that sawdust and rice hulls were pressed into the squeezed apple juice along with portions of apple pulp. When I asked about this I was told that it didn't really matter because everything was then boiled at nine million degrees Fahrenheit and then filtered clear.

This satisfied my curiosity until one day I saw bottles of natural apple juice with pulp and real fiber added. When I asked the man on the bottling line how they got the natural pulp and real fiber back into the juice. He said. "That's simple. We just don't filter it."

"Yes," I said, "but then what about the tons of rice hulls and sawdust that I'm throwing into the screw all night long?"

He answered me with a smile.

I have since noticed while reading the ingredients on a package of high fiber bread that the high fiber is also a product of Weyerhaeuser. So, stay healthy and eat a tree.

Another thing, did you know that a kernel of rice comes in a hull? Can you believe that? How in the world do they ever separate the zillions of tiny little hulls from the tiny little grains of rice?

In any case, whether justified or not, I don't usually buy high fiber bread. When I buy apple juice, I buy the filtered, thank you. If I feel the need for fiber these days, I go directly to the trees growing in my own back yard. At least I know that they are fresh and are not involved with the perils of roach and rat vermin that inevitably follow the storing of sawdust and rice hulls.

Another little problem that I experienced with regards to my new career as rice hull and sawdust dumper began on my very first day. My immediate supervisor, a young man of about twenty-two, presented before me a breath filtering devise. It was just a little paper thing with a rubber band that went over your head and held this paper filter over your nose and mouth. "You want one of these things?" he said. The manner of his question implied that if I did want one of these things I would be less of a man. Since I already felt as less of a man as I ever wanted to become, naturally I refused. "What the hell do I need something like that for?" I responded, manfully.

"I donno," he said, "one of them damn OSHA things."

I knew very little about OSHA, other than it was an organization that had something to do with the government, and their area of expertise dealt with worker safety.

After about a week at my new position I developed a cough. It was reminiscent of a smoking cough. I began hacking up this black-green ugly looking stuff from my lungs. I had completely forgotten about the paper respiratory device that had been offered to me on that first day of work until one day when I arrived at the jobsite I looked up at my station. The man who I was about to relieve at the rice hull and sawdust dumping station was standing in a wide beam of warm sunlight. The beam illuminated a thick cloud of dust engulfing the man and the whole working station. It was very clear to me how my cough along with the green-black phlegm from my lungs had developed. That evening at the peril of compromising my manly state, I requested one of the paper respiratory devices. Very shortly thereafter my cough along with the phlegm disappeared. I would show my wife the paper device at the end of each shift. It would always be coated with thick black soot. None of the other workers wore the paper respirator; no one on the first shift or on the second - not even the women - and they certainly shouldn't have been worried about not appearing manly. Oh well, so much for OSHA, and that interfering government of ours.

Life at the Sebastopol Cannery was a joy and a pleasure until one day somebody in authority realized that Carol and I were actually living in the Cannery parking lot. It wasn't like we were hanging our dirty laundry on the enclosing, ten foot, chain link fence, or adding an addition onto our camper. We were very discreet. The parking lot was full of cars, twenty-four hours a day, with their three shift operation. We were self-contained with our portable potty and all. We weren't about to give four or five hundred a month of our eight hundred a month earnings to someone for the privilege of parking our camper in their field - even if their field had electricity, and they called it a campground. But regardless of our discreetness and our resolution, a white hat (supervisor) one day informed us that we could only park our camper in their parking lot during the hours in which we were employed at the plant.

We were in a dilemma. We had often parked for one night here and there in our travels, but an attempt to live in the streets of Sebastopol would be rather ridiculous. But if we set up house keeping in a pay campground on the wages we earned at the Cannery, we'd be going nowhere. There would be very little money left over that could be saved for the future adventures of Dick and Carol. We would be like the majority of our poverty stricken co-workers. Earning just enough money at the Cannery to stay alive, and pay living expenses. We weren't about to give into that drab future. We hadn't come this far to be stopped now by simple necessity. Yes, we knew that this was the way that all of America lived. We did not want to live like all of America. Our attempt to overcome all of America was how this whole adventure had started in the first place.

That first night, we camped on a side street in a residential neighborhood in downtown Sebastopol. We could see from the looks on the faces of the people who lived there, as they exited in the morning to go to work that our camping van, though very attractive in our eyes, was not a welcome addition to their neighborhood. One night was alright, but any more than that and we would surely be having a visit from the police department.

We spent that next week visiting different neighborhoods in lovely metropolitan Sebastopol until one night we stumbled upon the Safeway Supermarket.

The Safeway had a very large parking lot. It had numerous cars parked in the lot, round the clock, due to their policy of an eleven to seven third shift shelf-stocking, cleaning and maintenance program.

Consequently, we ended up living in a Safeway parking lot in downtown Sebastopol, California. We spent a lovely ten weeks at the Safeway. I would also like the Safeway corporate owners to know, that in appreciation of their generosity we did buy all of our groceries and supplies at their store. This is the truth. We didn't even bother to comparison shop. Whatever price you guys put on that package was good enough for us. No questions asked.

The money we saved from working at the apple cannery, and living in the Safeway parking lot financed our tour of northern California, Oregon, Washington State, Idaho, Wyoming, South Dakota and more. It wasn't until we reached a little town called Mena, in the state of Arkansas that we again felt the pressing need for more financial backing for our unauthorized National Geographic adventure.

3 Peaches in Mena, Arkansas

We were strolling through the Wal-Mart in downtown Mena, when the local news flipped onto one of the TVs being displayed. A young, eager and very dapper announcer was heralding the arrival of the peach:

"Well, folks, it's that time of year again. And here I am, right in the middle of all the action at Barbrough Farms, in Polk County. We're out here at the Barbrough fruit stand, just off highway sixteen at the junction of state road two-two-two and highway ninety-eight. The folks out here, as you can plainly see right behind me, are as busy as they can be. Aren't you folks? (The camera pans and then zooms in on a fruit stand immediately behind the announcer. Men, women and teenage boys, all displaying colorful Barbrough aprons and ball caps, were bouncing about in all directions gleefully toting crates, baskets, and bowls filled to overflowing with succulent, rosy-red looking peaches ... 'We sure are!' everyone screams, as the camera gives them all another chance to be seen on TV by all of the folks back home.) So get out those Mason jars, and Aunt Tilley's peach preserve recipe, and shuffle yourselves out here to Barbrough Farms and pick up a couple of bushels of these wonderful, tree ripened peaches at just twelve dollars a bushel. You can't beat that folks - tree ripened, juicy, rosy-red peaches. A bargain by the bushel, just twelve dollars! Right here at Barbrough Farms on the corner of ..."

As we watched the young man on the screen peddling Mr. Barbrough's peaches, we couldn't help but to think of those yesteryears. The smell of peaches ripening in the cellar or pantry; those home made peach pies, coming hot from the oven. Grandma's hand churned peach ice cream, made with the chunks of whole fresh peaches paddled right into the cold sweet delight. Remember those peach preserves, peach cobblers, and peaches and cream? How about the luscious burst of those outrageous juices overflowing the corners of your mouth as you lean your head forward in an attempt to keep from staining mama's freshly washed and pressed school clothes? Peaches! How could anyone ever forget "the peach"? How could anyone not love a peach? Forget the apple. It had to be the peach that tempted Adam and Eve to revolution. Only the thought of the moist, succulent peach could have lured mankind's parents into the loss of Paradise. And at just this point our reverie was broken by the sound of the young announcer crunching into his pink peach.

Crunching? We both stretched forward listening more closely to the sound track.

Peaches didn't crunch. They squished. The announcer rolled his eyes and head with delight, as he nodded his approval and satisfaction to us viewers, while having the audacity to take another crunch from his pink, tree ripened peach.

"Why does he pick a green peach for his demonstration? What is the matter with this guy?" I screamed in desperation at the department store television set. "You mean to tell me, this man is at a peach farm and he can't find a ripe peach? I can't believe this! Wait until he gets back to the studio."

"Wait until Mr. Barbrough sees this commercial that he probably just paid twelve zillion dollars for?" added Carol.

"I just don't understand it. Hasn't this kid ever eaten a peach before? Doesn't he know what a peach is supposed to taste like? What does he think a peach is - a fuzzy variety of an apple?"

Although we were very dubious about any more John Steinbecking our way around the country after our experiences with onion topping and three-legged ladder Gravenstein apple picking, the lure of the peach was too much for us to overcome.

Within a week we were running behind the divots coughed up by diesel gasping, dust provoking, tractors, roaring along through rows of peach trees, at what seemed to be breakneck speed.

We again found ourselves immersed in a land of foreign speaking peoples. The predominant language was, once again, Spanish. Most of the workers were from Mexico, or came to this country via Mexico from other Central American or South

American countries. Carol was the only female fruit picker. There were other female general farm workers, though.

Peach trees are small. No ladders!

We were instructed that first morning by a rather spindly, tobacco chewing, Arkansan foreman, on the intricate art of peach picking. Here is what the man had to say; "Owa wapt! Blawabba dobablatter dumbwadder peaches." He then paused to spit some tobacco juice onto his assistant's cowboy boot, after which he held up a peach and tried to stretch his middle finger and thumb around it. "No blabba butter be!" he announced very sternly pointing to the peach wrapped between his middle finger and thumb. His middle finger and thumb were touching as they stretched around the peach. "Da blabba dubi daba dito aplapa troba," he added almost in a yell as he pointed over towards two pickup trucks and a van. Immediately all the workers started heading that way. Carol and I followed.

Well now, nothing to this. We had our instructions, and here we were in a van heading toward "Tick Hill". We rode over hill and dale, highway and byway, and then dirt road, followed by two-track. Finally there we were in a peach tree Garden of Eden.

Peach trees are wonderful looking things. They have these long narrow leaves and these delicate, awkward looking limbs. For a tree, they are sweet and gentle looking. They look so frail and fragile, one would think that nature would have incorporated a sign on them stating: "Be careful, you barbarian, this tree can be damaged easily."

A peach tree looks exactly like a tree that would bear such a sweet, soft, juicy, delicacy.

We were given these burlap sacks that strapped over our shoulders and around our backs, with the sack part flopped in front over our bellies. We were lined up behind a tractor which was attached to a long trailer. On the trailer sat three large wooden bins. They probably held between fifteen and twenty bushels. Then suddenly we were off.

The tractor jerked ahead with its two front tires lifting off the ground like a top eliminator at a drag strip. Thinking back on our instructions Carol and I had no idea what we were supposed to be doing. So we simply watched the others for the first forty or fifty feet.

The scene was one of literal carnage. It looked like a bunch of Huns bursting into a Playboy Bunny lounge - the Bunnies being the fruit trees. It was a disaster. The workers just spewed out from both sides of the tractor trailer, and raped the trees. They ran around the trees in frenzy, and if the worker was a little short, or the tree slightly larger, he would simply leap into it. The sound of limbs cracking, and separating from the peach tree trunk were secondary only to the roar and rumble of the tractor's diesel engine puffing along at breakneck speed.

The idea seemed to be to get as many peaches into your sack as quickly as possible, all the while, keeping within a reasonable distance from the speeding tractor. If you dallied too long, you would be forced to run a quarter of a mile chasing the tractor with a full sack of green peaches strapped around your neck.

All the peaches were green. I don't think that I saw a red, ripe peach that entire day. Some of the peaches were just too small to bother picking. Clearly one would never fill his sack if he grabbed the peaches that were the size of marbles, or Ping-Pong balls. So you ran around the tree as fast as you could, snatching at the largest peaches within reach and sight. Then you galloped after the tractor trailer, jumped up onto the trailer and dumped your sack into one of the bins.

I can still hear the clunking sound of those rock hard little peaches bouncing onto the wooden bottom of those bins. The assistant, who rode on the trailer, then handed you a token. It was a wooden token about the size of a quarter. We did this until about noon. At that time all the tractors, with their cargo of green peaches were routed back to our starting point and unloaded.

The bins were stacked on flatbed trucks, and we gladiators were all instructed to take a lunch break.

Carol and I got our tuna fish sandwiches and jug of Kool-Aid from the van. We then retired to the shade of an equipment shelter. We shuffled a couple of bushel baskets together. We stretched a dusty, paper sack we found laying on the ground across the bushel baskets in place of a tablecloth and sat down to eat.

It was a beautiful day. How wonderful it was, I thought, to be working out in this fresh air instead of some apple cannery, breathing rice hulls and sawdust through a paper filter. The scene was one of pickup trucks, dusty red farm tractors, forklifts and flatbed trucks buzzing about in the noisy, but enjoyable, atmosphere of production. The sky was bright and blue and littered with random white, puffy clouds. The still live, but semi-exhausted, bodies of peach pickers were sprawled about the area.

A tank truck was spraying ground crops in a field next to our peach grove. The truck's spray was being buffeted by the wind, and occasionally woofed up, and pushed across our lunching sanctuary. We ate in a cloud of dust and a hearty cough, cough, cough.

In between puffs of spray and dust, I noticed that our tablecloth had words and symbols stamped about its surface. One of the symbols was a rather distinctive skull and crossbones. I hadn't seen a symbol such as that since our last retreat to the Daytona motorcycle races. Why would they stamp a skull and crossbones onto a paper sack, I wondered.

As I munched on my tuna fish sandwich, I shifted and cocked my head around reading the lettering on our makeshift tablecloth. It went something like this: WARNING! This bag contains a highly poisonous material fatal to animals and human beings. The contents of this bag should be handled with extreme care and only in strictest accordance with the manufacturer's directions. This bag should be considered hazardous waste material and should be either buried or incinerated in accordance with federal regulations. Persons involved in the handling of this material should be trained and instructed in its proper use, and should wear the recommended protective equipment.

I nearly spit up my tuna fish. I stopped eating and pointed out the skull and crossbones to Carol. She began to read the package. Our lunch was over.

That next morning when we reported for work, we received a lecture from the management; "El jefe es no happy," garbled the Arkansan foreman. "Peaches mucho verde and too damn small. Mr. Barbrough ain't gonna pay you the forty cents a bushel that you were told. These peaches ain't gradin' to nothin'. All that you gonna get for these peaches is twenty cents a bushel, and if you don't do better today you might only get ten cents tomorrow. You folks knows what yer supposed to be doin'; so let's do it!"

Needless to say Carol and I were beyond shock. The fact that our wages were determined after the work was supplied, and even that price could be changed and manipulated according to the whim of el jefe was really of no consequence when one considered that even at forty cents a bushel this job didn't surpass the prime wages involved in the craft of onion topping. So forty cents, twenty cents, ten cents, or no cents at all, at this rate of pay what did it really matter?

We had already decided to hit the road that evening, but for some unexplainable reason we made the decision to stick around for a little longer. I don't know if it was the faces on those Mexican workers or just curiosity.

The Mexican workers were mumbling and shaking their heads sadly. They were not happy. But once out in the orchard, they attacked the trees with renewed vigor. Looking down those rows of peach trees at the end of each day would have made little Johnny Peach Seed sit down and cry. Broken branches, huge limbs cracked and split from the trunk, it was a genuine disaster. Not enough to make me feel compassion for Mr. Barbrough, but maybe for his grandfather, or great grandfather, or for whoever the poor man was who had enough of a dream to plant that first peach seed.

The next morning we got the "mucho verde" lecture again and we were then informed that we were all bad boys, and we were down to ten cents a bushel. Then for some unexplained reason we had two days off. I presumed that they must have wanted the peaches to "green up" a little. But when we returned on that third day, we met a very, very disgruntled group of workers. They worked the trees but with very little diligence and enthusiasm. The pace was not so much of a run as a walk. When we stopped for our lunch break, two of the workers came over to speak with us. They talked in their broken English about this and that and other trivia. Then one looked up at me intently and asked, while his compadre shuffled and fumbled behind him.

"Can you be shot in this country if you refuse to go to work?" My first reaction was to laugh. But my two inquirers were not laughing. Their dark black eyes were silent and sincere. The fear in their eyes upset me. I felt somewhat enraged that anyone would feel the need to ask that question in this country.

"No, they can not shoot you if you refuse to go to work in this country!" I said indignantly.

I laughed, but they didn't.

"I told you they couldn't shoot us," the boy who was shuffling in the background spoke up to his friend. Then he turned to me. "I told them that they couldn't shoot me. I ain't no damn wetback. I'm American. I live in San Antonio. I used to work in a restaurant. I've got working papers. I'm not illegal."

"Who said that they were going to shoot you?" I asked calmly.

"Mr. Barbrough and the foreman and some others came down to the migrant house in a pickup truck this morning. They all had rifles, and shotguns. None of us had gone to work for two days because we're not making any money here. We were told that we would make good money here picking peaches. I quit my job in the restaurant in San Antonio to come here to work. They told us we would make fifty to one hundred dollars a day. We ain't even making ten dollars. So we didn't go to work. They said if we didn't go to work, they would shoot us. Mr. Barbrough said that he could throw our bodies into a hole and nobody would even look for us because we were all illegal and we didn't belong here in this country in the first place. I told my friends that they couldn't do that in America, but everyone was too scared, especially when they shot the guns in the air and told us all to get moving. I'm no damn wetback. I live in this country. My family would look for me."

"This is ridiculous. If you guys don't want to work for these wages, just don't do it. Pack up and leave. If they threaten you, go to the police department. We have laws in this country. Nobody can shoot anybody here and get away with it."

I tried to speak confidently, but even as I said the words I felt the doubt seeping into my voice. Who would know if one or two of these illegal aliens disappeared? I was sure that they were all illegal, including the little restaurant worker. He was obviously frightened and trying to cover up his status.

Go to the police? If I was in a foreign country, illegally and this situation was put onto me, would I go to the police? This Mr. Barbrough was obviously a rich man. He owned a huge packing house, cold storage facilities, acres and acres of farm land, miles of peaches and fruit, buildings, trucks, tractors, houses. Why couldn't he do whatever he wanted? If he shot Carol and I, who the hell would know about it or even hunt for our bodies? Who were we; Dick the traveling gypsy and his live-under-a-bridge doofus girl friend. If WE showed up at the police department, they would probably arrest us for vagrancy. If we went to a newspaper would they believe us? In their eyes here were two potential hoboes, trying to cause trouble. How could we prove any of these allegations? Carol had a very serious look in her eye.

"They were probably just kidding these boys; just fooling around," I said.

"With shotguns? Do you call that fooling around? I think that we ought to go to the police."

"Yeah right. The police chief's name is probably Harry Barbrough. The judge is probably Ralph Barbrough. And besides that, take a look in the mirror. Do you think that either of us looks like a credible witness? Why couldn't we end up in a hole out behind the migrant house?" This was ridiculous!

My thought was that I had just gone from "Travels with Dick and Jane", to "In Cold Blood" or "Murder on the Orient Express", or "Of Mice and Men". I really didn't want to write a murder thriller. You know what I mean; just a cutesy little book about peach picking. Something that might appeal to the Culinary Institute, or some rich Republican Harvard undergraduates who wanted to rebel against Big Granddaddy Warbucks and run off and top an onion before they took over the firm. I didn't really need this.

For some stupid reason we decided to stick around.

That Sunday we took an excursion out to the migrant farmhouse. The Spanish boys had invited us to talk with them and the others.

The house that they stayed in was a disaster. It was owned by Barbrough and it was situated out in the middle of one of his orchards. It had no plumbing and no water. The area leading up to and surrounding the house, smelled like an open cesspool. For about fifty yards circumference around the house little sprouts of toilet tissue were growing everywhere. The guys were not allowed to go to town. They had no transportation anyway, but they were told that if they were caught in town they would be shot. They had been brought there by way of a friend, to whom they had paid a certain amount of money for the privilege of coming to America and making big bucks picking fruits and vegetables. It was a tragic scene. We knew not what to do.

We worked there a little longer nosing around trying not to arise suspicion. That was already impossible. Our presence alone warranted suspicion enough. We tried discreetly talking to some of the white working hands. Most kept their mouths shut. A few expressed discontent with the situation but said that they too needed a job. In a small town like this one, jobs were hard to find. Besides, it was no concern of theirs.

We met two women who were working as crew bosses. They drove the workers back and forth to the groves and, on occasion, drove the tractors or participated in the harvesting in one way or another. They had compassion for the position of the Mexicans, but felt basically that the Mexicans were no worse off than they were.

They said that they had started working for Barbrough years ago. He did not allow them to work anywhere else. In the past when they tried to move, he forced them to come back. If they went to work for another employer, he called their new boss on the telephone, and they were immediately fired. This whole thing was beginning to get out of hand, and out of mind. We decided to leave.

I don't know if Mr. Barbrough shot any Mexicans, or if those two girls were simply pathological nitwits. We did see Mr. Barbrough one morning having breakfast at a local restaurant. He was tall and slender, and wore western style clothes, cowboy hat and all.

I couldn't stop staring at him. My staring could not but have caught his attention. He leaned his head towards his foreman and, I presume, asked who we were. I guessed this because of the way they whispered and kept looking over at us sitting at the bar. When they came up to the register to pay their check, he glared at me. I'm sure that he could have cared less what I or my wife thought about him. Yet he peered at us for a good moment or two. He never spoke. He didn't even say good morning, or how are you. My wife has since suggested that he had no idea who we were, and that he only stared at us because I was staring at him. She could be right. What do I know?

4   The Chicken Factory

We decided that little Mena, Arkansas was a town worth exploring. It was situated at the base of the Ouachita mountain range, and had a beautiful parkway that tumbled along on top of the mountain and erupted its way into the state of Oklahoma. It should go without saying that we were still in need of money. Through no fault of our own, we left Mr. Barbrough's bank account virtually unscathed. Consequently, we found ourselves again seeking out our favorite people.

"I don't suppose that you have any jobs available in this town?" I announced, rather brazenly, as we stumbled into the little two employee downtown government employment office.

"We sure do! We have lots of jobs for people who are willing to work," one of the ladies behind the counter informed me with equal braze.

My wife was in "hearts and livers" and I was in "gizzards". We were now working on an assembly line in a chicken factory deep in the heart of the state of Arkansas - Ranis, Arkansas, to be exact; quite a spot to say the least. Large white chickens were roaming the streets everywhere. Every backyard seemed to have its own flock of little white chickens. Each and every dog, even the strays, invariably seemed to be prancing up and down the streets of Ranis with a large white chicken between its chops.

The assembly line went something like this. The chickens were strung up by the legs. As they dangled helplessly, their little heads were run over an electrified conveyor belt. After they had been stunned into an unconscious state, their throats were slit by this little fellow brandishing a very big, sharp knife. This poor or lucky fellow, depending upon your point of view, got paid fifty cents per hour extra for performing the dirty deed.

The chickens then went through some kind of hot water dip, and then into a beater room. They came out of this beater room minus their feathers. They then came sliding down a shoot into our department where they were re-hung on a stainless steel overhead rail system. This overhead system wound, back and forth, through our department, much like a waiting line at Disney World. People were lined up at various stations to do the essential jobs, after a special machine removed the oil gland from the poor bird's tail.

There was any number of fascinating, interesting, rewarding jobs to be done at "the Chicken Factory". With diligent and purposeful determination you could become a button-holer, a gut extractor, a fat puller, a gizzard snipper, a wrapper, a packer, a boxer, a loader - ah yes, the opportunities for advancement were endless.

The button-holer was the person who stood at the beginning of the belt system with a long pair of stainless steel scissors and - I don't know how to put this delicately - jammed one blade of the scissors into the chicken's rectum, and thusly snipped, in order to enlarge the hole to the point where the gut extractor could reach into the chicken and pull out all of whatever was stuffed inside there. The fat puller then separated the internals from the globs of chicken fat that protected them when they were once functioning happily inside our little buddy.

Hello? Do we have any chicken lovers out there; the Florida Defenders of the Chicken, maybe? How about Green Chicken? Can you picture a radical bunch of chicken freedom fighters bursting into a chicken factory and beating up on button-holers, and fat pullers? I can hear them screaming now, with tears streaming down their cheeks; "My God! How can you people do this? Does your mother know that you pull fat for a living? You over there? How would you like to have your hole buttoned lady?"

In any case, after the fat puller did her dirty business to this poor chicken, all of the chicken's insides would then be dangling there on the chicken's outsides. Oh, and by the way, all of this excess fat was not removed and thrown away. It was stuffed back inside the chicken a little further on down the line.

My wife, as I commented earlier, was in hearts and livers. She had a pair of stainless steel scissors and as the chickens came rolling by, she would snip off the heart and the liver and drop them into a trough that connected to a heart and liver conveyor belt. I performed a similar operation on the gizzard. In such a manner, the assembly line went along until all the vital parts were removed, and the chicken had no internals dangling from its externals.

We worked on the third shift, and all of our co-workers were from India, Afghanistan, Pakistan, Iran, Vietnam, Mexico, Argentina, Peru, or some other distant and foreign land. It appeared that the only legal workers were the foreman (Igor) and his second in command (Mrs. Igor), my wife and I, and four Choctaw Indians who were bussed in from Oklahoma each night. Oh yes, please don't let me forget the complete crew of six to ten Federal Government inspectors.

While my wife and I, along with this international peace keeping assembly of the world wide brotherhood of underpaid workers, struggled along this assembly line, these federal inspectors sat on stools and stuck their noses into every chicken's button hole. I never figured out exactly what they were looking for. At first I figured one of them had lost his chewing gum or something, but that couldn't have been the case each and every night.

These guys lived in a world apart. They never talked or gave instructions to any of the workers. They lunched in their own special, separate dining trailer. They spoke and socialized with supervisors and management only. I don't know if this was a government procedure, a worker management requirement, a social class thing, or just their personal preference. But, whatever, it was quite obvious that they were a group apart, or a slice above, or quarantined. In any case, they certainly didn't mingle with us riff-raff. I had never really seen anything quite like it. And clearly they had a don't look/don't tell policy with regards to illegal workers. It certainly was hard not to notice – but they managed to do it.

On that first night, I was put at the gizzard station. When I arrived, there were three of us snipping gizzards - myself, Mohammed and Mohammed.

Everyone from a Middle Eastern country is named Mohammed, or has Mohammed as some part of their name, or would rather have you call them Mohammed than listen to you mispronounce their real name.

This chicken factory was so loud you could hardly hear yourself think. The machines were banging and clanging, belts were rattling, motors were buzzing, and gears were churning. In order to talk to the person next to you, you literally had to scream into his ear. The job was so boring that if you didn't talk to somebody you'd go snip crazy; ... snip-snip ... snip-snip ... snip-snip.

Mohammed would take the first chicken. Then the second Mohammed would take one of the two that the first Mohammed let go by, and I'd get the third chicken. This system was working fine until Mrs. Igor figured that Mohammed, Mohammed and Dick were having too much fun.

Mrs. Igor was a little round shouldered, bony thing who always seemed to have a cigarette dangling from her mouth. She would stand each evening at the entrance leaning up against the doorway. With that cigarette dangling from her mouth, she kind of looked like Humphrey Bogart leaning up against a lamp pole - the only difference was Humphrey Bogart was much prettier. She always had this sarcastic, all knowing smirk on her face. I could never figure why, as a part of her gear, she wasn't given a bull whip to crack over our heads. I really think that she would have enjoyed the opportunity.

After about an hour or so, she wiggled her finger at Mohammed number one, and he went scurrying over to her in his most respectful, Middle Eastern manner.

So then it was just me and my good buddy Mohammed number two. Naturally, we snipped every other chicken, and things went fine until Mrs. Bogart wiggled her finger at Mohammed number two, and off he went.

So there I was by myself; snip-snip ... snip-snip ... snip-snip. I thought that I was doing fine until Mrs. Bogart suddenly appeared behind me. She tapped me on the shoulder and with her ever present cigarette dangling from her lips, she stuck out her palm and displayed to me a gizzard. It seems that I had missed one. She grinned, venomously.

For the next hour or so she popped up behind me periodically with a gizzard displayed in her palm. Being the gentleman that I am, I took the gizzard each time and placed it on the gizzard conveyor belt and thanked her for her diligence.

When she finally stopped bugging me with gizzards in her palm, the whole assembly line began to speed up. It was no longer; snip-snip ... snip-snip. It was; snip-snip, snip-snip, snip-snip. I was snipping gizzards as fast as my little snipper could go. There was Mrs. Bogart, back again, giving me her mean look. Her mean look wasn't really that much different than her regular look. The belt kept going faster and faster. I was snipping my little butt off - but, it was virtually impossible. I just couldn't keep up. Instead of just letting a chicken pass me by, with its gizzard still dangling, I decided to wipe a few whole chickens off the line and slip them into the waste, or feed trough. I felt like "I Love Lucy" at the chocolate factory. This was the only possible way that I could physically keep up with the machine.

Where the poor chickens went from there I didn't really know - unfortunately, Mrs. Bogart did. She found my discarded chickens. Suddenly, there she was standing across from me, cigarette dangling from her mouth and holding up four whole chickens.

I smiled and shrugged my shoulders, trying to give her the impression that I knew nothing.

She shook her head, then hissed at me, and walked away. Nevertheless, the belt didn't slow down. It got faster and faster. I was snipping, snipping and snipping when suddenly I snipped a good chunk off the top of my middle finger on my left hand.

I looked over and saw my wife hunched over her hearts and livers, snipping like crazy. Her biggest job related challenge was to avoid snipping the gallbladder while she was trying to snip away her hearts and livers. If she was unsuccessful in this endeavor, the world ended up with a green, gall-stained, grade 'B' chicken. She seemed to be doing all right. But, regardless, at that moment, I had pretty much decided that this job was not for us.

I yelled and screamed at the top of my lungs, trying to get someone's attention. All the while, I kept snipping, trying to keep up while my blood poured out the top of my finger splattering all over the chickens that I was trying to snip. No matter how I screamed or yelled, no one responded.

Then finally Mrs. Bogart showed up. When she saw that it was me who was screaming and yelling, she nearly had a convulsion. She looked at me; her eyes burning with outrage. At this point I displayed for her my bleeding middle finger - with no malice intended, of course.

Mrs. Bogart was in a state of panic. I was disrupting her whole factory. She stood there with her hands on her hips and glared at me. I displayed my finger to her once again, but this time I pointed to the chickens and shook my head negatively. Then I pointed to my finger and nodded my head positively. The message being - Let's forget the chickens lady, and get something for my finger.

Somehow she figured out my sign language and got me a replacement - then escorted me to the band-aid section.

A few hours after returning to my station that evening, three rather official looking gentlemen in suits and ties, popped in the front door. Everybody in the place began jumping out of windows. Everybody, that is, except Carol and I, the four Choctaw Indians, and the ten federally employed Government inspectors. The best that I could figure, it was break time. But why did people jump out windows when it was break time? Curious behavior to say the least.

Then one of the men at the front door held up a badge, and yelled - IMMIGRATION! - and all three men began laughing as they watched everybody in the place fall all over one another trying to make a mass exit.

All of the illegals exited safely. In fact, not one illegal employee was captured by the Immigration. Isn't that amazing? Actually the whole thing was somewhat of a ritual. The Immigration acting in response to complaints by local citizens, popped in about every two weeks to put on this show. Curiously enough, here was a whole industry operating in the heart of America, nearly entirely off the backs of illegal immigrants.

The Spanish speaking illegals came, of course, over our southern boarder, but the Arabs and the Asians were even more interesting. Most of them arrived here on student visas, usually landing in the Northeast. Many came right out of Washington D.C.

They found out about Ranis, Arkansas, and any other number of illegal employment opportunities throughout the United States by going to legitimate employment agencies. They paid these employment agencies hundreds of dollars, upfront, and then after they arrived, so much per week was deducted from their pay checks, and sent to the agency, automatically.

They had social security numbers. Social security taxes - along with federal income taxes - were deducted from their checks each week.

The illegal workers, who had managed to pay off their agency fees, were busy saving every penny that they could, to put towards the purchase of a green card. The green cards were selling for twenty-five hundred dollars at that time. My co-workers told me that these were legitimate green cards, purchased directly from our Government, in Washington D. C.

I don't know how much of what these workers told me was the truth, but the manner in which they volunteered this information, made it all very credible. They told me all of this as if it were all a matter of public information, not as if they were exposing some fraudulent behavior.

Payoffs and purchasing things from other people, or agencies, or governments was a part of their lives, and it went without question. When I expressed disbelief that social security and other taxes were actually being taken out of their paychecks on the basis of their purchased social security cards, they immediately showed me their pay stubs. Again, they were not trying to expose anything. They were trying to prove to me the legitimacy of their purchased papers, and establish the notion that all of this was really on the up and up.

Some of the Middle-Eastern boys informed me that they were here in this country because if they had remained in their homeland they would, most probably, be killed. When I asked why they would be killed, they very causally informed me that their parents were members of the opposition party in their country, and that in their country opposition meant opposition.

When I expressed outrage at this intolerance, they laughed. "You are American," they said. "You would not understand." By their tone I realized they thought I was very unworldly. For their part, they thought nothing of the fact that they were under the gun. They went on to inform me that if their families were to regain power back home, they would return to their countries and there would be a new group of escapees working at this chicken factory. It seemed that, they too, would be willing to shoot their enemies rather than discuss their political differences in public debate.

All of these young men, especially those from Afghanistan, Pakistan, India and the surrounding area appeared to be very well educated. Some of them told us that they had two or three college degrees. These degrees were almost always in the sciences. So then, why were they working in a Chicken factory, for less than minimum wage, in the middle of Arkansas?

Well, as we know, having student visas, they really had no permission to be working in this country, but with all of this education why weren't they working in their own country?

One, they were political refugees, as previously mentioned. Besides that, there were no jobs in their countries. They said that the Shah, or the King, or whoever ran the show over there, believed in education, and many, many people in their country had two or three different college degrees. In fact, education was free. As long as you could find the where-with-all for your basic needs, one could go to school as long as he wanted. But it seems, though the King, or the Shah was very much into educating his people, he wasn't that big on providing jobs for his people after they got their education. So consequently, most of them had to leave their country to find good jobs abroad.

I think of these poor, well educated people often. Especially, whenever I hear our politicians advocating education as the cure for all of our problems here in the States. Here were these very, very bright young fellows, all with degrees in chemistry, physics, math etc. They were snipping gizzards in a chicken factory in a little town in "Nowhere" Arkansas because their King graciously provided free education, but forgot to supply industry, and jobs. Which would you rather be – well educated and snipping gizzards in a foreign country or an uneducated bonehead earning twelve dollars an hour right at home in your own country?

These illegal employees who worked this federally inspected processing plant with a line of federal inspectors checking each and every chicken's button hole, had social security cards, had taxes taken out of their pay, and lived in trailer houses that were federally funded. It seems that the man who owned this plant got the trailers for free, or from a government program that was initially set up to relocate Vietnamese, who were brought here after the Vietnam War.

Four, five, or even six to eight individuals were housed in one trailer. The rent was one hundred and fifty dollars per month – that was per person, of course.

The person who owned this chicken factory owned, virtually, the whole town. He owned a clothing store, a grocery store, and a recreation center. The illegal employees purchased everything necessary for their existence without leaving the factory area - without even using money, in fact. They were given discount credit vouchers that could be used to purchase overpriced goods at company run businesses.

At this plant we were all paid minimum wage, of course. That is, as long as the assembly line kept rolling. When the line stopped, our paychecks stopped. Some weeks we would be on the job fifty, or fifty-five hours, and get paid for thirty-five to thirty-eight hours. In all the weeks that we worked there, we never got paid for a full forty hours, as I remember.

Another little point of interest to me was that many of the people who worked there had scabs and sores all over their hands and faces. These sores were so noticeable that I finally asked this one fellow what it was that he and everybody else had growing on them. I really thought that maybe they had a nuclear power plant in the area or something, and this was just a part of the local fallout. He looked at me rather matter-of-factly and said; "Oh, you mean this?" - pointing to a scab on the back of his hand.

"Yes that," I said.

"Oh, this is just chicken rash," he said. "Everybody gets it eventually. You stay here long enough and you'll have it too."

Periodically, the fans that cooled the live chickens as they waited outside in their crates would go off - power failure or something. Next thing you know, all the chickens on the assembly line start coming through filled with this green, pussy stuff. Then out came these vacuum cleaners. Each of the federal inspectors got one of these vacuum sucking things. They slowed down the line while each inspector stuck this suction thing into each chicken's button hole and extracted this green slop. (Hey? Let's all stop reading and run out and get ourselves a McChicken sandwich. What do you say?)

I've worked in food processing of one kind or another for most of my life. I've worked in meat packing houses, restaurants, sausage making shops etc., etc. Never did working in any of these areas stop me from eating any of the products that I worked with daily. But after just six to eight weeks in a federally inspected chicken processing plant, Carol and I didn't eat chicken for over six months. This wasn't a planned conscious effort. It was just that every time we saw a chicken, we were repulsed.

Do you think that the chickens know that the feed they are eating is, in actuality, other chickens?

Remember that movie where they processed dead humans into pellets which were used as sustenance for live humans in their fictional overpopulated world, "Soylent Green", I think it was called. Well, the heads, feet, innards, even the feathers of the processed chickens, are returned to live chickens in the form of chicken feed. The only thing that doesn't go into chicken feed is that little paper sack that one finds stuffed in the processed chicken's button hole - that tiny package containing the little chicken's heart, liver, gizzard and neck? That package most of us either leave in the chicken by mistake when we bake the darn thing, or put aside for future gravy or something, but which, more often than not, ends up in the garbage pail.

Believe it or not, that package of entrails is the sole reason for the employment of about ninety percent of the people working at the chicken factory. Almost all of us were involved in the processing and handling of that package. They even had this specially designed machine, the sole function of which was to remove the gravel or little stones from the gizzard.

I suppose I shouldn't say this, but if they simply dropped all of that stuff into the chicken feed trough, they could probably save themselves a million dollars a year - but if you don't tell them, neither will I. Maybe those people out there need those jobs - chicken rash and all.

We had no problem with our lodgings while working at the chicken factory. The factory was going twenty-four hours a day, seven days a week, and nobody cared where we parked our camper. But we were not completely satisfied at the plant parking lot. The factory was too darn noisy, and since we worked the third shift our sleeping time was during the day. If you want to sleep during daylight hours, you can sleep almost anywhere in America without a problem. We spent our days in parks and picnic areas, napping after grocery shopping in supermarket parking lots, by lakes and ponds, and often times just under a shady tree anywhere. This worked fine. We had only one rather upsetting experience.

We left work this one morning and went for a little excursion to the town of Mena. We had breakfast, did some grocery shopping, and then spotted a great, big, beautiful oak tree on this quiet little side street in the heart of the very peaceful looking downtown area. We decided to sack out for awhile in the cool shade of this lovely tree. We were both sound asleep, when we were suddenly startled to an abrupt sitting position by what sounded to me like the United States Marine Corps band.

Rat a tat tat - and the drums they banged and the cymbals they clanged - as we peered, droopy-eyed, out our camper bedroom window.

Within touching distance, was a full fledged parade passing; flutes, trombones, drums and bugles - the works! And we couldn't move. The street where we were sleeping had been completely cordoned off by the Mena police department. It wasn't the forth of July, or even George Washington's Birthday. But silly us, and I suppose we should have checked on our calendar. You folks will probably all laugh when you hear this. We completely forgot about Lum and Abner Day. Mena, Arkansas just happens to be the hometown of either Lum, or Abner, or both of these people.

5 Oranges in Altoona

Papa Charlie and his crew were poised and ready to strike into a grove of oranges along side highway forty-two in Altoona, Florida. Altoona is, of course, just north of Umatilla, Florida; which is just north of Eustis, Florida. Then we have Leesburg? Ocala? All of which are within an hour's drive of Disney World. I imagine with that last sentence, a number of people in Paris, France know, approximately, where Papa Charlie was located now.

We were on our way back to conventionalism. Our experiences with three legged ladders, sprays and pesticides, wetbacks and rednecks with shotguns had landed us in two, unimpressive, processing plants as the means of earning our daily bread. *Processing Your Way around America* didn't really sound like that big a seller to either of us.

Suddenly, without any debate on the issue, our van took a sharp left, and there we were, parked on a grassy knoll next to Papa Charlie's goat.

Papa Charlie was a very large Bahamian crew boss, with a deep voice, laced with that distinctive island-English accent, and a broad, warm, inspirational laugh. His face sparked with humor, and curiosity. I know this is a terrible analogy, but if you ever saw that childlike, curious, compassionate face that the movie men put on King Kong, you have a good idea of the physical appearance of Papa Charlie.

Papa Charlie's goat was not the kind with ears, a tail, and the propensity to lick labels off tin cans. It was a rather sophisticated piece of orange harvesting machinery. It was a great, big orange colored monster that rumbled through a grove like a tank over a sand dune. It had huge duel wheels in the rear, and was about the size of a ten yard dump truck. In fact, it was a dump truck, but a very unusual one. It didn't just tip up its load with a hydraulic lift, and have its cargo tumble off the rear. It scissored its entire holding box straight up into the air then dumped its tonnage of juice oranges off its side and into an open topped tractor trailer box. I don't know how many bushels of oranges the goat carried but it was in the hundreds.

In appearance it reminded me of something that Rommel might have used to carry troops in the desert during World War II. It had a cab with a seat, but no protective cover for the driver. Directly behind the driver, sat a heavy duty hydraulic arm, in place of a machinegun turret. The arm would operate to either side of the truck. It latched onto specially designed, twenty bushel, fiberglass tubs with metal rims. These bins would then be hoisted and dumped into the scissoring carry box that sat on the back of the goat.

There we were, stopped along the wood side on a sunny day with the prospect of continuing along the paved path back to nine to five, or taking the road less traveled. From what I could see, much less traveled, and for good reason.

As I looked out my van window at Papa Charlie's picking crew, I saw an accumulation of ninety-nine percent black people. There was one older, bearded white man, who strongly resembled Gabby Hayes, and one white hippie looking couple, who were openly sucking the last fumes from a joint which they were passing back and forth between pinched fingernails.

I thought that my bride had gone completely crazy. As they all stared at us, my only thought was a very large reluctancy to exit the protection of my van. I can still see Carol's beaming face, sitting behind that steering wheel. She was a grin from ear to ear, her eyes were sparkling, and her face was pink with the spirit of enthusiasm. What was wrong with this child?

I had no choice. She had already jumped from the van and was heading directly towards what looked to me to be a mongrel gang of Crypts and Bloods. They were all wearing peculiar headgear. Some had blue or red polka dot bandannas wrapped around their skulls. Others had winter type knit toppers pulled down over their ears. I mean, the Florida sun was burning down. This may have been December, but we weren't in Nova Scotia.

I jumped out of the van, and scurried after her. Clearly there was a protection factor involved here. She had left me completely unprotected in the van. I was all alone, for God's sake. What would you have done?

"Who do we have to see about getting a job picking oranges?" she screamed up to Papa Charlie who was perched atop his roaring desert troop carrier. His eyes were bulging with bewildered curiosity, but the noise from his equipment was clearly overpowering the tiny squeakings emanating from my little orange blossom. Unlike our Mexican friend back in onion territory, he didn't ignore us. He shut off his engine immediately.

"You would like to pick oranges, mum?" He queried in his strong proper island-British brogue.

"We don't know how, but we would like to try it."

"Well mum, that's all it takes. You come back here in the morning, and I will put you to work."

What, or who was Papa Charlie?

My guess would be that he was an uneducated laborer, who, through hard work, and a raw initiative managed to rise to a comfortable, but unenviable by white standards, position within the southern black community and the feudal Florida orange economy.

In our six seasons of orange picking in central Florida orange country, we met only one resident Florida orange grove owner. It was by pure accident that we stumbled onto him.

It was the week before Christmas and all through the grove not a creature was stirring, not even an armadillo. When suddenly with a huff and a puff we hear the putt, putt, putt of a farmer's cart. There in the dark and mist of night, we heard a choir of children singing Silent Night.

"Hello there anybody home?" A man, dressed as Santa Claus, sitting on a tractor that was towing a flatbed trailer loaded with hay and heaped high with cheering children, screamed to the front window of our van. I tumbled out the door hastily, not knowing what to say, but wanting to assuage any notions of trespassing or fears of burglary, but before I uttered even a single word Santa says; "You folks fruit pickers?"

"Yes sir," I say proudly, with no further explanation.

"Well you are perfectly welcome to park here in my grove. These are my oranges," he announced. "I'm the farmer who owns this grove. Enjoy yourselves, and have a merry Christmas."

I thanked our farmer Santa Claus and retired to the van. At the time I thought very little of this grove owner, other than the fact that he was a very proud and rather jovial citrus farmer. We would not meet another resident orange grove owner.

Papa Charlie had a home, we learned, and an additional property where he housed his crew. Papa Charlie was a crew boss. He was employed by a contractor. There were a number of contractors operating in the area. The contractors were actually the substitute farmers, who were hired by absentee owners, to plant, prune, spray, cultivate, and harvest the absentee owner's orange grove or groves. These contractors were large businesses with offices, secretaries, trucks, tractors, loaders, spray equipment, warehouses etc. As a picker, you received your paycheck from the contractor.

Our first problem that next morning hadn't even crossed my imagination. These juice orange trees were huge. It took a twenty to twenty-four foot ladder to barely bridge the peak of one. These ladders weren't your light weight aluminum, extension types that we all have at home sitting in our garages. These were one piece wooden things, cut from the still wet cores of heavy western oak trees. These monstrosities weighed a ton, and they were laying flat on the ground. You tell me, how do you get one of these things off its back and into a standing position?

We had arrived at the grove after sunrise and had unfortunately missed all of the experts in the action of performing this task. Carol and I harnessed all of our brawn to the challenge of erecting this so called ladder. In a good twenty-five minutes we barely got this thing to a forty-five degree angle, never mind perpendicular. Was this all a joke? Were we on Candid Camera? Someone with a camera had to be hiding behind one of these trees. Human beings didn't really pick these trees with a twenty-four foot ladder. They had a machine that did all of this. All of these people here were a part of a movie set.

Whenever we got the top half of this ladder up above forty-five degrees, the bottom legs would pop out of the ground and the whole thing would tumble down on top of us.

Finally Papa Charlie pulled up on his goat. He jumped down and, without a word, ran over to our ladder. He pulled one end of the ladder up over his head. Then he pushed forward on it until the other end dug into the soft beach sand in which Florida orange trees were planted. Then, step by step, rung by rung, hand over hand; he walked the ladder to a standing position. He hefted it up about six inches off the ground, and, balancing it as if it were a flagpole, ran it over to a tree and flopped it in. He did all of this, by himself, in less than a minute. Then again without saying a word, he jumped back onto his goat and plowed off into the orange grove.

Well, that was easy enough. Problem number two; how to get the oranges off this tree and into our twenty bushel fiberglass vat that sat at the bottom of our first orange tree. We took a stroll down the rows of trees to observe the other workers in action. Most of the men had picking sacks that they carried into the tree with them. We were given no such sack. We asked one of the black workers where he got his sack, hoping that they were supplied by the boss. No such luck.

"I bought it, maun," he replied gaily, without missing a beat. "But you don't need a sack, maun. You can just drop 'em, maun, like this ..." He started plucking oranges from their stems and releasing them to bounce through the limbs of the tree and plunk to the ground.

As we continued to walk about, we saw a number of other workers doing just that. They would race around the tree, moving their ladder from spot to spot as if it were a toothpick. Then after they had plucked and dropped all of the fruit to the ground, they would grab up a five gallon plastic pail and scurry around the base of the tree on their hands and knees, scooping the fruit into the pail. They would lug the pail over and dump it into the twenty bushel, orange colored, fiberglass vat.

So, there you go - easy enough. Now I had only one problem remaining. How was I going to get Carol up that damn twenty-four foot ladder? We debated the issue and it was decided that I was the boy and she was the girl. I don't quite know what that has to do with anything, but according to Carol that meant that I would be up in the tree doing the 'dropping' and she would be down, safe and sound, on the ground doing the picking up.

I won't say that I was afraid of heights, but how does one know, if he has never been perched on top of an orange tree? I don't remember exactly how long it took me to actually release both hands from the rungs of the ladder, simultaneously, to do my orange plucking, but it was no overnight condition.

My first transition from holding on with one hand and dropping fruit with the other, was the one arm through the ladder, or wrap yourself in the ladder technique. This technique I adopted for quite some time.

I overcame my initial fear of falling from the top of an orange tree by falling from the top of an orange tree. Before my actual full fledged tumble, I had a multitude of very close calls.

One common problem is that there is always that one elusive orange just slightly beyond your all out stretching position. It is the last orange left hanging on the tree. You can either stretch out and get it now; if not, you must go all the way down to the bottom of the ladder, hoist and move that redwood six inches. Then climb back up to the top of the tree in order to pluck that one last orange. You could leave it on the tree, but no one else does - no one! If you do, every picker sees it as he exits the grove for the day and shakes his head and smiles. He then looks at you, as the word amateur flashes in neon just above your head.

On this one particular occasion I left an orange in the top of a tree. As we were packing up all our gear making ready to exit the grove, a tourist passing by in his car, actually pulled off the highway, ran up to Papa Charlie and said with index finger of left hand raised and pointing; "You see that fourth tree in the fifth row from the right. There's an orange in the top of it." The entire crew, including Papa Charlie, turned and looked at me. No one knew what to say. It was a disgrace, like the washed sheet of a bed wetter hanging out his second floor window.

I saved a little face by telling the tourist that Florida law required that the picking crew leave, at minimum, one orange per grove, as seed stock. I do think that he believed me.

In any case, invariably, when you go that extra inch trying to snatch that last orange, your ladder does a flip-flop and there you are dangling wrong side up. From there you have absolutely no alternative but to call out to your wife who from her firm, safe position on the ground, helps you flip your ladder right side over.

Next the limb, on which you've braced your ladder, breaks. My reaction to this situation has always been to grab onto the ladder with both hands and both feet and scream. The difficult part of this technique is the screaming. It is nearly impossible to get out a good scream, when your heart is in your mouth.

After this happens to you forty or fifty times, and you realize that at worst the ladder will usually be stopped by another limb, or by the trunk of the tree, your Tarzan yelp pitters down to an - "Oh God!" - or something slightly less religious.

On one occasion, to my dismay, I ran into a tree with no trunk. Well, it had a trunk, but it was in the shape of a 'V'. No, actually it was more of a 'Y'. In any case, my ladder-holding outside limb broke from under me, and as we two friends tumbled through the tree expecting to be stopped in last resort by the tree's trunk, we arrived to the center only to find wide open space. I had the conductor punch my ticket at the tree's center and went straight on through. My wife found me with my feet still hooked under a rung and my head buried in the dirt at the bottom of (what used to be the top of) my ladder. The ladder had titter-totted over the pivot, and toppled me heels over head on the opposite side of the tree.

Now for some tips on free falling from the top of an orange tree. This might sound very dangerous, but actually - it is!

Just as if you were to jump off the top of the Empire State Building, you would probably hit somebody's patio five or six stories from the top and never float through the air for a mile to be splattered on the New York sidewalk. By the same logic even a running leap from the edge of the Grand Canyon, will not provide you with enough oomph to swan dive into the Colorado River. You will float, at best, fifteen or twenty feet where upon your swan dive will be interrupted by a big rock or ledge, abutting from the canyon's sloping walls.

Free falling from the top of an orange tree is similar in that you will not soar through the air for too long a period, before a tree limb will break your fall. From that point on, your fall will continue to be broken by tree limbs five or six more times before your body is actually deposited in the dirt at the base of the tree.

My biggest problem after such an event was finding my eye glasses which were usually clinging by leaf or limb halfway up the tree. Truthfully, my wife usually found my glasses, because without my glasses I would be very lucky to be able to find an orange grove, never mind a single tree.

We didn't rough and tumble our way into the big bucks of fruit picking immediately. But, our three bins a day at seven dollars per bin were enough to keep the concrete and asphalt of the big city from our camper door.

Theoretically, if you had the strength and stamina, you could pick oranges nearly seven days a week. Even if Papa Charlie wasn't in the grove that Sunday with his trusty goat, you could fill up all of the empty bins in the grove if you had a liking to and he would pick them all up the following day.

If you had any imagination at all, you could always find an excuse not to work at least one day a week. We made one priority early on - no working in the rain. It just wasn't worth the effort.

While I was mastering ladder moving, lifting, and placement, along with tree tumbling, and; Look ma, no hands on the ladder - Carol was organizing the ground work. Within two months of concentrated effort we were up to an average of five bins a day. This meant gross earnings of between thirty-five and forty-five bucks per outing.

We were ecstatic. We were accomplishing our dream. Here we were meeting our monetary goals, and spending our winter in warm, sunny Florida. This can't be considered all bad by any hobo's standards.

At this point, Carol had five to seven plastic pails. She would pick the bottoms of the trees, and as high as she could reach from the ground, and I would 'drop' the tops. We didn't know how well we were doing as compared to the other workers, but we guess-timated that we two were accomplishing approximately what one single hard working professional fruit picker did alone. To our total amazement, this was not even close to the truth. The average Bahamian in Papa Charlie's crew doubled our output - and then there was Lanzo.

Lanzo was Papa Charlie's good buddy. They came to the States from the Bahamas together, and through all these years, Lanzo picked only for Papa Charlie.

Lanzo, in appearance, was rather nondescript. He was average height, about five foot ten, and rather slender. He would arrive at the campfire at the edge of the grove every morning with a large can of Colt 45. Like his good buddy, he always wore a smile, but unlike his pal, Papa Charlie, he rarely ever said a word. The only thing that would distinguish him from the rest of the crew was his obvious maturity. He was probably two, to two and a half times the age of any of the other young men. He was the slow moving type, almost lethargic. He was never in a rush to begin working, and equally indifferent to stopping. In all honesty, we thought Lanzo was an over the hill picker, who worked for cigarette and beer money. Needless to say we were rather aghast when Carol, politely, asked Papa Charlie who his best picker was. "Well, that would have to be Lanzo, mum."

"Yes," I interrupted, assuming that he was speaking in terms of endearment and loyalty, "but who picks the most oranges?"

"Well, Mr. Noble that would be Lanzo. Lanzo has been picking fruit the majority of his life, Mr. Noble and, he's the best that I've ever seen, without question."

"Better than you?" I said with a smile.

"Oh, ha, ha, ha - surely better than I, Mr. Noble. That's why I drive this goat, maun. I couldn't stomach the thought of being placed aside Lanzo in the grove each morning." His laugh boomed as he cranked up his goat and plowed off into the orchard.

At this point we didn't know, nor were we concerned about how much money anybody else earned. We were primarily concerned with achieving our personal goals. We were not at any stage for competition. We were too busy trying to be the best that we could be. We knew that we had a lot of learning to do, along with building back, leg, arm, and shoulder muscles. We slept well each and every night, believe me. We were usually in bed before nine o'clock.

We had no idea how skilled a human being could become at such a relatively mundane task. But that's the "human being" for you. You take a human, well some humans; put two sticks in his hand at the age of five and forty years later you have Buddy Rich, or Gene Krupa.

You flop a little boy down in front of a piano. He starts out making noise and one day ends up playing Tchaikovsky or Erroll Garner.

Some boys and girls don't get the chance to sit behind pianos, drums, or musical instruments. They don't get palettes and paint brushes at Christmas time. They never learn to hear themselves sing. They, instead, apply their humanness into prying the meat from the bones of dead animals with a knife; pounding nails into boards until they become homes, businesses, or doll houses; or bolting, screwing, and stacking beam on top of beam to Empire State proportions. Each, in his or her way, develops the human art - just as Lanzo had done with the orange. His art wasn't painting it, or even growing one. His art was in the picking.

Even after Papa Charlie had praised Lanzo, we had no idea what it meant to be the best that Papa Charlie had ever seen.

One morning we found Lanzo plying his craft to the two rows of orange trees aside our assignment. By the time that we had picked two bins Lanzo had six. When we finally dumped our last exhausting bucketful into our fifth bin, Lanzo had filled fifteen.

This was beyond comprehension. If Papa Charlie had told us that Lanzo was capable of picking fifteen bins a day, we would never have believed it. This would appear to anyone who had ever tried, to be physically impossible. How quickly could the human hand move? What was he doing that we weren't? What possible tricks could there be to plucking a damn orange off a tree?

Now I had a new understanding of Papa Charlie's statement regarding his humiliation at being placed aside Lanzo each morning. These feelings were something again. For days after that experience, I had difficulty looking Lanzo in the eye. I kept thinking, for God's sake I was no damn wimp. My first job was unloading freight cars of beef. I could carry a quarter of a cow on my shoulder and still stoop down to pick up a cigarette butt. At one point I tried my hand at lifting barbells. I could press two hundred pounds over my head, and drag four hundred pounds up off the floor to my waist. I'm not saying this to brag, but here was this little man, who was probably three inches shorter, fifty pounds lighter, and thirty years older not only out performing me and my wife in an orange grove, but doing so to the point of ridicule. We had been doing this job now for a few months. How many ways is there to break an orange from its stem and put it into a box?

The man worked in a manner that would rock a baby to sleep. He never ran, skipped, or hopped. In terms of speed, the best one could boast is that he worked steadily. Every time I snuck a peek down his row, he was leaning on the side of a bin, pealing an orange to eat. From then on, I told my wife that we would have to stop at least three times a day and eat an orange. We did, but it didn't help.

It was at the morning campfires from that point on that I began to notice the mystique of Lanzo. When he approached the fire every morning with his can of Colt 45, a slow, respectful silence would settle in. Most of the younger men bowed their heads slightly, just as I did. In subdued tones, one after the other, they bid him good morning. What else could you do? He was 'the man'. Not the man to beat; that was not even in question. He was ONE HUNDRED BUSHELS PER DAY ahead of the best of them. It is one thing to be bettered one particular day by an equal. It is another thing to be knocked down and dragged through the dirt, day after day, by an old, grey haired man.

Carol had a much better attitude than I did about this whole situation. I went into a kind of pronounced sulk, and wanted my ladder at the opposite end of wherever Lanzo happened to be. But Carol ran, at each new grove, to have us placed beside Lanzo. And there was no waiting line for the position. All the young Crypts and Bloods were perfectly content to shuffle off down the grove. I did my best to ignore this fact. But every semi-free moment Carol had, she would watch Lanzo. She would talk to him every morning, and tell him how much she admired his abilities. He was more than humble in accepting her praise. He was actually shy. I really don't think that he was even aware of his achievement. He was a simple man, out to make a living, and I'm sure that he had met no one outside of an orange grove who was envious of his position.

In any case, the first tidbit of information she deduced from her observations, was, I suppose, a rather obvious one. Lanzo picked with a sack.

We analyzed what we were doing. It did seem kind of stupid. Instead of picking the oranges putting them into a sack and carrying them over to the bin, we were plucking the oranges from the tree, then tossing them onto the ground and picking them up again. Actually we were two people working as one. I was the picker and Carol was the sack.

It wasn't all that simple, though. Sacks cost money. This type sack held two bushels of oranges. I don't know how much two bushels of oranges weighs, but I would guess somewhere between fifty and one hundred pounds. Could Carol run around the bottom of the tree dragging a hundred pound sack on her hip? Could Dick negotiate a hundred pound sack of oranges on the top of a twenty four foot ladder? Dick, who had barely managed the art of balancing a ladder, and plucking with both hands, simultaneously?

By our way of thinking, picking with a sack was like adding weight to a race horse. It had to be more of a punishment than a benefit. Besides, a picking sack cost twenty seven dollars. Two sacks amounted to a whole day's pay.

We ordered two sacks from Papa Charlie, very reluctantly.

When he brought them that next morning, we were like two kids at Thom McCann's lacing up our brand new saddle shoes.

An orange picking sack is like nothing that I had ever seen before. The closest thing to it was the sack that I used as a kid to carry my newspapers on my delivery route. They both had a wide shoulder strap to distribute the sagging weight. They both draped over one shoulder, while the burden was slung down the opposite side of the body. The orange sack was narrower, but two or three times as long, and it had more hardware.

It had a metal hoop woven into its mouth. This hoop was half-moon shaped, and it kept the sack open, and taunt, so that it clung to your hip like an open barrel. This enabled one to toss the oranges into the sack without fumbling around looking for an opening.

The sack had no bottom. So, if you tossed an orange into it, the orange would slide through the sack, and tumble out the bottom and onto the ground. To prevent this from happening, a flap was designed into the bottom of the sack. The flap was triangle shaped, and had two pieces of rope woven into the triangle which went from the peak of the triangle, down both sides to the corners of the bottom of the sack. The ropes dangled out of the peak and were fastened to a metal snap. The snap would be then brought up and fastened to one of two metal hooks which were sown onto the face of the sack, one above the other. In this way the sack folded onto itself to form an artificial bottom. If you hooked the snap on the lower hook, you now had a bag that would hold two bushels of oranges. If you hooked it on the higher clip, your sack would hold, approximately, one bushel of oranges.

Now, when you lugged your oranges over to the twenty bushel vat, or bin, you simply hoisted the sack up onto the edge of the bin, unfastened the clasp which released the false bottom and watched your bushel or two tumble out of the hole in the bottom of your bag and disappear into the vastness of that twenty bushel orange-eating excavation called a bin.

A bushel of oranges in the bottom of that bin looked like a dozen raisins on the bottom of a two gallon mixing bowl. Dumping that first bushel of oranges into that bin was usually enough to discourage the first seventy percent of the humans who harbored aspirations of becoming wealthy professional orange pickers. But, Carol and I were not picking oranges to become wealthy, we were picking oranges because we ... ah ... because, ah ... Carol and I were picking oranges because we were ... Christians? We had a subconscious ethic to help feed the world? ... because we were reincarnationists and we believed that we needed to be purged of the sins of our past lives? ... because we enjoyed poverty and reveled in the notion of living under bridges and in forests with other similarly sick minded people? ... because we were Buddhist in search of our true dharma?

I really don't know, but to tell the truth we were truly happy to be doing what we were doing at that point in our lives. Besides, nothing that we had been doing in our conventional lives, up until this point, had filled us with awe or inspiration. Our days were not now being filled, quietly, with desperation, as an old friend once commented with regards to civilization in general. At bottom, we were alive, and we were having fun. We were sore, tired, overworked, and under paid, but we were having fun.

Nevertheless, even with the inclusion of our new picking sacks, our production did not increase. When we told Papa Charlie about this situation, he laughed uproariously and said; "Yes sir, Mr. Noble, I had the same problem, maun. When I first started picking oranges, I bought one of them new picking sacks, maun. They told me that a maun with a fancy new picking sack like that could pick himself twice as many oranges. Well maun, I hung that sack up in a tree and by the end of the day, maun, that sack hadn't picked even one extra orange." He stared me in the eye for a moment, waited for my smile, then cranked up his goat and drove off into the grove.

The moral of that story was a simple one. Sacks don't pick fruit, people do. If you don't know how to use the sack properly, it won't do you a darn bit of good. We were living proof of that fact.

So, what were we doing wrong? Well, it was plainly clear that Carol's production had increased. I, on the other hand, had been slowed down to a crawl. With the sack method, Carol was now five or six tree bottoms ahead of me. There was no question about it; I was the one who had to improve. I had to pick the top of the tree at least as fast as Carol could pick the bottom, or start out each day an hour or two ahead of her.

As time went on, I improved or Carol slowed down. Nevertheless, our production did increase. We contented ourselves to picking seven bins per day. This amounted in dollars to between forty-nine and sixty-three dollars per day. We weren't the best pickers that Papa Charlie ever saw, but we were making a living and accomplishing our goal. We were earning money to finance our travels about America. We were going places, and in an interesting manner. We were Steinbecking America. We were doing things, meeting people, and seeing parts of America that we two, and maybe you, would never have thought existed. And it was fun!

6 Peaches in Michigan

As is the case with most amateurs, we really weren't ready to take our act onto the road, but we thought we were. We had made a living all winter in Florida picking citrus. Not only did we earn a living but we saved money to boot. We even opened up a savings account in a bank in downtown Eustis. We had no phone but, Big Bass Campground, Ocala National Forest, was an accepted address. It seems that many people, with a much more substantial savings than we, were also using that same address.

I think that it is interesting to note, that in our entire career as migrants we never grossed enough money to qualify for payment of income taxes, our combined earnings not in excess of fifty-five hundred dollars. Yet we lived, paid our Social Security, traveled all over America, paid maintenance and repair on our van camper, had breakfast at the EAT in Umatilla, Kielbasa sandwiches and cold beer at our regular haunt in a bar in Hartford, Michigan, Pizza in South Haven, and all the chicken that you could eat at a cafeteria at the back of a small Roses department store in the Eustis mall. Of course, need I mention that we made our regular patriotic contributions to Hardy's, Pizza Hut, McDonalds and company. Still, we saved enough money out of our wages to buy a new 450 Suzuki motorcycle; pay twenty-five hundred cash money for a secondhand Airstream travel trailer; spend one summer vacationing in Saint Augustine, Florida; take a two week fishing trip with friends to Canada catching Pike and Walleye; fish for Salmon and Steelhead in Michigan; Rainbow Trout in New Mexico; Bass, Shell Cracker and Crappie in Florida and Arkansas; and pay chiropractors all over America to fix my wife's poor aching back.

You may think that this was impossible, and I won't argue with you. It is very hard for me to believe and I lived it.

The hot Florida summer was coming and orange picking was drawing to a close. We had conversations with members of Papa Charlie's crew and learned about the prospects of Georgia peaches, and "rough and tumble" apple picking in South Carolina.

The rough and tumble aspect, dealt with the notion that all of these apples were to be processed for juice. Therefore, you could handle them rough, not worrying about bruises or bad spots. If they happened to tumble to the ground before you got the chance to pick them, you could snatch them up and they would still be acceptable. Even with the rough and tumble option we headed North, all the way to the State of Michigan.

Okay, now close your eyes and think Michigan. What do you see? Well, if you're like me, you see hubcaps and chrome automobile bumpers. But Michigan south, west, north, and even somewhat east, is jammed packed with farm produce. Soybeans, corn, navy beans, squash, cucumbers, broccoli, asparagus, peaches, apples, pears, cherries, tomatoes - you name it, and we had our hands, knees, elbows and butts into it in Michigan. It all started at pick a peach daily, Daily Farms, in Hart, Michigan.

We heard about Mr. Daily from those two joint smoking hippies that we met along side highway 42 back in Altoona. To our good fortune, they had already "played" Michigan and had a long list of places to go and people to meet. Mr. Daily's name was tops on the list. I really thought that Mr. Daily was a rather nice fellow, until he introduced us to his pickle patch.

Pickles look a heck of a lot like cucumbers to me. It seems, if you don't pick them fast enough, they will be. Oh please don't throw me into that pickle patch, said bre'r Noble to farmer Daily - but he did. The man was without mercy. Truthfully, we had arrived too early for apples, and even a month early for his peach crop. But, since we were here with nothing to do, we could make a little expense money in the pickle patch, if we would like - informed Mr. Daily.

"Oh, okay, that sounds great!" said the fly to the spider.

This particular pickle patch was a half acre to a one acre square. Picking a pickle patch is relatively simple in theory. You start picking at one end, then continue to pick until you reach the other end. This process takes days, not hours. When you finally get to the other end, you take your tractor and twenty bushel bin and go back to where you started and do it all over again.

Low and behold, right there where you had diligently picked pickles a few days ago, there is a whole new crop of tiny little pickles waiting to be plucked. As you will remember; Peter Piper picked a peck of pickles. If Peter Piper picked a peck of peppered pickles, then where are the peppered pickles that Peter Piper picked?

This is the theory, but as is often the case, the "in practice" can differ greatly. For example, if you don't get your pickle picking butt moving, when you return to the beginning of your little pickle patch, you won't find pickles. You will find watermelons. If not watermelons, these big green things the size of which reminds you of a watermelon, at least in comparison to the tiny dill gherkins you plucked when you first arrived.

There is another very disconcerting problem that one encounters when pickle plucking. I don't know if any other pickle pickers have ever pointed this out to Management, but whoever designed the pickle, made it the exact same color as its vine and leaf. This, in my opinion, is an obvious design flaw; trying to find a little green pickle the size of your baby finger amidst a forest of green leaf and vine, borders on the ridiculous. If it were up to me, pickles would be red. No doubt about it. If people want green pickles, we could always dye them later, as with white Napoleon maraschino cherries, and green Satsuma oranges. I have no problem with this. Management and design team, please take note.

Fortunately, pickle picking didn't last long - at least not for us. Pickle season ended as soon as we received our first paycheck. We concluded that there must have been a mistake here somewhere. Mr. Daily was much too nice an individual to allow us to work his pickle patch for peanuts. When he handed us our first check, we handed it right back.

"Ah, must be some mistake here, good buddy. You forgot one or two hundred dollars on this ten day pickle picking extravaganza, my friend."

Mr. Daily took the check, walked over to a wall and unhooked a clipboard. With Carol over one shoulder and me over the other, he re-ciphered our receipts from the pickle factory.

"No," he said. "I'm afraid you got it all."

"Mr. Daily, please? Carol and I have dragged twenty bushel bins around that pickle patch for over a week now. With your tractor we loaded those bins onto your pick-up truck and then, free of charge, we hauled them for you down to the pickle factory."

"That's right!" interrupted Mr. Daily. "I didn't charge you a penny."

"Pardon me?"

"It's just like you said. I let you guys use my tractor, my bins, and my pickup truck, and not only didn't I charge you for the use of them, I didn't charge you for the fuel that you used. I gave you everything free of charge, just as you said. On top of all of that, I gave you every penny that I received from the sale of those pickles. I didn't make one dime. In fact, it cost me money to have you pick them. As I said, I had to put fuel into the tractor and into the pickup truck."

So we learned - the only thing green about pickles is their color. With Mr. Daily's aid we found our way that next morning to a neighboring farmer's tomato field.

Tomatoes and dollar bills have a similar disadvantage - neither grows on trees. Tomatoes grow on vines and are pretty much stuck to the ground as is the case with pickles, cucumbers and onions. In any case, the designers of the tomato did, in fact, make it red, thereby distinguishing it from its vine and leaf. Unfortunately, farmers insist on picking it while it is still green. "Why?" you ask. Well, there are a number of reasons. One, as the tomato reddens, it also rottens; ripening is a process of deterioration. Two, as it reddens or rottens, it attracts bugs, insects, and birds.

Birds are picky eaters. For some reason they would rather take one little peck out of fifty different red tomatoes than eat one entire ripe tomato. This has historically caused farmers to want to shoot little birds, and understandably so. Probably, more important than any of the above, tomatoes are picked green for reasons of storage, packing and handling. The hybrid tomato of today is designed for long storage, traveling, and durability in handling, which makes it perfect for selling, but not so great for eating.

Maybe there is a vicious cycle here. Hybrid tomatoes are purposely grown with a two inch thick skin, no juice, and picked green, disregarding flavor altogether. Maybe this is the reason that they have to be shipped so far and stored so long. Nobody eats the darn things. I cringe every time I see a young person lift the top of his or her hamburger bun, slip out the slice of tomato and throw it away. I've also heard kids of today say; I hate spinach, green beans, broccoli ... and TOMATOES. Tomatoes never made that list when I was growing up; a nice ripe tomato with a sprinkle of salt ranked next to a Hershey's bar and a Dixie Cup in my memory's eye. Sadly, that is not so today.

Harvesting tomatoes was reminiscent of onion topping and peach picking combined. As with onion topping, you were forced to master the "bent at the waist" technique in order to make any real progress. After eight or ten hours of tomato harvesting, it took another two or three hours just to straighten up.

Similar to peach picking, there was a tractor towing a flat bed trailer hauling two or three twenty bushel bins. You filled your five gallon buckets with tomatoes plucked according to size, as with peaches, and then ran them over to the flatbed trailer where you dumped them and received a chit for your wages. The tomatoes didn't clunk into the bin as the green, hard peaches did; they more or less bounced like a sponge rubber ball. You would think that by the time that you dumped the last five gallon pail of tomatoes on the top of that twenty bushel bin, all of the tomatoes at the bottom of the bin would be reduced to juice, but not so. These tomatoes were so resilient that they would literally conform to the shape of any space they were placed into. Yes, you can put a round tomato into a square hole. It will emerge with four flat sides, and without a bruise.

We left the killing tomato picking fields, for the tomato packing sheds. After picking pickles and harvesting tomatoes, we weren't really eager to do our next "gig" in a packing shed, but Mr. Daily had a very persuasive manner. When the offer was made, and our faces shriveled up, our shoulders slumped, and our smiles frowned, Mr. Daily said; "It's not piece work. You get paid by the hour. Only minimum wage though." Was he kidding? ONLY minimum wage! We were at that packing shed, before sun up, and with bells on that next morning. Finally, maybe we could earn enough money to get some bacon to go with our tomato and mayonnaise sandwich diet of the last two weeks.

Packing tomatoes was a lot more fun than picking them. I have always wished that I had taken a picture of that packing shed. It was a farmer's delight. It was strung together with bailing wire and Busch beer cans. It was a laugh a minute watching our tomato farmer friend in his frenzied attempt to keep the machinery rolling.

The packing system inside the old garage or walled in equipment shelter, consisted of a number of conveyor belts with motors, and three lazy Susan type sorting tables, also with a lot of belts and motors. The crew consisted of a number of women and children, obviously wives and the teenage offspring of our tomato farmer and neighboring farmers.

The tomatoes entered the building via a shoot and a conveyor belt. They tumbled off the conveyor, and down other shoots which deposited them onto our rotating lazy Susan type sorting tables.

The circular, rotating sorting tables were about ten feet in circumference and had, maybe, four or five packing stations bunched around them.

The packer stood at his station, belly up to the rim of the rotating table, with two empty cardboard tomato shipping boxes on each side. In one box went red, but not soft or over ripe tomatoes. In another box went pink tomatoes. In a third box went blush tomatoes. These were shy tomatoes, not even bold enough to be pink but just 'blushing' slightly on their cheeks. In the forth box - green tomatoes. The overripe tomatoes, which incidentally, were perfect for eating and tasted just like I remembered, went into bushel baskets that sat on the floor. These were removed periodically, and dumped into an open topped tractor trailer box that sat out behind the building. This tractor trailer box sat there for the entire packing period. It sat there, sun beating down, tomatoes crushing, rotting, and molding until the man from the ketchup factory came with his tractor trailer cab and towed it off.

Oh, by the way, did you know that one of the criteria for judging the acceptability of processed ketchup is the maggot count of the tomatoes being processed? That's right, so many maggots per million means umm umm good ketchup. I would imagine that if a batch of ketchup has too many maggots, they would just keep adding rotten tomatoes until the desired maggot count is reached, and vice versa, I'd suppose. Ah, excuse me - a little more ketchup with those fries?

But, around and around the tomatoes went, and faster and faster went the little hands; red, pink, green, blush; red, pink, green, blush; red, pink, green, blush.

Every time I took a quick look up from my sorting table, and saw the eager eyes of all the ladies and teenager, not to mention my wife, all glued and keyed into the tomato kaleidoscope, I had to smile. The whole process of industrious people is, really, like watching a symphony. The oboes, the bassoons, the violins, the horns, the tubas, the cellos - some playing, some not playing, but all intent with their eyes on the music - even the triangle player, anxiously waiting to tinkle once every hour or so. I can just imagine him following page after page, note for note, until finally he pings. My God what a relief!

Here we had the symphony of the tomato packing shed. All eyes and hands busy; the sorters sorting, the loaders loading, the haulers hauling. Every tomato in its proper place until it was eventually stacked in its box with hundreds of others, on a flatbed truck parked outside the packing shed door. All of us players, hypnotized by the music of our labor, as our conductor tried to synchronize a symphony of dollars and cents. Our conductor not only had the task of conducting, and orchestrating, but periodically he would be forced to jump down off his podium and replace a string on a violin, or tune a piano, or put a squirt of oil on a sticky tuba valve. I couldn't stop smiling.

Every so often, and it seemed more often than not, the farmer's wife would yell; "Eldon! The do-hickey on the flimflam is off again." With a look of panic in his eyes, Eldon would dive to the floor, with a ball of string, a clothes hanger, and two Busch beer cans. As I sorted enthusiastically, I could see him crawling from do-hickey to flimflam tying, pulling, and propping as he crawled all over the dirty, juicy, oil stained floor. When he would finally emerge from out some crevice, or hole, he would jack his jeans back up over the crack of his butt, and give his wife, who was working at one of the sorting positions, a smile and a thumbs up, only to hear her warn, with a loud shrieking voice, about the pinnarus slipping on the roustabout. Then down and scrambling he would go again. But, as he crawled, wired, tunked and banged, the music played on.

It was quite a scene to see him at the end of each day, strapping down his load of hundreds of boxed, sorted, labeled and sealed tomatoes, on top the flatbed of his almost devastated and slightly dilapidated truck. It would be with a smile that he would lift the brim of his John Deere, green baseball cap, and stroke his scalp. This was confirmation of a job well done, a day well spent, a crop cared for by the month, day and year. He would then jump into the cab and head off to the market with the last remains of sunlight, sparkling, hazily, through the dirt and dust of his slightly cracked windshield.

Ah yes, the symphony of the tomato shed, conducted by farmer Spike Jones, with a hiccup here and a gulp-gulp there, a piece of wire and a hank of hair and a whole lot of sweat, love, care and many an aching, tired, old bone.

Behind our campsite, and just beyond the giant cistern under which we showered nightly, was a mile long field, filled with nothing but ferns. When we asked Mr. Daily what he did with all the ferns, he said; "What Ferns?"

"The miles of them that you have planted right there."

"That's asparagus. You folks like asparagus?"

"We love asparagus!" My wife yelped.

To tell you the truth, I had never eaten any. Never ate it before in my entire life.

"Well help yourself," said Mr. Daily. "It is yours for the pickin'."

"Wow! A whole field full of asparagus; that's what I call a cash crop."

"Yes, that's what they told me six years ago when I planted it. First I had to tie up my acreage for three years, waiting for it to get to size. Then I harvested it one year out of the last three. It's a real money maker alright."

"But, I don't understand. A small can of asparagus in the store is nearly three dollars."

"That's right. And how many cans of asparagus did you buy last year?

"Me? I didn't buy any. I can't afford it."

"Exactly. At three dollars a tiny can, not too many other people can afford it either. That's why my asparagus sits there going to seed every year. I'm giving that field one more year, and if the cannery doesn't want it next year, it is going under."

"Why doesn't the cannery want it?"

"Well, my guess would be that they have a warehouse full of tiny little cans of asparagus that they would like to sell for three dollars each and nobody's buying them. I'd like to see asparagus selling for fifty-nine cents a can, myself. Then maybe I could harvest and sell some of this stuff. In any case, help yourself."

He pulled out a pocket knife, and strolled out into his fern field. We watched him cut off, at ground level, the little, finger-sized shoots that were popping up between the overgrown ferns. In less than a minute his hand was bursting with asparagus fingers. He handed them to us like a bouquet.

My wife steamed them that evening and served them with a little salt and a pat of butter. I had never had a green vegetable taste like that in my life. That rich nutty flavor comes to mind every time I see fresh asparagus sitting in the produce section of the super market, and I can't resist. I am now one of those freaks who buy asparagus, no matter what the price - at least occasionally.

We ate asparagus every night for weeks, and I never tired of it. We also had the good fortune of finding at a yard sale, an old woman who had finally given up on the fall home canning season. At a very good price, we purchased a classic pressure cooker, a book on how to put things up for the winter, and one hundred canning jars. The wonderful old woman would have given us more canning jars, but we had no place to put them. But it wasn't long before we had them all filled with delicious, over-ripe tomatoes that, if it weren't for us, would have been eating maggots out back of some ketchup factory. When we returned to the old woman's yard sale to show her what good use we had put to her book, pressure cooker, and jars, she gave us another hundred canning jars - and we took them.

At the Daily farm we got a little taste of everything. We picked peaches, pears, sweet and sour cherries, plums, tiny yellow apricots. We did pickles, tomatoes, cucumbers, ate our fill of asparagus, and even cut a little broccoli.

The Daily peaches were really an event compared to Mr. Barbrough's peaches in Arkansas. At the Daily farm we waited until a good number of peaches had ripened on the tree, before we were sent out puttsing on his old tractor, hauling a flatbed load of bushel boxes to that peach grove.

The peach grove was at the back of the farm and set down in a little valley. Riding out there each morning was truly like taking a tractor ride through the Garden of Eden. Fruits and vegetables of all types and sizes growing here, there and everywhere, and then, finally, those big, beautiful, rosy, red peaches. They were so ripe and juicy that the slightest pressure from a finger would put a welt on the poor thing.

We were Mr. Daily's only peach pickers and we had our instructions. "Pick only the biggest, reddest, ripest fruit on the tree. I don't care how many bushels you pick, or how long it takes, and I'll pay you by the hour," Mr. Daily told us. So each day we picked the biggest, the reddest, and the ripest. We left the greenest, the poorest and the smallest waiting on the tree for their moment of sweet, juicy greatness.

Our Daily peach picking was completely free of tension, anxiety, and stress. We were even told how to crate them. We were told to place them into the bushel boxes, as opposed to dropping them; and never, never fill the box over the upper edges. Because when the boxes are then stacked one on top of the other, one peach butting up over the edge will be squished down, and a chain reaction will ensue that will damage nearly every peach in the box.

It was a pleasure to pick Mr. Daily's peaches, rather than a chore. Each day when we came puttsing over the hill towards the makeshift, cold storage house that Mr. Daily had in progress, there was always a crowd of people waiting - some wanting to buy just a bushel or two, and others wanting to buy five, ten, or even fifteen, to sell at their roadside stands. Some days Mr. Daily had to actually limit the number of bushels going to each costumer in order to assure that every regular costumer got some and not one costumer got them all.

It was almost humorous, seeing the people anxiously waiting down at the bottom of that hill each day, as we puttsed along on our old tractor returning from our days labor out in the Garden of Eden. Interesting to note, never once did I overhear a customer arguing or haggling over the price. It was always,

"... and what do I owe you? ... That's fine; and, thank-you very much." That is all that we ever heard. It was all smiling faces, and everybody tickled pink, to be carting off those bushels of juicy, rosy red peaches.

We were almost like celebrities. When the people saw us bumping down that dirt road, their cheery faces beamed with smiles. I must admit, I really liked the feeling. Mr. Daily never uttered a negative word with regards to how few bushels we may have had, or how long it had taken us. His only concern was with the quality of the peaches. My guess is that these peaches were bringing top dollar, and everybody - picker, costumer, and farmer were satisfied. Oh, if only the whole economic world, were a Mr. Daily peach farm. What a pleasure life would be.

I didn't realize it at the time, but Mr. Daily was probably the only successful small farmer that we met in all of our migrant travels. We met plenty of small farmers, but, it seemed, they were either recuperating from bankruptcy, or swimming in it. If it wasn't bankruptcy, it was the children or grandchildren arguing over the remains of what was once a small farm. This is a sad observation that I am sure won't hold up statistically, or scientifically, but it was our experience. For the most part, small farming went just like the old nursery rhyme; Old McDonald had a farm; Ei - I - Ei - I OWE.

7 Michigan Apples

We were enjoying our stay at pick a peach Daily farms, but as we chugged by on our old tractor, pulling our little red wagon filled with crates of peaches, it was almost impossible not to notice the Daily apple orchard. It was very small. We asked Mr. Daily if he had apples growing elsewhere on the farm. He did not.

We were in a quandary. We weren't making very much money working for Mr. Daily, and from the looks of his apple orchard there wasn't much to come. Even with our amateur status as fruit pickers, we knew that we would be filling our last Daily apple bin with, at best, two to three weeks of picking. We had come a long way to pick apples. We were told that we could make fair wages for a minimum of six weeks, to a maximum of ten weeks. We would have to find greener orchards. We bid Mr. Daily ado and headed north.

To be touring the Michigan countryside in autumn could be no less exciting than a carnival funhouse slide through a rainbow. In fact, I would imagine the rainbow ride to be slightly less thrilling. For unless we could actually get into the rainbow as microscopic creatures and bound through the molecules of color; unless we could feel the cool mist of a purple moisture, or the warm splash of an atmosphere's red perspiration; unless we could see the shapes and textures of the colors as we slide through one shade and into another, it could hardly compare to the burnt-yellow-orange of a million maple leaves scattered across a horizon of blue and white sky. Nor could it compare to the sensuous hues of a hardwood autumn filled with the scents and essences of nature ripening along a Michigan country road.

I've lived now in the South for over twenty years. Yet when I feel that nip in the air, and the sun tipping in the sky, I wait with anticipation for those Northern Lights of Autumn; those lights that never quite arrive, and always, and probably forever, I feel a pain of longing - longing for the memory of an almost forgotten passion, or the innocent joy of a flowering youthful romance.

When we awoke from our autumn dream, we found ourselves talking with a friendly young man in the Hartford, Michigan employment office. He was exuberant. I had the distinct feeling that this was a new position for our young friend. He was glowing at the opportunity of finding us suitable work. When we told him that we were actually looking for farm work, and picking apples in particular, he seemed thrilled. Little did we know that our next employer had been in and out of this fellow's office for the last couple of weeks. He was anxiously awaiting the arrival of somebody - possibly anybody - who might be willing to pick the fruits of this, his first year's effort as a farmer.

Our new found friend was walking us to the door, to point out to us from the sidewalk, where we should make our first turn, when in walked Mr. Teachuum. He was a thin, full bearded fellow who always seemed to be bobbing in the bubbling rapids of unfounded joy. I think this man laughed from the time that we met him, until the time that we left. He was a wonderful fellow, if not the best and most experienced farmer on the block.

Before taking the big plunge into owning his own farm, he taught agriculture at the university. Most of his peers thought of him as a man frustrated with the dream of being a "real" farmer one day. The other farmers watched him dryly. They listened with a cynical ear as he ran about, slapping his thighs and expounding on his latest agricultural theory. His primary theory, as he expounded to us one day out in an apple orchard, was not so much agricultural as it was Malthusian with a slight touch of Will Rogers, and possibly Adam Smith and Ricardo.

He believed, like Will, that indeed land was a good buy. Not only because they were making no more of it, but also because population was growing in such a way that in the not too distant future there would be a severe scarcity of it. He felt that one of these days, the "landed" would again be the world's Aristocracy. Dollars just wouldn't hold up. Real property would be the only true wealth. If he could figure out a way to make this real property pay for itself, he would one day be remembered as the patriarch of the Teachuum clan.

I've heard lots of opinions to contradict this theory. People have told me about being "land poor" back in the days of the Depression, and many people have told me that nothing surpasses the simplicity and carefreeness of a wealth of dollars. One rich fellow even told me that he never knew the meaning of the word freedom until he unbound himself from the endless knots of material possessions.

I don't know who has the right point of view with regards to true wealth. As you have probably guessed, I have my own theories. I do know that all humans must have a dream. Without a dream life is barely worth enduring. One must stay active. Inactivity leads not only to sloth, as religious folks contend, but boredom and worst of all depression. On the economic side, that old adage that anything that pays for itself, is worth every penny that it costs, seems theoretically and practically true to me.

From what I could see, old farmer Teachuum had a number of good things going for him. He had a dream. He was very, very busy. If he could master the art of farming, the dirt and the trees would pay his mortgage. Ah yes, but as most farmers already know, it is all easier said than done.

Teachuum had apples; a whole season full of apples. He loved his apples - or did he love to spray his apples?

This man spent half of his farming life on a spray truck. If his apples weren't red enough, he sprayed them with something that made them redder. If they were too round in shape, he sprayed them with something that made them appear more like a tear drop. If he didn't want to pick them right away, he sprayed them with something that made them cling to the tree longer. If he wanted to pick them sooner, he sprayed them with something that loosened them from their stems. He sprayed them for scabs, for bugs, for birds, for disease, for fungus, for color, size, shape and quantity. If there were too many on the tree, he sprayed to thin them out.

This man knew his chemicals. His name should have been DuPont rather than Teachuum. He reminded me of the Lone Ranger. He was forever leaping into the saddle of his spray truck and galloping off through his apple orchard, with a cloud of dust, a waving hand, and a paper respirator over his nose and mouth. At first I couldn't believe it. How did these apples find the room to absorb rainwater after being saturated with all of these chemicals?

One day he asked me why I had a motorcycle. I told him about the smell of the road, and the wind in your face; the sensation of seeing the road rush by at your feet; the hot and cold pockets that caressed you and sent chills up your spine as you dipped and climbed a hilly country road. The smells - your senses alive as you rush from apple blossoms to peach nectar or from the sweet smell of his Niagara grapes, to corn fields or new mown hay. Finally, I told him of the adrenaline rush, with all your senses aglow and on edge, being well aware that at sixty miles an hour, you are a mere pothole away from instant death. He shook his head with admiration as his eyes opened wide with a passionate sparkle, and said; "Boy, that is exactly how I feel when I'm on my spray truck."

Teachuum had apples. He had all kinds of apples. He had early apples, late apples, and midseason apples. He had red apples, yellow apples, red and yellow apples. We started off with the first apple of his apple picking season, the Mackintosh.

It's funny, as a child we always seemed to have Mackintosh apples. My mother made pies from them, and we ate them for snacks or as a treat. As an adult the Mackintosh lost its glow. Every time I bought one in the store, it tasted like mush. Each time that I bought one, I tried to recall why as a child I liked them so much. I chalked the whole thing up to childish taste buds, a fading memory, and the nagging remorse that goes hand in hand with getting older. You know; Christmas trees just never seem big enough; never laughing until your sides hurt; and holding a hand, no longer providing the thrill of goose bumps. Mackintosh apples were just a blurry, half forgotten memory.

Then about halfway through our first day of Mackintosh picking, I twisted a ripe, red one off my tree, leaned up against my bin, and took a bite. It crunched so loudly, it made my ears ring. Suddenly I had visions of mom, apple pie, and goose bumps. It wasn't just like I remembered; it was more than I remembered. Then I realized, it wasn't all me, and my fading memory. It was THEM! THEY had been doing something to my Mackintosh apples. I wasn't simply growing old and senile.

THEY were tricking me. It was all a part of a national plot to try and convince me that the plastic world that I was now living in is what always was. They were trying to brainwash me. I had been living in 1984. [I was also living in 1954, 1944, and 1994.] I had been living in a George Orwellian haze. But now, I had discovered a real apple. Should I hide behind an apple bin and eat it before Big Brother's camera got a hold of me. Then it would be only a matter of minutes before the apple police arrived, and I would be locked up in a CO-2, controlled atmosphere with a billion mushy apples everywhere. Oh what should I do?

At the risk of being forced to have this book smuggled out of the U.S., and published in a foreign country, and myself whisked away into oblivion, I intend to leave this information, just the way it happened, exposed in print, right here in this book. To hell with the Apple Police! The absolute truth is: FRESH MACKINTOSH APPLES STILL CRUNCH! The only secret is, they must be fresh, and, of course, grown on a tree and not artificially inseminated in some Frankenstein fruit laboratory.

Mr. Teachuum was amazed at what we two could do with a straight ladder and a few apple trees. We were able to pick a lot of apples per day. It was clear to us both that we had truly benefited from our stay in orange country Florida, and from Lanzo. We knew the techniques. We could not only stand a straight ladder upright, but we now knew how to place it into the tree advantageously, with no back-tracking. We could hold and pick two, three and sometimes even four apples in one hand, and with one reach of the arm. Lanzo could actually pick five oranges with one hand, and one reach out. He had a huge hand for a modest sized man. This little trick is a real time saver, energy saver, and money maker in the fruit picking business.

The tiny, little half bushel apple sacks were a breeze to negotiate in the tree when compared to those huge two bushel orange picking sacks. The apple trees weren't nearly as tall, or as big as an orange tree. The ladders were shorter and tons lighter. Carol worked her own ladder and sack, and the sacks were provided by the farmer. Unlike orange trees, apple trees had no huge thorns growing along their stems. When you lifted the apple and twisted, as is the proper technique, the apple stem parted from its rooting, effortlessly. Here again, oranges left the tree much more reluctantly.

Picking apples was not only fun, it was actually profitable as well. Then again I suppose, it wouldn't have seemed so profitable if we weren't living in a truck under an apple tree behind one of Teachuum's old farm houses. We were very, very happy. Life as a migrant apple picker, at least in Michigan, was a joy.

On the days that we couldn't pick, for whatever reason, we bundled up warm, grabbed our waders and went Salmon snagging at a nearby river or damn. We caught Salmon; great big things that weighed between twenty and thirty pounds. We caught so many Salmon on these excursions that we ended up processing some of them in our pressure cooker and storing them under our bed in our canning jars. We ate Salmon for months after leaving Michigan.

On those off days, where fishing was out of the question due to rain or whatever, we usually found a little musty beer bar that sold sandwiches. It was on one of these off days that we met Ernie, a befuddled, confused, and socially lost World War II hero.

There had been a big storm this one particular weekend, and we had heard that the damage in downtown Hartford was considerable. We decided to take a spin down to the Hartford bar and grill and get ourselves a Kielbasa sandwich on rye bread with mustard and onions, and a couple of cold draft beers. We had our lunch, and then went out for a walk to survey the damage. The area had been struck by high winds, and there had been a number of tornado warnings. For the most part, though, the town had been saved. Other than the city park, and the streets littered with tree limbs and scattered debris, the damage was minimal. Yet there was an aura of gloom and misfortune that seemed to be hanging over the small town. The whole area felt strange and foreboding.

We walked through the park. Huge hardwood trees had been uprooted, or broken in half, and their trunks and branches were scattered about everywhere. It felt eerie, and I made the comment to Carol that the scene we were witnessing was probably comparable to some European village after a bombing during World War II. I barely had the words out of my mouth when a voice from a nearby park bench commented, "Not hardly, son. Not even close."

I looked at the man sitting on the bench. To my eye he looked pretty much to be a tramp, a bum, a homeless vagrant. He was wearing a long winter type overcoat. The kind one finds down at the Goodwill or secondhand clothing store. It was a good coat, but old, stained, and now, very much out of date. In that respect, it matched the rest of his wardrobe, except for the sneakers.

His sneakers were worn - and very red. They had no business hanging around with the rest of his outfit. I've known and have been exposed to bums most of my life. I have my roots in a neighborhood that bred a good many. Consequently, this type of individual didn't shock, offend or frighten me.

"You offer that comment as a man of experience, I presume."

"You presume right," he said with a smile.

I don't know how to explain this, but there are just some people to whom one has an immediate liking. This man was one of those types to me. He had that keen, aware, intelligent look in his eye - a smile that exposed a kind, loveable soul.

Then again this man could have had an addiction to eating human flesh as far as I knew. Yet, the only thing that made me keep my distance from him was the notion that his next statement would be a request for money. I don't have a problem refusing a bum money, but it does make me feel uncomfortable.

"You fought in World War II?"

"Yes sir, I did."

"And you were in Europe?"

"Yes sir. I was a paratrooper."

"I never liked the idea of jumping out of an airplane and trying to break the fall by clinging to a bed sheet."

He laughed. "Well, I never thought of it that way, but I've never missed the experience."

"I'll bet you don't." I laughed, smiled at the man and moved on.

We meandered down the pathway somewhat, and then sat down on one of the other park benches. Carol and I began to have a discussion about something or other, when the next thing we notice, our grey haired, grey bearded, paratrooper was sitting, crossed legged down at the end of our park bench.

There were any number of other park benches, and, of course, our friend could have chosen one of them. He didn't. Clearly, the smell of our affability had lured him to us like the smell of fresh cream to a stray cat. That is exactly the way I viewed the man. He was a stray - a stray human being.

There was just something about him that separated him from the bum class though. He looked more like Burt Lancaster, or Gregory Peck dressed up and playing the part of a bum. There was a class about him that set him apart from his meager frock. Everything about the man made me curious and put a smirk onto my face.

This was a man of position, disguised in a bum suit. He reached inside his overcoat and pulled out a pint of whiskey. He screwed off the lid and handed the bottle out towards us.

"Can I offer you a drink?" he asked.

"No thank you," I said.

"And you ma'am?" he said, pushing the mouth of the opened bottle in Carol's direction.

"Oh ... ah, no thank you," Carol blundered.

I laughed, and shook my head. This bum was definitely different. If he was going to hit us up for some money, a good bum would have kept his bottle hidden. Most of us upright citizens do not support drugs or alcohol with voluntary contributions - at least none that we are aware of. This fellow not only exhibits his bottle, but offers both my wife and I a drink.

He interpreted my laugh, and the shake of my head to be a criticism of his drinking.

"You're right," he said. "This is the stuff that has ruined my life."

"You really think so? I think it is that thing at the end of your wrist clinging to that bottle that has ruined your life."

He looked slightly confused; then looked down at his hand wrapped around his bottle and laughed.

"Maybe if you cut that thing off, your problem will be solved?" He laughed again. "You know, you don't look to me to be the type of man to be living like a bum."

"I don't consider myself a bum - a hobo, maybe."

"A hobo? There's a difference?"

"A hobo may be a vagrant and a tramp, or as you say, a bum, but he's a bum that pays his own way. I work. I earn my own keep."

"Oh? What do you do for a living?"

"I pick fruit." He uttered these words as if this method of earning a living was something for which he should exhibit shame.

"Really! That's what Carol and I do for a living, also." A glow of delight and confusion came over Ernie's face. He was clearly excited.

We sat and chatted with Ernie on the Hartford park bench, amidst broken tree trunks, and tornado debris for an hour or so. He was interesting. He had a style that made us laugh. Why he picked us as listeners, I have no idea. Then in the middle of it all, he got up, and extended his hand to us both. He told us what a pleasure we had been and how unfortunate it was that he had to leave. But he had things to do, and people to meet and had to be on his way.

As I watched him wander off in his dirty-old-man overcoat and red sneakers, I had the distinct feeling that we had done something for the old gentleman. For a moment, he had talked to the kind of people that he had been acquainted with in a life long forgotten and for the most part, lost. He was treated with respect, not ridicule. We laughed and sympathized. For that last hour, he was a real human being again; not a nameless tramp - excuse me, hobo.

He was once a man with a past, an identity, a real life. Now, at least as far as society was concerned, he was a nameless nobody, a social invisible. I had the distinct feeling that we were being used, psychologically. His time with us provided him with a free ticket back home, a bought and paid for dinner for two at the Ritz. The look on his face, when he excused himself and got up to shake our hands, was one of true satisfaction and pleasure. It made Carol and I smile simply to be a witness and audience to his temporary and imaginary transformation.

He had used us in some sort of way, but whatever it was that he had done for himself, it was painless to us. It had cost us nothing. If it weren't for the unique sense of satisfaction that we saw on his face and the strange manner in which he ran from us, we would have felt nothing.

As it was, he had gotten no more than a few yards up the path when I felt the necessity to stand and check my pockets. I had my wallet and the keys to my van. Nothing seemed to be missing. My wife laughed. "Do you feel like he has just stolen something from us?" she asked with a grin.

"I do, but I can't figure out what it is."

I guess Ernie had stolen an hour of respectability from us two strangers. He felt guilty and ran like a thief before he was discovered.

We thought about Ernie, and talked about him somewhat as we went about our free afternoon meanderings. Ernie was definitely a character.

Finally the sky clouded over and it began to rain. It began to pour, in fact. We made the decision to head on back to the Teachuum farm. We had wandered quite a distance away. We were a good fifty or seventy miles from where we had started out that morning. We consulted with our map, and chose to return to the farm via a small winding country road that eventually led to a main highway.

We were into this wilderness, no man's land for about ten or fifteen miles, when we saw hazily, between the rapid shifts of our windshield wipers, a long woolen Goodwill overcoat.

"Hey! Isn't that Ernie?" we both blurted, simultaneously.

Carol applied the brakes and we slid to a pretty quick halt up on the shoulder of the road. We tooted the horn in an attempt to garner Ernie's attention. Clearly, he was confused. He had never seen our van camper and obviously he couldn't see us sitting comfortably inside our van. I waved my arm out the window. We both laughed. In a moment he was bundling himself up to our truck like the wondering star in the movie, Doctor Zhivago.

"Ernie what the hell are you doing way out here in the middle of nowhere?" I yelled just as he was stepping up through our van's side door. With one foot in and one foot out, he stopped in his tracks. He then pulled his foot out of our truck and stood there in the pouring rain staring at us.

I didn't know if he was in shock, or if he was in a state of bewilderment as to who we were. He had no hat and his grey hair was plastered to his forehead. Then slowly a grin of recognition spread across his face. He had a very intriguing smile. His teeth were perfect in their alignment though slightly off in color. They were a kind of barroom coffee and back-alley, nicotine brown, but very much Burt Lancaster, or Kirk Douglas-ish in size, structure and alignment. "Well, get in man! What the hell, do you want to drown out there?"

Slowly and somewhat reluctantly, he climbed into our van. He pulled up a milk carton we had wandering about on the floor and slid it up, slightly to the rear, but between Carol and me.

"Where you heading, Ernie?" Carol asked. With his Lancaster grin still aglow, he burst into a huge laugh.

"You know," he said, looking about our van, like Willy Sutton finding himself on the floor of an unattended bank vault. "I like you people."

"Well thanks and we like you. Where are you heading?" He ignored our question for the second time.

"You people are all right," he muttered. "I've got to do something for you people."

"Yes," I said, trying to ease him out of his spirit of gratitude. "You've got to tell us where the hell you're going, so we can take you there. By the way, how did you ever get way out here?

"Way out where?"

"Well, you are about fifty miles from where we met you this morning."

"So."

"So where are you heading?"

"You know, you folks are good people. I've got to do something for you guys."

"No you don't."

"Hell yes I do. I've got some people out this way that owe me a whole bunch of money. If you people will take me out there, I'll give you half of it."

"Ernie, my boy, we will take you wherever it is that you want to go, but we don't want any of your money."

"Why's that, you folks rich or something?"

"Ernie, we are as rich as two people can get in this life. We've got each other, and we've got all the love that money can't buy."

Ernie's eyes opened up like silver dollars. Carol and I both turned and stared his multi-shades of blue down. He was in shock. He didn't know what to say. Before he could open up his mouth, I burst out with; "Oh, we ain't got a barrel of money, and maybe we're ragged and funny..." At this point Carol started laughing and joined in the next chorus. "But we travel along, singin' a song, side by side." Ernie tried to interrupt, but Carol and I were having too much fun. "Through all kinds of weather, whether it's rain or snow, as long as we're together, it doesn't matter at all..." At this point Ernie joined in. "Oh, we ain't got a barrel of money, and maybe we're ragged and funny, but we'll travel along, singin' a song, side by side."

We all laughed, and for the next ten minutes we, all three, sang the first couple of lines of every song that we ever knew. Including dashing through the snow and deck the halls with boughs of holly.

As we sang, Ernie kept pointing out right and left turns. To our total amazement, Ernie directed us into a huge parking lot that was situated in the middle of this under populated forest. We didn't know where the heck we were, but wherever it was, it was filled with people and pickup trucks.

The pickup trucks were all old, and the people were all Mexican, or Spanish. "Pull right over here!" Ernie said, very Douglas MacArthur-ish. "There are some people in here who owe me. You guys wait right here, and I'll be out in a minute."

Ernie exited the van, and Carol and I were still glowing with giggles as I popped open a bottle of liquid, alcoholic chuckle and began to review for her the major events of our day. She was roaring with laughter at my descriptions of what had happened to us so far, when I heard a little bird come a tap, tap, tapping at my chamber door. It wasn't a Raven. It was a rather unhappy, white, American woman in a $9.95 home perm, and a J. C. Penny woman's liberation, business suit. I was just releasing my lips from a warm embrace with the open end of an Old Milwaukee light when I heard this shocking screech.

"I've got a good mind to call the sheriff on you people." She was glaring at me through my closed window. I knew that I didn't really want to meet this woman, but when I saw Ernie standing behind her with a big smile on his face, I felt that I must.

"Excuse me?" I enquired, as I cranked down the window.

"Do you people know that it is against the law for you to accept food stamps from an unauthorized person?" I had the feeling that Mrs. Ichabod Crane was not asking me a question, but making a statement. My wife was horror struck, and I hadn't the slightest idea what the woman was talking about. Before I could utter a word in my defense, the woman stuck her long, pointy nose into my face, and sneered.

"People like you disgust me; anyone who can use a poor man like Mr. Pile here, for their own aggrandizement ought to be stood up against a wall and shot. I've met some slimy, underhanded people in my day, but you people slither in a way that makes my skin crawl."

I felt that this nice lady was in a point of anger that was beyond explanation. She was as they say in the vernacular of today - venting. I decided that it would be best to let her vent. As she proceeded, I sent a few sharp visual arrows towards Ernie. He had this pathetic, little smile on his face and seemed to be captured in a permanent shrug. I wanted to kill him.

"They talk about welfare fraud and begrudge a few poor people like these a paucity of food stamps, while garbage like you, go about a business like this."

She took a deep breath and calmed herself slightly and then went on.

"I've given Mr. Pile his monthly allotment which he has told me he is going to give to you "nice" people. Let me just say this. I am going to forgo calling the police department but if you slithering scum who are pretending to be of human origin, pilfer this man's monthly food allotment, I sincerely hope that your souls, if you have such, will rot forever in an eternity of HELL FIRE!!"

Well, what a predicament this had turned out to be. I had the sincere belief that if I went on to defend myself, this woman would completely lose it and proceed to literally beat me to within an inch of my life. Carol and I both sat quietly as Mrs. Penny Perm, swiveled and dink-toed her little butt back into the building.

We both sat there with chin in hand, staring at Ernie in our best Jack Benny outrage. Ernie shuffled about a bit. Then with a tentative grin and a hesitant arm he raised up for our inspection his book of government food stamps. I couldn't look at the man without harboring thoughts of biting off his nose. I rolled up my window and turned away. I stared at the dashboard for what seemed like an hour. I analyzed everything but could see no way to achieve retribution. He had baby stepped himself up to my window and was peering in at me through the rain with his nose pressed up against the glass. I lowered the window a slit and calmly screamed; "GET IN!!!" Once Ernie was comfortably inside the van, we slithered our "slimy butts" slowly out of the government food stamp parking lot.

Ernie defended his action at the food stamp office with the claim that; Them people owe me, man! I didn't argue.

As we continued down the road, we queried Ernie as to where he lived. We didn't know if he slept in an alley, on a park bench, or just behind an apple tree somewhere.

"Oh hell man! I can't go back there with all them damn blacks. You should see where I have to live. No white man should have to live like that, man." Ahh, this was good news. Be it ever so humble, the man had a "place". Now if we could just find out where it was, and how to get there.

"Hey, I've got an idea," Ernie said. "You guys pick fruit, and so do I. We could team up and travel together."

I was afraid of this. We did our good deed. We picked up a stray human being, and now he wanted to be adopted.

"Ernie, first of all - what am I talking about? There's no first of all here. Ernie? Where do you live?"

"No really, I like you guys. I wouldn't be no trouble. I could sleep right here on the floor."

"Ernie, there's no room on the floor. Besides Carol and I need our privacy."

"I understand," Ernie said. "And whenever you guys need privacy, I'll sleep outside."

"You can't sleep outside, Ernie. What happens when it rains or when it gets cold?"

"Hey, don't worry about me. Half the time them damn black boys back there at the camp, lock me out anyway. I'm always sleeping under that damn house."

"Ernie, I want to discontinue this conversation. Your proposition is impossible. Tell us where you live, and we will take you there."

"This proposition is not impossible. If you had a dog, you would let it sleep on the floor, wouldn't you? And you would buy it food and take it for a walk. I can walk myself, and I'll buy my own food. And I'll pay you rent out of the money I earn picking fruit."

Here was a grown man who wanted to be our pet. Carol kept looking at me, shaking her head and grinning. I kept thinking about what a life this man must have if he was willing to exchange it to become some other human being's pet. I could commiserate even with the feeling of being cared for by some nice people. I could even imagine giving up all of my freedom and dignity to become the love slave of Bo Derrick, or Marilyn Monroe. But, as bad off as I have ever been in my life, I have never asked anyone if I could sleep on their floor or under their house and be their pet.

Then suddenly, as we were passing through this small town, an image popped into my mind. I saw Ernie cuddled up on the floor of our van, sleeping with his head next to a bowl of table scraps. Here we were full circle, right back to John Steinbeck. Only difference being, we had passed through The "Grapes of Wrath", and were now in the prologue to, "Of Mice and Men".

"No, No, No!" I screamed. "Pull this truck over, Carol!" She gave me her confused, nervous look. "Just pull it over, don't worry about a thing." When the truck stopped, I got out and opened the sliding side door to our van. "Okay Lenny, you can get out here in this nice little village, or you can tell us exactly where it is that you stay and we'll bring you there. I'm afraid that I have already seen this movie. So, those are your two choices, pick one." Lenny looked around at the village I had chosen for him, disparagingly.

"What the heck would I do here?" he questioned pathetically.

"I don't know, Lenny. Wander around. Find Gregory Peck, and go kill a mocking bird, or something. That's your problem, my friend. I have my problems, you have your problems, and never the twain shall meet. You get me? I've got but one life to live and I don't want any talking pets."

"Okay, okay, I'll tell you where I live. But wait until you see it man. I know you ain't goin' to leave me there. You ain't that kind of a guy." I climbed back into the van and Carol pulled out onto the road. "The place is filled with dirt, garbage and black people, man. You ain't gonna believe it. And them damn blacks ... you know how they are; guns, knives, drugs. I'd rather be dead than go back there."

"Well, that is a third choice. I hadn't thought of it but it is a possibility - just don't do it here in this van. You wait until we let you out and then you can do whatever rings your bell." I looked at Lenny. A slow smile spread to his face.

It took us over an hour to finally arrive at Ernie's hideaway. We turned off the main highway and into somebody's fruit farm. We went along a winding dirt road that led out to the back forty. Then finally we pulled up onto a clump of buildings. Ernie was right. They really didn't look that great.

We had no sooner stopped the van in order to allow Ernie to exit, when an entire village of Cripts and Bloods came pouring out at us from every direction. How had I gotten Carol into this? Never mind Carol, how had I gotten myself into this?

I was reaching down behind the front passenger seat looking for a crow bar I kept there, while Ernie was stepping out of the van. I had no intention of staying around to socialize.

Before I could get my fingers wrapped around that chunk of heavy metal, I felt the impact of a big and powerful hand on my shoulder. I turned with a start to see what I was up against, only to be confronted in that dim twilight by rows of white, sparking teeth and a horde of black faces - all of whom were screeching my name, gleefully.

"Mr. Noble, Mr. Noble! What are you doing up here, Maun?" It was Lanzo, and the entire Papa Charlie crew. My island friends were busting at the seams to be seeing Carol and I in this white wilderness so far from our mutual Florida home.

Carol jumped out of the van, and one by one we shook hands and reacquainted ourselves with our fellow Florida orange pickers. Ernie was dumfounded. In the middle of all the gaiety, he asked. "You know these people?"

"Yes, we've picked fruit with them down in Florida." Lenny was at a total loss for words, or expression. He stared at me for a very long moment, and then meandered off through the crowd of smiling, black faces. I watched him walk over to one of the buildings. He pulled open a door, and just before he entered, he turned and looked back at me. He stared into my eyes. He was totally beside himself. In his wildest dreams, he just never could have imagined. I felt sorry for him, but we had no room - not for a dog, or even a human who aspired to becoming one.

8 The Teachuum Farm

I found out from Lanzo and the boys that they were having great difficulty in finding work in the area. After hearing Carol and I talk in favor of going to Michigan over North Carolina and their rough and tumble apples, the Islanders decided to follow our lead; "But every time we go up to a house, maun, the curtains close and the doors lock. I think that they don't like us black people, maun."

I left my co-workers and felt a little down hearted. Was it the example of Carol and I that made them think they might be treated better up in Michigan, than they were down in Florida, or over in North Carolina? They had come a long way, and now if they didn't find work, what would they do? I also felt a little disappointed in my white brethren, but why should that be? What should I have expected? It didn't take the imagination of a Jules Verne to visualize the lives of Carol and Dick as black migrant farm workers. I can't even begin to imagine what this book would be like, if Carol and I attempted to live this same adventure as two young black people venturing off to work their way around America.

Back at the apple ranch Mr. Teachuum was having a great deal of difficulty in finding a suitable picking staff. He had a few teenagers from the area who tried out for a day or two, and then left the bruised and damaged remains of their labors sitting under a tree somewhere. He had one out-of-work school teacher, who was at the moment between positions. He had two or three housewives who came to the jobsite complete with matching red bandannas, plastic aprons, white cotton gloves, jeans, jackets and steel-toed leather work boots. These women weren't quitters, but they weren't fruit pickers either.

At about eleven or twelve o'clock every morning, they would stroll over to wherever Carol and I were working and strike up a friendly conversation which invariably included the phrase, And how many bins of apples do you folks have so far this morning? Carol would announce our present number matter-of-factly and invariably the women would all gasp. We knew exactly how they all felt, but what does one say? If we offered tips on how to improve their picking technique, we would invariably be considered overbearing and egotistical. Everyone knows that picking fruit is "unskilled" labor. We could pick more fruit than they, because we were younger, or in better condition, or had more practice, and were, of course, willing to run around an apple orchard like a couple of monkeys. It would never enter anyone's mind that learned techniques and practiced skills would be so important in such a menial task as picking fruit.

Last of all, Mr. Teachuum had a few car people. One finds these car people in all parts of America wherever temporary farm work is taking place. These are for the most part white people who travel about with two to five small children, and live in their vehicle. They eat their meals on the hood or trunk of the car, and they spend their nights sleeping on the seats inside.

We've seen these type families everywhere. They usually stick around until they get a visit from the friendly little lady from the local H.R.S. office who is always shocked and concerned about their chosen lifestyle. As soon as this well dressed, and good intentioned lady taps on their window one frosty morning, and hits them with a bunch of questions and forms, they collect their pay and hit the road.

Mr. Teachuum, though always sporting a smile and laughing constantly, seemed distressed. When I asked what was bothering him, he expressed the notion that he didn't know how he was ever going to get his apples picked. I said; "Well, how would you like to have a crew of eight to ten fruit pickers here in the morning, each of whom, could pick ten to fifteen bins of apples per day?" He bounced up off the ground about sixteen inches (who says white men can't jump?) clapped his hands together and danced around like Al Jolson or Eddie Cantor. Then he started shaking me by the shoulders.

"Say you're not joking! Please, tell me this isn't a joke."

"No it is not a joke, but there is one problem," I said, hesitantly. He stood back, and braced himself, waiting for the blow.

"What?" He waited no more than half a second, then added. "What? What? For God's sakes tell me what's the problem?" I really didn't know if any disclaimer was necessary but, I didn't want to show up that next morning with a truckload of black people and find out that Teachuum was the head of the Michigan chapter of The International Federation of neo-Nazis. Somewhat embarrassed, I said. "These men, whom I have in mind, are all excellent workers, and very good people, but they all are as black as coal. They are island people, and they all speak with that strong British accent. But, I will assure you, they are not afraid of hard work." He paused for a moment staring into my eyes, after which he began to laugh so hard that I thought he was going to fall to the ground, rollover onto his back and start kicking his feet up in the air like a little bunny rabbit.

"Richard," he gasped through spurts of laughter. "I don't care if these people are purple or oxblood in color. If they can pick fruit like you people, or even half as well, you have them here in the morning and I will put them to work."

We had them there in the morning and from that day forward apple production on the Teachuum farm boomed.

We finished the Mackintosh, and then went into a grove of Jonathans.

It is funny; I always thought that an apple was an apple until I bit into a Jonathan. The Jonathan apple was a complete surprise to me. I had always known that there were sour under-ripe green apples and red ripe sweet apples. I wasn't really aware that there were a whole variety of apples ranging between sour and sweet, and that they were bred that way, on purpose. In other words, a sour apple isn't just an under-ripe apple, and a sweet apple isn't simply that same green apple that has been allowed to ripen. Some apples, no matter how ripe they are, will never be sweet. The Jonathan is a tart and tangy apple. I loved them, and couldn't stop eating them.

I was also not aware that the farmers had a system with growing apples. A small fruit farmer always had a variety of apples growing. He didn't just plant his whole sixty acres in

Mackintosh. The small fruit farmer had an early apple variety, a mid season type, and a late season group.

At the Teachuum farm, his early apple was, as I said, the Mackintosh. Then came the Jonathan, which was followed by the Golden Delicious; next came the Red Delicious. Finally, his last apple of the season was the Rome. Each of these apples had its own color, texture, shape and taste.

The Mackintosh was red and white, round, crunchy, and reasonably sweet. The Jonathan was more a milder shade of red, and an off or cream white. It was also round, but as I've previously stated, its sweetness is more towards the tart and tangy. It is crunchy and of a more firm texture when compared to the Mackintosh, or the Rome. The Golden Delicious is supposed to be yellow, but the Michigan variety tends to be more greenish. They ripen from their green origin, get more and more yellow, and then spread to a pinkish golden glow. When fully ripened they are a truly pretty sight.

To my taste buds, the Golden Delicious always seems to be sweet. Even when green, they taste sweet to me. Some of the Golden Delicious that we picked were as large as a softball, though somewhat longer in shape.

The Red Delicious is the apple's apple. It looks like an apple. It has that dark, rich, red color. It's the apple that one shines up to give to the teacher. It is big and red, and has that tear-drop shape. Every time that we passed through the grove of Red Delicious, I could not resist plucking a great big one from a tree. For the longest time, I was confronted with nothing but disappointment. Even when not reasonably ripened, they look so apple-ish. One can hardly resist grabbing one up, and just biting into it. But, if the sugar is not fully matured in the Red Delicious, it is actually bitter. For weeks I tried to figure out what was wrong with Teachuum's crop of Red Delicious. I cored them, washed them, peeled the skin off, but no matter what I did, they remained bitter tasting until the day we finally began to harvest them. When the sugar is right the Red Delicious can not be beat; the best apple that I have ever eaten. But for consistent quality and sweetness, I like the Golden Delicious. For a unique and different apple experience, I like the Jonathan. I'll never refuse a Mackintosh. If there are no other fresh apples available, or you want to make a pie, the Rome does fine.

As we picked each variety, it became my favorite, right up until we started the next variety, at which point that apple became my favorite. This little phenomenon took place with all varieties, excepting the Rome. The best I can say for the Rome is that when all other varieties of fresh apples are not available, the Rome is delicious.

I think I was actually more concerned about Mr. Teachuum's apples than he was. I became especially anxious when we got to the Golden Delicious. I felt my island friends were picking them much too roughly. They bruised so easily. The very next day after picking, the bruises and even fingerprints, were visible on the apples. Every dent or fingerprint would be an eventual brown spot on the retail product. I pointed this out to Mr. Teachuum often. I told him that he ought to have a talk with the crew, but he wasn't concerned. Either he wasn't concerned, or he had other things that he was more concerned about. He was very, very much involved in his grapes. In fact, grapes were his main income.

He had a contract with the Welsh's grape juice company. He had this huge grape harvesting machine. This machine straddled a grapevine row, and somehow extracted the grapes in bunches, and left the vine in tact. It was an expensive piece of machinery. It was an important part of the farm operation. Not only was it used to harvest his own grapes, but grape farmers in the area who could not afford one of these machines had to hire the service.

It seems that grapes are a touchy business. The sugar content is crucial, and the testing is meticulous. Then finally when the sugar is right, the grapes must be harvested immediately. When the grape harvest begins, these grape harvesting machines and their crews work round the clock, night and day, rain, cold or whatever.

Naturally when the announcement to "start your engines" was made it began to rain cats and dogs and the Teachuum grape harvester got halfway down its first row of grapes and took a crap. The boss was beside himself. He didn't sleep. He was up with the crew all night banging on that harvester. It was a tragedy. His first year in business and his main source of income went berserk. As far as us apple pickers were concerned, from that point on, Murphy's Law became the rule of the day.

When we went to get a tractor to move our bins, the tractor would be out of gas, or the hydraulic system would be incapacitated, or one tractor tire would be flat. It was one disaster after another.

One day all of us pickers were standing before an orchard of apples that were begging to be picked and we had no tractors in any condition. There wasn't an operable tractor to be found anywhere. All the bins we had in that grove were full. The only empty bins were a mile down the road. On top of that, it looked like rain. Teachuum was nowhere to be found. I already knew what he would say even if I found him. "Do the best you can! Do the best you can! I've got problems here. I've got big problems." The only conclusion I could come to, was that there had to be considerable money in grapes to simply disregard tons and tons of apples.

Apples had a time schedule also. If we missed too many days of harvesting, it would soon be cold. It could even snow. We would have to be through those Romes before the end of November. If the boss didn't get his act together, he would not only lose his grapes but his apples also. Something had to be done, but I was at a loss. So, Carol and I went fishing. This was one of the true benefits of being a hobo. "It's not my problem, man."

When we returned from our fishing trip later that afternoon, we saw a sight that neither of us could believe. The islanders were working. They were rolling empty twenty bushel bins that were sitting down at the barn, out to the orchard. Rolling a square, twenty bushel bin the length of a football field or two, was no easy task. That would have been enough of a day's work for me, never mind then climbing up and down the fruit tress harvesting the fruit.

We pulled off to the side of the road and sat there watching our friends roll those bins up and down the countryside. To this very day when anyone tells me about lazy black people the picture of those guys rolling those heavy wooden bins over hill and dale pops into my mind. How many bins could they possibly pick using this technique? It had to take an hour or so just to get one bin out to the site. This was ridiculous.

When it got dark, they stopped picking, but kept rolling. They were going to have bins in the morning come whatever. The following day they did it again. I felt embarrassed. Here were some men who really wanted to work and the intelligent white farmer was off somewhere in never-never land. The two white pickers in the group were getting ready to go fishing again.

"Well, are you ready to start rolling bins?" I asked Carol.

"No," she said, "but I am about ready to dive into one of them broken tractors down at the barn."

Within minutes we were at ground zero, toolbox in hand. We weren't expert mechanics but being on the road all this time, living in a van and earning very little money, had put us under the hood on any number of occasions. I had even bought a text book on the subject written by William H. Crouse, from a university.

We went from tractor to tractor looking for the obvious until finally we hit upon a tractor that simply had a bad ignition switch. We by-passed the switch with a screwdriver on the starter motor, and in less than an hour or two we were all back to working productively.

Tractors at the ranch were now in dire need. Teachuum had spotted Carol and I working this particular tractor, and that next morning when we went down to crank it up, there he was in the driver's seat clicking the key. He was in his usual state of panic. "What is the matter with this damn thing?" he screamed to us as we made our approach. We both knew that if we told him what was wrong with it we would all be back to rolling bins again. With barely a moment's thought, I said; "I can't imagine. It was running like a top yesterday." He cranked and cranked. Or should I say, he clicked and clicked. He stomped on the floor peddles like a drummer in a rock and roll band. Finally he screamed a few nasty words and jumped down.

"To hell with it!" he screamed. "I'll go borrow the Thompson's again."

We waited until he rounded the corner and was out of sight. Then we pulled out our trusty screwdriver and went to work.

Each morning, thereafter, we confronted a new tractor thief. Everybody on the ranch needed a tractor for something or other and everyday somebody would see us bouncing along with our apple bins. They would jot our trusty tractor down in their memory bank and then try to beat us to it the next morning. Luckily for us, none of them had read Mr. Crouse's Automotive Mechanics, seventh edition. After a few clicks and any number of kicks, they would rush off and go find something else to break.

We worked the remainder of that season with that particular tractor and our screwdriver. We had to get a little tricky or it would have simply been a matter of time before some minimum wage farmhand would figure it out. I knew none of the prosperous big shots would figure it out. None of them would ever have reason to be into screwdriver ignition switches, but every lowly farm worker carried one in his back pocket.

We would just leave our trusty tractor parked in an odd place. If anybody asked, we would simply say with a shrug of the shoulders, "That's where she stopped. We don't know what's bugging her today." We would have it artificially break down in a different odd spot every evening. Finally no one even asked us about it anymore.

It was actually snowing by the time we got to the Rome apples. Carol and I had orchestrated the whole harvest. We brought the empty bins out and the full bins back. At the end of the day we loaded them onto the flatbed truck and had them ready for market. We had no choice. If we didn't get the full bins to market, we would eventually have no empty bins.

I can still remember picking Rome apples in a flurry of snow, and the leaves falling from the trees in bushels. We got every last tree picked.

Teachuum was so happy with the results of everything that he threw a party and invited all of the farmhands and fruit pickers. He rented a room in a restaurant and treated us all to a big prime rib dinner with all the trimmings. The islanders had never experienced anything like it. "Dat's the softest steak, I ever eat, maun," was their only comment.

Working for Mr. Teachuum was quite an adventure. It was not always an enjoyable adventure, but it was certainly a memorable one. As an added bonus, he even gave us all a little extra money for gas fare back to Florida.

He was quite a nice fellow. I don't know if his adventure with farming, the dream he had fantasized about so often from out of some dreary campus window, eventually came true, but I hope so. I know that nice guys always finish last, but if they're anything like me, just finishing is happiness enough.

9 The Orange Grove Strike

At this point in our careers, Carol and I considered ourselves to be professional fruit pickers. Whether we were skilled at what we were doing or not was not the criterion for this judgment. The judgment was based on the fact that this is how we earned our living. Every penny that came into our possession was the product of our involvement in this industry. The government, on the other hand, most probably had us classified as migrant farm workers. Since we now earned our living by traveling from place to place helping farmers bring in their crops, this description would be accurate also.

Picking ground crops involved a lot of bending and a considerable amount of dirt, and it called for the lowest pay scale. Even a regular farmhand, who was paid an hourly, year-round wage, didn't make per hour what a good fruit picker was capable of earning. But yet, I remember no farmhand who expressed jealousy or envy for our chosen occupation. Most of them had tried it at one point in their careers and wanted no part of it.

The migratory part of our chosen profession eventually consisted of our yearly commute between the state of Florida and the state of Michigan. We left Florida each year just before the heat became unbearable, and landed in Michigan just in time to enjoy a little summer and the entire fall. We would then return to Florida for the winter.

According to statistics and verbal reports that we received from time to time, we could have wintered in Arizona, southern California, or Texas. All of these states claimed citrus crops, or farm work of one kind or another. We chose Florida. It had everything that we wanted, including lots and lots of Bass fishing. Although we always wanted to try our hand at peaches in Georgia, and apples in South Carolina, New York, Oregon or

Washington State, we just never got there. By the time that we tired of Florida and Michigan, we also tired of fruit picking.

We picked for Papa Charlie for two complete winter seasons, but at the onset of our third season we hit upon dissension in the ranks.

Although we picked the same groves every year, circumstances began to change. The trees seemed to be getting taller, our ladders heavier, and the fruit, poorer and poorer. This condition was due to a number of factors. Number one; weather conditions seemed to be getting worse every year. The area had experienced a number of severe cold spells - not nearly so bad for the people who lived in the area as for the orange trees. A few days of below freezing weather, and an orange grove could be in big trouble.

Orange trees are in the process of bearing fruit and producing blossoms year round. There is no "down" time for winter with an orange tree. It goes right from yielding fruit to producing buds for its next crop. This is one of the reasons, I've been told, why handpicking is mandatory. No one has invented a machine yet that is able to pick this year's fruit without destroying next year's crop.

Each succeeding year we saw more and more smudge pots dotting the groves.

Smudge pots are liquid fuel burners that fire with a small flame and a ton of smoke. They are used to warm the grove in an attempt to counteract the chilling effects of a freeze.

Another method of protection was to spray the grove via overhead sprinkler systems. This method would cover the tree and the fruit with a crust of ice and somehow insulate the fruit and or the tree from freezing temperatures. From our experiences picking fruit after a freeze, I presume that these methods of protection were for the benefit of the tree because the fruit was always devastated. Shortly after a freeze the leaves would dry up and begin falling from the trees. I have pictures of trees filled with clinging oranges but yet baron of leaves. They looked like ghastly things taken out of some frightening Halloween cartoon.

The oranges were no less a horror story themselves. The tree, in its struggle for life after a freeze, seemed to suck all of the juice and nutrients right back out of the clinging orange until it released its child to plunge to the ground as a pale piece of skin and pithy pulp.

Another factor affecting the care, up-keep, and health of a grove was the owner. From our experience Florida orange groves were not owned by Florida farmers. It seemed for the most part that they were investments for somebody. In any case, when the going got tough, the tough bailed out. When it came to maintenance, pruning, culling over-grown trees and replanting, it was obvious that there were better investments elsewhere. The grass in some groves was often knee deep. Unfortunately when it is "hamburger a-gain" up at the Mansion, it is fist fights in the fields and groves.

We didn't come to blows in the groves, but economic debates as to who deserves how much began to precede entry into every new grove. Some debates over a nickel or a dime went on for hours.

The system went like this. Upon arrival at a new grove the price would be announced. It would be so many cents per bushel. In the past, there was never a moment's hesitation. The price would be announced, the troops would pick up their ladders, march to their assigned rows and the competition would begin. But now, the price would be announced, there would be a grumbling and mumbling. Some men would go into huddles here and there. Other men would stand their ground staring, while still others would return to their automobiles or pickup trucks and light up a cigarette or turn on the radio. It was a totally spontaneous, unorganized revolution.

The experienced pickers could just look at a grove and know whether they were going to make a day's pay or not. The prices at every grove kept getting worse and worse. The best pickers were always first to give up ground. Even in a bad grove a Lanzo could manage a day's pay. But in a grove where a Lanzo could pick only five or seven bins, there would be others who could muster, at best, two or three.

To Carol and I the whole debate was completely academic. We could make the amount of money that we needed to survive in our lifestyle doing just about anything. If the crew wanted to pick, we picked. If they didn't want to pick, we went to breakfast. Our Thoreau-style poverty had made us independently wealthy.

As you philosophy students will remember, according to Thoreau, a man was as rich as the number of things that he could do without. Carol and I were comfortably without almost everything that most of America considered absolutely necessary. According to Thoreau, we two were about as wealthy as a couple could get.

To us the situation was almost humorous. Within an instant the debate over a few dimes turned everyone, black or white, instantly into a Karl Marx, or a Henry Ford. Not a one of the actors in this play had to read a script, memorize any dialogue or know Pragmatism from Dialectical Materialism. The actors were all legendary, and the dialogue instinctive. To see all the history books that I had read being re-enacted by the side of the road, and on street corners, word for word, by actors who weren't even familiar with the "play", or the "novel" was, to say the least, extraordinary.

On the left we had the "Mob". On the right, we had the controlling, invisible Capitalists. In between, we had the heart and soul of this dilemma, capsulized in the dark black eyes of two lovable and sensitive old friends.

Papa Charlie and Lanzo had great difficulty talking directly to one another or even looking one another in the eye. Invariably, no matter what the debate or price, Lanzo was the first to pick up his ladder and head for the grove. At first this was enough to start the trickle of production, but now Lanzo began to feel the pressure of angry, hurt eyes on his back. On one occasion Lanzo went so far as to pick up his ladder, place it into a tree and start picking, only to find himself completely alone. Carol and I never moved towards a grove until we saw a consensus of voting feet heading in that direction. From that defeat on, Lanzo relinquished his position as leader, and took his place beside Carol and me in the pack of followers.

The group had no real leadership. There was either a spontaneous general acceptance or a similar denial. The last act of this tragedy came to a head and an end for Carol and me, on the streets outside of this rather terrible looking grove hidden in the small town of Altoona.

We had picked this grove the previous two years, and each year it got progressively worse. On this day, what we looked at would make any real orange grove farmer's heart sink. The trees were overgrown, and the lack of care was obvious. Even the grass, under and between the rows of trees, was knee deep. This year's crop had obviously been damaged by last year freeze. The fruit was sparse. The trees all exhibited whole sections of dead limbs. It would be an act of kindness on the part of the pickers to even volunteer to pick this grove no matter what the price. Making good money here was totally out of the question.

The workers balked at the eighty cent per bushel offer and the street negotiations began. Some workers kept records of their picking from year to year. They informed us that we were paid one dollar and twenty-five cents per bushel to pick this grove last year. Not a one of us had any doubt that last year these trees were in much better condition. This grove was clearly in a state of neglect. Other workers told our group that crews had already been here, and had refused to pick this grove even at a dollar per bushel, never mind eighty cents.

The negotiations dragged on. Carol and I had already gone to breakfast and returned. Now it was almost time for lunch. This was the longest stall that we had yet witnessed.

The bosses had gone from eighty cents to ninety cents, and the workers had come down from a dollar fifty to one dollar and fifteen cents. Finally, a man from the crowd yelled; "Tell the man, one dollar, Papa Charlie, and we'll pick the damn thing."

It was bold on his part to yell this out, but a sigh of relief seemed to spread over the crew. It was clear that Papa Charlie could sense the atmosphere. He stood up on his Goat.

"If I get a dollar from the man for this grove, do you all agree to go to work?"

They mumbled and grumbled, but it was agreed.

Papa Charlie drove his Goat down the road to where the representatives of the invisible-hand capitalists were parked in their new automobiles. When Papa Charlie returned his face was glum.

"Da maun say, you can pick dis grove for ninety cent or you can go home."

I couldn't believe what I was hearing. What real difference did all of this make to the bosses? Every grove was more or less a matter of opinion. Without question they could get their dime back on a better grove down the road. They were simply forcing the worker's backs to the wall. A dime on one grove out of a thousand groves was virtually without consequence as far as I could see.

If the bosses had agreed to the worker's demands, the workers would have lost money but felt that they had won a small moral victory. They would have gone back to work. The rebellion would have been quelled, and the bosses could have made up their dime without question on any number of more marginal groves down the road. The workers needed their jobs, and it was clear by their last offer that they felt they had made too much of this situation and were looking for a way out. Their only hold out, now, was for dignity - and dignity had been denied.

I couldn't believe what I was witnessing. I didn't know what to say, but I felt I had to say something.

"Papa Charlie, don't you realize what these bosses are doing? They are completely destroying the morale and spirit of this team? How can these bosses expect these men to do anything but go home after that slap in the face? They haven't left your friends here a leg to stand on. Not even a false promise for the future. Even if they told them some outright lie, it would be better than this. Tell one of those bosses, sitting down the road there, to come up here and make that offer to these men personally." At this point a look came into Papa Charlie's eyes that I had never seen before. It was rage.

"Mr. Noble," he yelled, standing up on his Goat and pointing his finger down into my face, "you have got yourself mixed up with a bunch of evil people. These men are all trouble makers. They are a worthless lazy lot that has been run off every good picking crew in the area. You may not realize it, Mr. Noble, but there is not a man here who can walk away from this place and find himself another job. These men can either go to work, or go to hell."

I looked over at Lanzo who was smoking a cigarette and clutching onto his can of Colt Forty-Five.

"Does that go for Lanzo also, Papa Charlie?"

Charlie, looked over at Lanzo, as we all did. Lanzo's head was slumped towards the ground. He rolled his head up slowly and looked Papa Charlie in the eye. Papa Charlie stared back momentarily at his life long friend - the best picker that he had ever seen. He stammered, but then regained his drive.

"That goes for any man who refuses to go back to work."

"Does that go for Lanzo, Papa Charlie?" I repeated.

The two men now stared at one another for a long moment. Papa Charlie's eyes were in a rage of anger and confusion.

"That goes for every man here," he said almost inaudibly as he sat down on his Goat and drove away.

Without saying a word, Carol and I put an arm about one another and headed for our van. At that moment we were in agreement with another famous philosopher, Johnny Paycheck, when he said in a well known song; "You can take this grove and shove it." I don't know if he actually used the word "grove", but it was close enough for me.

10 Foster and the Padidiot

It wasn't an easy decision to pack up and leave Papa Charlie after two years of fellowship, but it really wasn't that difficult either. The bosses had sent a clear message to Papa Charlie's crew members. If any worker felt that he had skills and/or abilities that could provide him with greater income opportunities he should be advised to seek them out. Otherwise, he could take a deep breath, shut his mouth, decline his head, and pick.

For Carol and I, there was no choice here. To return to that grove under those conditions would have turned our adventure into a burden. There were dozens of other crew bosses and hundreds of different groves, not to mention several different competing contracting companies or bosses in the area.

We were back to picking oranges within the hour. We were working for another black man by the name of Foster, or Fosta. This was a nickname like "Papa" in Papa Charlie. We worked for Foster two years, or seasons, and never did find out his real name. It didn't matter. Everyone in the area knew who he was. He had a good reputation, and he was honorable and hard working. He was younger than Papa Charlie, and picked fruit himself along with the crew. He and the rest of his crew were Islanders also, and they spoke with that strong British influence.

Compared to the fruit we had been picking for Papa Charlie, Foster's groves were beyond our belief. The trees were shorter, bushier, and well cared for. We picked some groves for Foster where the trees were so short that we didn't need but a ten foot ladder. It was like we had left the barren wilderness and entered into the land of plenty. Production and pay went up, while work and strain went down. That very first Foster-grove was like a dream compared to the grove that we had just left.

We went to work without even asking the price, and when we found out that we were getting a dollar per bushel we nearly fainted. Sometimes the grass is greener.

I felt that picking with Foster's crew was distinguishable in a couple of categories. Sound and smell remain paramount in my mind's eye.

If, for whatever reasons, we could not find our fellow crew members' exact whereabouts within a large grove, like the American Indian we fell back upon our basic instincts.

If you will recall now those days of yesteryear, with a cloud of dust and a puff of smoke and a hearty ... You'll remember how Tonto would press his ear to the steel beam of a railroad track, in order to detect the distant rumblings of an on coming locomotive, or to the earth in order to anticipate a herd of stampeding buffalo? In like manner, whenever necessary to discover the Foster crew, Carol and I attuned our ears to the faint and distant sounds of the Bob Marley island band rupturing the quiet of the morning dew, and the distinctive odor emanating from the ritualistic burning of the sacred weed of the Rastafarian cult.

It is interesting to note that this particular branch of the Rastafarian island cult smoked joints the size of Cuban cigars. They actually wrapped the marijuana up in sections of brown paper, grocery store bags. We learned, latter on, that the members of this congregation actually planted, cultivated, and harvested this abundance of sacred weed, cost free. In truth, they got paid to do it. I am told that they planted their seeds under orange trees in groves that they themselves were hired to care and cultivate for wealthy absentee orange grove investors. Some of the group told me that they had grown plants, in and about orange groves, which reached a height of ten to twelve feet.

The next outstanding feature of the Fosterite experience was the language. When any of the Fosterites spoke to us, we understood them reasonably well. They, like Papa Charlie's boys, spoke with that distinctive, musically delightful, Caribbean-British lingual meter. But once into the grove, and up into the trees, they began to shout to one another in a language that sounded to Carol and I to be an indistinguishable blur. It was wonderful to listen to them chatter in the mornings. It was, to us, very much akin to the chirping of the crows, jays, sparrows and mocking birds. It was a delight. Like the birds, they had a pitch and tone resembling song. But, as with the birds, nothing was communicated to us beyond the joy that was obviously involved in their performance of it.

Carol and I eavesdropped on their conversations, the syllables of which dropped through the trees like notes tumbling from sheet music. We would struggle and strain and attune our ears to the beat and cadence, but the notes, though music to our ears, projected no communicative images.

One cool December, or January morning, as we stood about a fire warming our hands, I asked the crew, rather matter-of-factly, what language it was that they were speaking. They all looked at me as if I were insane. Some of them were shocked, while others slapped their hands together and laughed. Immediately Foster looked at me and, quite indignantly, proclaimed;

"What do you mean, maun! Dat's English. We speak English maun."

I shook my head. "No way man. That's no English that I've ever heard."

The crew erupted at my incredulousness, and bounced off into the grove, slapping their knees laughing and mumbling to themselves. For weeks afterwards each time one of them would pass us, they would ask with a smile; "What's a matter, maun, you don't understand English? Where you from, maun?" All of which brings us to the discovery of a man we named the "Padidiot".

The Padidiot was the patriarch of the only other white couple working among the Fosterites. He appeared to be a young man of about eighteen, who adamantly claimed to be no less than sixty eight years old. I suppose that he operated under the notion that if you are going to tell a lie, you might just as well tell a big one. He sported a slight stubble of peach fuzz on his chin which he tried his best to cultivate, and promote to the world at large, as a beard. He had a child bride, and I speak literally. Carol and I guess-timated that she could not have been past the age of fifteen, and possibly closer to the age of twelve.

She was a cute little thing who was growing appreciably more pregnant by the hour. They lived in a renovated school bus. He was about five foot tall, and had parentheses for legs. If he were only slightly taller he could have walked over a fire hydrant without disturbing it or himself.

His manner and attitude was his impersonation of an old farmer that he must have met and admired in his past, or, should I say, in days gone by.

He wore suspenders, jeans, work boots, an old dilapidated felt hat, and smoked a corncob pipe - obviously of his own construction.

He spoke broken English, and in a dialect I had never encountered. I realized later on that it wasn't really a dialect, but a language that he had actually made up himself. It was kind of a concoction of Pig Latin and general stupidity designed not only to baffle and confuse the listener, but to draw attention to the speaker. It went something like this; Mornin'. How you fadokes padoin' faday? Are you fadavin' your padennies? Fadell me, fadoo and the missus ever padake any padapple padies in your fradee fradime?

If and when you said ... excuse me? He would repeat the same dribble, dribble for dribble. He would repeat it as many times as you would ask him to. Then he would stand there and stare at you as if you were the stupid one. To tell you the truth, he was pretty good at this game, and he had me fooled for the longest time. I kept asking him what country he originally came from, or what his parents' nationality was. Sometimes I would ask him to repeat something five or six times, and he would repeat it flawlessly and unperturbed. From there we would kind of go into a pantomime quiz, until I finally got the gist of it.

For example, the dribble above would be translated thusly; Morning. How you folks doing today? Are you saving your pennies? Tell me, do you and the missus ever bake any apple pies in your free time?

I have once heard it said that the difference between a neurotic and a psychotic is that the neurotic builds imaginary castles in the sky, but the psychotic lives in them. Well this guy was without doubt a neurotic, with definite psychotic tendencies. But, all in all, he was harmless. At first we thought that maybe we should report these people to somebody. Who would we report them to and what would we claim they had done?

We could report him for abducting and impregnating a child.

Had he abducted her? She looked happy. My wife purposely questioned the young thing hoping to give her the opportunity of passing us a HELP note. In reality, she seemed more afraid of my wife than the Padidiot.

Then there was always the possibility that the Padidiot was not the oppressor but the young lady's rescuer. Maybe he scooped up the poor, young thing and carried her away from a Deliverance type family in which incest and sexual perversion actually provided some of the warmer moments of her childhood memories.

What were they doing living in a school bus in the middle of an orange grove?

Well, from that point of view, they were better off than we were. We were living in an orange grove, in a van. Then, what if they weren't that young at all? The older one grows, the younger everyone else seems. My wife always tells the story of her mother's comments when her younger sister informed her that she was running off for the purposes of raising a family with some boy from down the road. "Why you can't get married," her mother screamed. "You haven't even learned to make your bed yet."

Everyone is looking younger these days. Children are making children. But hasn't this always been so? To tell you the truth, I've gotten to the point in my evolution where I consider 'birth' an irresponsible act - not only on the part of humans, but for God as well. He, and we, should have given this existence considerably more thought. I don't care how old you are or what your motivation, when and if you decide to take the act of birth into your own hands, you have stepped beyond any bounds of decency and fair play.

In any case, we learned to live with the Padidiot, as, I suppose he learned to live with us.

11   Bill and His Dog, Larry

Bill Jones was what they call in the South - a good old boy. He was a big man, very tall and very heavy. Bill was the only fellow that I ever met who could sit in the shade under an orange tree and without making a move, sweat profusely - no matter what the temperature.

As all good old boys, Bill drove a pickup truck, collected guns, lived in a double-wide, and knew the art of survival, Southern style.

He had a small fishing boat that he used to trot-line for catfish. He hunted, and had a freezer filled to the lid with venison, wild turkey, ducks, wild hog, turtle, rattlesnake meat, shellcracker, bluegill, catfish, and bags of shelled field peas. When he wasn't contracting orange pickers, he could be found driving a tractor trailer or hauling and selling watermelons along side some main stretch of highway from the back of a rack truck.

He was a good old boy, surviving in any and whatever way he could manage. The only thing that Bill Jones didn't have that all good old boys are supposed to have, was a dog. Instead of a dog, Bill had Larry.

Bill and Larry were virtually inseparable. Larry was a stray that Bill had picked up alongside of the road one day. Larry was homeless, jobless, food-less, skill-less, school-less, speechless, transportation-less, and hopeless. He could neither read nor write, and was not too handy in handling numbers either. The orange picking crew had a party when they discovered this. Bill finally developed a system of lines and crosses. Four vertical lines and one horizontal line passing through the four indicated a total of five bins.

After being admonished by Bill a number of times and cheated by his fellow workers on numerous occasions, Larry learned the importance of these marks and adhered to the making of them with a strict self-imposed discipline. Despite all his short comings, as time went on, Larry became Bill's right-hand man. If Bill was contracting oranges, Larry was driving the Goat; if Bill was selling watermelons, Larry was loading the truck and checking the load; if Bill was catching catfish, Larry was tending the line. If you saw Bill driving down the road in his pickup truck, you saw Larry sitting there shotgun, drinking his "Pessi".

Larry also had a speech impediment. Pepsi was always Pessi. Larry spoke as if he had a hair lip - but he didn't.

He looked pretty much like everyone else - but he wasn't. He was a sad sack; the poor soul of the universe. Larry was the antithesis of Bill in nature and character. Bill was the capitalist, the businessman, the economic pragmatist. Larry was the peasant, the serf, the blue-collared, blue jean-ed worker of the world who saw only the idealistic.

Bill was shrewd and cunning. Larry was naive and simplicity itself. Bill was roundabout and diplomatic. Larry was to the point and childishly unsophisticated. If Bill said black, Larry said white. If Bill said right, Larry said wrong. What a pair!

Bill took care of Larry's every need, and was rewarded with Larry's loyalty. But this loyalty was certainly not blind or without questioning or criticism. These two went well past the tragic and comical, to the theatrically humorous.

I think that it all began with the ice water.

Old Bill, at first, brought out to the grove a five gallon cooler filled with ice water. He had it strapped to the back of his pickup truck. He even provided disposable drinking cups. It was only a matter of time before Bill's capitalistic creativity came to the surface. After all, this "free" ice water business involved a lot of trouble, time, and money. Bill, one day, added to the ice water, cans of Pepsi, Coke, Sprite, and Hire's root beer. He offered these to the crew for the current vending machine price.

Nobody seemed to have a problem with this except Larry who shook his head in disgust every time any crew member deposited fifty cents into Big Bill's open palm. Finally after one particularly long sigh on Larry's part, Bill turned to his constant companion and moaned pathetically; "Larry, what on earth are you groanin' about, boy?"

"You only paid twenty-five cents for those sodas, Bill. Why are you makin' everybody pay fifty cents?"

This was a question that bordered on the infantile or ludicrous to Bill. This was a question that was not what one would call stupid. It was not intelligent enough to be labeled stupid. Bill pulled out his handkerchief, wiped his brow, looked about the bed of the pickup truck and then into the eyes of the other listeners. He shook his head slowly back and forth asking the observers with this mocking gesture what one was supposed to do or say to a boy like this Larry.

"Larry, am I forcin' anybody to buy this ice cold, twenty-five cent soda for fifty cents?"

"No."

"Do you see me pushin' any man's arm behind his back, or intimadatin' anybody to buy these frosty, cold sodas for fifty cents?"

"No."

"Then tell me Larry, what in the hell is your problem boy? Honest and truly, cross my heart and hope to die, I really, honest and truly, would like to know? If you can splain it to me, son, please do?"

"It just ain't white."

"It ain't right, you say? What ain't right?"

"It ain't white to buy somthin' for twenty-five cents and sell it for fifty cents."

"Oh, it ain't! Well maybe you and me best get back to town and get the po-lice onto that dang grocer who sold me this ten cent soda for a quarter. Or how about the boy who sold me this twenty-five cent ice for seventy-nine cents?"

"You got the ice for free from Billy Bob. He always gives you things for free from the grocery store 'cause you let him shoot your machinegun some times." Everybody standing around the pickup truck laughed.

"Larry, what did I tell you about talkin' about that machinegun boy?"

Larry rushed his hand up to his mouth in embarrassment. "I'm sorry Bill, it slipped out. I didn't mean it. But that is how you got the ice."

"Don't you know Larry that a man can go to jail ifin he has a machinegun - which I do not!"

"You do so have a machinegun. You keep it in your trailer, right underneath your bed. You even let me shoot it once."

"Larry," Bill said, lowering his head, closing one sweaty eye, and staring very sternly in his hopeless little friend's direction with the other. "I do not have a machinegun in my trailer under my bed. If I did and other folks knew about it, they could tell the po-lice about it and I could end up in jail. Do you understand what I am sayin'?"

"But ..."

"DO YOU UNDERSTAND WHAT I AM SAYIN'?"

"Oh, I get it. But you didn't buy no ice."

"Okay, so I got this ice for free. Where did I get this fifty dollar cooler, do you suppose?"

"You got it off the Power Company truck last year, when they left it on the ground in the I.G.A. supermarket parking lot by mistake. Don't you remember? I told you that you shoulda followed that truck and give it back. And you said; 'Larry, the Lord giveth and the Lord taketh away' and it looked to you that the Lord had just chosen to giveth to you and taketh from those rich S.O.B's at the Power Company."

"Alright, alright, so I don't buy the ice and I didn't buy the cooler, but don't I get up two hours early every day, drive to town, and fill up my free cooler with free ice and store-boughten soda every day so that my pickin' crew can have ice cold soda out in this steaming hot grove?"

"No, not exactly."

"What do you mean, no, not exactly!? I don't know how you can say that when you're right there with me every dang morning!?"

"That's right. I'm not only with you every morning, I'm the one who goes over to your trailer every morning, two and a half hours early and gets you out of bed. I'm the one who drives you to town and drops you off at the EAT so's you can have your breakfast while I go over to the grocery store and fill up the cooler with ice and soda, and get gasoline put into the truck. And then I'm the one who picks you up after you've had your breakfast at the EAT, and drives you out here to the grove."

"Okay, okay. But who gives you the money to go to the store and get the ice and fill up the pickup truck with gasoline and so on and so forth?"

"You do."

"Well?"

"Well what?"

"Well, that's somethin', ain't it!? (a long pause from Larry)...well ain't it?!"

"I suppose. But it ain't exactly like what you said."

"Larry, you're the nit-pickinest little man I ever met. And you know if I wanted to have this kind of conversation today, I couldda just stayed home and listened to my wife. You're gonna make somebody a fine wife one day boy."

"Well, I sure don't wanna be your wife, she's already got more to do than you could pay me for, I'll tell you."

"Oh really? You feelin' sorry for my wife, Larry? I don't hear her complainin'. She's got a nice big double-wide. She's got a freezer full of food. She's got clothes on her back. Her kids is all taken cared for. She's got her own auto-mo-bile. She got a brang new washin' machine, and an electric dryer. That's right Larry, an electric dryer - right INSIDE the house. Rain or shine, she's got herself clean, dry clothes. Does she seem persecuted to you, Larry?"

"Well, she's got a washer and dryer all right, but the washer's been leakin' all over the place because of the broke hose on the back that you never had time to fix. And that dryer, she's afraid to use it because it lit on fire four times because of the way you hooked up the electric. And while you're drivin' this brand new pickup, she's drivin' that old junk box with the broken battery cables. Every time she starts it, she has to open up the hood and re-adjust the cables or it won't crank; and it's a standard shift, and the gears keep gettin' jammed; and in town, in the middle of traffic, she has to open the hood and with a hammer and a screwdriver she has to unhook the linkage. And then she has got to take care of your five huntin' dogs that you never have time for, and your six kids."

"Now hold on there Larry, only five of them kids is my younguns. She come to me with one of them boys, you know?"

"Ya, I know. You tell her that fifty times a day. Everybody knows. The whole town knows."

"Well, Larry, if I'm doin' such a terrible job, maybe you just ought to take over. I think Essee's likin' you better 'en me anyway. You always kissin' up and suckin' around, and no matter what, you always on her side."

"That's because she's always right, and you're always wrong."

"Okay Larry - okay you win. I'm always wrong. I never do nothin' right. I just come out here day after day, seven days a week, sweatin' my lazy butt off, dealin' with all the problems, and sufferin' through the likes of you. I'm just a mean old son of a bitch, who don't do nothin', cheats everybody and takes all the money. Why anybody can see that I'm one of the richest mans that is. Why I got money just crawlin' out my pockets. Don't I Larry?" (silence) "Well, don't I? Why everybody in the world is envin' me. Why I bet Mister Rocket-feller would like to be livin' in my double-wide, sleepin' with old Essee, and drivin' my new pickup truck. Why I can see him right now, rockin' in that chair out on my back porch, gazing at the view out over my septic tank and sayin' to hisself; 'Why I'm just the richest man in the world. There ain't nobody that's got a better life than me.' Can't ya just see him Larry?" (more silence)

Not too long after this discussion old Bill decided all that brand name soda he was bringing out to the grove was simply costing him too much money. So instead of Pepsi, Coke, and Hire's root beer, he started packing his cooler with the generic, no-name brand. None of the workers seemed to be overly upset, but Larry was outraged, and very shortly thereafter he had his own cooler, packed with ice, and filled to the brim with Pepsi cola. He wouldn't take the free ice from Bill's friend at the grocery store. He bought ice, and he refused to charge anybody one penny more than the exact cost that he paid for each can of Pepsi. Well, it wasn't too long before Larry had driven poor Bill right out of the soda pop business. Larry was sellin' "Pessies" like hot cakes.

"Well, you makin' a lot of money sellin' your Pessies Larry? Why don't you go out and buy a couple of more coolers; pack 'em with three dollars worth of ice every day and start yourself up a little route, goin' from grove to grove sellin' everybody Pessies at twenty-five cents a can. Why it seems that you got a real good little business there Larry. How much money did you lose last week – twenty, thirty dollars? Real good idea you got there Larry."

"I ain't tryin' to make no money, Bill."

"Oh I can see that. You don't have to tell me that, son. You know, the only thing that bothers me Larry, is why you want to stop me from makin' money. Is it 'cuse I've been so mean to you? I mean am I chargin' you too much to live out back of my place?"

"You ... you don't charge me anything Bill."

"What? ... what was that? Did you all hear what Larry done said? Would you say that again one more time - and say it a little louder, I don't think everybody heard that Larry?"

"I said that you don't charge me nothin' to live out back at your place."

"And did I hep ya fix up that old tool shed - put a bed and electric in there?"

"Yeah, you did."

"And did I take you down to the hardware, so's you could buy the paint like you wanted?"

"Yes, yes you did Bill."

"And did I hep ya pick out the radio that you liked so much?"

"Ahh huh?"

"And do I charge you anything to eat up at the house with me and Essee and the kids?"

"Nope; no you never do."

"And do I let you use the pickup truck, whenever you want to - even though you got no damn driver's license?"

"You ... you sure do Bill."

"Have I ever put a bite of food into my mouth, without offerin' you a share?"

"No, you always offer Bill. You're very good in that way."

"Well thank you. Thank you very much Larry. I think that's the first kind word you ever done spoke to me. But you know what I don't understand? Why, if you like me so much, and I'm so good to you - why are you tryin' to take the food from my younguns' mouths?"

"I ain't tryin' to take no food from the kids Bill."

"Ohhh, yes you are. Every time you sell one of them Pessies and I don't sell none of my soda, you costin' me money. And every time I lose a dime or a quarter or thirty-five cents that means that I have less money for the kids. That means fewer pieces of candy for the girls; that means fewer little toys for the boys; that means one less chicken leg on the dinner table. But I'll tell you Larry, it's all right with me. If that's the way that you feel; if you think I am such a sorry individual, you go right ahead. And when the kids come to me cause they hungry, I'll just send them out back to you. Maybe you'll sell 'em a Pessi for a quarter."

"I wouldn't make 'em pay Bill. I'd give 'em a Pessi for free."

"Well, that's real nice of you - you're a real good man. I'm sure God will be proud of you. Now let me just go back to the devil where I belong."

And that was the end of Larry's Pessi business.

Larry had lived with Bill for a couple or three years before it happened. Larry woke up one morning with a very sharp pain in his skull. Bill said that it must have really been hurting Larry because of the claw marks Larry had dug into the ground as he tried to drag himself from the shed up to the house. When Bill found him he was already dead.

The next time we saw Bill, he told us the whole story.

It seems that Larry had a family that lived back up north in the woods somewhere. The reason Larry couldn't read or write was because they had him declared retarded when he was still a little tike in order to get a check for his care from the government.

"The boy was a little slow, but he weren't no retard," Bill said. "So then one day Larry just upped and ran away. I judged that they was also not treatin' him too very well. And old Larry didn't like everybody around thinkin' that he was a dummy. So he become one of them street kids. I don't know how he got here to Florida, but you know when I met him I took a liken to him right off, and I put him to work. He was a good boy. I really liked him. Me and Essee put up the money for his funeral, you know. We felt everybody should have a funeral, and have somebody say somethin' nice about him, before they put him into the ground.

"We got him a little box and hired a preacher. We even found out who his folks were and where they was from. We felt it was only fittin' that we should invite 'em. When they showed up at the wake son, you could tell right off who they was. They was the sorriest looking folks I ever did see. They hardly gave Larry a look 'till one of them spotted that ring on his finger. It weren't much of a ring, price wise, but it looked like somethin'. I think that old Larry paid twenty-five dollars for it at a yard sale one day. It probably really weren't worth that much, but you know Larry. He weren't one to be talkin' anybody down on anything. I told him that he coulda gotten it for five or ten dollars if he woulda just bartered a bit. But no, he says he wants everybody to be happy. You know how he was. Everybody has got to be happy, even if old Larry has to pay extra.

"But no sooner did one of them relatives see that ring on dead Larry's finger than he decides that it belongs to him. He goes over to the casket and starts in to tryin' to pry it off old Larry's finger. Well when I seed that, I went right over to that boy, and I says; Son, you had best leave that ring right there on Larry hand, if you know what's good for you. But, he says ... 'that's my ring, Larry stoled it from me when he run away from home.' I told him that he was a damn liar and that I had been with Larry when he bought that ring. So, he backs off. But then a little while later, the whole damn family comes over to me and starts in to tell me that before Larry gets put into the ground, they want all of his valuables put into a bag so's they can take them on home with them. I tells 'em that old Larry didn't have no valuables, and that just about everything he had that was worth anythin' was right there in that box with him. Well, they told me that they want that ring. And I told 'em that ring belonged to Larry and that he was taken it with him to wherever ... wherever, he was goin'.

"Well you can bet that they didn't like hearin' that, but there weren't nothin' that they was going to do about it, I can tell you that.

"It was a nice funeral, and the preacher said some nice things. He didn't even know Larry, but I'll tell you what, he did pretty dang good. I really liked that Larry. He was tough on me, but he was a good old boy - maybe too good.

"They said he had a stroke - an aneurysm or somethin'. But he died pretty quick. He was into some real hard pain for a minute or two. You could see where he drug himself on the ground, clawin' at the dirt tryin' to pull himself up to the house.

"It was mighty hard for the kids and Essee - she and them younguns really had some feelin's for that old boy. We had a whole lot of cryin' goin' on, let me tell ya - mighty bad time. I'm goin' ta miss that boy. I'm sure gonna miss him."

12 Orange Juice in Umatilla

I don't know if we brought the orange growers in central Florida bad luck or it was simply their turn. But whatever, the orange picking business went rapidly downhill in the years after our arrival. There were freezes every year for three consecutive years. The first year we stayed busy in the groves, either picking the fruit off the trees before it withered and fell to the ground, or gathering it off the ground after it had fallen. We couldn't imagine why they wanted the fruit after it had withered on the limbs, dried up, and then fell to the ground, but they did. So we gathered it up, juice-less, sometimes pulp-less skins ... mold, rot and all.

The second year of freeze, the picking and gathering season was even shorter, but that year's earnings were supplemented by a new business - orange tree pruning. Only this pruning wasn't done from the ground with a pair of hand snippers, or even from a three legged ladder. This was man-sized pruning done with chainsaws, bulldozers and dump trucks. Where the bulldozers were employed, of course, they didn't need us with our itsy-bitsy chainsaws. They simply knocked it all down and then began constructing a housing complex, trailer park, or shopping mall. Where we went in with chainsaws, believe it or not, they were attempting to save the grove. I would never have thought that anyone could save a tree with a chainsaw.

Our job in some cases was to cut away all dead limbs, and in other situations to actually cut the tree back to a stump. Some groves ended up looking like orange grove graveyards, with a million stumps as individual grave markers. Within a year or two they evolved into stubbly little bushes with shoots sprouting all over the old trunk. Within three to five years, they were actually little orange trees again. But by the third year of frost or freezing temperatures the orange groves were in a state of devastation.

We went to the Citrus Tower, a tourist spot in central Florida where one could view orange groves far off to the horizon in any direction. When we got there we couldn't believe our eyes. All the trees, as far as the eye could see in every direction, were bare and leafless. We had never seen anything like this. We felt very, very sad to be viewing such devastation, but we knew not who to feel sorry for.

We saw no teary-eyed farmers hugging their wives, or frantic children bawling in fear. Everything was rather businesslike and matter-of-fact. Like some giant people-less conglomerate had just transferred its stock to another company.

We knew there had to be people suffering from this catastrophe. Certainly fortunes had been lost here. Millions, even possibly billions of dollars had to be going down the drain for somebody, somewhere. But whoever they were, and wherever they were, was matter for speculation. The hand of capitalism was invisible, the capitalist body was invisible, and no family and friends were to be found anywhere.

Yet somehow, somewhere policies changed, procedures were initiated, and men in suits and ties appeared here and there. They drove big new cars or tumbled out of fancy pickup trucks along side mutilated, abandoned groves and pointed, or walked about kicking at clumps of dirt with their polished Florsheims. Sometimes they shook their heads. Other times they just threw their hands and arms up into the air.

For two hoboes like Carol and I, all of this meant very little. We still had our van, a fairly comfortable bed, and lots of stately Florida oak forest, dripping with moss, to park under. Our big problem was our usual one - where to find another no future, dead-end, not particularly sought after, bad, but yet interesting job; a job that wouldn't tie us down, but would stimulate our interest and fill our pockets for at least a month or two. This was yet another positive, on the ledger for the choice of poverty in life.

Believe it or not we found just what we were looking for at the Umatilla orange juice plant.

Now, rightfully, you might ask with all of the orange trees dead, and no oranges to pick, what the heck were they squeezing at the orange juice plant?

Well, for awhile at least, they were still squeezing marginal oranges from peripheral areas. After that, subsidiary orange squeezing plants were closed, and oranges were being trucked in from even further distances. In any case, we were both working again.

Carol was working in the part of the plant that was squeezing the oranges, and I was involved in the processing of the peel and pulp. Carol pretty much hated her job, because it involved a good deal of cleaning and bending at the waist, and working with goopy diseased oranges that were apparently covered with slime and mold, according to her. As you've learned in the past, strange criterions judge the goodness and badness of your edibles in processing plants.

Dead, diseased chickens with their insides spewing with green puss did not necessarily constitute an inedible chicken. Unfiltered rice hulls and sawdust did not necessarily produce an unacceptable apple juice, nor did a few maggots eliminate truck loads of rotten, overripe tomatoes from being processed at your local ketchup factory. In fact, as long as the ketchup was under a certain number of maggots, per a certain volume, the ketchup was considered to be fine and dandy.

Orange juice was judged by a similar standard - a mold count. As long as the mold didn't surpass a certain percentage, it was okay. If, on the other hand, the orange juice was in fact moldy, new less moldy oranges would have to be added or barrels of less moldy orange concentrate purchased from Brazil would have to be added until the mold count was brought under acceptable limits. So there you go. Have you had your orange juice today?

The processing of the pulp was almost as important as the squeezing of the oranges. In fact, I remember someone telling me that even if the oranges were rejected at the squeezing part of the plant, they still would be chopped and processed for my part of the plant - kind of the tail wagging the dog sort of situation. Due to research and development projects, the skin and pulp was responsible for a whole slew of secondary products.

Now don't quote me but if my memory can be trusted at all, I think that out of the orange skins they were able to extract or concoct cattle feed, fertilizer, molasses, perfume, some kind of skin care lotion, and maybe some other products which I have now forgotten.

We both worked on the third shift.

My job was rather interesting, if not at times boring. Basically I was a sort of human switch, or cut off device. All night long I sat beside this big, long, metal trough that had a giant stainless steel screw which carried tons of orange peel goop and slop to processing boilers or something. The orange slop was transported from the squeezing section to my area via a giant overhead shoot. The shoot dumped the slop into huge, two story, funnel shaped vats. These vats were really gigantic. I don't know how much slop these vats could hold but it had to be tons, upon tons.

For most of the night, I just sat there reading a book, or talking to Leroy the forklift driver.

Leroy was a very affable, talkative, black man. He was tall, spoke perfect English, and seemed to be forever balancing on the edge of a smile and a booming laugh. He would come buzzing over to my area, silence the roar of his forklift, swivel in his seat, cross his long, gangly legs, light up a cigarette, and start in on shooting the breeze.

"How's the slop moving tonight?"

I'd answer with a shrug.

"I used to have that job. Hardest part of it is tryin' to stay awake. I see you always got a book, that's a good idea. Has that sucker overflowed yet, tonight?"

This was the adventure of my job - the over-flowing trough syndrome. Periodically, and for reasons beyond my scope of knowledge, the giant stainless steel screw inside the slop trough would come to a halt. When this would happen, I would have to heave-to on the chain fall.

I would lower this huge steel door, one of several, from whence the slop was exiting one of the huge vats. My goal was an attempt to stop the slop. If the slop was too loose, or backed up too high in the vat, the pressure of the backed up slop would make the closing of the five or six hundred pound door an impossibility, even with the assistance of a giant metal crowbar and the full weight of my body and sometimes even

Leroy's if he happened to be available. Consequently, when this situation would present itself, slop would come spewing through the crack in the bottom of the semi-closed door like a torrent of water from a fireman's pressure hose.

The slop would spew forth like orange colored projectile vomit from a sick, legendary, fire breathing dragon. At this point there would be nothing to do but step back, and watch the slop engulf the area like larva from an erupting Mount Vesuvius.

The first time I witnessed this horror, I thought that my job as slop controller and chief regulator had come to an end. I was totally panic stricken. I was on top of the precarious ledge of the screw trough at the peril of my very life, trying to get all of the weight of my body onto the huge metal pry bar when I heard a number of people behind me screaming. The screamers were all bosses. I could tell not only by their age, shape, and attire but by their color coded hardhats.

"Get the hell off of there you silly son of a bitch!"

"Stop that screw. Cut it off! Cut it off!"

This type of yelling only made me feel more insecure, and thus encouraged me to try all the harder. Finally, one of the executives walked up behind me, his shoes totally covered and his body, shin-deep in orange pulp slop, and yelled. "Forget it son! Just let it go." He reached up and grabbed onto my elbow in a guiding gesture.

I climbed down off the ledge of the trough and followed him through the almost knee deep slop that had engulfed the whole area. Everyone now just stood in silence watching the slop spew forth.

I thought for sure that this meant the axe for me. In the morning, I'd get my pink slip and it would be back to the ranks of the unemployed.

This was not the case at all. All the bosses and white hat executives stood around shooting the breeze, and talking small talk. No one got excited; no one got upset.

When the volcano finally stopped spewing, Leroy was ordered to go exchange his forklift for a scooper or front-end loader, which he used to scoop up the slop and return it to the screw trough once the screw was re-engaged. Finally with a hose and a push broom, I slid the remainder of what Leroy could not scoop up, down a number of conveniently placed storm drains.

At first this little adventure took place, with great regularity, once or twice every evening. Nobody ever said a word. No one got upset - nothing. This was just a part of the nightly routine.

Leroy was also involved in a nightly routine that peaked my curiosity. At first I was very flattered by Leroy's presence every evening. Being rather vain, and accommodating, I thought that the guy just liked me. He spoke to me with the familiarity of an old buddy. Just one of the guys, like up at the corner in my hometown.

I thought nothing much of it, until one evening it occurred to me that Leroy would often buzz off right in the middle of what I thought to be the most scintillating parts of our conversation. There we would be, discussing some pressing issue on the current political scene, or indulging ourselves in philosophic insight, when very abruptly Leroy would say. "Well, got to be on my way, duty calls." And varoooom, he'd crank up his forklift and off he'd go.

I thought not too much about it, but then found myself getting a little anticipatory. Should I continue speaking? ... was he about to run off? ... should I begin on new subject matter? This anxiety caused me to become more observant of Leroy's behavior. Was he nervous? Why was he always twisting and twidgitting in his seat? Was he not supposed to be here wasting time with me? Was he looking out for a boss or something? Why was he always looking at his watch?

The first thing I noticed was that Leroy would arrive at approximately the same time every evening. It was always somewhat before the break buzzer would blast over at the juicing plant. The juicing plant was within a stones throw of my working station. The majority of the employees at the juicing plant were women or girls. A few moments after the buzzer would blast, women and girls would come bustling out of doors and alleyways, heading for accommodating spots to sit and chat with their friends, and eat their apple or drink their coke. Some would sit on a stack of pallets, others would pull up boxing creates or bushel baskets. It would be at this point that Leroy would chirp; "Well got to be off ... duty calls." And off he would go. I noticed that for some reason he never left in the direction from whence he came. He always went off in this round about way, heading down towards the chainlink fence that surrounded the factory, off the asphalt, and down along the railroad track. It was a very bumpy ride, especially on the suspension of a forklift. I couldn't understand the necessity for the adventure. Until one night, I noticed that, just prior to Leroy's exit a young lady would go wandering down in that same direction. She would then disappear into a warehouse building. Shortly, thereafter, Leroy would be off on his bumpy little journey down along the tracks. He would stop his forklift, climb up onto the platform and also disappear into the warehouse building.

Ahh huh! The mystery was solved. My friend Leroy was engaging in a "rendezvous". Why a rendezvous in a dirty old warehouse? Why, on a fifteen minute break period? Then again, reflecting on my own youth, why not?

Were you ever not yourself a passionate person with an inability to wait for the proper place and time? Can you not remember those childish days of impetuousness - that lovely maiden; that glorious young man; the exciting wrongness of it all? A warehouse? A little league dugout in a public park at midnight, a back porch, a dark hall, a back seat, a drive-in movie, under a tree, behind a bush? A warehouse? Why not.

Nevertheless, the circumstances led to speculation. Especially when one is working on the third shift, and trying not to fall asleep between slop sweeping. Maybe Leroy was rendezvous-ing with a married woman. Maybe this warehouse, during break period, was the only safe time and place. This adventure was taking place every night. One would think that after two or three episodes in a smelly, dirty, old warehouse a more imaginative thought would come to mind. But, who am I to judge? Mine is not to reason why, mine is but to sweep slop and spy.

In any case, one evening, as I conducted my chat with Leroy, and I observed the little girl walking off in her tradition, it occurred to me that the little girl this particular evening seemed to be taller and of a different shape than the young lady of the previous evening. Then again, I could be wrong. It has happened. I decided to be more attentive. The following evening it appeared to me that there was a third girl tripping off down the lane to Leroy-ville. I was confused. I attributed my confusion to a lack of memory and under developed detective skills. But as time went on it became apparent. Leroy had a minimum of eight to ten different girlfriends - the short, the tall, and the fairest of them all.

One very beautiful girl, I remember in particular. I had noticed her on my way to my station on several different evenings. She was tall and stately, and walked with bearing, a Lena Horne type face and a figure to match. Her loveliness steamed through even her drab, khaki uniform. Her lace-up work boots, made her no less the ballerina of the loading platform. When I saw her tripping the light fantastic down Leroy lane one boring slopless evening, I was quite shocked. I don't know why. I guess that I expected Lena Horne to be a little more discerning - at least, not one to take her place in a line, as one among many. Yet, there she was, giggling and smiling, in the Leroy lineup.

All of this, night after night, week after week imbued Leroy with an aura of grandeur. I began to look at Leroy as if he were the John Henry of Fable and Folklore. He was a man among men, ten foot tall. When Leroy walked, the wooden loading docks trembled and creaked his name. The smoke in the smoke stacks whistled his fame. The men at the wheels hung their heads in shame, as the girls, two by two, strolled dreamy-eyed down Leroy lane.

Leroy, was he a man or a machine? What was this fatal attraction that led little girls to go skipping off behind the Pied Piper of Leroy-ville? I don't know about the rest of you guys out there but I was somewhat jealous. I began scrutinizing Leroy's physique, and looking for Errol Flynn demeanor. I had read Errol's, "My Wicked, Wicked Ways", basically because my eighth grade nun had come into the classroom waving a copy of the book over her head while admonishing all of us never, ever to read this kind of disgusting filth. Naturally I went and got myself a copy as quickly as possible.

But, what was this with Leroy? I had heard stories of men who were irresistible to women, but I had never met one. I had read about women jumping off the tops of buildings the day that Rudolph Valentino died. I had even skimmed Tom Jones as a teenager, but I had never met such a fabled character face to face, much less striding atop a forklift, in torn jeans and doffing a scrapped and dirt-smudged plastic hardhat. Leroy was rapidly becoming my idol. Each night he began to grow in stature right before my eyes. I began to just stare at him, until finally I had had enough of the mystery.

"What is your story?" I challenged.

"What do you mean?" he stammered.

"I mean, what's with all the different chicks? Every night I see a new broad strollin' down Leroy lane. You're a petty good looking guy, I suppose, but you're no movie star. You don't drive a Porsche. I don't see you flashing hundred dollar bills wherever you go. You look pretty much like an average Joe to me. What's the story here?"

Leroy burst out laughing. "Oh, it ain't got that much to do with me." He sputtered. "Most of them just wants to get their own apartment."

"Oh, and you've got a lottery goin' or something? The girl who treats you the nicest gets to move into your apartment?"

"Hell no man! They get pregnant. They get their own apartment. You know, man ... the social services gives them an apartment when they get a baby. That way they can move out from under their old lady. Get out on their own. You know, become independent. Start their own life."

"Oh. Well, that's interesting. But, ah, why you? I mean they could get sperm donated from any number of sources, couldn't they?"

Leroy laughed again. "Yeah, you right there. But you see," he jumped down off the forklift, and stood before me at his full height. "I'm six foot four and still growin'."

"So?"

"So, all the young chicks want to have a little Magic Johnson man! They think that if they have a baby by me, it will grow up to play basketball for the L.A. Lakers. You know, man! Magic Johnson, Michael Jordan! Grow tall, play ball! Make a million dollars man!"

"Well huh, that's somethin'. I never would have guessed."

You know, from that night on, Leroy grew shorter and shorter in my estimation, and his girlfriends lost their sex appeal. As the nights, and the girls, rotated in their turn, even Lena lost her charm. I felt nothing but pity and a profound sense of sadness. One can only feel sadness for anyone so self involved as to bring a child into this world with the above mentioned motivations. Neither Leroy nor his various girlfriends had very much to be proud of in my estimation. Even the "accidental" births of my generation loom up with compassion, if not with virtuous morality when placed beside this behavior.

It wasn't long before our jobs at the orange juice plant petered out. First, Carol got laid off. Then a week or two later the whole third shift was done away with. It was back to ground zero for the Happy Hoboes. What would we do now? There were lots of ding dong jobs around, but any ding dong job just wouldn't do. We had our standards. There had to be at least an implication of adventure. The job had to be different. It had to be something that would surprise the listener. We really didn't want to put any boss out on a limb either. We didn't want to pretend that we had a serious intention of being milkmen or busboys or waitresses for the rest of our lives. In effect, we didn't want to lie to anybody. Worse than all of this, we had the whole winter to kill. It made very little sense to be heading North in January.

We began making inquiries, and reading the advertisements in the newspapers. Not the help wanted columns. Most of those opportunities were either phony or involved a job that we had no interest in doing. We looked at the ads that touted things for sale or services rendered. People in service orientated businesses often run into periods of over commitment. I knew this from my brother-in-law. He had a pool service business in Fort Lauderdale, and although he rarely ever hired any help, whenever we showed up for a visit he always had some kind of work for me - something that he didn't want to do or something that he usually farmed out to a contractor. People who had things to sell and could afford to advertise in the newspaper often had odd jobs for odd people. We qualified under both those criterion.

The first thing we noticed was an ad for mushroom compost. The guy was selling mushroom compost by the pickup truck full, and for a very cheap price. Our first question was; What is mushroom compost? Then where would somebody be getting such a supply of it that they would be selling it by the pickup truck full? This was worth investigating.

The next ad that we noticed was by somebody selling ferns. We had heard they raised ferns somewhere in Florida, and that sounded interesting. You know; How I found fulfillment at a

Florida fern farm; or ... farming ferns can be fun. In any case, we hopped onto our 450 Suzuki, low-rider motorcycle and buzzed off in search of ferns and folly.

In our frenzy to find fun and frolic fern farming, we got lost. We took a left when we should have taken a right or vice versa, and ended up at the base of some dead-end road. At the end of this road there was a dirt parking area and a building. The building had a familiarity about it. It was the kind of thing that one would see on a farm, a packing shed or something. We had seen a multitude of these. It had a four foot high, concrete loading dock and stacks of wooden pallets piled here and there. Beyond the building were furrowed fields filled with, not ferns, but what appeared to be carrot tops.

We parked the "Easy Rider" and started walking around. The dirt that these carrots were growing in was like nothing that either of us had ever seen before. It was very dark, almost black in color. It looked like mud, yet when you picked it up it crumbled in your hand and turned to dust. It was so dark. It looked as though it had been saturated with oil, or was at the bottom of a lake at one time or other.

There was a late model pickup truck parked over by the building. We decided to find its owner and make some inquiries. The loading dock, except for the stacks of pallets and a couple of old forklifts, was deserted.

It is kind of "ghostly" walking around a business that, for whatever reasons, is not functioning at that moment. The still and silence of things that should be active and moving, makes everything seem out of place, and one felt like an intruder.

We tip-toed from one area to another, not wanting to disturb any gremlins or ghosts of harvest days past. We entered through a creaking door into the main building. It was a great, big two story, cement block structure. It was two stories high but there was no second floor. It was just a great big hole, twenty or thirty feet high. Yet, once inside, I felt safe and comfy. Although nothing was recognizable, I knew that I had been here before. Ah yes, the decor' - American ingenuity. The walls were covered in a tapestry of inventive necessity and the furnishings were mechanical American farmer. It was another Rube Goldberg's farmer's paradise. Machinery, belts and pulleys, straps and motors, metal walkways, steps, ladders, handrails, gears and chain falls, things with rollers, and rubber wheels, vats and holding bins, bags, boxes, tags, toolboxes and the smell of burnt grease or gear oil permeating the atmosphere.

On the floor, sticking out from under a piece of mechanical apparatus, was a pair of legs, wrapped in dirty jeans, and capped at the hoof by a worn and equally stressed pair of genuine cowhide work boots.

"Howdy?" A voice vaporized from the floor. "What can I do for ya?"

"Well, I'm lookin' for work."

"Well, I've got plenty of that, only not much money to go with it."

"I didn't say that I was lookin' for money. I said I was lookin' for work." The pair of dirty jeans lying on the floor began to vibrate with laughter.

"Well, I've certainly got plenty of that, let me tell you." And then the jeans and a dirty T-shirt began to snake out from under the machinery. The man was a mess. His everything was covered in fresh grease and oil - face, hands, clothes, hair, the works. He had a beard and was wearing a pair of glasses. His glasses were ridiculous. They were splattered with drops of oil and smears of grease. It was a wonder he could see anything. Naturally at this point his nose itched. Lacking any appendage clean enough to scratch it, he attempted to relieve himself by wriggling his nose into his arm pit. He laid there on the floor staring up at me and my wife. He was quiet for a long moment, and suddenly I was observing our reflection in his face.

Both Carol and I were no longer teenagers. In fact, we couldn't even brag about being in our twenties any longer. We had left on this adventure in our early thirties and now, years had past. We were on the dark side of our thirties, and our friend on the floor, though older than we, was not older by much. He would be more in tune as an older brother than a father. He was lying there, and obviously weighing our whole lives, using his own as a balance.

These people were old, not spring chickens, he was obviously thinking. They didn't look stupid. What were they doing looking for work that paid no money - dirty, physical work? What kind of people would be in this kind of a position at this stage of their lives? But then what was he, a man in his forties, doing lying under an old piece of machinery, covered in muck up to his ears, involved in a job, which by this time, he should have success enough to pay to have done. A slow smirk spread across his face as he stared up at us from his supine position. "You know anything about electric motors?"

"Not a damn thing."

He hesitated slightly, and then laughed. "That makes you just perfect. Be here tomorrow at eight o'clock." Before I had chance to utter a response, he was already back under old Betsy banging and pounding away.

I looked at Carol. What more was there to say? Be here tomorrow at eight o'clock, the man said. So, let's go before he changes his mind. We were off and once again ... working.

13   The Carrot Factory

That next morning I learned I had become maintenance manager - well, assistant maintenance manager. I filled conveyor belt motors with the proper level of oil, and learned how to operate a grease gun.

It is always amazing to me that in certain areas of endeavor in this life, one actually finds uniformity, or, at least, a reasonable quotient of similarity. Like, there were actually people who came before you and who thought this whole thing out; there was actually a system. I mean, it's not like politics or government, or human relationships, or religion or philosophy, or falling in love - there was actually something sensible going on here.

For example, in order to tighten a nut onto something, you turn it clockwise. Wow! Doesn't that make you feel secure? If you want to remove a nut from something, you put a tool onto it and turn it counterclockwise and it will come off. This is the same deal on bottle caps, and pickle jars. In any case, before I get too excited, this is the situation on lots and lots of things. This all says to me; Hey, we're not here alone. There must be a God, or at least other thinking creatures in the universe. I love it. Every time I make a discovery like this I feel like a man excavating a pyramid and finding - "Kilroy was here" - scratched onto one of the hidden inner vaults. It's ecstasy.

I remember the time I first did anything electrical. My title was electrician's helper. I had this big belt with all sorts of tools hanging onto it. I didn't know what half of these tools were, but it didn't matter because I was working, at the time - for the government. Besides, there was always a crowd of us walking around together, all of whom knew as little as I. Within the mess of us there was one older man with a belt of tools who could actually fix things and make them work again.

He was kind of a rough guy; you know the type. He swore a lot, and drank a lot of coffee. He always treated us other guys, with belts full of tools, very abruptly; like we were all stupid or something. He had all of these mean, nasty sexual kinds of expressions.

Well, in any case, I was helping him fix something this one morning when he told me, in his usually gruff manner, to hand him the "female" end of an extension cord. My first reaction was to pretend that I understood the joke. This was obviously some kind of manly, sexual thing - naming inanimate things, male or female, I thought. So I looked at him, smirked knowingly, and tried my best to laugh in a dirty, sleazy manner. He stared at me, rather dumfounded, for quite a long time. When he finally realized that I didn't have the slightest idea what the heck he was talking about. He walked towards me, took me by the arm and led me to a pile of extension cords that were lying on the ground.

"Those, sonny boy, are extension cords," he said very sarcastically, I thought.

"I knew that, sir," I informed him.

"You did?"

"Yes sir."

"Ah, well then, do you know how to distinguish between the male end and the female end of an extension cord?"

Again, I grinned sheepishly, and then smirked with as much sleaze as I was capable of mustering at the time."

"What in God's name are you smirkin' at, Sonny?'" he belched. "Can you show me the female end of that cord or not?"

It was at this point that I determined he was not joking. There was obviously something sexual about these wires lying on the ground.

I looked down at the wires and began scrutinizing with all my might. This long orange extension had a sexuality about it? What in the hell was it about an extension cord that should remind me of a female?

I think, very appropriately, the first thing to enter my mind was - breasts. I began looking for bumps on the cord, or something that would symbolize "two", as opposed to "one". Females have two breasts, and males have one - well, you know what. Suddenly I had it. One end of the electrical cord had two prongs on the end of it; how obvious, and how stupid of me. I proudly picked up the end with the prongs on it and handed it to the boss. For some reason his face got very, very red. He started to question my integrity as an honest, sincere human being.

"Are you putting me on? Because if you are, you little wisecracking, overeducated, little puke, we can go back outside this building and discuss this like two men."

By the way he said "men", I knew that he had no intention of having any kind of serious discussion with me about this. I also knew instinctively by his last statement that he was not only jealous of my education but of my youth also. These were things that I had no control over. I had no idea of what grade he had completed in school, or how old he was. I tried to make friends with him by telling him that neither of my parents had graduated from grammar school either, and that not having an education was nothing that he should be ashamed of. In my opinion, if he was making enough money to care for his wife and family he was as good as anybody else.

It was at this point in our dealings together that he stopped talking to me somewhat and resorted to a kind of sign language. Initially, he just stared at me for a very long time but finally he bent over and picked up both ends of the extension cord. He then took the pronged end and with both ends as close to my face as he could possibly get them, he inserted the pronged end into the end with the two holes in it. Then said; "Get it?"

As much as I hate to say this, I didn't get it. I shook my head and in as calm, controlled and pleasant a manner as I could muster, I replied;

"Sir, now don't take this the wrong way. I'm no electrical expert. I'm only here to help, and you are the man - you are the main man. I know that you know more about electricity than I will ever learn in my entire lifetime. Even if I started studying now and never stopped reading until the day that I die, I am sure that I will not know half of what you already know. But, I do know - and I'm not trying to be critical - that thing ain't gonna work like that. You've got one end of that cord plugged into the other end of the same cord. Even I know that one end has to go into a wall socket or nothing is going to happen."

It was my turn to become a little annoyed, I thought. He, almost without hesitation, started running away from me. In kind of the manner of a discus thrower at the Olympic Games, he flung that cord into the air. Reading this body language, I knew that I had erred once again. He stood with his back towards me and his hands on his hips for a very long time - but then finally he returned. He picked up another cord from the floor. He took hold of the two ends and dangled them again in front of my face.

"You see this end with the prongs on it? This is called the male end." All that I could think was - How strange, the one with the two things on it, which should be symbolic of the female breasts in my opinion, was actually called the male end - at least according to my good buddy here. Then wiggling the other end he said; "And this is the female end. Looking at these two different ends, do you have any idea why they would be named thusly?" I shook my head negatively. He nodded knowingly. "Well, you see," he went on, "this end," he dangled the end with the two prongs on it under my nose, "goesinta this end." He then dangled the end with no prongs on it under my nose exemplifying the process. "You get it? The male end - the one wit the prongs on it - goesinta the female end . . . the one wit the holes in it. The male goesinta the female." He kept inserting the pronged end into the non-pronged end over and over while repeating; "Male goesinta female; male goesinta female; male goesinta female."

Well, believe it or not, I got it. But for the longest time I thought that this notion was simply the invention of my crude electrical friend's perverted imagination. I could not believe that intelligent men of learning and educated training could be as crude, and rude as to make reference to things in such a debasing manner. It wasn't until years later when I overheard two men in a hardware store actually making the same references that I realized that this was common electrical language.

Well, getting back to my grease gun experience, my new boss told me to crawl under each and every mechanical conveyer belt and give every "nipple" that I could find two or three squirts. I had no idea what a "nipple" was, but when I crawled under my first belt there, to my surprise, was a grease fitting just like the ones on my van. I was ever so happy that I didn't have to get into the "nipple" story. A grease fitting seemed to me to be more of a male goesinta type thing than a female nipple sort of a thing. If I were to name a grease fitting sexually, I would be more inclined to call it a . . . well, I'll leave that to your imagination.

It was only a day or two later that my maintenance management position was relegated to a part-time experience and I was demoted to the carrot packing assembly line. Actually the carrot harvest had just begun, and my greasing and oiling was the precursor to the assembly line production in this Florida farmer's packing house operation.

The place was then a bustle with people. Carol was hired to work inside as a carrot packer, while I was outside arranging fifty pound bags of carrots on pallets.

Carol was inside with the banging and clanging machinery, standing along side of a conveyor belt with a number of other women. She was now a carrot packer. One thing that we learned from Carol's carrot packing experience is that a one pound bag of carrots is not necessarily one pound. A one pound bag of carrots can actually weigh from three quarters of a pound to one and three quarters of a pound. There are a number of reasons for this phenomenon. God or Mother Nature does not grow His or Her carrots in portioned controlled increments. But this is obvious and should not account but for the smallest discrepancies. When I asked my wife, she gave me a bunch of sorry excuses; The belt goes too fast - We're just too busy - My scale was broke - It is too nosy - We're all tired - The work is too boring - The boss doesn't care - Nobody checks anything anyway. In any case, the next time that you go to the grocery store and buy a bag of carrots, take five or six of them over to a scale and you will see what I mean.

The carrot operation was pretty much like the apple cannery. The carrots were cleaned in a water bath. Conveyors carried them around and about. They were then dumped onto the packing assembly lines. The girls stationed there, who were all equipped with their own personal scale, proceeded then to disregard its advice and stuff the carrots haphazardly into approximate one and two pound cellophane bags. At this point the girls put the wrapped product onto another conveyor line. This line took the carrots around and around, where upon they finally exited the building and rolled out - like little soldiers - onto a long conveyor belt that stretched out into the loading dock. This is where my job began.

The outside area or loading dock was a bustle with forklifts, and wooden pallets, and male and female employees. The little bags of unevenly stuffed, supposed one and two pound bags of carrots, rolled out on a conveyor belt before a line of carrot bag stuffers. The stuffers were females, and it was their job to extract the unevenly portioned bags from the line and stuff them into these large, heavy-duty, plastic sacks. These large sacks were hanging on an apparatus that held them open and in place. The bottom of the heavy duty plastic sack was sitting on a platform scale. The weight balance was set at fifty pounds. When the sack tripped the scale, it then became my job to remove it, spin it around and hog tie its mouth - then heft it, and wrestle it onto a pallet behind me. I stacked the pallets five, fifty pound, sacks to a layer, then five layers high. They were stacked in a kind of interlocking weave pattern, with two sacks going one way, then three sacks laid perpendicular to the two. The next layer would be laid just the opposite - interlocking the layers in the manner of laying up a brick wall. If you have ever worked this type job, you know exactly what I mean; if you have never done this type of work, you probably never will, so don't worry about it.

There were three pallet loading stations lined up along side this outdoor conveyor. Each station had one girl stuffing and one boy loading and stacking the pallets. I was one of the pallet stacking "boys". Each girl had two platform scales at her disposal. When she tripped her first scale she immediately went to her secondary scale where a bag would already be waiting. This was also a part of my job. Every time that I removed a full bag, I would re-hang an empty one. Needless to say, it was very hard work to stand there hefting fifty pound sacks all day. But, I had done worse, and this job had its advantages. One, I was working outside in the fresh air. Two, there always seemed to be a cool breeze blowing. Three, there were a number of quite attractive, young female, carrot bag stuffers. Four, my wife was working inside.

It was at this job, placed as I was, in this unique position, that I gained a previously undiscovered insight into my inner workings - my subconscious motivations, if you will.

I had always thought of myself as an extremely non-competitive type individual. In fact, when I picked up the autobiography of the famous writer, Pearl S. Buck, and she stated on page one that she was a person born into this world without a competitive bone in her body, I was thrilled to discover that there were two of us. I immediately liked Pearl and considered her a personal friend from that page onward. Don't get me wrong, I always considered myself a complicated, interesting individual; a kind of multi-faceted composite of any number of famous, recognizable personages. In examining my personality over the years I had discovered myself to be a little bit of Albert Schweitzer, with a dash of Bertrand Russell, a pinch of Tom Paine and Thomas Jefferson, a light sprinkle of Socrates, or Aristotle, topped with liberal doses of Confucius, Buddha, Jesus Christ, and Mahatma Gandhi. I have always considered this to be a fair and objective self-analysis. Of course, there have been others who have disagreed, but the most of them were extremely jealous, competitive type individuals - that type of which, I am not.

In any case, this new insight was brought about, or stimulated by my observations of this Venus-Adonis type male who was working at the first loading station. He was without question a good looking young fellow, and I suppose that his muscular appearance was deserving of the inordinate attention he drained from the females - almost against their will. The girls kept saying things like; "How would you like to wake up next to that muscle-bound creep in the morning? I know one thing I would have more than one mirror in the house or I would never get to work in the morning. I hate men that have all of those muscles sticking out like that on the outside. I would much rather have a man that looked like you, Dick."

What bothered me about that last remark is that I thought I looked pretty much like he did. I just kept my shirt on - you know what I mean. But when thoughts of actually taking off my shirt entered my mind, I reconsidered.

This guy was a case study in narcissism. Whenever there was a moment to pause on the assembly line, he would start fingering his abdominals, or flexing his biceps with his fist pressed against his forehead - the Thinker - yeah right. If this guy were a female, he would be a blond. I must admit that the only place I had ever seen a body like his was in a magazine. Even so, he was a little much, if you know what I mean. Every time you looked at him in a slack moment, you felt embarrassed for intruding. His playing with himself should surely have been reserved for a bedroom, or bathroom at minimum. This guy was ridiculous. But as ridiculous and obscene as he was, the girls seemed to be unable to avert their envying eyeballs from his sweaty body.

It was embarrassing. I mean, I would be talking with one of them only to look up from my task at hand and find her drooling over in Hercules's direction. At first, I simply smiled in my noncompetitive, totally disinterested manner. Then, very shortly thereafter, I found myself wishing Herk the Jerk a very unpleasant next Odyssey.

But what did all of this have to do with me? I was married, and happily - at least that's what my wife told me. Besides, I was ten to fifteen years older than anyone else there. This was not my territory. If little girls want to drool over little muscular boys, what had this to do with me? What did I care, and besides, I didn't have a competitive bone in my body. There was absolutely no reason that I should want to pick a fight with this little bastard. What purpose would it serve, even if I could rip off his head and stuff it down his latissimus dorsi. I mean, it's a free country. People have the right to be handsome, good looking and muscular. Yes, but could he do Geometry? Did he know obtuse from abstruse? How about, A square plus B square equals C square. Ah, forget it! He's not worth getting upset over.

In any case, as the days go by, I observe a curious phenomenon. If you happen to get positioned at the third loading station, you hardly work at all. You spend most of the day talking or flirting with your assigned carrot stuffer. This depended, of course, on your marital status, and - as you already know - I was married, so, ah, - there you go; nevertheless, this did seem curious to me.

Even at the second loading station, the task was relatively minimal. Herk the Jerk, at station number one, was doing all of the work. My first thought was - good. Obviously, Herk the Jerk, was, as I had suspected, dumb as a board. He probably liked to sweat, and since sweating was a matter of indifference to me - who cared. For a week or so, I just smirked and laughed. It wasn't until I sat down with the foreman one day and expressed my notions with regards to the dumbness of Herk the Jerk that I found out about the piecework bonus system.

It seems that Herk was making double and sometimes triple my minimum salary because he was working by the piece. He was getting a dollar-fifty per pallet, and filling between forty and fifty pallets per day. But, when I asked if I could also work by the piece, the foreman informed me that it would do me no good, because whatever pallets Herk let go by didn't amount to the minimum hourly wage anyway. In other words, the only guy to work piecework was the guy who worked station number one. That station belonged to Herk, and no one had ever challenged his authority.

When I asked if station number one could be rotated so that we all could get a chance at making more money, the foreman actually looked a little frightened by my audacity. Was I actually suggesting that I, the burnt out old fart that I am, was capable of filling as many pallets as Herk? No one prior to this had ever suggested such a notion. I had been the first to be so bold. I had thrown down the gauntlet without even realizing it. In my mind, I was merely suggesting rotating the number one position so that each loader might in turn earn a couple of extra dollars - instead of one guy making it all. I thought that even if I only stacked thirty pallets on my day at number one station, this would be a half a day's pay more than what I was presently earning. What could it hurt?

In other words, when I or the other guy were at station number one, Herk, at station number two, could still make bonus, but one of us would also make the bonus too. This is what I thought I was saying, but this is not what the foreman was hearing.

The next day when I arrived on the scene, a hush had descended upon our world. There was what appeared to me to be a host of total strangers hovering about the loading dock. They all seemed to be pretending to do things. Even the owner was there. He had a bunch of tools and was screwing around on his pickup truck. I had done it once again, it seems. What to do now, Ollie?

The foreman took Herk aside. They had a little discussion, after which, Herk walked over to station number two. He took off his shirt, sat down on a stack of pallets, and began admiring himself, as usual.

The foreman then called me over to station number one. Before he left, he put his hand on my shoulder, and said in a voice just above a whisper, "Whip his ass man! If I were ten years younger, I'd do it myself." The funny thing about that statement was that the foreman was, in my estimation, at least ten years younger than me, anyway - oh well.

There was an attractive blond girl standing at station number one. She was the girl that usually worked with Herk. She stood there for a moment looking me up and down, then shook her head and smiled; "I think I will just mosey on down the road, Pop." She slid over to station number two. My guess is she felt that would be where the action was going to be, anyway.

The other two girl stuffers just stood there. I had worked with both of them. The first one just looked down at her shoes. She was obviously not up to the humiliation of the impending loss. The third girl was a not so attractive, tall, spindly type thing. She wore her hair in pig tails and reminded me of Olive Oil in the Popeye cartoon strip. She had been telling me for at least a week that she needed a new freezer, and was saving her every penny for a down payment. "Well," I said, "do you want to put that freezer on layaway, or what?" She smiled, then shrugged her shoulders, as much as if to say; Hey, what have I got to lose. I've been rejected by better people than these in the past.

So there we were Olive Oil and Archie Bunker, about to challenge May West and Arnold Schwartzenegger. But actually there was no real pressure on me. Yes, everybody was there watching, but nobody really expected that I was going to beat Herk, or break any records - nobody, except Archie Bunker, his self, of course. I told Olive Oil not to let a bag of carrots go by, if she could help it. She slipped up next to me, put her hand on my shoulder and whispered, "Do you really want to do this?"

"Hell yes, I really do."

"Okay," she said. "If you say so."

And we were off!

As Olive Oil stuffed and I packed, I proceeded to analyze the nature of competition, or the competitive instinct as they say.

Whenever I hear people say that they like to compete, or hear some famous person on TV announce, with pride; "I'm an extremely competitive person." I cringe. I mean, what is that person actually saying? To me it sounds something like this; "I like to beat up other people. I like to destroy their pride in themselves. I like to display my God-given talents in a way that humiliates my fellow man. I like to dominate and be abusive. And if I don't win, I would like to, at least, break somebody's bones or cripple them for life."

Strange as it may seem, losing has always been a more pleasant experience for me than winning. If you win at something, you know deep down inside that nobody is really happy for you. The person or people that you beat do not really think that you deserved to win. Those that praise you are usually not filled with feelings of love for you, but are harboring feeling of envy and jealousy. They smile, and may even pat you warmly on the back or shoulder, but you know, deep down, the emotion that they express is insincere.

On the other hand if you lose, you have the satisfaction of knowing that those that won were really very, very lucky. You also know they aren't half as good as they think they are. You know next time you, or somebody else, will come along and beat them as badly as they truly deserve to be beaten, and hopefully even worse. As a loser, your friends will express genuine compassion for your loss. They will hug you and kiss you, and tell you how deeply they associate with your feelings, because in their lives they too have been losers and they know exactly how you feel.

This emotion is for the most part sincere because losing is the common experience of mankind. Life is a losing experience for everyone. No one survives it, and no one can truly and honestly predict that it will end or be resolved, finally, in a happy, satisfactory manner.

So, if you win, you will have heaped upon you; envy, jealousy, criticism, vindictiveness, hostility, vengeance, ridicule, and sometimes hatred by, even those, closest to you. But if you lose, you have a whole world of losers to commiserate with you.

I remember I used to play poker with a bunch of fellow workers after our week of hard labor. Every time that I won, I felt terrible seeing my workmates and friends going home to their families without their hard earned money, or a portion there of. After one of these sessions, when I would see their wives or children, I would be filled with guilt knowing that junior went without his fried baloney that week, or the Mrs. was forced to miss her layaway payment on the new washing machine, or vacuum cleaner. Consequently, I found myself playing poker and hoping to lose.

This didn't make sense. I may not be the competitive type, but I'm no masochist either. As a result of these feelings and observations, I stopped playing poker and gambling in general.

I have often criticized myself for thinking along these lines, primarily because I never met anybody who expressed similar feelings and because it makes coming out on top in any dealings with other human beings very difficult.

Interestingly enough though, one day my wife and I were at a supermarket when a neighbor came running up to us. She had just won a drawing that bestowed upon her one week's free groceries and one hundred and fifty dollars in cash. She was so happy. She was in a state of ecstasy. She was bouncing up and down. She was laughing and screeching. My wife and I were very happy for her, and we expressed ourselves so. At least I thought we had, but when the woman looked at us, in-between bounces, she had a searching look in her eyes. Suddenly, without missing a bounce, she dug into the money in her prize winning envelope, pulled out ten dollars and stuffed it into my wife's hand. "Here, take this," she said. "Go out and have lunch or a treat on me."

"No, no!" my wife exclaimed. "We don't want your money."

"I know, I know," she said, "but I want you to have it, because I want someone else in this world to be truly happy that I won." Then she ran off into the crowd.

I never stop thinking about that woman. She had the correct analysis and a good solution.

Suddenly I found myself in the middle of a crowd of expectant fans. I tried to convince myself that it was the extra money that was motivating me and not the need to be competitive or combative here in the carrot packing assembly line. I mean this wasn't the Orange Bowl or Yankee Stadium. Was there really a need for any of this at all? It was too late now. I had opened my mouth, and precipitated this mess. It was too late to turn back.

Needless to say Olive Oil and Popeye stuffed and stacked their little butts off. We worked really hard. As hard as we worked, I really didn't feel that over-stressed, but yet Olive seemed to be very concerned about me. She kept looking at me and asking if I felt okay. She kept suggesting that we give up this challenge. I really couldn't figure out what was bothering her. Her stuffing job really wasn't that demanding in my opinion. Why did she want to quit? And why did she keep looking at me in such a concerned manner?

When the break period came, I went to the men's room. When I passed by the mirror, it was clear why my work mate was so concerned. Obviously my radiator was over heating. My face was as red as a beat. I had taken my blood pressure pills, and my gout pills, and my aspirins. Everything, internally felt O.K., but what was I doing here?

This whole adventure, for Carol and I, started out as an escape from the killing pressures of the dog-eat-dog competitiveness of our daily lives in the everyday, work-a-day world. Now what the heck was I doing, out here in the middle of nowhere? Here I was banging heads with some muscle-bound Hercules who was probably half my age. We were competing for wages, even with the bonus, that ten years ago I wouldn't even have accepted as a starting pay. This was rather insane.

So the question loomed; Was it really the competitiveness of the dog-eat-dog, work-a-day world, or was it the inner workings of Dick and possibly Carol? Maybe, more so Dick, because Carol certainly wasn't inside trying to out bag any carrot baggers.

So was the competitiveness that I hated all around me, really not all around me but in me? Ah yes, and what a terrible thing to discover - it's not the world, or "they" that is to blame; but you, yourself.

I stared at my beat red face in the mirror. I visualized myself having a heart attack right out there in front of everybody. The horrible young muscle-man that I was trying to beat would probably end up saving my life with mouth to mouth resuscitation. Poor Olive Oil would be horror struck, standing over my dead body with her delicate thin hands pressed to her trembling tear stained cheeks. All of the other employees would be bunched around. Some would be standing in horror watching me die. Others would be shaking their heads in disgust at the stupidity of an older, supposed mature man, acting like a child and killing himself. If this wasn't the dumbest thing I had ever done, it had to be second.

I stuck my head under the cold faucet and soaked my weary brow. Then I took off my T-shirt and soaked it in the sink. I wrung it out then put it back on while it was still soaking wet. It felt great.

When I returned to the arena and saw the faces of all of my hopeful admirers, and heard everybody whispering about how well I was doing, all my bathroom meditations disappeared. I was again the gladiator. I couldn't believe myself as I ran about stacking fifty pound sacks like a crazed maniac. I remember, in the midst of it all, mumbling audibly to myself; Well, stupid, if you die, you die.

It was a difficult day for me all in all. I mean, not only breaking Herk's record but discovering that deep down inside, I was actually one of ... them. Yes, I was one of those people who all of my life, I truly hated. I have continued to make similar discoveries day by day and year after year to the point where I can barely tolerate myself. Is this the wisdom of old age, or am I a manic depressive?

In any case, after his staggering defeat at the hands of a potbellied, beer drinking, middle aged loony tune, Herk was too embarrassed to return to work. He didn't show up for three days. During all that time I felt worse and worse even though everybody kept patting me on the back and telling me all the nasty feelings that they harbored inside for The Horrible Herk. I was the hero. I was the unlikely wimp that had KO'd the giant. I was the knight who had slain the dragon. I was the Boss, the big man on campus, the admiration of all my peers.

When Herk finally showed up that fourth morning, the place was a tremble with anticipation. What would happen now? Would the battle start anew? Would Herk flex his muscles, return to position number one, and out stack the mad-middle-aged-monster. Would this become like one of those wrestling bouts on TV? Would we be crashing pallets over each other's heads or tumbling off the loading ramp wrapped in an antagonistic hug of hate and horror. Would we duke it out like Victor McLaglen and John Wayne in the Quiet Man. What would happen?

Well, Herk showed up a changed man. The muscle shirt was gone, and replaced by a long sleeved sweatshirt, and a pair of baggy pants. When the line started up, he went to position number two, and left number one open to me. I called to him and suggested that he could have the production spot if he wanted. He waved me off, with a smile and a shake of the head. I felt kind of funny, much like the lady in the supermarket who had won the drawing. I had won the battle but was there anyone there that was truly happy for me?

I told the foreman that Herk and I would both work production. I kept my eye, all that day, on station number two, and adjusted my pace so as to come up "even" at the end of the day. There would be no big winner from now on - just two better than average paychecks.

By lunch period, Herk figured out what I was doing. He came over to where I was sitting with my wife. He put out his hand as a token of friendship and asked if he could join us.

As it turned out, he was a very nice young man. He confessed to us that he had gotten himself into a position that was not happy for him. Because he had such a bold physique people naturally expected more of him, and consequently he had developed an image for himself. His defeat at my hands had now given him the opportunity to be a regular guy like everybody else. He was looking forward, very, very much to having no images to now live up to. He thanked me for sharing the piecework with him. He did really need the extra money to help out his parents at home, neither of whom was in very good health. This was part of his incentive in trying to live up to the muscle-man role.

Well, as it all turned out, I had won the prize but decided not to plunder all the profits for myself. I think, I ended up, not all alone and lonely in a personal happiness of self indulgence. Maybe I'm not as bad a guy as I thought I was.

14 Cherries and the Old Mission

"The Old Mission", it is called. It is located on the northwest portion of the lower peninsular of the state of Michigan, just north of Traverse City.

Whenever I think of this spot, one phrase continually comes to mind; One of the most beautiful places that we have ever been. Yet every time I say this to myself, I am shocked. How can I say such a thing, I ask myself, when we have driven on mountain tops in Virginia, North Carolina, Arkansas, and Oklahoma; when we have traversed both coastal, scenic highways, route 101 on the West and route 1 on the East and traced the Gulf of Mexico from the Florida Keys to Port Isabel, Texas; when we have seen the mesas of New Mexico, the Grand Canyon in Arizona, the Mississippi and the Rio Grande rivers; after we have chugged up one side of the Rocky Mountains and down the other; after we swam in the Atlantic, froze our butts off in the Great Lakes, bathed in the Gulf of Mexico, and traipsed along the craggy cliffs and picturesque inlets along the Pacific Ocean; after we have seen fields the size of small countries filled with wheat and soy beans; the Florida Keys, the Thousand Islands of upper state New York, the wilderness of the North West and the upper peninsula of Michigan; Skyscrapers from New York to San Francisco - and on and on.

How can it be that this little, not so familiar, isthmus can be ranked as; One of the most beautiful spots that we have ever been? I feel as though I should go back and examine the area again before I make such a statement, but whether it is true or false, it is the phrase that always comes to mind whenever I think of our stay there. I guess if you don't believe me, you will just have to go and look for yourself.

We hung a right somewhere in Traverse City, and then drove up the two lane highway that wound through the Old Mission.

Both sides of this lovely little road were trimmed with cherry trees, quaint older farm houses, and over-views of possible pirate hideaways cutting into the landscape.

All the lawns were a dark, rich green and trimmed meticulously. Wherever there were no green lawns, there were cherry trees, spotted liberally with their tiny bright red fruit. I felt there should have been a gate leading into this wonderland, and stationed armed guards. Yet there we were, two hoboes chugging along a pathway through heaven in our scruffy brown van towing our classic 1965 Airstream travel trailer with no authority giving our trespass a second thought.

It was only a matter of minutes before we spotted Eldon and Marge camped along side the road next to the cherry stand that we were going to help them operate this summer.

We had met Eldon and Marge in central Florida, and for reasons quite beyond my understanding we became immediate friends. How strangers become immediate friends, is as baffling as the phenomenon of love at first sight. It has happened to us several times. I see no explanation for it, yet there it is. As I reflect on our personalities now, with the advantage of twenty years under my belt, I can see many reasons for the bond.

Marge is very much like Carol. Both Carol and she are self-sufficient, take-charge kind of people; the kind that any boss loves to have in his employ. You just never see them idle, or at a loss for things to do ... busy, busy, busy. They are always in charge. They are always directing people to their proper positions without the people even realizing it, whether it is at the home business or at the Thanksgiving family reunion.

Eldon and I were clearly worker bees, inexhaustible plow horses, who could only be turned to another task, but never stopped. We both had one common principle, if we could make a nickel doing it, we did it. Over the course of our friendship we had all worked together in apple orchards, orange groves, tomato fields, and now cherry orchards. On our first outing together we gathered wild mushrooms, along side a stretch of dirt road in the middle of the Ocala National Forest. Marge still talks about the stuffed mushrooms we made that evening.

Whenever Eldon and I were idle, we fished. I couldn't tabulate the number of fresh caught fish dinners we ate together. We met one another all over the country. They showed up at our forty acres in Arkansas during our "back to the land" period. We had them as overnight guests in our tiny van camper when we first started out on our hobo-ing America, working tour of the U.S.A. We slept on the floor and gave them our mattress, no box spring bed. We took up residence in their Florida home one summer when they went back to Michigan. It seems as though we have known Eldon and Marge all of our lives. We know their children, their families, their relatives, and friends, either through actual encounter or conversation. We know their religion, their political views, and what they value in life. They seem more like family to me than my actual family.

Marge, unlike Carol, was loud and emotionally expressive. Marge never had a second thought about hugging, laughing, or saying anything that came to her mind. When she saw our hobo caravan inching along the narrow two lane highway, she immediately began to bounce up and down and scream for Eldon. I've never had anyone as excited to see me, not even my mother or my wife. Whenever we showed up, the first thing we would hear would be Marge's scream. "Eldon! Eldon! They're here! They're here! Come see who's here Eldon, quick. Can you believe it? Look at this!"

I can't tell you how wonderful it is to be greeted in this manner, by anyone.

There was Marge at the cherry stand, screaming and rushing about. She had a dishpan in her hands, and was either washing cherries for a cherry pie, or soaking trout fillets, I don't remember which. Marge was one of those people who could make a five course dinner almost instantly, and out of absolutely nothing. I've seen her do it a hundred times. She would say; "Is anybody hungry?" Then immediately bounce up, look into what would appear to the average housewife, as an empty refrigerator, and like a genie start concocting.

Then, in what seemed to be a minute or two, the table would be laden with gifts from the gods; mashed potatoes, gravy, rolls, buns, toast, meat, soup, home canned green beans, peas and corn, pudding, fruit cocktail, and apple pie. She was amazing. Carol and I, in contrast, took at least an hour to make a canned tuna fish sandwich. All the while that Marge would be scurrying around she would be apologizing for the scant provisions. "Oh, I don't know how this is going to turn out, but at least it is food."

We had our camper parked right on the front lawn of this farmhouse, or farm worker house, just off the little roadway. We set up our awning and lawn chairs and there we were campers in paradise. We had only one rather minor problem - how to make a living in this paradise.

For the first week or two we picked cherries for the roadside stand that Marge and Eldon were running. The cherries were called Bing, but in truth, they were a substitute, or some type hybrid. Nevertheless, they were delicious. We also picked some sour cherries. I never really knew there was such a thing. In my ignorance, I had assumed that all cherries were sweet. I mean, why in the world would anyone want to grow a cherry that was sour?

My wife informed me that sour cherries were used to make cherry pies. But cherry pie is sweet I replied. "Well of course it is, silly. They add sugar to it."

So there you have it. Truth is stranger than fiction. They have actually bred a sour cherry tree. Sugar must be added to these sour cherries, in order to make them taste sweet enough to be eaten as a pie. Now if that doesn't seem strange enough to you, try this one on for size. They have a special breed of white cherry called a Napoleon, which they bleach, then die red in order to manufacture the little maraschino cherry that we find in our Manhattan, or on top of our banana split. Go figure, huh?

We had soon supplied the little roadside cherry stand with a temporary, over abundance of saleable product. In other words, we were temporarily unemployed again. So, while Carol and Marge "womaned" the cherry stand, Eldon and I went out on a crabapple picking extravaganza.

Crabapples are funny, ugly, green things that really aren't very good to eat. Why anyone would want to grow them, and what one did with them after they were grown, I haven't the slightest idea. I only know that for whatever reason there was a human being out there who was willing to pay money to have them picked. We picked a few crabapples, but didn't make very much money. Little things may mean a lot, but it sure takes a whole lot of little crabapples to amount to anything in terms of dollars and cents.

With enough cherries supplied to the roadside stand, and the crabapples all picked, we were idle once again. Marge suggested that we might truck some cherries down into the big city, and see if we couldn't sell them along the road someplace. We did. It was fun, but once again, we didn't really make any money, but we were getting by, enjoying ourselves, and seeing the sights. What more could one ask?

The craft of hand picking cherries was almost obsolete. In fact, the farm that we were staying at was one of the few farms on the Old Mission that still engaged hand pickers. It seems to me that the inevitable course of competition leads invariably, to the gradual and sometimes very rapid replacement of human beings. I have never read an economist who has stated exactly this principle, but this does seem to be the course in every industry I have ever worked.

At present I have always been able to find something to do in order to stay alive, but it does appear, that my fellow man is trying to get rid of me.

Regardless, good or bad, someone had invented a cherry tree shaker. As Carol and I were out picking cherries on the back forty somewhere, we witnessed a cherry tree shaker operating on the farm across the road. It consisted of a clamping ramrod type of device. It grabbed onto the tree and punched the heck out of the tree's trunk. A large trampoline, of sorts, wrapped around the trunk of the tree and caught the falling cherries. The trampoline cushioned their fall, and then dumped them onto a conveyor belt. The conveyor carried them up and into a container sitting on the back of a forklift or truck.

My first impression was that when this device would be removed from the tree, the tree would simply tumble over onto its side and die. The action of this machine was that violent. This was not the case. The tree did remain standing. I did find out this shaking process cut a tree's longevity considerably.

On the other side of this equation, while Carol and I spent the whole day picking, maybe, three or four trees, this machine shook an entire grove - a task that would have taken, in my guess-timation, hundreds of men. There would certainly be no John Henry to contend with this technology.

A very interesting and entertaining couple owned the farm where we were working. The man's first name was Toliver. I forget his wife's name.

Toliver had run the farm all of his life, and his wife had been a school teacher. He was a very big guy. He was obviously once robust and powerful. Today, he was withered and severely weakened by the effects of arthritis and old age in general. His wife was still active and busy, but unfortunately the effects of her aging were detrimental to her mental state. She was seriously deaf, though it did seem, as Toliver often criticized, she could hear perfectly clear when she wanted to.

Another problem was her forgetfulness. I suppose that today this problem would be called Alzheimer's. Let me describe for you our first trip up to the old farmhouse attempting to collect our wages.

I knocked on the door. I knocked with a reasonable force, but not abusively. We heard someone inside begin shuffling about, but no one came to the door. I knocked a little more forcefully. Nevertheless, I got no response. I knocked harder and harder, but still got no response. I could hear the old woman inside moving about. It sounded as though she were shuffling herself towards the door. Then, the shuffling would just wander off again. I began to call aloud, along with my knocking, feeling that possibly she couldn't hear me. Very shortly, I was up to pounding and screaming. I knew she was in there. I could hear her distinctly. It is hard to walk away defeated when you know most definitely that someone is right there within a reasonable hearing distance. I felt I was being annoying. But?

Finally Carol and I both gave up. We turned from the door, and were just beginning to walk away when it opened. The old woman was standing there. She had, draped over her shoulders, a colorful, hand-crocheted shawl, and was carrying her egg carrying basket. Every morning she shuffled out to the barn to gather fresh chicken eggs from the nests of her hens. The chickens were scattered haphazardly, or should I say, at their own discretion, about the barn. We stopped, turned and smiled at the old woman. She stared at us with a look of shock and dumbfoundedness.

"Can I help you?" she asked.

It was clear that she hadn't heard any of our pounding and screaming. She simply decided that it was time to go out of doors and do her egg gathering and there, to her surprise, were two strangers standing in her doorway.

"Yes," I said. "We've come to collect our wages." She exhibited a look of great bewilderment. It was sad to see this sweet woman, once an educator, now struggling so with her mental facilities. We had met her and even been introduced on several different occasions, but it was obvious she had absolutely no idea who we were. It did seem that the word wages meant something to her.

"Oh yes, of course," she said. She smiled warmly, then turned, stepped back inside and closed the door.

I smiled at Carol, she grinned back, sadly. We waited for about two minutes. Then we waited for two more minutes.

After what seemed to be an additional four or five minutes we began to worry. What if she had gone back inside and fell down or something? I began to knock and call once again. We heard a shuffling inside, and as the shuffle seemed to draw closer and closer to the door, I knocked with increasing volume and began to shout. The door then opened. The woman was standing there. I looked at her and smiled, querulously. She smiled warmly and stared up at me in a like manner, and then said; "Yes?"

I looked at Carol. It was plain that the old woman had absolutely no idea who we were. Carol immediately filled the awkward gap. "We've come for our wages? You remember, we just spoke to you a moment or two ago?" The old woman's eyes darted back and forth between Carol and me, puzzlingly. After what seemed to be an enormous pause, a light seemed to come to her eye.

"You've come for your wages," she stated matter-of-factly.

"Yes!" We both repeated, enthusiastically. The old woman then smiled warmly and knowingly, turned, stepped back inside the apartment, and then closed the door once again. We were sure that this time we had struck a vital chord. She was most likely on her way to get Toliver, or our paychecks. We were confident. As we stood in the hall waiting, our confidence began to wan. A good five to ten minutes went by as we stood considering.

She's old, we thought. It takes her a long time to get anywhere. Maybe she had to go to the other side of the house. We should be patient. We should also be understanding. The day may come when we will find ourselves in a condition similar to this woman. Life has a terrible way of doing things like that.

We were both very pensive as we stood meditating upon our future and thinking about Toliver and what's-her-name.

The waiting went by very quickly this time. There was so much to think about - so much to be sad about. What a wonderful time it was in our lives to be together, and still cognizant, in love, and capable. Standing there thinking about this old woman and her Toliver put us both on the verge of tears. It may have been an hour or two that passed as Carol and I stood there staring at one another. Eventually the door did open again, and it opened this time without our even knocking.

We were elated! She must have remembered us this time, on her own. There she was in the doorway, once again. This time she was re-equipped with her shawl and egg basket. At the previous sighting, she appeared without these items. We looked at her, each of us bearing a warm, sympathetic smile, beaming optimism. She stared at us, then suddenly smiled warmly and broadly, and said quizzically; "Yes???"

She was obviously gone again into never-never land. "Okay, your guess is as good as mine. What should we do now?" Carol was more persistent than me.

"Hi, ah you remember us?" she said pleadingly. "We've come to get our wages. You remember? You were just talking to us a moment ago? You went back inside to get the money for us? You remember that, don't you?"

"Why, of course, of course," the old woman said positively. Then she turned and started into the apartment. We both had a very good idea of what was coming next. She would go inside, close the door, and we would soon be "lost" once again. Simultaneously, we both grabbed at the door, and then followed the old woman inside the apartment. We no sooner got inside the apartment than the woman turned and looked at us with that now familiar dubiousness.

"The money! The money!" we both burst in chorus.

"Oh yes! Of course, of course." She turned and began walking again. We followed her around the house, from room to room. Periodically she would stop, turn and stare at us as if she had suddenly discovered intruders in her living room.

Instantly, we would both burst once again; "The money! The money!"

"Oh yes, of course, of course." Then she would giggle and resume her shuffle.

Finally she led us into the living room, then stopped and looked at us once again. After a chorus or two of "The money! The money!" from Carol and me, she pointed towards a couch. We presumed that she wanted us to sit down. Suddenly I had the overwhelming feeling that we shouldn't even be here. What if she suddenly didn't recognize us at all, became frightened, and started screaming? What if she then had a heart attack or something?

We were both sitting there on the couch, staring up at her when she turned and started walking away again.

"The money! The money?!" we screamed.

"Yes, yes!" she scolded, and then she wiggled her finger towards the couch once again. "It's right there! It's right there! Just take what you need."

"The money is where?" we inquired.

"It's right there, right there behind the couch," she said impatiently.

"Behind the couch?" I said to Carol.

We both got up and then slid the couch away from the wall. There on the floor behind the couch were piles and piles of money. We were in shock. What now?

Somehow just helping ourselves to our pay did not seem like the right thing to do. We slid the couch back up against the wall. We scurried our butts out of there and found Eldon and Marge. They called the old folk's son. He came over and was equally shocked. It seems that the old lady had been cashing her Social Security checks for the last few years, and just dumping the money behind the couch. They really didn't have a great need for money. Their children brought them everything they needed. The kids knew that mom was a little off, but they presumed that dad had things under control.

Not quite.

Our next experience with Toliver and his bride, what's-her-name, came one day when good old Toliver got the notion to have an ice cream cone. He came pulling up to our campsite in his big old Cadillac and invited us to go with them. The idea sounded inviting, so we dropped what we were doing and jumped into the back seat. Carol then tried to make conversation by asking Mrs. Toliver a question. When she got no response, she asked again. Greeted once more by silence, she asked again. At this point Mr. Toliver interjected; "There is no sense in trying to talk to her. The old bat is deaf as a door nail."

"Who you calling an old bat, you old bat! I've been listening to your babble for fifty years now, haven't I."

"See, I told you," offered Mr. Toliver. "She hears what she damn well pleases to hear."

"You're right you old goat, and I damn well don't please to hear you."

The old man laughed uproariously while Mrs. Toliver went into a little giggling spasm. While they were engaged in this bantering, I couldn't help but notice that Toliver was driving his Cadillac right down the center of the two lane roadway. Oncoming cars were swerving off to the shoulder while a line of cars was beginning to bunch up behind us. The cars were bunching up behind us because Toliver was traveling at a speed of about eleven miles an hour. Carol and I were both embarrassed, agitated, and, of course nervous as hell. I kept quiet for as long as I could. Then with as much calm and politeness as I could muster, I said; "Ah sir ... do you ah realize that you are driving down the center of the highway?"

"Where are you kids from?"

"Well, my wife is from Lansing, Michigan, and I am originally from Massachusetts."

"Mass-a two-sets huh? Never been there."

"Well it's ..."

"Don't want to go there, either."

"Well I can understand that, but don't you think you should steer the car a little to the right? You've got the center of the car traveling on the white line. You are supposed to be to the right side of the line."

"And how about you young lady?" Toliver asked Carol, ignoring my request.

"I agree, sir," offered Carol. "You should be more over to the right so that cars can go by on the left."

"You've been to Mass-a-two-setts?"

"Ah, no I haven't," Carol responded nervously while looking back over her shoulder at the long line of cars with all of their horns tooting.

"Don't worry about the darn cars!" Toliver screamed. "I've been living here longer than all of them and their cars. In fact, I have been here longer than this road. I helped build this road - should never have done it neither. Besides, everyone in this town knows me."

"But the other people ..."

"All the people here know me. And I've been here longer than all of them."

By either a blessing from God, or a positive turn of fate, the big Cadillac pulled off the road and up to a small ice cream stand.

Toliver pulled his big Cadillac right up to the front door. In fact, he almost drove right into the front door. He turned off the ignition and then leaned on the horn. As the horn roared, he continued to make small talk.

"So you kids like ice cream, do ya?"

"Yes sir!" I screamed over his blaring horn. I could tell by the look on Carol's face that she wanted to crawl right under the seat. Actually, under the seat didn't sound all that bad to me either. There were two middle aged people working inside the ice cream parlor. One could easily discern from the expression on their faces that they were not exactly in the state of ecstasy at the sight of Toliver and his bride.

The horn was still blaring as one of them exited the ice cream parlor and stepped up to the side of our vehicle. Toliver was not immediately aware of the woman's presence. His head was turned to the rear of the car where he was still involved in making small talk. He finally noticed the woman and lifted his large palm off the horn. The horn had stopped but I could still hear it ringing and shouting in my ears.

"You've got any ice cream in there?"

"Yes sir."

"What flavors you got?"

"Mister Toliver, we have over thirty different flavors as you well know. It might be easier for you to tell me what you like and I will tell you if we have it."

"Got any honey dew melon?"

"No sir. I've never heard of it."

"How about Tapioca?"
"No sir."
"How about licorice? You got any licorice?"
"No sir."
"How about frozen pudding or rum raisin? You got any rum raisin?"
"Ah, no sir, we don't."
"Well what the hell do you have in there anyway?"
With an exasperating sigh, the woman said;
"We've got vanilla, chocolate, strawberry, butter pecan, cherry, coffee, rocky road, peanut butter, raspberry, maple walnut, peach, black cherry, mocha, butterscotch, six different varieties of lite, low fat type ice cream, four varieties of sherbet, two French sorbets, three varieties of Italian ice, and our special of the day, vanilla caramel maple fudge crunch."
"Yaaahhh, well give us four vanilla. You got vanilla, don't you?"
The lady turned and went back inside. She had a very, very unpleasant look on her face. When she returned with our four vanillas, Toliver said with his usual finesse; "That's on the house, ain't it? You know I send a lot of people down here to this little, dinky, hole in the wall place."
The lady simply shrugged her shoulders, shook her head negatively and went back inside. "I own this damn place," Toliver then added by way of explanation.
We ate our ice cream and then started on the perilous journey back home, straight up the middle of the road at eleven miles an hour.
When we got back to the ranch, there was a crew of migrant pickers packed up around the entrance to the old farmhouse. For the last few weeks they had been picking Toliver's sour cherries. While Toliver straightened up and fumbled for his canes, we slipped out of the back seat as Mrs. Toliver shuffled off into the house.
By the time Toliver hobbled up to the front door, three or four of the Mexican picking crew confronted him. They had not received their wages. The old man got hostile and accused the workers of doing a bad job and stealing his picking sacks. He went into the house and returned with a shotgun.
At just about this time, Toliver's oldest son pulled into the yard. He ran up to the front porch steps.

"Dad, what are you doing?"

"What the hell do you care? And what are you doing over here? Nobody called for you."

"Well, it sure looks like you should have. Now get inside the house with that shotgun before the police are up here to arrest you."

"They can arrest me if they want to. I'd just like to see 'em try."

The son went up the stairs and reached down to get a hold of the old man's shotgun. The old man pulled away, gave his son a stern look, then with a big laugh, spun around and went back inside the house, grumbling all the way. The frustrated son looked down at us, and then shook his head. "Ain't he something?" he said with frustration and dismay.

What was there to say? I could think of nothing to do but laugh. We both shrugged our shoulders, then turned and headed for our campsite.

The next couple of weeks after that event, I remember as being quite pleasant. Every morning we had breakfast in the great out of doors. We were, for some reason into an egg feast. We had eggs with grits, fried eggs, scrambled eggs, eggs with English muffins, hard boiled eggs, soft boiled eggs, eggs with cheese, eggs over easy, eggs every way that one could imagine.

As we ate our eggs each morning, we would watch poor, old, Mrs. Toliver shuffle over to the barn for her morning chore. Watching her reminded me of the thousands of times I had watched my grandmother. My grandmother was perpetually old, and just like Mrs. Toliver it took her forever to get from one place to another - her hand bracing up her hip, traipsing around in her bathrobe and slippers, taking those tiny, obviously painful, little steps familiar to all the older folks.

What was the old woman thinking about? Poor Mrs. Toliver always looked so confused. She seemed to be in a struggle just trying to remember anything. Maybe it was a task for her to remember how to get from the house to the barn. When she got there, did she even remember what she was looking for? All our eyes were on her, inadvertently, as we watched her shuffle in her arthritic way. One can hardly imagine being in her shoes, or slippers.

I asked my grandmother once what she thought about. Did she look forward to going to heaven? Did she have fears of going to hell? She just smiled at me and explained that it would be pleasure enough to just not have to wake up every morning - to not feel all the aching muscles and the pain. This alone would be good enough she told me. She said not having to endure the length of the day and the loneliness of the night would be more than enough of a reward.

I wondered as I watched Mrs. Toliver. Is this what she was thinking? Is this what it eventually comes to for all of us? As I watched her on this day, she headed towards our picnic table. After what seemed an eternity, she finally arrived at our breakfast spot. She sat at the end of our little picnic table. Marge began talking with her, and then I asked gently; "Tell me ma'am, on your daily journeys between house and barn, what do you think about?" She looked at me very seriously. Then after a long thoughtful pause, she stammered in her shaky voice;

"Well, mostly I wonder what is wrong with my chickens. They haven't laid many eggs now for almost two weeks." For some unexplainable reason, Eldon gathered up his plate full of bacon and eggs, and abruptly left the picnic table. "I miss my eggs in the morning. Me and Toliver have had eggs for breakfast nearly every morning since we've been married. I'd hate to ask Toliver to kill the chickens, but what good are chickens that don't lay eggs?"

"Eldon!" Marge screamed.

Eldon appeared at the door to the camper.

"Ahhh, anyone feel like sweet corn tonight?" he mumbled.

"Sounds good to me," said I, and we were out of there, on our way to rifle some sweet corn out of an absentee farmer's garden down the road a piece.

For weeks after old Toliver had died poor Mrs. Toliver wandered around the farm looking for eggs, and then looking for Toliver. She would call out to everyone that she encountered asking if they had seen Toliver.

"Where is Toliver?" she would whine. "Where's Toliver? Has anyone seen my Toliver?"

One afternoon we were all sitting outside at our picnic table when poor Mrs. Toliver came wandering by.

"Where's Toliver? Have you seen Toliver? Where's Toliver?"

"She can't find Toliver," I said.

"I know," Marge said. "It's sad isn't it?"

"Where's Toliver? Has anyone seen Toliver?"

"Somebody ought to tell her. Not to be mean, but just in a way that she will understand," I said.

"Where's Toliver? Where is that man? Where's Toliver?"

"Honey, come over here and sit down," Marge said." She paused while Mrs. Toliver sat herself down. "Toliver died, sweetheart. You remember? We had that big funeral?"

"Toliver died?" The old woman responded quite distressed.

"That's right sweetie. You remember now don't you?"

"Toliver died?" The old woman looked into Marge's eyes. Then she looked at all of the other faces about the table.

"That's right. Yes, some time ago. You remember? Remember, we had that wonderful funeral with all the cars?"

The old woman paused thoughtfully. She stared off vacantly into the cherry orchard. Then she turned and looked into Marge's eyes. Her eyes were plaintive, then slightly tearful and then suddenly wide and frightened.

"Wh ... wher ... where's Toliver? He was here just a moment ago. Have you seen Toliver?" She asked probing into Marge's eyes. Marge stared at the old woman for a moment. Then with a crack in her voice, and tears coming to her eyes, she said;

"I don't know sweetie. Maybe you had best look for him. He was here a minute ago. I saw him myself. Maybe he's out to the barn." The old woman looked at Marge and smiled.

"You know, I can never find that man when I want him. I think I will just keep looking for him."

"Yes, maybe you better. That's a good idea," Said Marge.

The old woman smiled again and then rose from the table. She shuffled her bedroom slippers across the lawn and towards the old farmhouse. We all watched as she slowly shuffled off.

"Where's Toliver?" she cried out, warmly. "Where's Toliver? Has anyone seen my Toliver? Ohhh ... where's Toliver?"

There was a huge silence at the picnic table.

"You did the right thing, Marge," I finally said. "People just can't go on living in a dream world. Everybody has got to face up to reality one day."

Marge looked at me, and as she started to laugh at my sarcasm, she also started to cry.

15 Celery Packing

The winter oranges depleted from another freeze, and the Umatilla Orange Juice Plant relegated to memory, we discovered another new and interesting enterprise one winter. It was a packing shed or factory. I had never heard of the man who owned it or the company, but I was informed that this company or individual was the largest farmer in the world.

This packing shed, on a back road in the middle of nowhere central Florida, was involved in the project of packing and blast freezing celery. We were out on our motorcycle exploring when we just kind of bumped into this place. The first thing that impressed me about this factory was the fact that when they hired us, they not only checked our social security cards, but took a photograph of us and placed it in our file along with our numbers. I presumed that they were either upright, honest citizens, or they had already been hassled by the federal government relating to the hiring of illegal immigrants and wanted no further aggravation. I think somewhere along the line here, the federal government had passed a law that involved a fine for businesses who made a practice of hiring illegals. This was the first place of employment we had ever been where the boss took this law seriously.

Working within the plant were blacks, whites, Hispanics, older women, teenagers, corporate manager types and simpletons. The foreman was Hispanic, and for that matter, probably still is. His name was Juan.

Juan was a sweet, kindly, sympathetic little fellow. He didn't appear to be more than a teenager, but since he was married and had children, I would presume that he was at least in his twenties. When he asked you to do something your tendency was to want to comply so as not to hurt his feelings. He could not in anyway be described as intimidating. One just wanted to please him. If you were a woman, your tendency would be to just hug him and pinch his pudgy little cheeks. If you were a man you were inclined to ruffle up his hair and bestow upon him fatherly advice. Carol and I both took a liking to him, and got to know him personally. He even invited us to his home to meet his wife and family.

The next character was the plant supervisor. I really don't know if he was the plant supervisor, but he always wore a shirt and a tie and walked around all day with a clipboard and with what appeared to be, nothing to do. I assumed that he must have been somebody important.

My next Celery Plant caricature is that of Baby Huey. He was an enormous guy, well over six feet, and built as broad and as powerful as a line backer for the Green Bay Packers. He was as strong as an ox, but completely unaware of this quality. He would grab hold of anything, lift it as if it were weightless, and never express the least notion of achievement. He was obviously, as they say, not aware of his own strength. Couple this with his child like mind and attitudes and you understand why I named him Baby Huey.

When he didn't get his way he would curl up his lower lip and pout. He was white but yet all his features were that of a black man. He even had kinky hair, but it was blond. They said that he was an albino, but I really don't know.

Baby Huey was definitely mentally incompetent. I hesitate to say that he was retarded, but I don't have a better word. How about simple minded? Dealing with him was like dealing with a five year old - a six-foot-three, two hundred and fifty pound, strong as an elephant, five year old.

Finally one day after I had exited a forklift, Baby Huey jumped up into the seat and started pulling levers. He got it going and then began buzzing it around. I ran after him yelling warnings to everybody. He nearly drove it through a wall. People were diving for safety in every direction. He smashed the side of it into another wall, and then backed and banged it into equipment everywhere. I really thought someone was going to get killed.

Finally Baby Huey got the forklift onto the loading slab in back of the building. He got a little close to the edge of the concrete area and the forklift began to tip.

I had seen a boy killed on a forklift. It was tipping over and he tried to leap from it. He didn't leap far enough and the rollover cage caught him and crushed his skull. I could envision the same thing happening once again, right now.

Baby Huey was petrified. As the forklift started to tumble off the edge of the ramp, he just sat there and held onto the steering wheel for dear life - exactly the correct thing to do. It went over onto its side and he went over with it.

He was very, very lucky. To my astonishment, Juan took it upon himself to teach Huey how to drive the forklift correctly. I really felt he was doing exactly the wrong thing. But, Huey eventually became a forklift operator. Amazing! Believe me I never turned my back on any forklift that was being driven by Baby Huey. He had several other close calls in our stay there, but by the time we were leaving, he was still alive, and hadn't yet killed anyone.

As I looked at the human cross section of this plant, I wondered if it wasn't in reality some sort of sociology experiment. I had never seen so many incompetent, virtually untrainable socially and mentally stressed people clustered together in one spot in my life. It was like having the entire cast from *One Flew over the Cuckoo's Nest* as your staff. Everybody had a serious problem. Nobody did anything well. They would try to lift things that they couldn't, or dump things where they shouldn't, or fix things that weren't broke. Flipping light switches was often a big deal.

Juan tried to have Carol and me working everywhere. He would show us a task, we would say fine, and just do it. This was obviously a new experience for him. He loved us. He even invited us to his home one Sunday afternoon for supper. We became friends.

The celery plant, itself, as I have said was quite interesting, and somehow things did get canned, packaged, spindled and filed.

I helped Juan operate the blast freezing machine. It was really a simple looking thing. It looked like the automatic dishwashing machines we had back in the restaurants where I once worked – but bigger.

It was a giant stainless steel box, with an opening north and south, and a conveyor belt on each end.

The raw diced celery went rolling in at one end and came out like little individual stones at the other end. Then the celery would go round and round until it dropped into a shoot.

Under the shoot was a plastic lined cardboard box into which the little individual frozen chunks of celery would tumble.

The box sat on a scale. When the scale read twenty pounds, you slid it off and quickly slipped in another box with plastic liner. While that one was filling up, you tucked in the plastic liner on the full one and shoved it down the line. This job really didn't require a college graduate, but Juan was very happy to have Carol there on a regular basis. Two young colored girls tried their hand at it and it was a disaster. Between the two of them they couldn't manage getting the full box out of the way and the empty box in place without dispensing frozen celery all over the floor by the ton. After each uncoordinated effort they would both break up into uncontrolled laughter. Carol could do the entire job alone and carry on a conversation at the same time. She appeared to Juan to be a genius.

The next guy folded in the tops of the box and taped it shut. Then the box was stacked on a pallet.

When the pallet was full, along came Baby Huey with his infamous forklift and carted it off, and into a freezer or onto a freezer truck. The blast freezing machine had all kinds of dials and doohickeys. It blanched the product exactly to a set of specifications and then zapped it with nitrogen.

While we were zapping and freezing on one side of the room, another crew was on the opposite side cooking and canning. I never worked on the canning side but they had huge stainless steel vats where the celery was cooked, and then automatic extruders, I guess you would call them, shot the celery into the gallon sized cans. The cans were then sealed and rolled on down the line where they were boxed and palletted.

Even with all of the strange people, we had a good time. Juan liked us, and most of the management was friendly. I guess that made the difference. We fully intended to return to that plant the following winter, but, for whatever reasons, we never got there.

16 Canada Fishing

Well, as you can imagine it was coming to crunch time in our lives. Time had been racing by. We were still fairly young and healthy, but we were getting older. This lifestyle of ours though interesting was not providing for the future. Actually it was barely providing for the present. A comparable model of the old van that we originally bought for thirty-four hundred cash was now selling for around ten or fifteen thousand. We couldn't go on living like this. We must of necessity return to the "real" world, if not this minute, someday soon. We were very despondent with this thought, especially Carol. How could she live, without a dream, with only the life of a work a day, day-in day-out human?

We didn't want to think about it. But, our decision was to bite the bullet. We would return to the big city, probably Miami, or Fort Lauderdale. But before we took such a horrid, depressing final step, we would have one last fling. We would take Bob and Rose up on their offer.

Bob and Rose were another retired couple that we met while we were traveling. They had retired a little early. They were supplementing their early retirement doing odd jobs, like picking oranges.

Bob's hobby was working on automobiles. He had a complete workshop, he had told us, and had overhauled many a sick engine. This conversation had come up when I told him that I was now buying oil by the case to keep our old van running.

Another of Bob's hobbies was fishing. He especially enjoyed going to Canada. He had been making fishing trips to Canada from his home in Michigan for over twenty years. He had made us the casual offer of going with him and Rose to Canada on a fishing trip, along with the opportunity of overhauling my engine with his help at his garage. We would pay our own expenses on the fishing trip, and in exchange for his help on my engine, I would help him to overhaul his. This to me sounded like an offer that we shouldn't pass up. So we called Bob and Rose and made the arrangements.

Bob was in the infantry during World War II, and believe it or not one of the biggest loves of his life was hiking. He never spoke about his experiences in the infantry in Europe other than this one comment. I had asked him if he enjoyed hunting. He said he didn't because he had gotten his fill of killing during the war. I then asked him why this same attitude hadn't carried over to walking. He laughed but had no explanation.

Bob's home, his attitude and his whole life, at least what I knew of it, was kind of an inspiration to me. He was always smiley faced, thoughtful and agreeable. I rarely saw him lose his temper, or let his frustrations get out of control. Then again, maybe I just didn't know him well enough. He had this beautiful farmhouse. When he originally purchased the property, it was hardly more than a wheat field with a chicken coup on it. His advice to Carol and I was to buy anything that we could afford. "Don't worry about what it looks like he said, you will grow into it."

I guess what I really liked about Bob was his easy going demeanor, and calm steadfastness.

We parked our trailer out behind the main house, nestled under a couple of comfortable trees.

Now overhauling an automobile engine, may not necessarily be your idea of a trip into wonderland, or a traipse in ruby slippers down a yellow brick road. But for me, it was the true fulfillment of a boyhood longing.

Bob insisted that we work on the engine of my van first. I argued that we should do his pickup first but it was to no avail.

It was clear that Bob had done this overhauling business before. He had the "system" all laid out.

When you detached anything from the main body of the engine, you refastened everything back to it. In other words, every nut, bolt, wing nut, screw, clamp that you had to undo to get the dohickie off, had to be reassembled to the dohickie once you had it off. You did this so that later that day, or two or three days later, whatever the case may be, you would have everything necessary to re-attach whatever it was that you had unattached originally.

At first, I thought this was really kind of unnecessary because I felt that I could remember where I got what. But when we began the reassembly, let me tell you, I was ever so grateful. There was so much stuff, if we hadn't had this system, that engine would have been a part of some scrapheap somewhere.

But Bob had the system. He even had racks made where we put the valve stems, indicating right side, left side, front and rear. It was a wonderful experience and a miracle. I had naked pistons from my own engine right in my palm. I had valve stems and O rings.

Oh, that reminds me. Our van had always burned oil, even though we bought it new. We had even brought it back to the dealership, but he gave us a ration of doubletalk and we never got any satisfaction. As time went by, it simply got worse and worse. We now measured our travels in quarts of oil. But that aside, there were these little rubber things that were on the valve stems, or valve stem guides. We bought a new set of those things. They cost about forty-two cents. When the guy at the auto parts saw our old ones, he immediately said;

"You've been burning a little oil?"

"Not a little, a lot!" I said.

"It is no wonder with rubber O rings like this," he said.

And when we did finally get everything done and reassembled, we never burned a drop of oil again as long as we had that van.

We disassembled, and reassembled everything - dohickie by dohickie. We got the heads off, and then took them down to this machine shop where we left them to have the valve seats ground, and the heads themselves x-rayed for hairline cracks or any defects. We took the bearings off the crankshaft, but I can't remember if we had to replace them. Bob could just look at everything and tell if it needed replacement. We replaced all the rings on the pistons. I chipped all the burnt-on carbon deposits off the piston heads. Then I scraped and sanded them down. We replaced all the sparkplugs and bought new sparkplug wires.

I don't know how long the whole operation took us, maybe a week. But it was really something! It was actually fun. We replaced everything that looked like it needed to be replaced.

Bought all new air filters and fuel filters and then put it all back together.

After we had it all back together we had only one remaining problem to deal with.

It wouldn't start.

We did everything. We checked this, cleaned that, bought new points, tried new sparkplug wires, checked the fuel lines, bought a new battery, everything. Yet for three whole working days, almost as long as it had taken us to do all the labor, we couldn't get it to go.

I was never so depressed. What had we done? Did I ruin the whole thing? Maybe Bob really didn't know everything. What was I to do now? Bob said that if I wanted to give up on trying to solve the problem ourselves, we could always tow it into town and have a mechanic look at it. When I expressed interest in that notion, Bob's spirits dropped instantly. I realized afterwards that he had only said that as a confidence builder. He had no intention of giving up himself, and, I think, was very disappointed that I had even harbored such a notion. He convinced me that we should give it a couple of more days of experimenting before we abandoned ship. I agreed.

That evening after supper Carol asked, "Could the distributor cap have anything to do with it?" I looked at Bob, his eyes flashed.

"Well Carol that is about the only thing that we haven't checked or changed."

We were out of the living room in a flash and off to the department store. I bought the distributor cap. I had it out of the box and was looking at it on the way home. I had the old one also. They looked exactly alike to me. In all honesty, I could not see how this was going to make much difference. The old one didn't even look worn to me. Bob had a more optimistic look on his face. I didn't say anything. I didn't want to hurt his feelings as I had done earlier when showing enthusiasm for his idea of going to the town mechanic.

We returned to the garage, and put on the new distributor cap. I got into the cab, inserted the key, took a quick look at everybody's hopeful eyes and with total dubiousness and doubt in my heart turned the key in the ignition.

The van literally leaped to a start. I mean it roared. I would just love to have a picture of all of our faces at that moment. I can see all the others as clear as a bell right now. That was a Kodak moment, let me tell you. Eyes all wide and beaming, all smiles up front and positive. Carol's face glowing with relief, and I know mine must have been also. Bob was aglow with satisfaction and "I told you that we could do it, didn't I?" pride. The look on Rose's face made me feel ashamed that I had ever doubted her husband's ability. I can only hope one day to see the same look on God's face as I approach the gates of heaven.

The next morning we started in on Bob's truck. When we began on his truck Bob's whole personality changed. All the while that we were working on my truck, Bob never showed the slightest bit of aggravation or frustration; he was the epitome of control and self restraint, always poised, confident and business like. But when we got to his vehicle, it was almost as though our roles had been reversed. Bob grumbled, gruffed, banged, cursed and kicked, while I assuaged, calmed, and cooled my way through the whole thing. It really felt good to me and I had a big grin on all the while. Bob was human. I laugh just to think about it now. It was a great experience.

We then began preparing for our fishing trip to Canada. On this issue also, Bob and Rose had everything down to a science. The trip would last so long; we would be in the woods away from any grocery stores for so many days. We would need so much money, and X number of provisions. They even had a menu prepared for our days in the woods.

One of the traditions of the trip was pancakes and fish for breakfast. If you didn't catch any fish, it would be plain old pancakes. But, Bob added. "We have never had that happen yet in twenty years of fishing trips."

I didn't realize what a fortunate opportunity Carol and I had actually stumbled into. Bob and Rose were truly professional fishing guides when it came to Canada. They had been exploring these regions of Canada now for twenty years. They had found their own special lakes out in the wilderness, and remote forest roads. They knew which lakes contained what species of fish. They had hiked and mapped out destinies in the remotest regions. They knew exactly where we would have to set up camp, and what paths and directions through the woods we would have to take in order to get to the best fishing lakes.

This trip involved canoeing. Carol and I had our own canoe. Oftentimes on this adventure we would have to portage our canoes over hill and dale, to arrive at that secret destiny. This was really some kind of adventure for Carol and me. A trip like this would probably cost some sport enthusiast thousands of dollars, but because we had met these new friends, it was just a matter of sharing a few dollars worth of expenses - quite a wonderful happenstance for us.
   For Carol and me this would be our first trip into a foreign country. I suppose that a lot of people wouldn't consider Canada a foreign country, but it wasn't the United States. At that time we didn't need any passports, or special shots or anything though. But there were certain requirements. You had to declare any guns or weapons. You had to give a basic destination, and approximate length of stay. I don't remember that there was anything else necessary to get across the border.
   Once across the border and into Canada, it really appeared to me as a different world. We had by now been pretty much all over the United States, but I could remember no scenery quite like this section of Canada, just north of the state of Michigan.
   First of all, it was very sparsely populated. There just seemed to be more trees, more rocks, more landscape. As we kept going north, the distances between gas stations and eateries got more and more spacious; until finally we headed off into the land of no gas stations, no eateries, and only trees and dirt roads. Believe me when I say we went miles and miles into nowhere. And once we got to the designated camping site, the one selected by Bob and Rose from their experiences in past adventures, we saw nobody and nothing. I take that back. On one occasion we did hear and spot a small biplane buzzing over head. That was the furthest that either of us has ever been from civilization. If you have ever had notions of going off and living the life of a recluse in the wilderness, Canada is your territory. No telephone poles, no electric lights, when darkness fell, there was nothing but the light of the moon and the stars above.
   We got up and went to bed with the sun - no radio, no TV, no newspapers. You don't realize what a stress we all live under until you spend a few days in the wilderness. The bombings, killings, murders, earthquakes, forest fires, floods, wars, stock markets, even mail at the post office, all have to

take second place. All that there is, is you, the trees, an occasional eagle or hawk soaring over head, your immediate companions, and of course FISH!!

And did we ever catch the fish! I have never had an experience like that in my life. Carol's first cast in that first lake had actually netted the largest fish of the trip.

We had just finished traveling up and over the hill and through the woods to Grandma's lake with our canoe on our shoulders. We dropped the canoe into the lake, pushed off from shore, and as we waited for directions from Bob and Rose, Carol just couldn't wait to try her first cast - and wham-mo!

Carol had always been something else when it came to fishing, but this was really something else. The tip of that pole just rolled over, and that line began to run every which way. There were five of us on this trip, Carol and I, Bob and Rose, and Lanney, an older friend of Bob's.

Lanney and I manned the smaller canoe and Bob, Carol and Rose shipped out in the larger. We had no motors up here. In fact, I don't think that motors were allowed. When Bob finally netted the fish for Carol, he was quite taken aback.

"We better tie this one out," he said.

Since you were only allowed to take so many fish back with you, they had devised this technique of tying the big ones off along the shore someplace, until the last day.

"Isn't it a little early to start tying off fish?" I said. "Why don't we wait a day or so? I mean, that's our first fish."

Bob was already at the shoreline and in the process of tying off the fish. He turned, and peeked at me over his shoulder, the sly grin on his face told me that we had something special.

"Well, Bob said; "We have been coming up here for twenty years now, and this may be the biggest pike, I have ever seen."

Whooaa! I just shut my mouth and looked at Carol. That look on her face was something to behold. And as it turned out that was the biggest fish of the entire stay.

Another interesting phenomenon was the black flies. There were zillions of them. They didn't bite or anything. They were just everywhere. For the most part they came out around sundown, and by that time we were ready for bed.

Fishing for Lanney and me went pretty well in our little canoe also. In fact, it was ridiculous. That was the first and last time that I had ever caught too many fish.

We released most of the fish and only kept the giants. The water was so clear and pristine that Lanney would just dip his cup down into the lake and drink it. I remember at one moment I actually got bored with just catching the fish. I started looking down into the water and watching them. They were right there. You could actually sit and watch them swimming around. On one occasion, I played Toreador with this one aggressive pike. I would lower my lure into the water, and jiggle it. This pike would see it and literally make a beeline attack for it. When he would get to about a foot from it, I would pop the lure out of the water. We used what was called a red and white daredevil lure. I played this little game with this particular pike for a good eight or ten runs. Then we moved to another spot and I played the same game with another one.

We caught a lot of fish before and after that trip, but I have never ever seen anything like it again. That was without a doubt the catching-est fishing trip I have ever been on.

My boat partner Lanney was very much like me, the tall, dark, strong, silent, handsome type. (That reminds me. You guys out there who are in charge of designing the jacket for this book, no pictures of the author please.) We really didn't have too much to say, but the little that we did have to say clings in my memory; especially this next little anecdote.

Lanney had just hooked into a big one and I had helped him net it and get it into the boat. As we sat there admiring the fish and basking in the glow of our achievement, Lanney said. "You know, I am sure glad I came on this trip this year."

"Why's that?" I said.

"Don't you know?" He stated matter of factly.

"Ah no, how would I know?"

"Well I'm seventy-two you know."

"So?"

"So this might be my last fishing trip, people don't live forever."

"Well, you never know. You might be the first."

"I don't think so."

"Well from the way I see you hefting this canoe around man, you look like you've got a good many more fishing trips in you."

"Hell, I've been letting you carry the canoe most of the time."

"That's nothing. I've wanted to."

"Yeah, I know. But in past years, I would never let anybody do that. Nobody ever had to carry my load."

"I didn't carry your load, man."

"Oh you did so, and I let you do it."

I didn't know what to say. So I didn't say anything. I just let the conversation drop, but I kept thinking about it all day long. I really don't think that I have had a day go by since my father died when I was thirteen or so that I didn't think about death. I try never to forget that at any moment, and for no apparent reason the people and the things that you love can be taken away from you - instantly. But how many times have I thought that my own life could be over at any given second, like my buddy Lanney was doing here? How many times do you think; Hey, this day could be my last.

All of a sudden I started looking around me. The sky was suddenly brighter and bluer; the trees were all green; I saw birds where I hadn't noticed any moments before. The water seemed so fantastically clear, and beautiful, I thought that I might be having a religious experience. I sucked in every sight and every moment as if it might be my last. I had a very exhilarating, intense afternoon, let me tell you.

When we got to shore, I got out of the boat. I grabbed the poles and the sack of fish. I looked at Lanney. "Your turn to carry the damn canoe," I said. He turned and stared at me with a shocked look on his face. He smiled, hesitated momentarily, and then patted me on the shoulder in a gentle grandfatherly way.

"That's okay," he said. "It's alright. It don't really bother me."

"Well it bothers the hell out of me," I said. "I've been carrying you on my back for a week now, and I'm getting damn tired of carrying your load, old man." Instantly he straightens up and his eyes got big and his jaw got tight. For a second or two there I thought he was going to give me a poke in the eye. Then suddenly he just went loose, and roared with a big laugh.

"I'll bet you don't think I can carry that darn canoe do you?"

"Well I don't know if you can or not, but I know you are sure as hell going to." And I just took off walking into the woods. It wasn't thirty seconds later that old canoe with Lanney under it came zipping past me. I couldn't see his head tucked inside, but I could hear him laughing his butt off.

On the last day of the fishing trip, I ran into a similar thing with my buddy Bob.

On this day we had to gather up all of the huge fish that we had been tying out all week. We cleaned and gutted them, stuffed them in plastic bags, then loaded them into a back pack. It was plain to see that one of us three men was going to have to carry that backpack. It was heavy. Even with the fish cleaned and gutted the sack had to weigh over one hundred pounds. I immediately grabbed the sack and began the task of getting it onto my back. When Bob saw what I was doing, he said.

"That's okay, Dick. I'll get that." Naturally I assumed that he was just being polite. Lanney was seventy-two, and though I didn't know exactly how old Bob was, he was certainly old enough to be my father.

"No, I think that I can get it," I said, very casually.

"Well I know damn well that I can carry it!" Bob said with quite a bit of agitation. In fact, he was angry.

"Well, I didn't think that you couldn't carry it, Bob. I just thought that since I was the youngest the job would naturally fall to me." We stood there staring at each other for a moment. Bob was seriously angry. I could see it in his eyes. "Hey, I'm sorry; if you want to carry the damn thing you are welcome to it." I made the statement but I made no motion to remove the sack from my back. Bob just stared at me for what seemed the longest moment. He was getting over his initial anger and was now thinking. Momentarily the anger in his eyes dissipated somewhat. Then, without a word, he marched passed me and started clogging off ahead at about forty miles an hour. I looked at Rose. I shrugged my shoulders and said. "Did I do something wrong?" She smiled and chuckled a little, then said.

"No, you didn't do anything wrong." I started walking and shortly she came up beside me. "It's just that until now, Bob has always been the youngest."

"Well, what was I supposed to do, let him carry it? He is old enough to be my father." She grinned.

"You did the right thing," she said. "Don't worry he'll get over it. You will probably know how he feels one of these days yourself." And so, I do unfortunately. I understand only too well.

When we got back to the "States" and Jackson, Michigan in particular, we got busy preserving our catch. We filleted the fish. We canned the rib area thus dissolving those troublesome little bones and smoked the remainder of the body in Bob's spiffy little smoker. We ate Canadian Pike for a number of months into the future, and at every meal our trip came back to life.

You know, we almost missed that trip. At one point it was simply a matter of a yea, or a nae, and it was almost a nae. We didn't have very much money. It seems that we never do. We calculated and weighed our alternatives very closely. Right now it seems very clear to me that there will never be another fishing trip like that one again in my life - certainly, not with Lanney, Bob and Rose.

Lanney is no longer with us, but in retrospect, I'll have to say that I most heartily agree with his sentiment, when he said; "You know I'm really glad that I made this trip. Folks just don't live forever you know."

17 Butchering Meat, in Miami

Our Canada fishing trip over, Carol and I were both in agreement. We would return to the world of nine to five. We would both go find jobs. But what kind of lifestyle would we now choose to lead? Carol had a couple of friends, who had married and bought an old house. We went and visited with them.

They had bought an older under priced home, in a modest neighborhood. They had turned it into a really neat place, we thought. They had a little woods for a backyard. They had cut a path winding through it. They had built a big ten foot fence sheltering them from the main street. They decorated inside with plants and all kinds of goofy stuff. It was kind of like a hippie pad from out of the sixties, psychedelic lights and all.

The basic idea appealed to us. They had made their own little world within a world. When they came home from whatever type boring, uninteresting, annoying work that the adverse, unfortunate circumstances of their hopeless lives had forced upon them, they could hide away and have peace and comfort cowering in their little cave.

We supposed that to be some sort of consolation yet this thought of going back to the world of "boring" convention, was not settling in gently with us. There would be no way that we could live a conventional life, even adorned in hippie accouterments, ever again.

We could see absolutely no hope in trying to glorify this failing attitude, with a half-way house fantasy.

This return was no dream or fantasy. This was a nightmare, or horror story. We weren't back to the big city a week before we had devised a whole new plan.

We would become back-to-the-landers. And we knew just the area that we would want to settle in ... Arkansas.

The northern part of Arkansas was beautiful. It had mountains almost as beautiful as those on the Blue Ridge Parkway. The people there were friendly, and the land was dirt cheap. Certainly we could buy all the land that we needed to become back-to-the-landers for ten thousand dollars or less. We could clear the land and become pioneers. We could farm, build ourselves a log cabin, raise chickens and sell the eggs.

When I was growing up, I had a friend back in Massachusetts whose uncle made his living peddling fresh eggs door to door. He seemed happy. And, as you'll remember Carol had fond memories of her Uncle Merton's farm, Ei-I-Ei-I-O!

Believe it or not that became the basic plan. We figured we needed about ten thousand for the land, and about another five thousand for the first year's expenses. Then after that, of course, we would be raising or own chickens, and butchering our own hogs. We would have a big garden, with all kinds of vegetables, and it would all be free. Well, you know, we would have to grow it, but how hard can that be? There are a million books written on that sort of stuff.

We rented the cheapest apartment we could find. Well, not exactly the cheapest. The cheapest was an old trailer in this dumple-down trailer park in North Miami. You could see right through parts of the floor. And it wasn't all that cheap either. I couldn't believe that people were actually living in this so called park right behind the high risers and just down the block from massive and elegant hotels. But there they were, poor people who couldn't afford to pay their first and last months rent in advance. Not to mention, their security deposit.

We found a fairly nice apartment, with a reasonable rent. We put down our first, last and a security deposit which amounted to nearly fifteen hundred dollars. We had traveled around the country for almost a year on that amount of money, but ... but what?

Carol was immediately hired back at her old job at a north Miami Beach hospital. I decided to give the restaurant business a break. Actually, working as a manager of a restaurant wasn't a job it was a career.

Minimum hours in a restaurant were sixty, and to tell you the truth I never worked only sixty hours. It was always eighty to a hundred. And, of course, since you were in management, you didn't get paid overtime. You received a salary.

I decided instead to try something I hadn't done in years. I would make an attempt to get back into the butchering trade. It seemed like a reasonable thing to do. There was a massive supermarket on every corner it seemed.

Well, the first thing I learned was that supermarkets didn't really need butchers anymore. Meat no longer came to the markets in the form of fore quarters, and hind quarters. Everything now arrived in neat little boxes. It was all cut, trimmed, chunked up, and packed into airtight bags. Real butchers were no longer necessary. Most of the work could now be done by unskilled labor. One simply had to take a chunk out of a bag and slice it up, and then wrap it and put it out into the display case. Anyone could learn to do that within a week or two. This, of course, translated into minimum wages.

But then I thought how do the chunks of meat get into these little bags? Steer don't come in boxes. There must be some place where the meat is processed, and certainly there, they would need experienced butchers.

I looked up meat processors in the yellow pages, and I started calling. It was really very discouraging. I felt like Rip Van Winkle. I didn't think I had been asleep that long, but already the whole world had changed. Every place I called told me that they didn't use butchers. They had all their meat shipped to them in boxes from out west or some such thing. They sold it by the box, never had to open the cryovac bags inside the boxes. Cryovacing was a process that I was familiar with. Actually, I had operated a primitive cryovac machine way back in the good old days.

In cryovacing, one puts the product into a plastic bag, and then by the use of a tool or some kind of a machine, simply sucks the air out of the bag. Having the meat snugly wrapped in a semi-airless environment greatly enhances the shelf life, or the refrigeration life of the product. Cryovaced meat will keep for as long as six months under proper refrigeration. Could it be that all butchers now worked in Chicago?

I finally gave up on the phone, and went back to my door to door technique with the supermarket chains. In the course of being told the same sad story, store after store, I did eventually bump into this store manager who thought he knew of a place that might be able to use me. He gave me the phone number and directions to the shop and low and behold it was an actual processing plant. I had an interview with the plant manager and started work that next morning.

This place was a real meat factory. I had never seen anything like it. Of course, as a butcher, one always works inside a large refrigerator. But, in Miami, working inside a refrigerator didn't sound all that bad.

In the center of this refrigerator sat a huge conveyor system. The refrigerated room was itself about fifteen hundred to two thousand square feet. Adjacent to this large room was the beef storage area, which was another large refrigerator of about the same dimensions. Inside this refrigerator was the overhead rail system on which the beef quarters hung on moveable rolling meat hooks. This was what I was accustomed to - a standard meat packing house arrangement. What I wasn't familiar with was the conveyor belt system.

A steer is slaughtered, skinned, and then cut into four sections. The front section, minus the head is called the fore section. It is split in two, along the backbone. These sections are called fore quarters. The rear section, minus the tail, is divided similarly. These two rear sections are called hind quarters.

On the fore quarter you have the chuck or back, shoulder, neck, and rib sections. On the hind quarter you have the loin and round sections. The round breaks down into what is called a bottom, top, eye, and face. The loin is divided into two parts, a short-loin and the rump. These are all large wholesale chunks of meat.

After the bones are removed from these basic wholesale cuts, they are cryovaced, boxed then shipped out to your local grocer. He then basically slices them up into steak or roasts. Some of these wholesale cuts can also be purchased with portions of the bone still attached. They can then be sliced on a band saw and packaged with the bone displayed. This is done to give the appearance of a lower price, or to give the impression that fresh meat is being processed, or simply to satisfy costumers who like meat with a bone in it.

The meat quarters at this plant were broken down into smaller sections with the bones in, and then brought out to us butchers who were stationed at the conveyor belt operation. The bone-in meat would be thrown onto the conveyor, and as it rolled up the belt, butchers on either side would grab a chunk, pull it off the belt and onto a work bench or area where we would then remove the bones with our knives. This was a very sophisticated operation compared to anything that I had ever seen in the past. It was very efficient, very Henry Ford-ish. You weren't allowed to leave your position along this assembly, or should I say dis-assembly line, without requesting permission. Even then, permission was usually denied. They didn't want the line to be stopped. You were given a number of knives that you sharpened before or after your shift. The same requirement applied to bathroom calls.

For the first few weeks inside this place, I felt as though I had been put in prison. The work was very heavy and very hard; I had forgotten just how hard it was. Every inch of my body ached. It is curious how different jobs require different muscles. This job reworked muscles that I had obviously lost somewhere out in an orange grove. Each morning when I awoke, my hands would be clinched together like a fist, and it would take five or six minutes for me to get my fingers functioning well enough to hold a coffee cup once again.

This condition was caused, I presume, because of the necessity of squeezing the meat hook in one hand and grasping the knife in the other. Of course, the thirty-eight to forty degree temperature inside the boning room didn't help the matter any either.

Everyday during lunch break, I talked to my fellow workers about my future chicken farm and log cabin in Arkansas. They laughed. At night Carol and I would meet at the supper table and stare at one another like a couple of zombies.

I knew what Carol's job was like in the emergency room at a busy Miami hospital. She had described to me in the past, the Saturday night, sucking chest wounds; the broken skulls, gashes, and knife wounds; the battered faces and bodies of men, women, and children. We were oh so glad to be back to the real world, and our steady dependable paychecks. Yeah, right!

At least I thought they were steady and dependable. A month or so had gone by on my new job, when I was called into the boss's office and told that I was fired. I was shocked. I had never been fired from a job in my life. I asked for an explanation, and I was given what seemed to me to be a series of outrageous lies. I was so disappointed, because after this initial trial period, I would have had the opportunity to join the union. The union representative had even spoken to me. But that was it. I was fired.

I asked if there was anything I could do to make up for my so called short comings. I told them that I would work even harder if I were given a second chance. It was no go. I had all day to wander around and think about what I would say to Carol. I was embarrassed. I was ashamed. I couldn't face her.

I went to a payphone and started making calls from the yellow pages again. I felt that this job had gotten me in shape. I could physically handle butchering once again. All of my recollections about taking the bones out of meat had been brought back to me. By my third telephone call, I had a job.

A man had answered the phone. I asked if they used experienced butchers at his shop. He said, "Are you working at the moment?" And I said.

"Well, up until about ten minutes ago, I was."

"Where were you employed?"

"At the Great Union processing plant," I said.

He instantly broke into a laugh. "The Great Union wasn't so great, was it?"

"No, it wasn't," I said.

"Well, I've just had some people quit me. How soon can you start?"

"Tell me where you are located, and as soon as I hang up this pay phone, I'll be over there."

The man laughed again. I didn't realize it but I had been talking directly to the owner. He had just stepped into the office. He usually didn't answer the phone. If I would have called at any other time, I might not have spoken to him and I might not have been hired. But, I was at the right place at the right time, and off I went.

This place was down in the Cuban section of town. The owner was not Cuban, but the majority of the butchers were. The only non-Cubans were myself, this black kid, and an older white Jewish guy whose name was Lenny Silverman. Believe me, after my experiences at the Great Union, I was glad to be there. The owner's name was Tommy. He was a young fellow. He was probably in his early thirties. He was a nice guy, but very inexperienced. I don't know if he started this business, or he inherited it from his father or something. But whatever, he was very naive as to the workings of the common laborer's mind. He just didn't seem to know what made people tick. The place was not operated efficiently. We constantly experienced slack time, most of it because of a severe lack of communication between him and his foreman.

No work started until Tommy arrived on the scene. If Tommy was late for work, or got caught in traffic or something, we all just stood around looking at one another. I never understood this, because the work was all basically the same everyday.

The meat quarters were unloaded off the truck and into the breakdown room. There, with the help of some large circular shoulder harness saws, and some standard old fashioned reciprocal cutting saws, the quarters were broken down into smaller pieces. From there they were pushed out to the boning table, where the bones would be removed; then, to the cryovac machine, where they would be processed and boxed. The boxed and labeled product then was carted into the storage room. That was it - the same thing day in and day out. What was the problem? Why did no work commence until Tommy got there? I never got it.

My opinion was that the foreman was playing some kind of game. For whatever reason, Tommy went along with it. My real concern was that because of this foolishness, this guy was going to go out of business. I was going to lose my job before Carol and I had saved up enough money to go to Arkansas and start raising chickens and building our log cabin.

I had already sent for a whole slew of books. Books dealing with subject matter like; how to be self-sufficient on your own five acres; how to raise chickens for fun and profit; how to build your own log cabin; how to build a house out of stones; how to preserve your food in the wilderness; survival in the wild; solar energy; peddle power your own electric, and how to start your own business on fifty dollars or less. I mean I was getting ready, and Carol and I were saving every penny. I didn't need this meat company to shut down on me.

In any case, this situation came to a head one day. Tommy didn't show up and neither did the foreman. What to do, what to do, what to do? Everybody stood around staring at one another for five or ten minutes. One guy suggested that we sit down and wait, and another suggested that we go home. I said,

"Wait a minute here. I don't know about you guys but I know exactly what to do. I've been doing the same thing here, day-in day-out, for the last six months."

I went into the breakdown room, and started chunking everything up. As soon as I would get a quarter done, I would push it out to the boning table. The first one to start working out there was Lenny. Then the black guy, and then the rest finally joined in. I didn't think very much about the incident, but as it turned out, it seems that I had quelled a minor revolution. The boss was extremely happy with me and called me into his office to thank me. The foreman was back to work the next day, and he never missed a day thereafter for as long as I was working there, anyway. From that day on, work began everyday whether Tommy was there or not.

The next incident was the sausage episode. Tommy had decided to go into the sausage producing business. He bought some grinders, racks, funnels and other apparatus, sectioned off a room, and then began interviewing us employees, one on one, as to how to make a sausage. This guy was really strange. He had purchased thousands of dollars worth of equipment for the purposes of making sausage, and he didn't have the slightest idea of how to go about it. When he asked me if I knew anything about making sausage, I told him what I knew.

Years ago, when I was starting out in the business, I had observed this fellow making sausage in his own wholesale sausage making shop. None of my knowledge was very specific. I knew that most sausage was made from pork. The pork involved was primarily butt, or pork shoulder meat, to which spices and more pork fat were added. One thing that I did know was that sausage contained a lot of fat. I also knew that the spices varied according to national origin and ethnic background.

Every country in the world seems to have its own unique type sausage. Tommy wanted to make Italian sausage. I told him the first thing that he ought to do, probably, was to buy a cook book. What could I say? I had never been in this situation before. I did ask Tommy, why he decided to go into the sausage making business when he didn't know the first thing about it. He said; Why not?

When Lenny came out of Tommy's office he was exceedingly bemused. When I asked him what was so funny, he said; "That moron don't even know how to make a sausage."

"Do you?"

"Do I know how to make a sausage? Do you know what I did for the twenty-five years before I came to work in this dump?"

"No, what?"

"I had my own sausage business, that's what."

"All right! That's great! Then I guess you are going to be in charge of the new sausage department, huh?"

"Like hell I am. Do you think I am going to give away twenty-five years of my life to some little, rich punk who don't know pork butt from his elbow, for a few bucks an hour?"

Lenny was funny. Every couple of hours or so, he would take a spin into the sausage making room. Then he would come back and tell me all of the things those stupid S.O.B.s were doing wrong.

"You're not going to believe this, kid," he would say, "Dem morons is trying to grind sausage without no ice."

"What's ice got to do with grinding sausage?"

"Go in dare and take a look at that sausage, and come back here and tell me what you think."

To make sausage, first, the fresh pork meat must be chopped then put through a coarse grinder. Next, the coarse ground meat would be blended by hand with whatever mixture of secret herbs and spices. Then it would be put through the grinding machine once again. By means of a funnel attached to the mouth of the grinder, it would then be stuffed into a casing. When this sausage that these guys were making came through the funnel and into the casing, the sausage ended up looking like a fat roll of Pepsodent toothpaste in a see through wrapping. It didn't look good at all, not the least bit appetizing.

"You gotta grind it the second time wid ice," Lenny told me. "Or else you get that white mush, like they got in dare."

Lenny did know his sausage making business, but I thought it rather amusing that although Lenny wouldn't tell Tommy "nothing'" for even less an hour, he was willing to spill the beans to me.

Actually Lenny and I became more and more friendly. I got a kick out of him. He was a tough little Jewish kid from the

Bronx. Every other word out of his mouth was a cuss word, but he had a good heart, even "dough" it didn't include tellin' Tommy nuttin' about makin' sausages.

After work, me and Lenny would go out and have a couple of beers, and shoot the breeze for an hour or so. Then one day he asked me if Carol and I would like to go out to dinner with him and his wife. We did, and from that time on it became pretty much a ritual.

Lenny was Jewish, but his passion was not for Israel, but Italy. He loved Italy, and everything about it. He drooled over opera. He could sing Italian Operas by heart. His home was filled with books about opera, the classics and Jewish and Italian history and culture. Listening to him talk on these subjects was like getting instruction in the classics from Jimmy Durante.

"Ya know ... ya know Caruso? He was a poor guy. Ya dat's right. He come outta da slums in Naples. He was the youngest and the oldest of eighteen kids, all the utters died. You know Mario? Mario Lanza. He's a nutta one. Ya, he useta deliver pianos. Dat's right. You'd be surprised about opera. It's real people music. It ain't so fancy like people tink. It's right offa da streets. You'd like it if you got into it."

Every week when we went out, we went to this same Italian restaurant. I don't think that anyone else ever went there. We always seemed to be alone. Whenever we came in the front door, the owner, his wife and the six kids would all come running out to greet us. I don't even know if they spoke English, because Lenny would always speak to them in Italian.

"Bona beana culchunee maranonie piconi polanni," Lenny would say.

Lenny's wife was another contradiction. She was not only well mannered and sweet, but very sophisticated. She was very attractive. Lenny called her his Jewish princes. I don't really think that she liked it so very much. She loved Lenny, but it was plain that they had their moments. In the few minutes that we were able to talk to her alone, she would try to explain Lenny to us, and to herself.

"You know, Lenny really doesn't have to work anymore. We've got enough money. But, Lenny always has to have a job. Do you know why? So that he can meet people like you, I think." I didn't know how to take that, was it a complement or not? "I don't mean this in any denigrating way, but Lenny doesn't like people his own age. He won't mix with any of the people from the condo. He only associates with working class people like yourselves. I'm not saying there is anything wrong with that, but don't you find that peculiar?

"Lenny reads all the time. He is a self educated man. He's a wealth of information, if you get to talking with him. He knows everything, but he has no respect for educated people. He loves the opera and the classics, he can speak Italian, French and Yiddish, but yet our whole social life is surrounded by truck drivers, butchers, sausage makers, and floor sweepers. Don't you think that's strange?"

Lenny loved that Italian restaurant. Every week he got the same dish, mussels with marinara sauce, and pasta. I had the dish a few times myself and it was great, but the rest of us were getting tired of Italian every week.

We finally convinced him that we all needed a change. To his wife's delight we went to this fancy well known Jewish restaurant in downtown Miami Beach. It was quite an experience for me. I felt like I was in a different country.

Eventually, the boys in the back room did learn how to make sausage, and without Lenny's help. Lenny and I also had another common aspect to our background. We had both been fired from the Great Union. Lenny's contention was that because of all the benefits that the union offered, the company was hiring only temporary employees. As soon as a new employee became union eligible, or expressed the notion that he would join the union, he was terminated.

I don't know if that story was true or not but it made me feel better. It was made more believable by the fact that Lenny was one of the best butchers I had ever seen.

I had yet another interview with Tommy, in fact, we all did. Tommy had a problem. He wanted to know if we could tell him why production had dropped ever since he stopped his policy of piecework. This piecework policy existed before I had been hired, and I didn't know that much about it. I told Tommy I didn't really think I had the right to comment on the subject because of my lack of knowledge. He insisted on explaining the whole deal to me in search for my opinion nevertheless. I found his confidence flattering, so I listened.

It seems that in the past, Tommy had devised this totally new concept. I had never heard anything about it in my experiences as a butcher. He devised a price per hind and per fore quarter, and the butchers were paid a certain price according to how many of each they de-boned each day.

The problem with this, according to Tommy, was that when he paid the workers by the piece, he would be able to process seven to ten truck loads of beef a week, but since he went to salary, he was lucky to process three to five truck loads.

My first question was did he have the same number and caliber of butchers? He said that he thought their abilities were about the same, now as then. In fact, some of the present workers were employed under both systems. At present, he had even more butchers than he had back in the "piece" work days.

"Did they work the same number of hours?" I asked.

"Actually," he said, "the old crew worked fewer hours."

"Which group made more money?" I asked. "The ones that worked by the hour, or the ones that worked by the piece?"

"Oh, there was no comparison," he said. "The piecework guys were making considerably more. I was writing out checks to some of them for a thousand dollars a week, and now, as you know, I pay everybody by the hour."

I was once again dumfounded by this guy. Was he serious? He couldn't figure out why the work production had slowed down? One week some of the guys out on the floor were making a thousand dollars a week, and the next week they were making three hundred. Was Tommy nuts, insane, or senile? What was he talking about? I was getting nervous just looking at him. I mean, a man in his mental condition could possibly attack me at any moment. Should I actually say something to him, or should I express sympathy for him and the indisputable paradox of his quandary and try to escape from the office, unharmed?

"Sir, you're kidding me, right?"

"No, that's the truth."

"I mean your joking about not being able to understand why production has slowed down?"

"No. Do you think you know why?"

"I could pretty much guarantee it."

"Really? Well please, give me your explanation."

"Well, one week a man is taking home a thousand dollars a week, and the next week he is working more hours and taking home three hundred."

"What's money got to do with it?"

"Pardon me?"

"What's money got to do with it?"

"Why do you think workers come here everyday; because they are lonely?"

"Are you saying to me that the only reason people come to work here everyday is to get a pay check?" He was now bent forward in his chair and leaning on the desk between us. He had this intense emotional look in his eyes. I had the feeling that if I said yes, he would start to cry or something, but I said it anyway.

"Yes."

"That is a very cynical point of view, don't you think?"

"Would you consider it cynical if I said to you that one day you, your mother and father, your brothers and sisters, and even your own wife and children will be dead?"

"I don't know if I would call that cynical. I would be more inclined to call it cruel, or mean."

"You would? That's strange because I would call it a simple fact of life. Don't you realize that one day everybody is going to die?"

"Well, of course I do. We all do. But that is no reason for you to say that one day all of my family will be dead. So will yours."

"I didn't say that your family will one day be dead, to be mean to you. I was trying to impress upon you that coming to work everyday for the purpose of getting a paycheck is not a curiosity, but a fact of life, just as death is."

"I don't come to work everyday just to get a paycheck, in fact some weeks I don't even earn a paycheck."

"You don't?"

"No."

"Then why are you here?"

"Well, one, I would like to create a successful business."

"Why?"

"Personal pride - to promote a sense of achievement within myself; to make my family proud of me; to give my children someone to look up to; to assist other people in making a living; to gain respect from my peers; to participate in life and the community; to see if I can take an idea from my own imagination and make it grow into something that not only myself but everyone in the community can take pride in ... Do you want me to go on?

"Yes."

"Well, I would like to be a part of something greater than just getting along in life, or just getting by. I want to build something. I want to plant a seed and see it grow. I want to be in control of my own destiny. I want to own something. I want to be the boss and not have to answer to others. I want to think up an idea and be able to put it into practice. I want to prove to myself that I have the ability. I want to discover my limits. I want to go beyond the everyday ... I ..."

"Okay, you've convinced me. You don't work for money. But I do. And most everybody that I have ever met does also. I have never heard anyone in my entire life describe what they do for a living as you have just done. Most people do not have such lofty goals. Most everyone that I have ever met, have goals and aspirations that are simpler and more basic. They would like to be able to provide for themselves and their families. They would like to be able to take care of their loved ones when they get sick, at least be able to pay the doctor bills or hospital bills.

They would like to live in a nice neighborhood. They would like to, one day, be able to afford their own home. They would like to have a car and some of the other material things that make life more enjoyable. Some of them might like to be able to send their children to college so that they can get an education and then maybe go out into the world with goals like yours. But for the most part all of their goals center on how much money they can earn. The less money, the further they are away from these basic goals."

"And what about you? What are your basic goals?"

"Well, at the moment, my wife and I are living as frugally as possible, in the hopes that we can save enough money to go to Arkansas, buy some land, build ourselves a log cabin in the woods and raise chickens."

Tommy laughed. "And you think I have goals that are unrealistic? Okay, thank you for your opinion. I appreciate your co-operation and your honesty." We both got up and shook hands. Just before I opened the door to leave Tommy said. "And good luck with your chicken farm plans."

"Thank you. And I wish you success in curing the common man of his wage mentality." Tommy laughed.

After a number of months passed, Carol and I figured that with our previous savings, and what we had been able to add to them over the last twelve to fourteen months, we had enough to hit the road for Arkansas. I put in my notice.

Tommy actually threw me a small going away party. He bought a big cake and brought it into the break room at lunch time. I was quite shocked. No one had ever thrown me a going away party. Actually, no one has ever thrown me a coming back party either.

18 Back to the Land, in Arkansas

Hallelujah, it was almost over! We had approximately fifteen thousand dollars saved. We had our van and our camping equipment in tip-top shape. The van ran like a gem. The body was in excellent shape, and now, with our overhaul we felt that it would be going strong for possibly another ten years. We had a few goodbyes, a couple of big city ends to tie up, and we would be on our way!

Our last big city obstacle was the reclaiming of our damage security deposit. The woman who owned the apartment complex at which we stayed migrated between New York and Florida. At this particular time she was in New York and we were instructed to deal with a realty agent who was managing the property in her absence.

The first thing we learned was that the property would have to meet a list of requirements before our money would be returned. We had between four and five hundred dollars on deposit. The list was not unreasonable. It included cleaning and the maintenance and repair of anything that we may have damaged while living there. After these demands were satisfied, the apartment would be inspected by the realty agent, and he would then notify our landlady.

We met the demands, and then called the realty man for our inspection. He inspected the property and gave us a glowing report. But when we asked for our check, he informed us that we would have to call the property owner. When I called her, I was never so shocked in my life. She literally laughed at us when I told her we had satisfied all of her demands through the realty and we were now waiting for our check.

She seemed to be a very nice lady. She never bothered us all the time we were living there. She wasn't friendly either, but we never had one unkind word or any conflict of any kind. I couldn't understand her attitude. I explained to her that we had the carpets shampooed; we had scrubbed all the floors and had all of the appliances in working order. The refrigerator and the oven were spotless. How could she legitimately refuse us our money? She told me her position basically as follows.

"Whether or not I refund your money is wholly up to my discretion. I can give it to you or not give it to you, as I choose. I am not going to give it to you. If you like, you can take me to small claims court. They have a six month waiting list. If I am not mistaken you are about to leave the area. You will be required to return in person, at the appropriate time or the judge will not reward you the money and I will win by default. So Mr. Noble it is up to you and you can do as you please."

I started to tell her, as politely as I could what I thought of her attitude, when she abruptly interrupted me.

"If you don't like it Mr. Noble, sue me ... Otherwise you can just go to hell. I have many more serious problems in life than to worry about the few dollars that I owe to you." And then she hung up.

Well, have you ever had an experience like that? I felt that it was only because of the miracle of the telephone that anyone could get away with talking to me that way. But, nevertheless, what could we do? I guess that it was a fitting way for us to exit our lives in the big city.

We huffed, puffed and sputtered all the way to the panhandle of Florida at which point the exhilaration of our new adventure overpowered all of our past struggles and sacrifices.

We were on the road once again. We were footloose, and fancy free. Our coffers were full and our imaginations were bursting with the wonder of what might happen next. What would we find?

Carol began relating her fantasy of being a pioneer in the days of the Wild West. I could only think of how much luckier we were than the pioneers. We had an automobile, not a covered wagon. We were traveling on paved highways, and not just wandering towards the sunset over hill and dale, fording streams, rivers, and mountains. We could stop and eat at McDonalds, or Wendy's rather than shooting a buffalo. If we were pioneers, we were certainly pioneering in comfort. We had to be two of the luckiest pioneers that ever were. And, we knew right where we were going.

We had selected either Arkansas or Oklahoma. The northern section of Arkansas and the northeast section of Oklahoma were filled with mountains, lakes and streams. Snowfall was minimal. Best of all, land could be bought there, cheaper than anyplace in the United States as far as we could tell by our research.

We didn't know how much land we would really need to become self sufficient pioneers. But I had books that advocated a minimum five acres. We figured that we would start off with at least five acres, but, of course the more the merrier.

I also had books on how to buy country land. In these books they told me about all of the things to look out for. You had to be sure that when you purchased the land it was intact with all of its natural rights, and that there were no liens or encumbrances and that the title was free and clear. One of the biggest things to be concerned with was title insurance. As long as the insurance could be had, it was at least safe that you could get your money back if anything went wrong.

Living and surviving on the land would be relatively easy. We already knew how to pick, can and harvest fruits and vegetables. Now all that we had to do was plant the seeds and stuff like that. We had already discovered the magazine, "The Mother Earth News". This magazine basically told you, everything you would need to know about going back to the land. And, everybody was doing it. It wasn't like we were the only two people in the world who were heading this way. In fact, there were already famous pioneers who had laid out the basic pathways to rural self sufficiency; for example Ma and Pa Nearing.

These two people were in the Mother Earth News nearly every issue. This guy had written books about all of this stuff. He and his wife were both, at present, about one hundred and sixty three years old. They credited their longevity basically to this back to the land lifestyle and a healthy diet of grass and blueberries.

These two old people could do just about anything. I mean there were pictures of them right there in the magazine, hauling boulders to build their new stone observatory. They didn't have to build houses or barns, or anything like that.

They had already done all of that stuff a hundred years ago. Now they were into observatories, and planetariums, science foundations and things like that. They could repair and fix anything they owned with basically a needle and thread. They had instructions right in the magazine on how you could fence in your whole property with nothing more than blades of grass and Nestorium roots. They had made a combine harvester out of a fiberglass septic tank and some grape vines.

These people were unbelievable. And they were both, like I said, two hundred and sixty three years old. So if they could do it, what could two people like Carol and I accomplish?

The future of Carol and Dick, the back to the landers, was definitely without limit. We could see no way that we could be stopped. Not even common sense had a shot at us. Carol and I, the Nearings, and The Mother Earth News could conquer just about everything.

We spent our first month or so exploring northern Arkansas and Oklahoma and stopping in at every realty office along the way. Let me tell you, the admonishment, "let the buyer beware" took on a new and vivid meaning. Land prices varied somewhere between the ridiculous and the sublime. We saw land covered with rocks, with no trees, mineral and timber rights withheld, with no access, sloping on the side of a mountain at a seventy-five degree angle selling for mucho dollars an acre. Almost every property we looked at was being sold by a guy who looked and spoke like Mark Twain. Why, they were all the most friendly, good humored, down to earth people you ever met. Most every real estate adventure was a trip into goofball land, a total waste of time and effort.

Finally we devised our own strategy. We decided that we wanted forty acres of land, and we would pay ten thousand dollars. From then on, when we entered the realty office we simply stated our demand, and waited for a response. Most realtors just shook their heads negatively, some had maybe one property to show, but many others just laughed. I felt that this was a very good plan. It sure ended a lot of Mark Twain tours through dopey-land.

Then we landed in this little town of Mena, Arkansas. We had been there before as you remember.

When we were there, it was just plain old, down home, tobacco chewing, chicken raising, no hippies or pot heads allowed, Colonel Everybody, Mena, Arkansas.

We went into this realty office, asked the Colonel sitting behind the desk if he had any forty acre parcels of land for ten thousand dollars or less.

"Sure do," he said.

"Got about eight of them."

"Great we would like to go see them."

"Let me get my hat, and we're gone."

He put on his Colonel cowboy hat and we were out of there.

We spent the whole day touring the countryside and looking at one forty acre parcel after another. Then finally we headed out into the boonies. We turned down one dirt forest road after another. Crossed two beautiful shallow streams, then as we approached the third the Colonel said. "Now, I got four forty acre parcels beginning right here just ahead of this stream."

The road that we were traveling on was a National Forest road. It was wide, covered with gravel and as traversable as one could want. The road just about bisected the property, and the property was really as pretty as could be. It was covered with hardwood trees and pine. It had two or three streams running right through it. It had a slight southern slop to it but for the most part, we considered it to be flat.

The back side or northern end of the property sat at the foot of the Ouachita Mountains. Our eyes were just bugging out of our heads.

"Now this may be just a little too far out into the boonies for you guys," the Colonel muttered. "But you won't find a prettier section than this."

"Oh, this ain't too far out for us; the further out the better."

Our year in the big city had left us very un-lonely for human contact. I felt pretty much like the character in Sartre's play "No Exit" when in the end he concludes that Hell is "other people".

Ah yes, other people can surely be a pain in the butt. Out here, there would certainly be no other people to bother us. Without any doubt, this was it. One of these parcels would be our back to the land paradise.

We decided that the second parcel along this beautiful roadway would be ours. What really sold us was the poke salad.

We saw this plant that looked like spinach growing all over the place. We asked the Colonel what it was.

"Why that's poke salad," he said. "Let me tell ya, you take some of that there poke salad, dip it in a quart of lard, fry it up in a pan with about a pound or two of bacon, then put it in a pot with some butter beans and black eyed peas, throw in some pig snout and a little hog jowl, and oooouuu weeee, you got some real eatin' there son. Let me tell you, it would make you want to slap your mama up side the head."

Well, even though neither of us had any desire to slap our mothers up the side of their head, the fact that we had poke salad and blueberries was enough to settle it all. Ma and Pa Nearing move over, here we come.

We told the Colonel to go and write it up. In the meantime, we set up house keeping on our new wilderness.

It was wonderful! We gathered up some stones and built a combination fireplace and make-do outdoor oven. We were cooking breakfast and baking bread over an open wood fire in no time. I made a bath tub out of our canoe. I set the canoe in a sunny area, filled it up with water from one of our mountain streams, and just waited for the sun to get it toastie warm. Every morning we were up at the crack of dawn exploring our forty acres.

Forty acres of land, is more land than I would ever have believed. One acre is about the size of a football field. So imagine forty football fields stretched out side by side. And these football fields were all covered with trees, and streams, and beavers, and turkeys, and blueberries, and poke salad.

What more could anyone ask for?

We hiked the borders of our property several times. We had machetes, axes, and hunting knives with us. We found hand built stone walls, a half acre pond, a large stream running parallel with the road, which was being fed by our two other streams that were running down from the mountain. The view from the hill on the northern slop of our property was spectacular. We were simply beside ourselves with joy. This could be nothing less than miraculous, and for just ten thousand dollars, it was all ours.

We would have to make a plan in order to become self-sufficient as soon as possible. First we would designate an area for a garden and then get the planting done. While our vegetables were growing, we would pick out a homesite. Then start marking, cutting, stripping and stacking our hardwood trees for our future log cabin. After that we would consider what type of animals we would like to raise.

We figured chickens for eggs and meat to eat, some pigs for eating and to sell, and maybe a cow for milk. Bacon and eggs, milk and vegetables, poke salad and blueberries, how much food can two people eat? Why we would probably be forced to open a restaurant just to get rid of our surplus. Who said that man would have to live by the sweat of his brow? Not Carol or I or Henry David Thoreau. We would no longer be one of the crowd living lives of quiet desperation. Not us, Henry old boy. We were doing it to it, buddy! We were not only traveling on the road less traveled, Mr. Frost, we bought the darn thing!

Can you believe it! What a book this is going to be! "How we found heaven on a dirt road in Arkansas"; "How eating high off the hog can be as easy as falling off a log". They would have to change the expression of "living the life of Riley" to "living the life of Carol and Dick". This was it. This was definitely it! It would be downhill sailing from now on.

My first project was to clear an acre or two for a garden. We had a good piece of open ground.

The first thing that I figured I would need would be a pick and a shovel. That would have to be the least expensive way to go, and I had plenty of time, so what did it matter.

I found out immediately that the ground in Arkansas was filled with stones. I don't mean pebbles. I mean boulders. Every time I bonked my pick into the ground, it bonked right back up at me. Then I would get down onto my hands and knees, and start digging around the buried boulder with my hands and a garden rake. At one point, I actually thought I was in the process of excavating an entire Mayan village. Did the Mayan's ever get that far north? Well then maybe it was the Inca's or the Aztec's or maybe the Pueblo Indians. The Pueblo's were just up the road a way in New Mexico.

After about a week, I had a garden plot cleared that was about the size of a bedspread - a twin bedspread.

Carol had her own projects going. She was baking bread, and picking blueberries; soaking poke salad in bacon fat; making a refrigerator in one of our streams; trying to develop her own turkey calling technique, and looking up beaver recipes in The

Joy of Cooking cookbook that someone had given us as a going away present.

With all of our problems we were not in the slightest discouraged. These were all just minor setbacks, that with a little thought we would soon overcome. In the mean time what if we took a little break and went for a ride to get a couple of brewskies and a meatball sandwich.

About three hours, and a hundred and fifty miles later we found ourselves in Oklahoma. Unbeknown to us we had settled into a county in Arkansas that was dry. Dry means that they don't sell alcoholic beverages in that county. Man! Trying to imagine Dick and Carol without beer is like trying to imagine Moscow without Vodka. I didn't know that there was such a thing as a dry county. This was America; I mean prohibition ended sometime back in the dark ages.

Except in Arkansas, we found out. The closest liquor selling establishment was just over the state line in Oklahoma. So there we were in Oklahoma, sitting in a log cabin barroom.

They had no meatball sandwiches though. The guy behind the bar had never heard of one. In fact, he had never heard of a meatball, and as I described it to him, I thought he was going to puke. So instead we ate pork rind, and smoked beef jerky with our beer. And for beer, they didn't have any Pabst, or Narragansett; no Black Label, or Schlitz. They had Lone Star, Coors, and Bubba's. So there we were in Oklahoma, drinking Bubba beer and eating smoked beef jerky and hot and spicy pickled pig's feet. I'll tell you what - any port in a storm.

After an hour or two of discussing our personal situation, we decided that some changes would have to be made. The pick and shovel would have to go. Maybe we could find a secondhand rototiller somewhere.

At just about this time my body requested a trip to the men's room. The men's room was out the back door and up the side of the mountain about a quarter of a mile. It was a country style outhouse, a two-holer and it was real neat. They had all sorts of good smelly stuff in there to keep down the stink. They had regular city style commodes, sinks and stuff like mirrors, and little curtains adorning the window over the sink. They even had a bookshelf and magazine rack. It was great! I could have moved in there.

As I was washing my hands - using the jug of water and soap that was left there for that purpose - I saw out that bathroom window a rototiller. This was unbelievable. It was obviously a "sign". God wanted us to be here in Arkansas. He must have made us thirsty for beer, just to get us to this log cabin barroom on the side of the Ouachita mountain range.

This tiller obviously existed in a state of abuse. The ratcheting, pull-rope-starting thing-a-ma-gig was cast upon the ground next to it. In general, it looked to me that someone had just left it sitting there in disgust. I hiked back down to the log cabin barroom, and asked the bartender what he intended to do with that old dilapidated, worn out rototiller up there by the men's room. Actually I was pushing for my side. The rototiller looked pretty darn new, but I was already building my case.

"I don't really know. Let me call my folks."

When the bartender returned, he said. "They don't want the darn thing. They said that they hadn't been able to get the useless thing to run for more than a half hour straight since they bought it. If you want it, just pack it up with you when you leave."

Oh man, this was unbelievable! You tell me? Was this a sign or was this not a sign? Even Moses didn't get any straighter talk than this. I'm not the most religious fellow, but neither was St. Paul. Listen, an abandoned rototiller, behind an outhouse, on the side of a mountain, in Timbuktu Oklahoma? Come on now? Somebody up there had to be liking us? What do you think? Be honest now? And the guy gives us the rototiller! When is the last time that a total stranger gave you a rototiller?

Yeah Really! To say the least we were inspired.

The first thing we did after getting back to the ranch and unloading our new rototiller, was go down to the Wal-Mart in Mena and get a book on small engine repair.

I followed the instructions, and redid the rope-pulley ratchet thing-a-ma-jig, and that wasn't easy, let me tell you. But the real work was probably just beginning. It had probably been run without oil and the pistons were welded to the cylinder walls. The cylinder heads were most likely caked with carbon. It would probably need a whole overhaul, just like I had done to our truck - with Bob's help of course.

But before I got into all of that, I thought that I should crank it once or twice, just to see what would happen.

I gave the rope one giant tug, and brummmmm, it was off and running. Carol's eyes nearly bugged out of her head. She couldn't believe it, nor could I. Those folks at the log cabin barroom had thrown away a rototiller because the ratchet was broke.

Okay, okay just stay calm. After Carol and I hooted and hollered and danced around the fireplace two or three times, I decided to hit the dirt and till up two or three acres.

I quickly found out that the rototiller really wasn't much better at breaking new ground and turning over hidden, underground cities than the pick and shovel.

After another week of pick and shoveling, in combination with rototilling, I had cleared a spot about twenty foot square. It wasn't much, but it was a start.

We decided to go to town, buy some seed and talk to the man at the feed store. We told him about all the rocks we had discovered in our potential garden, and he said, "You're kidding! Rocks here in Arkansas? Wait until I tell the neighbors."

After he was through laughing, he did have some good suggestions. His first suggestion was to call Cladius Thalmudge, and if he was not available he gave us the number of Coolmidge Fostle. These were two local people who cleared land and such for people.

We got a hold of Coolmidge, who sounded very much like Will Rogers.

"Well," he said. "I'd sure be glad to come on out there, but you gotta remember, you a long way out in them boonies out there. Now I don't mind travelin' out there, but it will cost ya."

Oh oh, here it comes. Nine million dollars and forty-six cents and he would be right there to sock it to us city slickers.

"You guts to remember, I got my blader and my prongfoger that I'm havin' to haul out there. And then, of course, there's my flatbed hauler and fuel for the tractor and my pickup truck. You know all of these things cost money these days. Then you gotta rake it too. How much land did you want to clear?"

"Well, actually, all we wanted was about an acre or two. All that we really want to do is plant a garden. We got this big field; there's no trees or nothin' on it. In fact, it might have been a pasture or something at one time."

"I know exactly where you're talkin' about. In fact, I used to know the folks who originally owned that property. Old Horace Askkisser was the man. He was a good man too; died of dysentery back in thirty-nine. At least that's what they called it back then. Today they probably have some new fangled name for it. But whatever, when you're dead, you're dead."

"That's true, that's certainly true; but tell me, what do you estimate that it will cost us, Coolmidge? You don't have to be exact, just give me a ballpark figure."

"Well, okay. Let me get my pencil and pad here. You say you need about two acres now? Is that right?"

"Approximately."

"Well, best I can cal-kalate it here, that will probably run ya about twenty-five to thirty-five dollars." (Long Pause)

Needless to say old Coolmidge was out to the ranch that next morning. He had a tractor and this giant ground breaking thing. I guess it would just be called a plow.

"Now ya sure that you want two acres? That's going to be a mighty big garden?" advised Coolmidge.

"That's okay. We might set ourselves up a vegetable stand out on the highway and sell our excess to passers-by."

"Now, there you go. I like that kind of spirit."

So first he plowed it all up, and then he ran over it a couple of times with what he called a disker. By the time he was done it looked great.

As you watched Coolmage with that giant plow and disker, you had to wonder about those pioneers once again. How did they ever do it? They didn't have giant tractors, plows and diskers back in "the good old days". They must have really been something else.

Now I could start in with my new rototiller, because all the big clods still had to be broken up, and there were yet numerous branches and rocks and boulders that had to be carried out by hand to the boundaries of the garden. But, it was finally beginning to look like a garden. We were on our way.

Carol started right in planting seed. The sooner the better, we thought. The quicker you get those seeds into the ground, the sooner it would be tossed salad time out on the back forty.

We also figured that because this was practically virgin land, we shouldn't need any fertilizers and stuff like that. And with our Mother Earth News as our guide, we would, of course, not pollute our virgin land with chemicals and pesticides.

We planted our first garden in the very early spring, March or something like that. You were suppose to wait until the ground warmed up, and in March it felt plenty warm to us. We could always plant some more later on. So what difference did it make?

Our first disaster came with the spring rain. They called it spring rain, but it came down in Biblical proportions. You know, like Noah and the flood.

Our slightly sloping land suddenly looked more like the downhill of Olympic Games fame. Our seeds were on a downhill slalom. A three day deluge and our garden was no more.

So we remembered the Romans and the Chinese - we would terrace, and canal our next garden.

We bought a couple of rakes and hoes and began scraping up furrows. Every so often, we would leave a space in our furrows, to let water run through, forming little canals. We staggered the spaces in our furrows, so that the water would run in and out when the next deluge came. We waited and it worked. Then we planted garden number two. All the while, of course, I was rototilling my little butt off, clearing more garden space.

Our seeds sprouted immediately, but then just stopped dead in their tracks.

Back at the feed store, our friendly pick, shovel, rake, hoe, land clearing recommender, advised us to take a soil sample over to the farm bureau adviser at the court house. "It don't cost you nothin'."

So we did, and it didn't cost us a penny. We brought in a sample as our farm bureau advisor had recommended, by taking a little dirt from several different spots in our garden area and mixing them together in a bag. When our sample came back we found that our little garden was far from virgin. In fact, it had been plowed, re-plowed, and then plowed once again. It was worn and weary and deplete of all vitamins, minerals, and enthusiasm.

The first thing we would have to do was lime the whole thing. It would then need a good dose of a combination fertilizer. We limed, planted and fertilized once again. This time all our little seeds sprouted, and then continued to grow. In fact, it wasn't long before we had rabbits, deer, birds and other little animals visiting us daily.

In the midst of all of this we were also involved in the construction of our log cabin.

I had gone down to the feed store and bought myself a nifty Poulan chain saw. With Carol holding our back to the land instruction book, we began felling trees. We zapped down about four or five hardwood, Red Oak trees. On our property we had Red Oak, White Oak, Sweetgum, Loblolly Pine, Post Oak, and several other varieties.

Once we felled and trimmed the trees, we ran into our first setback. For those of you who may not realize this, a thirty foot tree is very, very heavy - and a hardwood tree even more so. We certainly couldn't lift up a thirty foot log. We couldn't even roll a thirty foot log. So we decided to cut the trees up into ten foot sections. Ten foot logs wouldn't make as pretty a log cabin but necessity is truly the mother of invention.

After we had the logs cut up into ten foot sections, we ran into our second problem. A ten foot Red Oak log, that is about twelve to fourteen inches in diameter, must weigh about half a million pounds, as opposed to the thirty foot log which weighs about forty six million pounds.

Then we had our best idea yet. We would keep cutting the logs down until we got to a reasonable size that we could lift.

At this point, I remembered reading an article in one of our Mother Earth News magazines about how to build a cordwood cabin. Carol felt that a log cabin made out of cordwood, would just not be the same thing. So now in my spare time I began reading about Archimedes.

Archimedes was certainly quite an admirable fellow. He was able to defend the walls of his hometown against a large enemy with nothing more than a handful of men and a barrage of weaponry all devised from pulleys, levers, and inclined planes. If Archimedes could do that, we could certainly figure out how to heft a few measly, old logs.

While on our way to town to purchase some levers and inclined planes, we noticed that a good many houses in and about town were built out of stones. These stone homes were not only fascinating but beautiful. Some of them were works of art. We began researching stone construction. I sent away for a number of new books. The first book dealt with laying stones as one might in laying and layering a redbrick wall. It was very interesting but extremely difficult.

I opted for the slip-form method. This was a method whereby one made wooden frames and kind of layered the stones in a bed of cement. Actually it looked just as good from the outside and if you wanted you could have a stone facade on the inside also with a layer of insulation in the middle of the wall. After doing our required reading, we were pretty much sold.

A stone house would be just the thing. Certainly, it would be consistent with the environment, naturally aesthetic, in addition to being practical, and physically and economically feasible. We went to the feed store and bought a wheelbarrow.

As we wandered around our plowed, disked and partially tilled garden gathering up what we considered the prettiest stones, we continued our research on stone house construction in the town of Mena.

We discovered this one house in particular that we both thought was exceptionally lovely. Every time we rode by, we stopped to look at it. It was so nice and to our liking that Carol decided to sketch it. We wanted to get basically the floor plan, how the porches were added, where the windows and doors had been placed, along with the basic roof design.

The house was on a corner, and we parked at every possible angle so Carol could do her best work. After a week of intensive design research an old woman came out of the house, stood on the porch, arms folded across her chest, and glared at us. We rather quickly felt like complete idiots. What had this poor woman been thinking in her observation of us circling about her house? We both instantly jumped from the truck and walked up to the woman to explain ourselves. As it turned out she was delighted with our interest. She invited us to come in and tour the inside.

The home was built by her husband about sixty years earlier. She was very proud of it. We were especially captured by the beauty of the exterior. The type of rocks used were just perfect to our eye. We asked her if she had any idea where her husband had found such a lovely selection of rocks. She said that she knew exactly where he found them because she had helped in hauling them from out in the boonies to their homesite. We asked her for directions to the site because we felt that even if the land were owned now as opposed to a vacant forest, the new owner probably wouldn't mind at all parting with a few troublesome stones.

She sat down and drew us a map. The map was a detailed instruction on how to get to our newly purchased property. She had given us directions to our forty acres. She talked of a stream on the south side of that new forest road that now cut through the property. Sure enough, when we got back to the ranch, we followed her directions right down to a stream bed on our property. There they were; piles of beautifully washed and polished stones and boulders. It was amazing. We couldn't believe it. Obviously, this was another sign. How could it be denied? We began hauling rocks that very day and our forest could now be left for posterity.

The garden? Ah yes, back to the garden. With all the little animals and birds suddenly discovering our garden, we realized how the notion of a scarecrow had evolved. What I couldn't figure was that with a whole jungle of green stuff out there in the middle of this forest, why did these little creatures have to pick on our bean sprouts? What's the story? Isn't that a little ridiculous? Believe me there were whole divisions of black birds or crows circling our garden. Why? I mean the world was full of wild blueberries, and poke salad patches abounded. What was so attractive about our little string beans?

But, be that as it may, we began scarecrow construction. And it worked! Not to perfection, but reasonably well.

Everything was growing fine until the early summer drought came. Nobody said it was a drought, but everything started drying up. Only our rock quarry stream bed maintained enough water to take a bath in. All our mountain tributaries were gone. Our babbling brooks and tiny waterfalls were no more. What could we do? Between the animals and the heat, our garden was disappearing as fast as we were tilling and planting. We got out our Mother Earth News and decided that our best alternative against the heat and sparse rainfall was mulching.

Mulching is a technique whereby you surround your little plants with water retaining material like woods chips, or leaves.

Leaves? We had a forest full of them suckers. We began hauling leaves from our hardwood forest in our wheelbarrow.

We mulched our mulch, man. And it looked good, and it seemed to be working - right up until the tiny grasshopper eggs in the mulch starting hatching.

Our garden was once again a religious experience. You remember the plague of locust story. Oh man, did we have grasshoppers. When we went to the feed store and asked our friend for something that killed grasshoppers, as much as we hated to do it, he simply smiled and shook his head. "No such thing, neighbors. Grasshoppers are simply something that you'll have to contend with. But I'll tell you one thing I'd get them leaves off of there. That is most likely where they are all coming from."

Back at the ranch we were busy with our little wheelbarrow once again hauling all of our leaves back into the woods. But we weren't discouraged.

Well, yes we were. We were really very, very discouraged. Would we ever see a homegrown tomato? You know, there are only two things that money can't buy and that's true love or a homegrown tomato.

We kept tilling and planting, despite all the setbacks. At about this time we began calculating our costs. We decided that we had better get out our back issues of the Mother Earth News and start in on possible ways to make some bucks out here in paradise.

They had a million ideas in the magazines, but small engine repair seemed to us to be the obvious thing. Hadn't I just recently overhauled our truck engine? Didn't I get our rototiller up and going in less than a day? Certainly my mechanical ability was blossoming. Besides, Carol always wanted to be married to somebody mechanical. Why couldn't it be me?

Carol was very critical of the idea. She has really never thought too much of my mechanical inclinations. In her heart of hearts, she respects me, but does not really feel that I have mechanical common sense. For example, she offered; "It took you three weeks to figure out which side of the canoe to paddle on, in order to change its direction to the right or the left, and you still consider the term "clockwise" to be a confusing concept. Maybe we should try another business, other than small engine repair?"

I was totally shocked by her lack of confidence. I couldn't believe she could actually say something like that to me. She saw my shock and disbelief, but insisted on continuing.

"You know we have been traveling for a long time now, and you still can not read a road map."

"What has that got to do with being mechanical?"

"What about that director's chair you bought, and ended up throwing in the dumpster because you couldn't figure out the directions?"

"Those directions were ridiculous even the people who wrote them couldn't figure out what language to put them in. I mean they were written in five different languages."

"Yeah, but you only had to consult the one that was written in English. You didn't have to take lessons in Spanish, French, and German. That was your choice."

I was not going to sit there in the middle of the wilderness debating minutiae. I immediately went to town and came back with four junk lawnmowers, and one junk rototiller all of which I had purchased for under fifty dollars. Carol surveyed my purchases. She immediately went to the Lawn-Boy mower that I had bought.

The mower was intact. The man had assured me. The reason that all of its internal organs and electrical equipment were thrown together in a sack, was simply due to a shortage of time on the part of the original owner. Carol examined the sack with its array of pistons, wires, and dufenflops.

"If you get this one running," she said. "I will personally make you a sign and hang up your shingle."

Then she snickered and walked away.

It is very disheartening to have the person with whom you have chosen to spend the rest of your life, feel this way. Other great men have had similar setbacks. Oh they laughed at Columbus, when he said the world was round, they giggled at Mosconi when he invented sound.

And so I began.

Within a week or so, I had the rototiller and all of the lawnmowers, except for the Lawn-Boy buzzing happily. Carol was very, very impressed. But she was holding out on the shingle until the Lawn-Boy was running.

The Lawn-Boy was different. It was a two stroke engine, rather than a four stroke. I don't really remember if that made so much of a difference now, but it did have a lot of different, unidentifiable do-dads floating around in the sack.

I had the schematic of the mower. My conclusion was that there were just too many parts in this darn sack. So I just used the ones that I felt fit. I stuffed the thing together. I remember using a cut up beer can as a piston ring compressor, but finally I had it all assembled. I brought Carol over to my working area for the grand start up. First she examined the mower. She nodded her approval. Then she took a peek into the sack.

"What's all this stuff?" she asked.

"Extras," I said calmly.

"Extras?"

"Yeah extras; they just had too much stuff in the bag; probably from some other lawnmowers or something."

Carol stared at me for a moment of two, and then walked away laughing.

I cranked it two or three times, but it didn't go. Carol peeked back over her shoulder.

"Oh, wait a minute. I forgot about the fuel."

The oil on the two stroke engine had to be mixed together as one does in an outboard motor. I did that, and then filled up the tank. Carol had chosen to ignore my project entirely. She was over at her oven, baking bread or something when I gave the Lawn-Boy its next crank. It sputtered, ran for a second, and then stopped. Carol was back looking at me very skeptically.

"Was it that motor I just heard?"

"Yes."

"You've got to be kidding?"

I cranked it again, and it ran.

There are very few times like this in the life of a man. In fact, I can think of none. I just stood there while Carol went bonkers. She was really beside herself. It was clear to me that she seriously felt I would never be able to get this lawnmower going. To tell the truth, I really never thought I would actually get it to go either. Then why did I attempt it, you ask? I don't really know. Why am I writing this book? I don't think that I really believe it will ever be published, or that I will ever become a successful author. But here I am.

For the next few months we not only transported rocks, tilled the garden, repaired lawnmowers, baked bread, built scarecrows, fought off the seven plagues of locust, flood, drought and who knows what else there was to come, but we mowed our driveway with our Lawn-Boy, came-in-a-sack, mower.

We had also put up a mailbox at the end of our road. We did this at the postmaster's insistence. For whatever reasons, he was really pushing rural Star Route number 35. I think it must have meant a job for a relative or somebody in the family, but besides making our postmaster happy, I kind of thought it would be neat to have company. It wasn't really like having company, but it would be somewhat neat to have a chat with rural route driver number 35 once or twice a week. I was looking forward to the social interaction. Other than the man at the feed store, we met practically nobody.

But we had another problem, before we could enjoy this social contact at our ranch out in the boonies, I would have to get some mail. People had stopped writing to us years ago. After all, we never had an address. What were they supposed to do? We never wrote to anybody ourselves, we were always too busy. I thought of a solution. I started sending off for seed, gardening, and fruit tree catalogues. It was kind of neat. I would walk down to the mailbox, put in my catalogue requests, close it up, and then lift up the little red flag on the box.

For the first few times, it was kind of exciting to just go down to the box and find that the flag had been lowered. This was, of course, proof positive that another human type creature had actually been out this way. As time went on both Carol and I had the urge to actually see this creature. It was kind of like the Bigfoot thing out west. You know, we've seen the tire tracks, had the outgoing mail disappear, but wouldn't it be something to actually see Star Rural Route driver number 35? I don't know about you folks, but Carol and I were both excited.

We waited down there several mornings with our coffee cups. We even brought a thermos and a third cup, anticipating that Star Rural Route driver number 35 might want to stop and chit-chat. But we just couldn't seem to get the timing right.

Finally, one lonely morning as we sat on a log behind our mail box contemplating the universe, a yellow Toyota pickup came blazing down the road. He zoomed up to our box and skidded to a stop. By the time the dust from the dirt road had cleared from our eyes, ears, nose, and throat, he was gone. I saw nothing man! I didn't really know if Star Rural Route driver number 35 was a man or a woman. We had to throw our coffee away. By the time the dust had settled, it was like river muck.

"Did you see him?" I asked Carol.

"Are you kidding?" She said spitting and coughing. "I still can't see anything."

We were a little annoyed, but it wasn't really his or her fault that the road was dusty. Star Route Rural driver number 35 wasn't responsible for rain. We would just have to be more patient, and prepared.

The next morning we were there once again with our coffee and thermos. This time we added to our wardrobes two pairs of goggles and two red polka dot bandannas that we tied over our noses and mouths as protection from the dirt and dust. On this morning the Toyota slowed as it approached the box, but even with the little red flag up, didn't bother to stop.

The next morning, we were there polka dot bandannas, coffee, and goggles intact. The Toyota rounded the bend, skidded to a stop. A hand reached out the side window through the thick cloud of dust, extracted my seed order requests, flipped down the little red flag, then skidded to a start once again. A new cloud of dirt and dust engulfed us, but suddenly we heard the Toyota's breaks squeal once again. We saw the dim glow of backup lights through the dust. Suddenly we heard a voice. It was a man's voice, and it was speaking to us.

"Your blank-ity-blank mail box is too damn high. Lower it or you won't get no mail!" As the truck sped away we heard the faint rumbling of the man's voice sputtering something about weirdos and goofballs.

We brought our new posthole diggers out to the mailbox site and lowered the box. Needless to say we no longer continued the coffee and donuts idea. We can take a hint.

As the months droned on in the wilderness, Carol and I began to run out of things to talk about. We longed for a newspaper or TV; even news of a famine or a new war sounded appealing. We went on long walks, each of us taking an opposite direction.

The garden had actually come to pass. We had zucchini squash the size of watermelons. How many damn zucchinis can two people eat a day? We had cantaloupe and cucumbers coming out of our ears. We had tomatoes, radishes, and leaf lettuce. We had pole beans, okra, and soybeans. Why we planted soybeans and okra I can't really say. We may have gotten the seeds as a free gift from one of the hundreds of seed catalogue companies I had written to. Okra? ... yuk! The more you cook it the more camel saliva it seems to puke up. Who ever invented that slop?

Finally one morning, as we sat by the fire burning seed catalogues, drinking boiled coffee and spiting out the grounds, Carol said. "What the hell are we doing here?"

Within a half an hour we had the truck loaded up with every harvestable, edible vegetable in our garden. We stopped at the first farmhouse that we came to. Told the couple who were living there, where our property was and that they could help themselves to the six rototillers, thirty five lawnmowers, and as much of the two acres of garden vegetables that they could eat.

Free at last! Free at last! Thank God Almighty; we were once again ... free at last!

19 Harvesting Oysters in the Florida Panhandle

November was approaching rapidly. We knew that we were going to head south, but where? And when we got to 'where', what then? What would we do? We felt that it was time to sit down and discuss this. The question was, if you could live anywhere in the United States, where would it be? The question was not really - what would we do. We would do whatever was available in the area, that's what.

We listed our priorities. We wanted to be near or around some kind of water. It could be a lake, a river, a bay or an ocean.

Next, we both agreed, snow was out. Neither of us were winter sport enthusiasts. We were both raised in cold, snowy, winter areas, and it just didn't seem to us to be worth the effort. Our choice was not restricted by job opportunity as with most folks, because there was always another lousy job right down the road. In fact, every place we have been in the U.S. always seemed to be overflowing with one lousy job after another. So, if our choice in life was to do lousy jobs, one locale seemed to be just as good as another.

In the back of one's mind, I guess everyone hopes to find that perfect place, just as we all seek that perfect mate, but end up settling for each other. And a lucky thing that is, because otherwise most of us would have nobody.

We also had a second notion. Let's find a neat retirement place, and beat the baby boomer rush that would be coming after they all got their children raised and off to work. If we got there first, we could establish something at a reasonable price. By the time the frenzy started, we would be all paid for and settled.

So, where were we? No snow; water a must; what else did we want? Carol wanted to be able to grow a garden, and I wanted trees. I liked touring out west, but the thoughts of living in a land of deserts, boulders, and mesas didn't really excite me.

We had just left Oklahoma, and Arkansas, what was left? Southern California, or someplace in the South seemed to be about it. Southern California was much too expensive, and much too crowded. It would have to be someplace in the South.

Mississippi, Georgia and Alabama seemed to us to be pretty much a family affair. Atlanta was growing but we really didn't want any big city.

The Gulf coast of Texas was a possibility, Corpus Christi, Padre Island, Port Isabel. But all we could remember about those places was the wind, even when they weren't experiencing a hurricane.

What about good old Florida? Florida did feel like home. Carol and I had met and married in Fort Lauderdale. Central Florida was a beautiful area, even if we did something other than pick oranges. Southern Florida was just too crowded. What about the Florida Panhandle? We had met Marge and Eldon and camped on an island one time. What was the name of that place? ... Saint George Island, yeah, that was it. That was really a neat place. It somewhat reminded us of the Keys, yet not so touristy.

The Island itself was pretty much deserted, no high rises anywhere. It was a little too far north for most Snowbirds. But as southern and central Florida got more and more jammed where would they go next? There were a number of campgrounds in the area, and there seemed to be some goofy job opportunities to explore.

This one little town on the mainland called Eastpoint had all of these little oyster shacks lining the waterfront. We had observed people catching oysters when we were there. They had quaint, little boats that dotted the bay, right by the St. George Island Bridge. Many of the boats had a husband and wife team working them. We had met a few on our stay there way back when. It was right on the Gulf. It had lots of trees and no snow. It did seem that there was work there; work that looked interesting, at least to a Mr. and Mrs. Hobo.

It was agreed. We set our compass for St. George Island, Eastpoint and Apalachicola Bay.

Our first night back in Florida, we camped aside a stretch of roadway overlooking the Gulf of Mexico. The sunset that evening was so spectacular that it made us wonder why we ever considered living anyplace else. The only place that I had ever seen a more dramatic sunset was from the road outside the apple cannery in Sebastopol California. The size of the sun in California was, without a doubt, the biggest that I had ever seen, but the colors of this Florida sunset were really beyond description. I mean purple, rouge, flaming red, yellow, green, blue and various shades in between, all melting together. The whole sky, all along the horizon, was lit up.

"Welcome home," I said to Carol as we stood there on the shore line with the traffic buzzing behind us as if nothing were happening.

"We've always got to remember to do this," I said. "These are the moments, the ones that you will remember. Days, years will all be forgotten, but moments like this will linger on for the rest of our lives."

We didn't know if the oystering industry would be all wrapped up and a family sort of an affair. But certainly, I could get a job unloading trucks or working at one of them little, oyster houses or something. That is, if there weren't too many restrictions on the oystering itself.

We really figured that oystering would be like lobstering up in Maine. The permits and licenses alone would cost you a fortune, more than likely. Then, what about a boat and a motor? And then, how would one find the oysters, and all of that sort of stuff. You know - Murphy's Law.

We arrived in Apalachicola on the first Saturday in November. That is the date of the annual Apalachicola Seafood Festival. It was cold. We took a spin down to the festival on our motorcycle, after we had found a campground to stay at.

Basically we pulled into the first campground we came to. It was in the middle of Eastpoint, and it was right on the water, but you wouldn't know it for all the campers crowded along the water's edge.

That next day we began nosing around. The man who owned the campground struck up a conversation with us.

"How does one go about getting into this oystering business?" I asked. The man gave me a strange look, and then asked.

"Why would you want to do that?"

"It looks like fun," I said.

The man pondered us both for a moment. Then he led us into the street and pointed down the road.

"Take your first left down there at the dirt road. There is a campground down there. You talk to the guy who owns that place and he'll set you up."

"What do you mean ... he'll set us up?"

"Well, he rents oyster boats and the stuff that goes with it."

"You're kidding? You can rent a boat? We don't want to be like tourist, you know. We want to make a living at it."

The man laughed.

"I'm sure you do. And that man down there is the one you want to talk to. He'll help you get at it."

We packed up everything and carted ourselves over to this dirt road. The road dead-ended at the water's edge. From there you could look out on all the oyster boats lined up along the island bridge.

This so called campground was something out of a Steven King novel. There were lots of ramshackle temporary dwellings in there, but none that I would consider a legitimate camping apparatus.

Some of them were shells of old campers with no wheels and drift wood additions. Others were combinations of old trailers and anything that might be laying around. Most had broken doors, aluminum foil on the windows and a dog suffering from the mange sleeping underneath.

There were live people wandering around this place. They all were wearing white boots, and carrying a beer can or a pint, whiskey bottle.

The inhabitants were the raggediest, most fearsome band of riff-raff that I had ever seen anywhere in my travels. You could put a dozen of them together and you wouldn't accumulate one full set of teeth. Thoughts began to enter into my mind that I hadn't had for quite some time. Like where had I stored that shotgun? Was it in the bathroom closet, or was it above the bed? How could a person forget something like that anyway? What about my pistol? Where had I stored that? Why hadn't I ever taken karate lessons? Even little kids today knew Karate.

What was I thinking? I began checking my path for retreat out of this Pirate Cove. One guy even had a patch over his eye, and another guy had no nose. No nose, man! People from each of these hovels began crawling out to check us out. I turned to Carol with a dubious look on my face, but she wasn't there. She had gotten out of the truck and was "mingling".

I had married an insane person. What was wrong with her? I watched for a few moments. No one was attempting to rape her and cut her up with a broken beer bottle. Some of them were even beginning to smile. What could she possibly be talking to them about? Very reluctantly, I exited the truck.

"This is it!" Carol exclaimed.

This was what? I thought. What in the world is she talking about?

"This is it!" she exclaimed once again. "What a place this is, huh?"

Was she serious? I took another look around. There was what looked to be a public bath just behind us. Both doors were broken off, but yet still hanging there. The entire area was littered with beer cans, broken glass, spent wine and whiskey bottles, old wooden boats, and random pieces of outboard motor.

But, Carol had me curious. She was a smart girl, as far as I was concerned. She even had artistic tendencies. She could paint and draw. Oftentimes she saw things that I wasn't seeing. Could I be missing something here?

"What do you see, Carol?" I said putting my arm over her shoulder.

"Look at this place!" she said enthusiastically. I looked around once again. This time I saw more debris. I saw garbage bags that had obviously been torn apart by mange infested dogs in search for food and as I scanned the area, my vision stopped on the face of a man not more than two feet away from me. He was drinking a can of beer. His face was beat up like he had just been bludgeoned in an alley the night before or something. He was wearing no shoes, and his feet were black with dirt. He wasn't wearing a shirt, and every inch of him looked to be muscle. Not bulging and rippling like some body builder; just hard and firm, workingman muscle. He was smiling in a very friendly manner. He nodded; then moseyed on past us.

"I'm looking, Carol, I'm looking."

"Look out here," she said. "Look out at the water. Look at the little boats out on the bay. Look at the island off in the distance. Can you imagine living right here along the water's edge. Can you imagine our camper parked right there. We just crawl out of bed every morning listening to the water roll up onto the beach. We drink our morning coffee while we walk the beach and watch the sun come up behind the island. Can you believe it? This would be like living on an island in the South Pacific."

I began feeling a big shortage of imagination. My wife was an artist at heart, and she was painting a picture. She was brushing out all the negatives. She was painting in, all the beauty, and ignoring all of the ugly. Why couldn't I do that? I took another look at the place, brushing out all the ugly in any way I could.

It was kind of like this planet earth; trashed all over by us humans, but yet still, the beauty shining through, if you had the vision for it. Here, in this spot in particular, that was a big "if" and not an easy one to swallow. Again though, wasn't this like all of our relationships? Wasn't this like Santa Claus and the Tooth Fairy, and Tinkerbell. All one has to do is believe.

Wasn't this like everybody? First you see their big noses, then their misshapen heads, then the wart on their forehead, the hairs growing out of their noses and ears, their skinny legs, or big butts. Then after awhile, after you get to know them a little better, all that you see is the sparkle in their eyes, the joy of their grin, and the warmth of their friendship. Suddenly there are no warts; there are no misshapen heads and skinny legs - there's just people. People pretty much like you. How does that happen?

Well, it does happen. It happened to us right there at Harrington Billinger's campground by the sea. We lived and worked right there for the next three years. I can still remember standing there and watching Harrington Billinger, throw out his old crankshaft anchor, jump into the water, turn, snatch his tiny wife up off the deck, and carry her to the shore. Not a sight that you see everyday in the real world. They were laughing and giggling all the way.

I could paint that picture: Visualize a choppy sea in the background; the winter tide out; the naked bay bottom exposed for twenty five, fifty yards; Harrington in his slicker suit and waders; his wife in his arms; she, all bundled up, a white apron smeared with oyster mud, over everything, and both of them laughing and giggling all the way to shore.

I think that this picture of a couple coming home after a hard days work, laughing and in each others arms, was a part of the allure. Years later, when Carol and I were both established "Oyster People" Carol would joke from our boat's walk rail, as she pretended in a helpless petite way, to be Mrs. Billinger ... "Carry me honey?"

Carol was no Mrs. Billinger. In fact, she has joked of weighing more than Mrs. Billinger on the day of her birth.

Finally one day, as she petitioned petitely, I snatched her up around the knees, flopped her onto my shoulder, and lugged her to the shore like a sack of potatoes. I can still hear her screams and giggles and her belly bouncing up and down on my shoulder as I hauled her in.

We had our first interview with our prospective new boss right there. He told us he had a boat and a pair of oyster tongs that he could rent to us right then, but he didn't have any motor.

That next morning we were off about the country-side shopping for a twenty to twenty-five horsepower outboard motor. We went to every motor dealership in the area, but could find nothing in our budget. We didn't want to spend a bunch of money, just to find out that we didn't like oystering. We had just about given up our tour and were on our way home when we saw a sign tacked to a tree advertising outboard motors for sale.

The man showed us this old twenty-five horsepower, Johnson outboard. He demonstrated its seaworthiness by putting it into a fifty gallon drum filled with water and "cranking" it up. It started, it accelerated, and it went into forward and reverse.

"How much do you want for it?" I asked.

"How does three hundred dollars sound?"

"Sounds like you made a sale."

By that next morning, we were once again productive citizens. We were not only employed, we were self-employed. The rent for our boat was one bag of oysters per trip out on the bay.

We had absolutely no idea what we were doing. The first thing we found out was that the oysters were all stuck together, and somehow had to be broken apart. We had brought our tool box, just in case our motor had a problem. We got out a hammer and a screwdriver, and began operating on the oysters. The oysters themselves, in many cases, were almost indistinguishable. Some of them just looked like balls of coral. Many of the balls were just six or seven oysters all grown together into one mess. With that hammer and screwdriver we made mince meat out of those things that day.

But we were out on the water, in a boat; a boat with a motor, and we were doing it. We were oystering.

We named our boat, bail-a-little, sail-a-little. The boat leaked like a sieve. After I would finish tonging up a bunch of oyster balls, I would go to the back of the boat with a plastic bucket and bail the boat down to a point of security.

For those few of you out there who may never have had the experience of catching oysters, I will explain.

First, finding an oyster bed is very simple. All you have to do is find another oyster boat working on the bay. Secondly, you don't really have to "catch" an oyster. They are not really running around on the bottom out there. In fact, a baby oyster, or spawn or larvae swims for less than twenty four hours in its entire life. As soon as it is born, it immediately looks for something to grab onto. And you would too, because everything else out there is trying to eat you.

A larvae or spawn attaches itself to something, a bridge piling, a rock, and old tire, anything. From that point on, it is called a spat. A spat's favorite thing to attach to is an oyster shell; hence, all the clusters or clumps of oysters that I was telling you about.

If an oyster bed is not cultivated, it will grow into one huge mass of shell, like a coral reef, I guess. The oysters in Apalachicola bay have been cultivated for decades. The oysters in Apalachicola bay and the Gulf of Mexico, in general, rarely live much longer than one year.

The warm water in the Gulf of Mexico makes the oyster extremely prolific, but also mass produces its enemies.

Among its enemies is a parasite named Dermo-cistidium-marium, or Dermo for short. It gets into the oyster, originally by way of the bonea snail, they think. But, for the most part, the parasite is transferred from one oyster to another by the infected meat of other dying oysters.

Dermo eventually weakens the oyster muscle. The oyster then becomes too weak to keep its mouth shut. Predators then devour it. Sloppy eaters that predators tend to be, they spread it everywhere.

Once an oyster bed is infected with this parasite, it is, for all practical purposes, impossible to eradicate. This parasite is not harmful to human beings so the trick is in catching the oysters, before they become too severely infected and become fish food rather than people food. That means catching the oyster at a size of three inches or less. Actually two and a half to two and three quarters inches would be the size that would yield the greatest abundance.

But, you ask, how does one catch an oyster? Well, as you have just learned, you first need a boat and a motor. Next you need the hand harvesting implement known as a pair of hand, harvesting tongs. Criticism of this age old method of hand harvesting via tongs has led many to refer to these harvesting tongs as idiot sticks. I myself would not be inclined to use this term, as far as I have seen, they have not yet been able to devise a more efficient, safer, non polluting method of harvesting or cultivating oysters than this method.

All attempts at aquaculture techniques in oyster growing and harvesting have been abysmal failures in the Gulf of Mexico. Such an attempt was made not too long ago here in Apalachicola bay.

This extravaganza cost the American taxpayer millions of dollars, and grew relatively few oysters. The big problem here is that Mother Nature can successfully sacrifice a million spat in order to sustain the life of one full grown oyster. But one must remember Mother Nature has many other mouths to feed and does not consider this a sacrifice at all. But to an aquafarmer who must buy his seed or spat, such a sacrifice is not economical.

These tongs are anywhere from ten to twenty feet long. Traditionally the handles were constructed of oak, or ash, but today most are made of pine.

The "heads", or the part that goes down into the water and sits on the bottom, are constructed of metal. I think they would be best described as two interlocking rakes. These heads have teeth on them similar to a garden rake.

The wooden handles have a pivot point in the center. The man operating the tongs is standing on a walk-way extending along the side of his boat. When he separates the handles, the heads open up on the bottom. He then bounces, scrapes, and digs the tongs along the bottom. He gradually closes up the handles and bunches up oysters inside the heads. The teeth on the heads eventually close and interlock, thus trapping the oysters in a kind of basket. He then hauls the heads, by way of the handles, up to the surface.

He dumps the clumps, and mounds, or as the harvest improves into the season, the "single", cultivated oysters onto a plywood sheet called a culling board.

The "culler" then has the job of separating the catch into legal three inch size oysters, and smaller illegal size oysters. The legal oysters are put into a crocus sack, or burlap bag via a bottomless five gallon plastic pail, or a similar bottomless ten gallon metal garbage pail.

Believe it or not, they actually sell these bottomless garbage cans at the local hardware store here in town. I wonder what tourists must think when they see these garbage cans with no bottoms.

On our first day we caught four bags of oysters. The oysters were selling for four dollars a 60 lb. bag. We earned a gross of sixteen dollars; less one bag for the boat, and whatever it had cost us for gas and oil. Not to mention the thirty dollar fine we received for not having the proper lifesaving flotation devices. We were told by Harrington that a floatable seat cushion was adequate, but the Marine Patrol Officer who checked us didn't agree with Harrington.

Harrington and the other observers at the dock thought we would be ready to quit for sure, but strangely enough Carol and I were thrilled. We were doing it! We had actually netted twelve dollars, approximately - not counting the fine. And this was just our first day!

We knew that we would improve. We knew, as with orange picking, our techniques would get better. Ten bags a day seemed entirely possible. On the second day we caught six. The third day we had eight. Carol had switched from culling with a hammer and screwdriver to a small hatchet. Without doubt we killed and destroyed more oysters than we ever got into a bag.

Finally Harrington took pity on us. He pulled up along side of Bail-a-little-sail-a-little, squatted down onto our culling board and demonstrated the technique of separating the oysters, with a real culling iron.

A real culling iron was just a long flat piece of metal, about two inches wide and eight to ten inches long, with a piece of rubber hose wrapped around one end for a handle or gripping area.

The way he tossed that formless clump around in his hand, and tapped lightly here and then lightly there, and dissolved that mass into five or six acceptable oysters without killing or destroying one live oyster was amazing. We were lucky to get one live oyster out of a clump, and it took minutes of banging and bitter pounding to do that. Harrington did it with grace and skill, no pounding, no banging, no cursing.

Honestly, this may sound crazy, but watching Harrington at work was like watching an artist play the piano, or Charlie Bird plucking his guitar. Carol and I had huge grins on our faces, and by the end of that day alone, we were immediately up to twelve bags. Within the month we were harvesting fifteen acceptable bags per day. Within a year, we were up to twenty. As time went on we got better and better. The most bags we ever harvested in one day was forty. The most money that we ever made in one day of harvesting oysters was three hundred and sixty-five dollars. But that was because the price of oysters had risen to seventeen dollars a bag due to a drought or something, and we were lucky enough to stumble onto a spot that had been passed over by everybody else.

Needless to say we were in love with oystering. It wasn't long before we had a new forty-horse, workhorse model, Johnson outboard. That next year we had our own boat made to our personal tastes. The next year we had our own trailer made, so that we could travel to the best spots. At this rate of pay it sounds like we were becoming wealthy, but that was hardly the case. There are other factors in the oystering business that limit one's income. Weather was a factor. Season of the year, was a factor. Whether or not the dealer to whom you sold your oysters had orders that week or not, was a large factor. All in all we made more money oystering than at any migratory job we had thus found – which really was not all that much. Most likely we were still in the "poverty" category.

We found an acre on the outskirts of town and put a down payment on it. The man was willing to do the financing himself. Little by little we improved the land while still living at Harrington Billinger's campground by the sea. We adopted a pair of kittens that we named Bogie, and Buddy. Buddy was the true love of my life. She was a super special kitty. I miss her.

It took us a year to get a septic and a light pole put onto the property. After that was accomplished we pulled our travel trailer onto the property, and stopped paying rent. I consider that to be a major accomplishment in my life.

It is something I know most people don't think about. Probably because they have always had it or because they think they will never have it. But, it is very, very important. When I think about it, one of the reasons we left the Miami-Fort Lauderdale area was the fact that it would have taken us twenty to thirty years of fulltime employment to pay for a home. The home that we have today may not be the envy of society, or even my neighbors, but it is ours. I pay no rent to anyone. We accomplished the whole deal in six years of working at what would amount to minimum wage jobs.

I have always thought of the oystering business as the perfect factory system. Truthfully, I have never been involved in anything to compare with it.

If for example, you can imagine a factory in which the owner could become a millionaire, as many have, or just get by, as others have done depending on their ambition and ability. And the workers could pretty much do as they pleased, you have the oystering industry.

As a worker, you could go to work or not go to work. You never had to call in sick. If you were ambitious and wanted to make a goodly amount, you could work everyday that was available, and as long as you wanted between the hours of sunrise and sunset.

If the orders were there, you could work everyday of the month. But, if all that you wanted from life was a pocketknife, a baloney sandwich and a six-pack of beer, you could do that also. It was all up to you. There aren't or should I say weren't many factories in America that could make such a boast.

Those that love oystering say that it is not a job but a way of life, like you hear farmers say. I never understood what that meant, but I have a better understanding of it now.

I shouldn't leave this section, without a few words about life at Harrington Billinger's campground by the sea.

Harrington was himself quite a character. I consider him to be a real classic type American. He was older than I and had served in World War II. He told me that he was in the first wave of soldiers to land on Normandy Beach in France. Yet he wasn't a wave-the-flag kind of a guy. He was very critical of the government and its policies. To be honest with you, from my experience this seems to be a universal all American characteristic. This tradition goes back to Will Rogers, and before him Mark Twain, and before him Tom Paine. But, without any doubt, being critical of American Government, whatever your political view is as American as apple pie.

I like this story about Harrington and the Marine patrol in particular.

Harrington had just come in from a hard day of oystering. He was storming up the dock like Winston Churchill. He was waving in his hand, a ticket he had just received from a Marine Patrol officer for undersized oysters. This type of fine was very common. He was sputtering, screaming, yelling, and cursing in the true tradition of a seafaring man. I had never seen him quite so vocal or so animated. His face was so red I thought he was going to explode. His speech was so hot that it was slurred, and he was nearly spitting over himself to the point of a drool. I don't know why but the sight of a man in his condition just makes me laugh. Believe me, I have been there many times myself. Harrington's outrage was beyond description.

"Harrington? What happened?" I asked. He related the whole outrageous story to me. Of course, the story was only outrageous in his opinion. But his punch line was;

"So I told them SOB's to get the hell off my boat."

This may sound rather strange to you, but every oysterman was a Captain. This courtesy was even afforded to the Oystermen by the Marine Patrol. For example, when a Marine Patrol would pull up along side of your boat he would say. "Captain, may I have permission to board your vessel?" This I always thought somewhat funny. You know, like a traffic cop stopping you and asking permission to approach your vehicle. Like you can say no, right! What can you do about it?

In any case, Harrington told the Marine Patrol to get the hell off his boat. I wondered; does this have something to do with the law of the sea or something? You know, like they need a search warrant to defile the sanctity of your home. You know, a man's home is his castle, and in it he was King. Was this Captain stuff something like this? Could a Captain actually throw a Marine Patrol off his boat and then they had to go get a search warrant or something?

"Can you really do that, Harrington?"

"Of course you can do it. I just told you that I did it, didn't I?"

"Yes, I know you just told me. But when you tell the Marine Patrol to get off your boat, is there a law that says that they have to get off?" Harrington paused for a second. The wind from his sails was slightly deflated, but then with a huff and a puff, instantly regained.

"Hell no, he don't have to get off your boat ... BUT YOU CAN TELL HIM! You're damn right you can tell him. This is America. I can tell anybody any damn thing I want!"

"Yes, but what good does it do? You can tell him, but he don't have to go?"

"Done me a lot of good; saved me a lifetime in prison. It stopped me from killing him, didn't it?"

Here is another Harrington Billinger gem.

Some camping friends of ours stopped by the campground one day to say hello. They had just recently retired, and had celebrated their retirement by taking a trip to Europe. They were just thrilled. Harrington had joined us and was sitting in one of our lawn chairs sipping on a can of beer. When our friends had just about exhausted themselves expounding on their wonderful adventure, one of them turned to Harrington.

"Have you ever been to Europe, Mister Billinger?"

"Yes, I have."

"And what did you think of it?"

"Well, to be quite frank, I didn't care for it."

"Really, and what in particular didn't you like about it?"

"Well, the thing that annoyed me most about it was the fact that every time I poked up my head to try and get a look at it, somebody tried to shoot it off."

20 Shucking Oysters, and Troubles in Paradise

We lived in our travel trailer on our acre for some time. Today, I don't think that it would be permitted. But back in the good old days, nobody seemed to care. We had a septic and a light pole and we weren't bothering anybody.

To tell the truth we didn't really intend to live in our travel trailer as long as we did. But no sooner had we gotten ourselves into debt, with monthly payments on the land, than the town of Eastpoint got hit with both barrels. Hurricane Elena and Hurricane Kate both struck within months of one another. We weren't damaged, personally a great deal, but the bay and its oyster beds were hurt severely. In fact, the damage was so bad that we were all put out of business. They closed the bay to oyster harvesting for an entire year.

Believe it or not, Carol and I are really economically conservative. We always stayed out of debt. We felt that there would be no way to maintain our Hobo lifestyle and cart around a payment book. You can't imagine the debate and soul searching that we engaged in when considering the purchase of our land.

To be honest, I was against settling permanently anywhere. I considered gypsy-ism a perfect way of life. I actually wrote an article about it that was purchased by the Mother Earth News. As far as I know, they never printed or published it.

We added everything up to the penny and dime. We weren't going to buy something on time and lose it. After months of calculating and debating, we finally put our butts out on a limb to buy our little acre out on a dirt road at the end of town. And, no sooner do we get moved onto it, than whammo, we are out of work.

Compared to most, we had a very small debt, but we also had a very small income. With no oystering, we had no income. Since we were self employed, we had no unemployment compensation either. It was a very "scrappy" year. But when we bought the land, we decided that this would be our home, so for the first time in our careers we had to dig in like a couple of moles, or like everyone else, I suppose.

Many oystermen went to Alabama to catch oysters out there. We decided to get a job downtown shucking oysters that were imported from other states. Most jobs were taken, but the new fellow we were now working for, had decided to try his hand at the shucking business.

I really, honestly and truly thought that shucking oysters would be a picnic when compared to the difficulties involved in catching oysters. To catch oysters you had the expense and maintenance of a boat, a motor, gasoline, tongs, gloves, culling irons, slicker suits, waders etc. On top of that you had bad weather to contend with. I don't know how many times we found our boat washed up along the shore due to a bad storm during the middle of the night.

That first three hundred dollar motor was constantly under repair, and we repaired it ourselves. We had that motor torn apart as often as we had it running. In fact, at one point we had to carry it to shore every night and work on it, in order to have it in good enough shape to get us out in the morning.

Sometimes I would be working outside the trailer in the dark with a flashlight or light on an extension cord until ten or eleven at night, after working ten or twelve hours catching oysters all that day. But to tell you the truth, we never really thought that much about it because everybody else in the business did pretty much the same thing. It was all just a part of "the oystering way of life".

Now we were going to get the opportunity to shuck oysters; no water, no boat, no waves, no white caps, no lightening, no thunderstorms, no side seas, no getting seasick.

Believe it or not Carol got seasick everyday that we oystered until she discovered Dramamine.

Shucking oysters had to be nothing but a joy and a pleasure compared to the perils of life on the treacherous high seas.

We couldn't understand why all the local people were so hateful of shucking. A boast of many an Eastpoint citizen was that no matter how bad things got in life, they never had to stoop so low as to shuck an oyster.

How hard could shucking oysters be? You're inside a building, out of the weather. You stand in one spot all day. You sit down or take a break when you feel like it. What's the problem here?

After a month of shucking oysters, I began to truly have my doubts about the existence of God. Oh man! It didn't take long for the old "chicken back" to be re-awakened.

Chicken back is the name Carol and I had given to the pain that occurs between your shoulder blades when you stand in any one place for a long period of time with your arms held out in front of you. I think this was once a Nazi concentration camp torture. We first experienced this type of pain when we worked at the chicken factory in Arkansas. A knot forms right between your shoulder blades, and then just cramps. It feels very similar to the night cramp that might knot up your calf, or the back of your thigh, but this cramp just doesn't go away, and you can't reach it to rub it.

Then there's the pain in your legs and your feet, and your hands and your fingers. I don't know why but this job caused me so much pain and in so many different places, that there were times I actually went pale, and had to stop for a break or I would have puked. And now that you know the basics, let me tell you how to shuck an oyster.

The traditional way to shuck an oyster is with a block and a hammer. The block was made out of metal or iron. The block sat on the counter in your shucking stall. The shucking stall, as it was called, was concrete. Today the stalls are stainless steel. The stall is more or less a cubical, or a counter with three sides. It stands at about waist high. The oysters would be shoveled up onto this counter.

At the front edge of this counter would be a hole, and inside the hole, a shoot. The shoot was a six inch P.V.C. pipe. After you shucked the oyster, you would throw the shells into the hole. They would then slide down the P.V.C. pipe shoot, and land on the ground outside.

A backhoe would load the shells in a dump truck at the end of each day. From there they usually went somewhere to be stored and dried. Then they were sold for fill, or drain fields, or driveways, or whatever.

The metal block that sat on the counter was about an eight inch square block. It had a three inch perpendicular metal tongue sticking up on the top of it. You would place the bill of the oyster so that it overlapped the edge of this tongue, and then you would chip it off with your hammer.

An oyster has two sides or ends. One end is called the heel, and the other is the bill. Most people who are shucking oysters for a raw bar or for personal consumption, heel the oyster. When I shuck them at home I heel them. In this process you use the shucking knife like a combination wedge, and pry bar. But for most people involved in commercial shucking, heeling is not fast enough. So they either use the block and hammer technique, or they buy a shucking machine.

After you chip the bill end of the oyster off with your hammer and block, you then insert your shucking knife into the small hole that you have caused. You slide your knife along the inside of the top shell, cutting the top part of the oyster muscle away from the inside shell. Then you flip the top shell into the hole and roll your knife under the oyster and cut the muscle away from the bottom inside shell. If this is done quickly enough, you won't even hear the oyster scream.

You do know that the oyster is alive while you are doing all of this? In fact the next time that you eat fresh raw oysters at a restaurant or raw bar take a good look at the oyster before you eat it. If it is really fresh, at the center you will be able to see the oyster's heart still beating right through the semi-translucent membrane. But even then if you act quickly enough and get it into your mouth, while the oyster is still in shock, you will not hear it scream. You may hear a tiny little whimper or groan, but that is usually coming for the other quests at your own table.

Now you slide the oyster off its bottom shell and into a stainless steel one gallon shucking pail that is usually half filled with ice water. This is done in lieu of refrigeration.

Carol and I tried the hammer and block technique for a week or two, but we really didn't do that well. So we went out shopping for shucking machines.

The shucking machine, as I understand it, was actually invented right here in Apalachicola bay. We met one of the two partners who claimed to have invented the machine. Our machine consisted of an all brass, non rustable framework topped off with a half horsepower sump-pump motor. All the gaskets and seals were adapted from local outboard motor parts. The later model shucking machines are adapted from conventional bench grinders.

An oyster machine doesn't really shuck the oyster for you. All that it actually does is replace the block and hammer. You still have to flip the shells and cut away the oyster.

At one end of the machine sits a rotating star shaped blade. The edges at each point of the star are blunt edged chipping devices. As the motor on the top spins the blade at the bottom via a connecting shaft, you slide the bill of the oyster along a protective guide until the chipping edges of the star blade chips off enough of the bill to leave a hole. At that point you do your thing with the knife as I explained above.

Okay, now that you have this information, you should be able to go anywhere within these United States wherever oysters are being shucked, and within a month or two of concentrated effort, be able to work yourself up to minimum wage.

A complete year of oyster shucking had finally drudged by. We had managed to make all of our payments on our land and we were happy. The bay was getting ready to open. The entire oystering community was excited. People who had gone to other areas were returning home. The streets and highway were beginning to look alive once again. Outside of fishing and oystering there was no other industry in the county.

We had gotten our boat, motor and gear all ready to go when the dealers announced the price that they intended to pay the oystermen for opening day. It was six dollars per bushel. This announcement caused a very serious rumble throughout the county. For the last year the dealers had been paying anywhere from fifteen to twenty-five dollars per bushel. Oysters were scarce and the demand was high. Apalachicola bay was responsible for ninety percent of the oysters that were consumed in the state of Florida, and ten percent of those consumed in the entire United States. Local oystermen had been driving the trucks that were hauling the oysters here from out of state, and doing the shucking and the processing.

All the numbers were now public information. The oystermen knew what a dealer paid for an oyster, and what he sold it for. The oystermen knew how many oysters it took to make a gallon, and what a gallon sold for. All the economics of the oyster business were now public information. The oysters were in high demand, costumers were begging. Since the bay had been shut down oysters were a restricted commodity all over the state of Florida. The oystermen and their families had been discussing for months the prospects of a good price for oysters when the bay opened. Six dollars per bag was considered a rock bottom price. Even if there were a lot of oysters out on the beds, after a year of neglect, they would need a lot of work before anyone would be catching any record amounts.

None of the oystermen knew what to do, but nobody ran to their boats. Talk of a strike was hot and heavy. Carol and I didn't even bother to put our boat back into the water. It was too discouraging. Besides, we were now accustomed to shucking oysters. We were getting by and we didn't have all of the expenses of oystering. Our boss asked us when we were going back to our oyster boat for our living. We told him that we were not, and that as long as there was oyster shucking to do, we wouldn't.

I guess that was the wrong thing to say because within the week oyster shucking was shut off. Our boss suddenly decided to buy his shucked oysters from somebody else. Now we were without any income at all. There were virtually no other jobs within this community.

We thought of leaving town and going south to pick oranges until this whole thing blew over. Tempers were really getting hot. When we had made the decision to put our first down payment on our land, Carol and I had both decided that Franklin County would be our home. To pack up now seemed somehow a sign of defeat. We had made it here in Franklin County for a number of years, now. We had even gotten through this last very difficult year.

"If we are going to stay here," I told her. "Let's develop a framework for our own success and safety. Don't get involved with the oystermen and their problems, and don't get involved with the dealers and their excuses. Let's just concentrate on our own personal goals. There are always problems. No human beings are ever satisfied with what they have in life, no mater how much or how little. So let's not become like them. Let's just do our own thing and mind our own business. Smile, say good morning to everybody, don't take any side, and just go on about our own business."

That was our original plan, but as the tension mounted, it was decided that if we were going to stay and make our home here, it would be necessary to take a side. If the whole town were to go on strike, what were we to do? Sit home and watch TV? We felt the dealers decision to pay low prices was not warranted. We were a part of the working community. We would do whatever the other workers did.

It wasn't long before the whole county was shut down. This strike had to be the biggest strike in Franklin County history. Oystermen were picketing in Apalachicola, Eastpoint, and Carrabelle, twenty four hours a day. If I'm not mistaken the strike lasted two or three weeks, my wife says three of four days, but I know that it was longer than that, too many things happened.

I don't know what the dealer's point of view was in this situation, but in their defense many of them were probably hurting economically themselves. They probably looked at this as an opportunity to make up for lost ground. But whatever, it got very, very serious. Many dealers had guns. Some came out into the streets with revolvers and guns threatening the crowd. Many other dealers, it was reported around town, stayed up all night guarding their property and buildings against vandalism and threatened arson. This was also a hell of a time for the local sheriff's office.

Throughout the whole ordeal I kept admonishing Carol to keep a low profile. She won't admit it now, but she looked to be a little suffragette. It wasn't that she was so vocal or anything. It was just that every time I turned around she seemed to be in the middle of everything.

One day we were assigned by the "union" guy to picket in front of this one oyster house. Nobody really wanted to go there because this particular dealer was acting somewhat violent. This may be selfish, but if anybody was going to be shot, I wanted it to NOT be my wife.

In any case, there we were. We were out in front of this guy's building marching up and down with our little picket signs. I don't even know what the sign said. All I can remember was that whatever was written on it was spelled wrong. But who cares, everybody was getting the point. Suddenly a TV news truck pulls up and the cameramen and guys with portable microphones start running over towards our picket line. I ran over to Carol.

"Don't talk to anybody! Don't say a word! If one of us is on TV we will never work again in this town. You can kiss the land goodbye. You can kiss our future here in Franklin County goodbye. If they try to take your picture cover your face with the sign, and just keep moving."

As a last warning, I told her to get at the end of her line. She nodded her head up and down and did exactly what I said.

My line was marching north and her line was marching south. I was happy. My line came to the end of the guy's property that we were picketing and then just kind of snaked and curled back around. When I looked down at Carol's line, I couldn't believe my eyes. There she was right up front. She was the first one in the line as it came back. For some reason their line didn't snake around. Everybody just did an about face, and there was Carol marching straight for the TV camera. Not only that, one of the owners was out there in the street taking film of her with his personal home video camera.

I was in shock. There was Carol with her stupid misspelled sign high above her head, marching towards the camera with a big smile on her face, looking like a modern day Susan B. Anthony. And don't you know it; the man with the mic picked her out of everybody for his interview.

That night Carol was on the phone calling all the Florida relatives instructing them to watch the channel six news, to see if they could catch her interview. And that weekend her picture was bottom front page in the Panama City Herald - just what we needed in our personal struggle for survival in our newly adopted home. And you know everyone in town was already in love with us "Yankees", as they called us. The next thing I knew, the rumor was that it was all of us damn Yankees who had started this whole mess. Believe me that was the furthest from the truth.

But, I will tell you, this was a strange strike. The families who owned the buildings were the relatives of the people in the streets holding the signs. I was standing with a couple of guys one day, when one guy says;

"We oughta just burn down Biggie Turner's whole damn place."

"Oh no," the other man said. "Uncle Biggie ain't really that bad. He's just bein' a little greedy at the moment."

"This building belongs to your uncle?" I interjected.

"Oh yeah, well, it's his cousin too," my co-striker said pointing to the man who suggested burning down the building. "He didn't really mean it when he said he was going to burn Biggie's building down. He'd just like to, but he won't."

At one point, one of the owners came out into the street, and slapped his striking sister in the face.

I thought I had seen everything when one morning a window opened on one of the oyster houses. The woman who owned that particular house stuck her head out and yelled;

"Elroy! You get your butt up here right now."

"No way, mom!" Elroy, a striker in the street, yelled back up to his mother. "I signed up for four hours of picketing, and I'm going to do it."

The next thing I knew there was Elroy's mom, down in the street. She had a house broom in her hands and was swatting old Elroy every which way. Nevertheless, Elroy wouldn't leave the line. He picketed his four hours, and I imagine got no supper when he went home that night.

One day the fellow next to me started yelling at a woman who was crossing the picket line to shuck oysters in one of the houses.

"Don't you go in there, Helen! You get home with the kids where you belong."

"Don't you tell me what to do," The woman said with tears streaming down her face. "You may be my husband but you don't own me."

"But you're making me look like a damn fool standing out here, while you go in there and go to work."

"You are a damn fool. And if I follow you, none of us will have anything to eat, and we will both be out of a job."

It was quite a bad time, but as far as I know everyone lived through it. Carol and I survived. Not only that, we managed to pay off our land and re-establish our debt in the form of a new mobile home. I had never lived in a home of my own. It really meant something to me, and still does.

But no sooner had we established this new mobile home debt when the oyster crop began to fail. As I have since learned, we were experiencing some drought years.

Drought caused the fresh water content to drop in the bay, and the saltwater content to increase, or something like that. In any case, the oysters were dying by the ton. Oystermen were leaving the bay in "bushels". Carol and I were seriously considering quitting.

I began to wonder to myself, if this was the course of all people who try to settle down? I mean it just seemed to be one hardship after another, just like when we were out in Arkansas. Wasn't it better to be just living the life of a Hobo? Going from here to there, not giving a darn, and just packing up and leaving when the going got tough?

21 Oyster Farming

Oystering got so bad on the bay that the area was actually declared a federal disaster. The D.N.R., Department of Natural Resources, along with the Marine Patrol - the local fishermen's favorite government agency - were called in to protect the public's resources ... the oyster, that is, not the oystermen or the local Seafood Industry. To say that things gradually deteriorated in the local oyster industry from that point forward would be a gross understatement.

The upside of all this disaster and government intervention was the initiation of a federally subsidized program to re-train oystermen into a new skill or trade. I guess the determination was that the public oyster beds were being over harvested, hence the drastic lack of oysters out on the beds lately, and in the last few years. The government's solution was to teach all of us oystermen, via an independent, non-profit, expert organization in the field, how to grow oysters. When they had accomplished this, they could then petition the local government to issue leases for the purposes of establishing this new aquaculture miracle, as a legitimate business opportunity for the local citizenry.

It sounded great. Carol and I thought it was the opportunity of a lifetime. For once we were actually in the right place at the right time. We had been working the bay for over ten years at that time, and more than met any qualifications for enrollment in the program.

I think most all of us have the inner desire to be the owners and operators of our own business. And here was our chance. Not only did we have the chance of establishing our own business, but the success of the venture was just about guaranteed by the United States of America. Can you believe it? How lucky can you get?

This program had more government agencies involved in it than I previously believed existed. In fact, I think that they invented some new agencies just to make sure that everything was covered.

Carol and I went to the town hall and watched movies about the "science" of growing oysters and the success of this type of aquaculture throughout the world. We were very impressed and pretty much led to believe that this was not a theoretical experiment but a proven technology. All we had to do, was pay attention, do as we were told and we would one day be growing oysters right here in Apalachicola bay.

We were told at one point in the indoctrination that oysters could actually be grown anywhere. Scientists had grown them in vats; you could grow them in your bathtub if you wanted to. Oysters had been discovered growing out in the middle of the ocean somewhere. The Japanese had been growing oysters for centuries. We saw pictures of huge, successful oyster farms established since after World War II on the west coast of the United States. This was going to be like falling off a log. Since conditions were slightly different here than on the west coast, certain minor adaptations were necessary. But don't worry about a thing. We've got it all figured out - so said the Government and their aquaculture business advisors.

Carol and I talked of putting our land in Arkansas up for sale. This could be the opportunity of a lifetime, and sometimes opportunity only knocks once. We had best not miss it.

But, I still had one problem lurking in the back of my mind. I wasn't convinced that the problem on the public bed was over harvesting.

In the ten or so years that I had worked the beds, I had witnessed a reproduction and growth pattern that looked to be impossible. Some years there seemed to be more oystermen working the beds than there could possibly be oysters. Though, at the end of every season, the oyster beds would be harvested down to a scant and scrappy few, that next year when the beds reopened the crop would once again be renewed.

People of a spiritual nature who had lived in the area all of their lives, considered it to be somewhat of a miracle. I myself had no good explanation for it.

The oyster harvest and the oyster beds were divided into two seasons, a winter season and a summer season. So like in farming, the beds were given a time to rest - a time when no harvesting was permitted on certain beds, while you then went and worked other beds.

The system obviously seemed to be working very well. The harvest, of course, varied from year to year. Some years, the harvest was definitely better than others. But in these last few years something strange was happening. When we returned to the oyster beds to begin our new season, the oysters were dead. Not all of the oysters but the vast majority. The harvest in terms of bushels had fallen drastically.

The aquaculture experts contended that the oysters were being eaten by predators, and it did seem that there were more fish swimming around the beds than we had ever noticed before. Carol and I were aware of the fish around the beds, because Carol loved to fish. We always kept fishing poles on board. In fact, most days while Carol was culling oysters, she sat on the handle of her fishing pole which she had dangling off the side of our boat. Many of the fish ate the little crabs that were in abundance. Carol would capture some of the tiny crabs off our cull board as she culled through our oysters, and then bait her hook with them. We ate a steady diet of fish and oysters.

In fact, for our first year, I think we ate a pail full of steamed oysters every night before supper. It became kind of a ritual. We had a pail or pot that we brought in with us every evening, and as we went about cleaning up and taking our showers, we put the bucket of oysters onto the stove. By the time that we were cleaned and primped, we were ready to eat our bucket of steamed oysters, dipped in butter, as our appetizer.

We caught lots of Drum Fish, and Sheepshead, and on occasion Speckled Trout. At other times we caught Croaker and Catfish, and sometimes Flounder. Talk about dying and going to heaven. It really hurt to see the bay dying, and this way of life giving out. I don't think we will ever forget the good times that we had oystering. I think we ended up catching oysters for about thirteen years - which has turned out to be the longest that I have ever worked the same job in my life.

Getting back to the reason for the dead oysters, it was my contention that the predators were always there. These oysters were dying from something else - something that no one was telling us about for some reason. I didn't know what it could be though. I kept bringing half dead oysters out to the aquaculture farm area, and showing them to the scientists and instructors involved in the program. They had no explanation. Oysters die from a million different things I was told.

I wasn't looking at this problem as a scientist. I was looking at it as a potential entrepreneur. The program that we were learning in this aquaculture technique was based on the successful system that was operating out in Washington State.

The oysters were to be grown in bags. The bags were of a plastic material and were porous. The idea being to let water flow through, but keep predators out.

But what if the oysters out on the beds were not dying from a new abundance of predators, but some type of disease, or what about pollution? And more important than that what if I sold my land in Arkansas and invested it in this program? What if I bought all the bags and paraphernalia, invested in thousands of dollars worth of seed, and all my oysters died, just as they were dying out on the public beds?

I kept bringing oysters and samples of sick oysters half opened with the meat still inside, out to the aquaculture experts, but I got no response. I went to the library trying to find books on oyster diseases, but no luck. After I had exhausted all local sources, I started sending off letters to research institutes. In the meantime out at the farm, I convinced them of the necessity of providing more information about the oyster and anything relating to its demise. I was very much interested in having my own oyster farm but I had no intention of running off halfcocked and losing all my money - my life's savings.

A lending library of research information was established out at the aquaculture center. I read everything they put in the lending library. And one day there it was, a word for word description of exactly what I thought was happening on the public beds. There was a disease, named Dermo-cistidium-marinum, or Dermo for short.

I thought this disease described the situation that had been plaguing us all on the public beds for these last few years. I called the Aqua-farm scientists. I left my number. I told them what I had discovered. I asked them to contact me. I went out to see the scientist in charge. He never seemed to be around anymore.

From that point on, a new adventure invaded the lives of Carol a Dick. I became convinced of a conspiracy. One suspicious thing just led to another. To explain what then happened in the lives of Carol and Dick would take a whole new book. I'll do it here, just briefly.

My idea of an oyster disease was not given a lot of credibility. One area university scientist had been saying for years that the bay was on a course of gradual deterioration due to development and the problem of a gradually creeping saltwater intrusion which was primarily caused by a cut that had been made through the barrier island years ago. This gave even more credibility to the predator theory.

The fact was that most people didn't want to hear about any disease, and that included other oystermen and dealers. The last thing anybody wanted to hear was a whole lot of publicity about a "disease" devastating oysters out in beautiful Apalachicola bay.

This would not be good, and I realized that. It didn't really matter that this disease was not harmful to people and only affected the oysters. It sounded bad, and would certainly not help the sale of oysters. But as time went on, I became so outraged by all the stonewalling I received, that I decided to take matters into my own hands. I had gone to everybody whom I thought should have a stake in this controversy.

I went to the dealers association, the oystermen's association, the local newspapers, the state legislature, the Governor's cabinet, and the local radio station. I even wrote my state and federal representatives. I contacted the attorney general's office. Believe me when I say this, I contacted everybody. As time went on I found many allies within the scientific community, and elsewhere. I began to have a steady correspondence with several different research groups and universities. But all of my efforts were to no avail.

The program had bigger obstacles to overcome than my theory. If the program were to be successful, a system of leasing of the bay would have to be devised in order for the newly trained farmers to be able to ply their craft. The established order of fishermen and oystermen had a long standing opposition to the idea of leasing. The bay had been open territory to anyone for, what seemed to be, forever. Now to start dividing it up into little privately owned portions seemed sacrilegious.

A large hue and cry was heard throughout the county with regards to this issue. There were debates at city hall and in the newspapers. Even if the program had been a complete success, this issue would have presented a huge obstacle. Along with the notion of leasing comes the issue of who is going to get the leases. This brings in all kinds of arguments - one being the rights of the general public at large.

Would leasing interfere with the general public's right to enjoy and pursue their recreational interests on this, their public resource? What about our free market capitalism? Could you grant leases to local residents, and not to everyone else who might have an interest? Would it be Constitutional to grant leases to displaced, unemployed oystermen, and not others within the community? How would such a division of public property be handled to everyone's satisfaction?

All of these questions became pretty much moot when the oysters out at the farm project began to fail. The failure of the majority of the oysters to grow successfully began to cause rumblings and discontent among the farmers themselves. The majority were experiencing drastic death rates in their experimental crops. The establishers of the program complained they had been given a poor location, but critics countered that they had initially claimed to be able to grow oysters anywhere.

In any case, all arguments became null and void when the local county commission voted in a three to two majority that there would be no leases granted in Apalachicola bay, now or ever.

In my heart of hearts, I am still convinced that the failure was due to the effects of the disease, Dermo. I seriously don't think that oysters could be grown by this bag and seed growing system that we were being trained with, anywhere in the Gulf of Mexico. I do think that some type of oyster farming could be successful in the Gulf of Mexico if one, the leasing, public use, and fair play issues are overcome; and two, some sort of transplanting technique is coupled with a smaller harvesting size. Without the smaller size, I am convinced that under most conditions a very large percentage of the harvestable, saleable crop would simply die.

The transplanting technique, which is harvesting small oysters from wherever they are presently growing and transferring them to more advantageous lease growing areas, would let Mother Nature take the gigantic losses that occur in the seed and spat stages. An oyster farmer, buying and attempting to cultivate his own seed, is not cost effective at present. And it would go without saying that the present policy of public bed harvesting would have to be discontinued. I see no way that public harvesting and leasing could exist side by side. The problems would be immense.

In any case, with the failure of the government program, and the continuing decline of the oysters on the public bed, Carol and I were confronted with the inevitability of once again finding new employment.

I would miss oystering, but the truth of the matter is that oystering at our age was getting to be more and more challenging. I was enthusiastic but Carol and her oyster bush were making things more and more difficult. Oh, I never did tell you about Carol's oyster bush.

Just outside the bedroom window of our trailer, we had a little bush growing. If we looked out that window and saw that bush swinging in the breeze, Carol was convinced that the bay would be much too rough for us to ply our craft. As our bag count went down and down, and our paychecks got smaller and smaller that bush seemed to be swaying and swishing more and more often. There were days when Carol didn't even get out of the bed, she would simply rise up on one elbow, peek out the window, and say "No oystering today, Richard. That bush is blowing like crazy." After a while I began to think she had some sort of mechanical devise attached to that bush. When we did get up to go, it seemed to me that our preparations to go oystering actually took longer than the time we spent working out on the bay. It was clear we were suffering from the oysterman blues ... more commonly known as burnout.

22 Restaurant Work

I use the term "burnt-out", with regards to our oystering career, but the fact is that it was more than simple weariness or boredom that precipitated our decision.

Oystering is, of course, physical. A bushel of oysters weighs sixty pounds. The last duty of a long, hard physical day of oystering is to unload the boat. This alone was rapidly becoming a dreary dreadful thought.

First you must lift each bag from the floor of the boat, and place it up on the walk rail of the boat. Then you climb up onto the walk rail of the boat, and hump the bags up onto the loading dock - a dock which is usually about chest high. Then you heft the bags off the dock and into a wheelbarrow or onto a two wheel cart. Then you run them up the dock and into the house. There you unload them from the wheelbarrow onto a pallet. That's a good deal of hefting right there, but when you think of this task after eight to ten hours of tonging or culling all day, it is not a pleasant thought.

Culling is one of the jobs that doesn't really look hard to an observer, but whenever any observer ever tries to do it for an hour or so, they very quickly learn they would probably starve to death if this were their sole means of making a living. But human nature is a very peculiar thing. I remember this example in particular.

There was this middle aged man who came touring through our little campground by the sea. He had an older, yet attractive motor home and was obviously from the class of hard working American better offs. He was big, burly and it was plain that he had experienced physical work in his past life. He claimed to be semi-retired in some fashion. He wanted to go oystering to learn what it was all about. He complained that no oystermen would volunteer to take him out with him, even though he had agreed to work for no pay. When I explained to him that a new inexperienced man working on a boat was a detriment and not an asset, he laughed. Then clearly, making reference to my wife, he exclaimed jovially, "Certainly I could do a woman's work, couldn't I?" This was not meant to be a question but a statement. My wife was standing right there beside me when he made the statement. This was not only a male chauvinist insult to women in general, but a personal insult to my wife.

My wife is not only a woman but one of the hardest working women that I have ever seen or met. My wife carried her share of the workload in every endeavor. She hefted her own ladder in the orange groves and did tonging when necessary on our oyster boat. In as far as speed, effort, and physical strength are concerned she was second to very few men, and far ahead of most. In terms of mental quickness, determination, and ability to withstand pain and discomfort, I have met very few men who can compare, including myself. Before I even had a chance to get warmed up on my wife's behalf, she piped up and invited the gentleman to accompany us on tomorrow's "cruise".

On that next day, my wife instructed our new friend in the technique of culling, and I instructed him on the fine art of tonging oysters.

I've often tried to calculate by physical definition how much work a man actually does in a day, tonging oysters. In Physics, distance times weight equals work. If each tong load of oysters weighs approximately fifty pounds let's say, and it is carried over a distance of ten feet, then that would be, fifty times ten equals five hundred foot pounds of work each tong full. An average tonger tongs about six loads per minute. There are sixty minutes in an hour. So that would be, six times sixty, times eight hours, times five hundred equals approximately one million four hundred forty thousand foot pounds of work per eight hour working day. I don't have any comparative figures, but my guess is that this figure is quite substantial, and compares favorably or above the hardest of physical laboring efforts.

During that next day, our trainee worked very hard - by his standards. By our standards, he really hadn't accomplished very much, but we thought that teaching him a lesson would be worth our effort. He had said that he would work for nothing simply to have the experience, but we felt that we should be generous. It would only be a one time affair anyway. We paid him a straight third share of the catch, taking nothing for the boat, motor or the free instruction. We had caught eighteen bags that day. The price was six dollars per bag, so we gave him thirty six dollars. When I gave him his money, his face shriveled up like a prune. By the look on his face, I thought he was either having severe gastronomical upset, or a heart attack. I asked him if something was wrong. He nodded his head and with a wise smirk, sputtered. "Cheat a man once, shame on you. Cheat a man twice, shame on him."

"Hold on, hold on," I said. "Nobody has ever accused me of cheating him on anything yet in my life. You don't think that a third is a fair share? How many bags out of our eighteen do you think that you culled by yourself today."

"Ten."

"You think that you culled and tonged ten bags of oysters by yourself today?"

"At least, maybe more."

I really couldn't believe it. I understand that as human beings we all have the tendency to pull for our own side, and to over value our own personal efforts when compared with others, but when your own inadequacy is demonstrated for you right before your own eyes, I would figure that some humility and objectivity should be called for. I guess I was wrong. He had obviously calculated my wife's efforts as zero, and his personal output as slightly above my own. Sometimes it is hard for me to get a grasp on the human ego, my own included, but its fantasies are sometimes overpowering.

"Well," I said as civilly as I could muster. "I'll tell you what I'll do. I'll take you out again tomorrow, if you feel up to it. But tomorrow you will work one side of the boat and my wife and I will work the other. You'll fill your own bags, and you'll tong your own oysters. How does that sound?"

"Fine with me."

That next day my wife and I caught twenty three bags of oysters and he caught two. I was really surprised that he only caught two. I thought he would at least get three. But when he saw how badly he was losing, he pretty much quit. Of course, he was very slow as a culler, but his tonging was even worse. He kept tonging up old cull piles and dead oysters. There is a skill and a knack to even the most simple of looking tasks, believe me.

When we got to shore, he stumbled around waiting for his pay. It is kind of funny but suddenly I felt like mister Daily of pickle picking fame.

"What are you waiting for?" I asked. I don't have to tell you that he wasn't about to help Carol and I unload our twenty three bags. In fact, he didn't even bother to heft the two that he had caught, up onto the dock.

"My money, friend."

"Well, I don't know how you figure it, but by the way I figure it, you owe me sixty-six dollars.

"WHAT??"

"Well, standard boat and motor rent is one bag for the boat, and one bag for the motor. You were really only capable of doing two bags per day as we see from your efforts today. So in two days you caught four bags, that leaves us even on the boat rent account. But yesterday, I gave you thirty six dollars for what amounts to you doing nothing. So I think if you were any kind of a decent man you would return that money to me. Beyond that, it should be clear to you that your presence on our boat cost us at least five bags production for yesterday. You probably cost us another bag or two today just getting in our way, but I won't charge you for that. So if you add the thirty dollars that you cost us in production yesterday to the thirty six dollars I already paid you out of the kindness of my heart for yesterday, you owe us sixty-six dollars."

I figured that if he got mad, I'd let my wife beat the hell out of him. He didn't. His experience with us triggered something inside him. He ended up buying himself a boat and motor, and periodically thereafter we saw him out on the bay. We never saw or heard of him catching more than two bags on any given day. We nick-named him "The Two Bagger".

Oystering was more than simply hard. The weather could be rugged. A "light chop" as they describe it on the weather station doesn't sound too bad. But, in the winter with the temperature between thirty and forty degrees, and a ten to fifteen knot wind blowing from the north; out on that bay in your damp clothing, boy it can feel like Antarctica.

Then there was a host of new and continually revised government rules. It got to the point that even the Marine

Patrol couldn't give you a definite answer as to the exact code rules for everything. The bay seemed to be closed more than it was open, due to one government management excuse or another. On top of all of this, there seemed to be a never ending stream of negative publicity with regards to eating seafood and raw oysters in particular. If anybody died or even got sick, or claimed to have gotten sick, it was all over the newspapers and the TV. There were even special exposés on 20/20 and Sixty Minutes about eating raw oysters, and illegal harvesting practices out in Louisiana and elsewhere. On one occasion ten or so people claimed to have gotten sick at a particular oyster bar, and with no further corroboration than their word, the whole Gulf coast oystering industry was shut down. The people involved in the complaint, if I remember correctly, never went to the hospital or even to a doctor's office. They were later found out to be friends to the owner of a rival restaurant. It did seem to me, as it did to many other oystermen, that someone was involved in putting us seafood workers out of business. To be honest, it still seems that way to me.

But between difficulty, bad weather, more rules and permits, and an endless stream of enforcement agents, negative publicity, and fewer and fewer orders; it did, for a while there; seem that the oysterman was public enemy number one. Even many local people had nothing good to say about oystermen. Oystermen were all dirty, uneducated, drunken, rowdy, violent and lazy. Carol and I felt that the hand writing was on the wall. If we didn't get out of the oystering business, it probably wouldn't be long before we would be driven out.

But, all in all, Carol and I were still happy with our progress living here in Franklin County. We were poor but comfortable. In just six years we had set ourselves up in a little home that was all paid for. In the big city, the same accomplishment would have taken us thirty years. We had everything paid for, owed nobody nothing and had a few emergency dollars in the bank. We were living the good life right here in downtown paradise. We had our bought and paid for home out on a dirt road, one block up from the bay. And to tell you the truth, if I didn't go to work, or could find nothing for the next whole year that appealed to me, we would still have enough money to get by. But, I caution, most Americans wouldn't consider our lifestyle actually living, but we were happy.

In our little community of ten thousand, if we have one, we have fifty different places to go out to eat. When I go to the big cities, it is almost mesmerizing. You can get your hamburger cooked in the style of twenty different countries. I don't know how many people are now employed in the food service industry or related fields, but it must be millions, possibly tens of millions.

I think statistically people now eat more meals out of the home than they do at home. It is unbelievable.

The restaurant business has always fascinated me. I have been involved in some facet of food service all of my life. And now I can say that I have literally done everything from harvesting to gourmet preparation. I incorporated my gourmet experience right here in Franklin County, but let me start at the beginning.

The family decision being pretty much in, with regards to ending our oystering career, I got my first job at a local restaurant as a fry cook.

That first night when I arrived home, my wife nearly collapsed into hysterics just to look at me. It seems I had somehow gotten covered from head to foot in flour and grease. Believe me, it was a tough night. The "kids" were really rough on me. I say kids because that is exactly what they were. I felt like a sixty year old man working at McDonald's, and believe me the children working at this McDonald's didn't like me one bit.

They had a built-in mistrust of anyone over twelve years of age. I was filled with all of these very stupid ideas about cleanliness and organization and they were going to have none of it.

They weren't the least bit impressed by any of my credentials. They had all been privy to my application and everybody seemed to know everything about me. They had no intention of letting some older know-it-all, ex-manager type from the Stone Age, tell them what to do.

The owner of this particular place was the original invisible man. He knew nothing about cooking, and made it a point never to set foot into the kitchen if he didn't have to. The young man in charge of the kitchen at the time was about thirteen years old, maybe fourteen. I don't really do that well at guessing ages these days. He was a computer whiz, and felt that a good kitchen was a microwave, and a wooden spoon. He seemed to have the unique ability to cook anything and everything in a microwave. I had been out of the restaurant business so long that I didn't even know what a microwave oven was, never mind how to operate it.

I was a big city restaurant boy. I knew about stainless steel and cockroaches. Everything in this kitchen was pretty much wood and white wash, which had been outlawed in any of the places I was at, twenty years ago.

On my first evening, I inherited the job of fry cook. I was assigned this position because this was obviously the month that they had allocated to the changing of the grease. The grease was drained from the fryolators into a giant pot. Then carted down a mountain of stairs, and out into the parking lot where it was then dumped into a grease dumpster. The fryolators were then scrubbed, cleaned and soaked with a grease dissolving chemical, which was also drained and dumped.

In any case, after I had changed the grease, I was ready for my nap. But, of course, that was out of the question. I opted for washing my hands and slapping a little water onto my face, but first I would have to find a sink. When I asked Junior, who was at that moment busy making a pot of gumbo in the microwave, where I would find the sink, he pointed to a huge sack of dirty laundry that was stacked against a wall.

I saw no sink, but decided to go over and investigate. As I examined the area, it did seem that the top of the dirty laundry sack had a porcelain lid. I foraged through grease stained aprons, and piles of cloth, hand towels infected with goo, until I came to what appeared to be a chunk of porcelain. But it was difficult to tell. The whole bowl - ledge, walls and whatever - were encrusted with six inches of caked on dirt and flour. This was the sink that the fry cook used. They hand battered all of their fried food. The hot and cold water knobs on this sink looked like little snowmen with propellers for heads. I was able to rotate one, and get a little water to tumble into the bowl, but it certainly wasn't going anywhere from there. A drain hole was not to be observed. I decided to scrap the idea.

As the evening progressed another young man of about six to nine years of age, instructed me on the delicate art of fry cooking. Within six to eight minutes of frying, this kid looked like the Pillsbury Dough Boy, and everything around him for six to ten feet looked like a winter wonderland. No one in this restaurant ever heard the notion of "back up".

For example, when this fry cook would run out of scallops for his presently cooking seafood platter, he would simply make an Olympic sprint into the freezer, grab a bag of frozen scallops, and toss them into the sink with the water running. In a few minutes the scallops would be floating up over the rim of the sink and into the laundry bag and onto the floor - because as you remember no water could possibly drain out of the sink. The "Chef" would then gather ye scallops as he may; toss them into this liquid he had sitting in a bowl on a card table; then toss them around in a bucket of flour, then into the grease by the handful, flour and all.

When this concoction came out of the fryolator, it looked something like one of those fried Elephant Ears you get at the fair or the circus. The seafood platter looked like a big mound of half browned, pasty goop. In between accomplishing these culinary masterpieces, the fry chef would retire to a corner; pull up a milk crate and read a paperback novel.

At about this point in my training, a plate was returned to the kitchen, the customer complained of discovering a cockroach floating in her Shrimp Divine. I examined the plate, and sure enough, there was a little cockroach doing the backstroke in the cheese sauce. Though no one else seemed very concerned about this incident, I was somewhat curious as to where, in particular, the cockroach had come from.

The dish had been prepared in the microwave, so I took a little peek in there. It was quite dirty, but I saw no roaches. I started looking around the counters, when I saw another frightened little roach make a dash from underneath the microwave into a stack of platters. I then took a peek into the little half inch crack or space under the microwave. And there, I saw what appeared to me to be a hundred little eyeballs peering back at me in terror.

I felt sorry for the roaches. They had found a good home, and now they had been discovered. Where would they go from here? But to be honest with you, I had an even bigger question, where would I go from here?

I took a trip to the bathroom. It was easy to find the bathroom from the kitchen. I simply followed the floured sneaker prints from the kitchen, through the carpeted dining room, and into the men's lavatory. There was even a floured hand print on the wall, next to the trough where my instructor had obviously been standing to relieve himself. On my way back to the kitchen, I observed some of the customers foraging through their food. The ash trays on all of the tables were filled with balls of goop and semi-fried things. The people, and yes, there were people eating in here, were saying things like;

"What is this, Ralph?"

"I think that is what they call a corn fritter?"

"No, no, this is a corn fritter," someone would yell while tossing the thing in question from the ash tray on his table to the ash try on the next table.

"But what is this massive pancake looking thing?"

"That's a fishcake," someone would yell.

"But it tastes like scallops or shrimp to me."

"Really, you mean you are actually eating this stuff? Boy, you've got more guts than I do."

I had serious misgiving with regards to maintaining my position at this restaurant. Besides the obvious, these kids were seriously abusing me with every physical task they could think of. It was even more amazing to me, that everything they could think of didn't include cleaning.

The restaurant business is an interesting business. Anyone and everyone can open up a restaurant. Actually, it seems that today just about everyone has.

In my old ethnic neighborhood back home a restaurant of some sort was a stepping stone for many a poor immigrant. I was raised on Italian meatball and veal cutlet sandwiches, French napoleons, and lemon tarts; German sauerbraten, fried potatoes and real potato pancakes; Chinese egg rolls, and fried shrimp tempura; roasted or grilled lamb, and baked kibbie; Polish stuffed cabbage, perogie, kapusta, and Irish stew. I was exposed to every kind of bread and pastry imaginable. I've always had great respect for food and good cooking.

But really, restaurants are kind of like hospitals. They say that a hospital is really the last place you want to be if you get sick. In the hospital you will be exposed to every type of sickness, disease, and bacteria available. Well, sometimes I think the last place you want to be if you are hungry is a restaurant. Working and managing restaurants at different phases of my life has exposed me to every type of malpractice imaginable in the food handling area.

When I first started my working career, I drove a truck and made deliveries to grocery stores and restaurants. This was over thirty years ago, and I can still remember some of the horror stories that existed back then. Believe it or not, I think that things are better than they were thirty years ago. But, one must still advise ... let the eater beware.

My next experience in the local restaurant business was really like night and day compared to this last one. Certainly, everything was far from perfect, but it was a serious learning experience for me.

I was introduced to a whole new world of cooking. For the first time in my life, I started buying cookbooks and reading up on the history and science of cooking.

I started reading about people like Marie-Antoine Careme, Aureate Escoffier, and Brillat-Savarin. I learned about the incorporation of air, and emulsifiers, and lecithin. I learned about browning and caramelization. I learned about rue, and reduction. I learned the art of sautéing food. I learned about artistic presentation, bordelaise, and mousse; escargot, and burre blanc, hollandaise, béarnaise, béchamel, espagnole. I learned about Osmazome, and concepts of flavor enhancement. I learned about thyme, turmeric, garlic, ginger and other spices.

I worked for a new guy who had recently arrived in town. He and some friends were about to shock the community with a new eating experience. And they did. The food was excellent - far above anything I had ever experienced. The local crowd in general, being of the grits, biscuits and gravy, and fried mullet type really didn't frequent the restaurant all that often. But the restaurant drew from all over. Since then a rash of gourmet type restaurants have tried their hand at things in the area.

This restaurant was the first in the area to offer such things as sautéed shrimp in roasted garlic cream sauce, angel hair pasta, blackened salmon, roasted red peppers, tomato basil and other herb butters, sautéed garlic tuna, baked stuffed scrod, feta and gruyere cheeses, roasted duck, lamb, prime rib, pesto, Dijon, marinara, bordelaise, cream and other traditional French sauces; bisque and volute, chowders, and heavy cream oyster stew. It was far and away the best restaurant in the area, and without any doubt the best restaurant I ever worked at. I had great hopes that this would be the last job I would ever need. I had found my home and now I had found a career, and an interesting career.

But nothing in my life has ever been so. It seems that my destiny is in writing about my never ending encounters in Hobo-ing America.

This restaurant was plagued with personality problems. The Chef was one of the most eccentric and hyper people that I ever met. He had some problems that plagued him, and at some points in my stay, I actually thought he was going to experience a nervous breakdown. But with all of his problems he was a great cook. He could cook anything. He was far and away the best Chef that I had ever met.

He had two other partners, and the three of them and their families were constantly at odds. Trying to organize my loyalties made me feel like a ball in a pinball machine. Eventually the partnership disintegrated.

23 Hobo's Ice Cream Parlor

It was at this point that my wife got the bright idea of going into our own business. I was almost totally opposed to the idea. I had already tried being in business for myself on several different occasions.

I had opened my own butcher shop when I was just into my twenties. I had tried my hand at a sandwich shop. I had a seashore, hot-waffle, ice cream stand. And I had tried and failed at a number of others. If I knew one thing, I knew you didn't go into business to get out of working hard, or to make, instantly, bunches of money.

I argued diligently against my wife's notion. I felt that all of her motivations were wrong, and not thought out. I told her of all my bad experiences with trying my own business, including the story of how it took me five years of time payments just to pay off the debts I had incurred from my efforts. Going into business for one's self was a dark cloud looming up from my past.

But as always, with Carol, I was fighting a losing battle. She had her mind set. She would find the perfect idea for us to embark on a career of fame and fortune. I decided to do as all husbands do. I would humor her. I would pretend to go along with whatever she said. Then, let her go about exhausting herself with the mounting problems that inevitably arise with the notion of establishing any idea.

This technique worked for a while. But it wasn't long before she had me figured out. She did admit, that my complaints about not having enough money to start a business were justified, though. She begrudgingly agreed to stop pestering me about it, at least until she thought up the perfect means and method.

It was at this moment the strangest thing that had ever happened to me in my life, occurred.

I got a letter in the mail. The letter was from some lawyer's office up in Massachusetts. The letter informed me that an aunt of mine had died. Her estate was being settled, and would I have any objection to a particular uncle of mine being appointed executor of her will.

To tell you the truth, I didn't know any of these people extremely well. My father was pretty much the black sheep of his family, and this aunt, was his sister.

As the proceedings rolled on, we kept receiving information from the lawyer's office. Finally we received a complete breakdown of all of my aunt's finances. My Auntie Dot had accumulated in her lifetime, over a million and a half dollars. I couldn't believe it.

I took my wife to visit my hometown in Massachusetts a few years before my Auntie Dot died. So Carol actually got to meet my aunt Dorothy. My aunt even took us out to eat.

We had a very nice visit. We told her all about our travels. We even brought a scrapbook and took her vicariously on our adventures. I think she liked it.

In any case, after all was said and done, I had inherited approximately twenty thousand dollars. I was very pleased, to say the least, but now I could never again complain that - nobody ever gave me nothin'.

But with this new found luck, my wife's thirst for fame and fortune in a business of our own was reinvigorated. And to tell the truth, at this point, it sounded like a good idea to me too. I mean, a bunch of money just fell out of the sky. If we didn't invest it in something, I was sure that it would be piddled away somewhere. And doesn't having your own business sound more exciting than getting a job at a fast food store?

We both certainly had lots of experience. Couldn't we be successful at something out there in the business world? And wouldn't this kind of be in tune with our original Hobo-ing America idea? Wouldn't it be the ultimate dream of two Hoboes to end up in their own business?

Really, to even think that we would be where we were at this point was beyond my wildest dreams. To think that we would be even looking forward to such a dream seemed somewhat humorous to me. I mean just to be in this position? But realistically, what kind of a serious business could we buy or enter into with the finances at our disposal? But, my Taoist spirit was willing to go with the flow.

Where would we start? Carol had the first good starting point, I thought. She said; "We have been all over the United States. We have seen all of the different things that they have elsewhere. What neat things that we have seen elsewhere, are lacking here in this our newly adopted hometown?"

Wow! I thought to myself, she is really good. That is a wonderful approach.

My first suggestion was an airport. They had no La Guardia here in Franklin County; no Kennedy for that matter either.

She didn't like that though.

My next idea was a shopping mall, preferably one with a bowling alley and a multi-screen, movie theater.

Next I thought of a high rise condominium on the water's edge.

Carol liked that better than the airport, but felt I was still shooting a little too high. She then suggested selling chewing gum and cigarettes in a little empty space that was for rent across from the courthouse.

It is easy to see who has the real imagination in this family, isn't it?

Her next idea was getting permission from the people at the local bank to sell Popsicles and Eskimo Pies in their lobby.

My next idea was a golf course, or a theme park.

Carol said she had never played golf and that as far as she could see ideas like Disney World were slipping and starting to slide down hill.

My next idea was a steak house restaurant, featuring prime rib and fillet mignon.

She thought that was a good idea, but didn't think that we could quite swing it financially.

Her next idea was to buy a mobile sandwich cart that she saw advertised in the local newspaper and sell chili dogs out in front of the grocery store.

I felt that the wagon was over priced.

Her next idea was to open a baked potato stand. But I told her Wendy's had already beaten that idea into the parking lot.

Next we thought of making our own hand cream, or peddling home baked goods door to door - remember the Cushman man?

Then we thought of a mobile knife sharpening unit; then a barb-que restaurant; then a Pizza Hut, or a Burger King. We even wrote to Subway sandwich franchise – sixty-five thousand to get started talking.

I then thought of peanut vending machines, and Carol thought of a big, and even bigger, sized clothing store.

I then thought of selling tapes and CDs. I sent out letters to every music company in the business, I never got a reply.

By Halloween we were experimenting with candy apples and a cotton candy machine. Then we thought of a fish and chip stand, like Arthur Treacher's, or Captain Kids, but Franklin County already had at least twenty seafood restaurants and only ten thousand people on a sunny day in the middle of May.

In the midst of all this brain busting, we decided to take a trip down to Fort Lauderdale to visit the relatives. It was very hot in the car and the air conditioning wasn't working properly. I wanted an ice cream cone. I told Carol to stop at the next ice cream place that she passed. We drove all the way to southern Florida looking. I really couldn't believe it. What was more American than ice cream? I mean, maybe apple pie, but certainly ice cream had to be a very close second. And I could understand maybe not bumping into an ice cream parlor in Alaska or Siberia or some place, but how about Florida? No ice cream parlors in Florida, what is this?

We felt that we had found a void. Now, how would we go about filling it?

Carol wanted to just rent a place in a good location and give it a try. But, I felt that I had already been that route. When I had spent my life's saving over twenty years ago opening up a butcher shop in my old neighborhood, I had rented the building and bought all the equipment. When the business failed, I was left with a bunch of equipment that wasn't worth ten cents on the dollar, and a long term lease agreement that the people wanted payment on whether I was there or not. I wasn't about to make that mistake again. If I was going to blow my entire, once in a life time, inheritance, I wanted to, at least, make some kind of real estate investment. We began looking for property. My goodness, our twenty thousand began looking mighty small.

I had inherited twenty thousand dollars. But when it came to a business and a piece of property, it seemed hardly worth considering - everything we looked at cost hundreds of thousands. We saw almost nothing that was priced under one hundred and fifty thousand. We began to come rapidly to the conclusion that if we were to have a business it would be a rented business. But, we didn't give up looking.

We began researching ice cream and ice cream companies. We also began eating all kinds of ice cream. It's tough, but somebody had to do it. We went and visited local ice cream distributors. We then went into trying to figure out how many scoops in a gallon and so forth. I've got another hot tip for you and your future business; Don't base your sole success on the notion that you can beat the other guys price. It won't be long before you will find out why that son of a gun was charging all that money for that little bit of something.

Of course, I bought books. I read all about Ben and Jerry, and the Colonel, and Ronald McDonald, and J.C. Penny. Did you know that the original J.C. Penny stores were called the Golden Rule Stores? Now my next question is; Do you know what the Golden Rule is?

I had always wanted to have my own business, and I really, really wanted this try to be a successful one.

Finally Carol came to me with the information that there was a cement block building, on the main highway over in the next town for sale for a very reasonable price. A price, that with my inheritance and our personal fortune, we might be able to swing. As she was driving me over to look at it, all I could think was that at this asking price the place must be a real gem. I mean we had been looking all over town at what two hundred thousand dollars would buy, and it wasn't necessarily very pretty. What could one possibly get for the money we had?

When we drove past the place and Carol said there it was, I laughed. I didn't laugh because I thought the place was a joke. I laughed because I thought Carol was kidding me. Actually, I was almost sure she had picked out the wrong piece of property.

"Are you sure that is the place?" I asked.

"Ah Huh," she answered positively.

I'll tell you what. Take me over to the realty right now, do not pass go, and do not collect two hundred dollars. If this building is selling for what you say it is, we will buy it right there, on the spot.

"Really?"

"Yes, really."

"But, what if the roof is no good, and what if the furnace doesn't work, and ..."

"Carol if they are selling that piece of commercial property for the price you are telling me, from what I have seen, we can turn around and double our money tomorrow; unless I am completely out of my mind."

Sure enough, when we got to the realtor's office, the young lady told us that the selling price was nearly triple what Carol had discussed with me. I laughed.

"I knew it was too good to be true," I said to Carol as we exited the office.

By the time that we got home, the phone was ringing. The girl on the phone said that she had spoken to the lady who owned the property and she wanted to know what we thought the property was priced at. So we told her.

That next morning we got a call. We were told that if we wanted the property at the price we thought that it would cost, we could have it. So we bought it.

But after we bought the property, we heard about town the property did have flaws that one couldn't tell by just looking.

The first supposed flaw was that the property was "low", and the second flaw was that it was in an area that was considered a wetland.

I had no idea what a wetland was, but I did know what low meant. When you looked at the property from the highway, it certainly did look as though the folks who had built it had set it right in a hole. But, in a hole, or not in a hole, we had bought it and it was now our problem.

One former renter told us that during the rainy season, he used to canoe out of the front yard. Another renter told us not to bother putting down any carpet because when the water started coming in under the doors we would just be throwing it out. "Get a good sump pump," he advised.

But tell me, do you think any of this scared or worried Carol or I? Come on, you can tell the truth, you know the two of us well enough by now?

You're darn right we were worried. But, that wasn't the half of it. The wetland business was an even bigger concern. You know, you have heard the story about those poor people who bought a property only to find that it was home to the last double-headed, pecker toad in the whole world. And when they tried to cut down a tree, fourteen thousand folk singers showed up on their front lawn holding hands and singing; He's got the whole world in his hands, he's got the whole wide world in his hands. He's got the whole world ... holy molly, what have I gotten us into now Ollie?

We fretted about everything for about a week or two. Got excessively depressed, and then came up with a plan.

I knew and had figured that if we were going to turn what was really a two bedroom, two bath home rental property, into an ice cream parlor, we would need a new septic system, or at least the one that we had, would have to be upgraded. The plan would be ... First, we go down and talk to the man who issued the permits and proceed as if we had never heard any rumors about wetlands, bald eagles, tsetse flies or two headed toads. If it were true that the property flooded when it rained, we would just raise everything up off the floor or close up shop until the flood waters subsided.

That next morning, we were down to the permitting office. We met the man in charge. He greeted us from behind the counter and said;

"Okay, now what hopes, aspirations and dreams of yours can I reject, trample on, and totally crush into the ground right here at your feet."

He had obviously been working this job for some time. We told him about our ice cream parlor, and he said;

"Uuoohhh, that sounds like something we destroyers of the American dream down here at the permitting office can really get our teeth into. Do you have any other fantasies that you would like to tell me about before we get started?"

We gave him the description of our property. He looked it up on his board, and then told us to meet him there tomorrow morning at eight. After he looked at the property he would be able to give us his prognosis.

That next morning, he was there at the proper time with his group of advisors from the E.P.A., and E.T.T., and D.E.P. and the C.C.C., and who knows what else.

Carol and I were really in a bad state. What would we do if our septic system permit was rejected? Worse than that, what if they looked at our property and all their maps and charts and said ... What's that house doing there? This is supposed to be an empty lot man. How long do you think it will take you guys to disassemble that house and get it out there? ... Or ... Isn't that a double-breasted, conch sucker's nest over there, Elory?

"Well, be darned if it isn't, Clivis. Sorry folks, but there will be no ice cream parlor here, not at least until the year two thousand forty-three. Have you ever thought of donating this property to the state, as kind of a national bird watching monument or something? You could probably deduct it from your taxes."

But, we never heard a sputter about wetlands or whatever. Everybody seemed more concerned on giving us suggestions about how to get started. We did have one problem though, the property being low, it would take a lot of fill for the septic, unless somebody had a better idea. Well, the septic man had a better idea. Thousands of dollars later, we had a sewer system to qualify us for a twenty eight seat restaurant.

But, we had lots of work to do. The inside of the place still looked like a house. We had to change it. First we made a window into a doorway; Carol designed and built a door with a big ice cream cone in the center of it. Then we knocked down a cement block wall with a skill saw and a sludge hammer, and converted a bedroom into a sitting area. Once again, Carol made all the tables and chairs, basically out of two by fours. There was this rather large cedar closet that we reconstructed into a booth. The back bedroom we redesigned into a music room. In our travels Carol had spotted a secondhand Juke box filled with old forty-fives from the fifties and sixties. So with that juke box and some album covers from my fifties record collection on the walls; we had the music room.

We struggled for a name. But wasn't this place really the culmination of all of our Hobo dreams. Why don't we call it Hobo's ... Hobo's Ice Cream Parlor?

Now we had the music room, the front door, a dining room, a new state of the art septic system. What about a parking lot? We were right on a corner lot, but it was covered with pine trees. With my Arkansas tree felling know how, I began clearing the corner for the parking lot. Trees cut and then about ten loads of fill dirt and we had a parking lot.

Now, what have we forgotten here? Let me see? Oh yeah, how about some ice cream. Getting some used ice cream display cases was a book in itself, but eventually we found a couple. We hauled them in our pickup; unloaded them and put them where we wanted them. Of course, we had to re-do the door, just to get them into the building. Then the refrigeration man had to replace the compressors. Then we needed a sign. Carol built one, and painted it herself. She also painted ice cream cones all over the building. How was anybody going to know that we were selling ice cream in this old house?

During all this effort and expenditure, we did, of course, have a terrible need for some words of encouragement from our friends, and relatives. In our time of need everyone was there with everything we needed.

"You're going to sell ice cream? I get all the ice cream that I need at the grocery store."

"Happy days are over kiddies. Nobody goes to ice cream parlors anymore."

"Aren't you afraid that those trees will fall on top of your building?"

"What are you going to do when the flood waters come? This place is going to be under water you know."

"It takes at least five years to make any money at your own business these days. Do you have enough in your savings to last five years?"

"Do you know that four out of five small businesses fail every year?"

"I hope that you are not going to sell ice cream cones for nine dollars each, like everybody else?"

"Why did you buy a place so far outside of town? Do you really think people will drive this far, just to buy an ice cream cone?

"You're not going to make it with just ice cream. You're going to need soup and sandwiches. Why don't you open a pizza parlor instead?"

But even though our friends weren't too confident, it seemed that everybody else in the county liked our idea. A new place opened up in town. It was to be a pizza parlor and sandwich shop, but suddenly they had a big ice cream cone out front, along with a picture of a banana split. The little ice cream parlor in the back of the drugstore over in the next town, renovated - another big ice cream cone hanging on the outside wall. For some strange reason after two years of being empty, the ice cream parlor out on the barrier island found new owners and it was up and running. A local diner previously selling bacon and eggs and hot roast beef and gravy sandwiches, put in a dipping well and ice cream case. And three local convenience stores added hand dipped ice cream to their list of ten million things. We couldn't decide whether the whole community just loved our idea, or they simply hated our guts.

Our first year in business was rather dreary. Our whole idea was to sell ice cream at a reasonable price, and hopefully do a big volume, because really, we were just about the only place in town ... Yeah right!

Our first year in business was a total loss. I had thoughts of writing a book about our experiences. I was going to call it *Living Out of the Tip Jar*. I never really got started though. It was too depressing.

That first year, we stayed open all winter long, and all I can say is that I felt like the Maytag repairman. It was a very lonely experience. Every sort of imaginable rumor had been spread about the small town concerning us. We were foreigners. We were rich Yankees, who had more money than brains. We bought rejected ice cream from the discount bins at the grocery store. We had old ice cream. Our ice cream had been frozen and refrozen so many times, it tasted like snow cones.

That first year we had our biggest bursts of business, after every heavy rain. Everybody came in wearing rubber boots. They all just knew our place would be flooded. How could it not be? Almost everyone in the community had a relative who used to live in this old house. "Have you had any trouble with the bears out there yet?" was a very common question.

I remember this one guy came walking in with his rubber boots and slicker suit during a real downpour. He never looked at the ice cream, or anything that we had for sale. He just kept looking at the floor and the ceiling.

"Can I help you, sir?"

"You poured a new floor in here, didn't you?"

"No sir."

"Oh come on. I didn't just fall off a turnip truck. This place used to have water in it up to your knees when it rained. You poured a new floor, didn't ya?"

"No sir."

People are still upset at that one. It seems that nobody locally would buy the building because of that very reason. It was "low". Whenever anybody asked me where Hobo's ice cream parlor was, after my explanation, their immediate response would be ... Oh yeah, that place is low ain't it? I've pretty much given up on an explanation. No matter what I say, everybody looks at me as if I'm lying. Many people still think that we walk around the place in rubber waders and slicker suits every time it rains.

Those people who said that we wouldn't make it selling just ice cream were right. Our idea about selling things cheap and doing volume was also right. I just never realized how much volume it really takes to do "volume".

A year or so after we originally opened, we added a whole line of sandwiches and snacks. And we looked for more and better things to sell every year.

I always loved books, as you have probably figured out by now. So I started selling secondhand books at Hobo's also. That was a lot of fun.

First of all, because I had books all over the walls, many people wanted to know if we were a library. Other people assumed that I had read all of the books. They would come up to me with a book entitled, "Gremlins from Star Group Seven" and want me to tell them what it was about.

But, in any case, any time my wife or any friends of mine were out and scrounging about, if they saw books they would buy them for me.

A lady came into the ice cream parlor one day. She was very talkative and somewhat eccentric. She told my wife that she had just purchased an older house in the area, and was having an "everything must go" estate sale. My wife and her sister went to the sale the next day. There were a bunch of old books for sale, so naturally they bought them. I priced them and put them all up on the shelf. That next week the woman who had the sale came in and started looking around. "Oh I just love old books," she said. Then she proceeded to buy just about every book we had gotten from her estate sale. Some folks just aren't paying attention.

It seems also that because you sell a particular book people think that whatever the book contains must be a part of your personal philosophy. For example, I have sold any number of books written by Rush Limbaugh. I really have never seen or heard the man speak. For the most part, I only read books that are a hundred years old or more or are about people who have been dead for a hundred years or more. I suppose if I live long enough, someday I will read a book written by Rush Limbaugh. But I bought this secondhand book entitled, *Rush Limbaugh is a Big Fat Stupid Jerk*. I thought that to be a catchy title. I bought it and put it up on the wall. One day this man came in; ordered a milk shake and started looking around. He saw the book in question and started talking out loud to the book on the wall.

"Oh you think so, buddy!" he screamed up to the book on the wall. "Well, Rush Limbaugh has more brains in his big toe than you have in your whole head. If anybody is a big fat stupid jerk, it is you. I don't even know you, buddy, but I know you must be an idiot. I know Rush Limbaugh, and he is one of the smartest most brilliant men in America today. So you can take your book my friend and shove it …"

By this time I had the man's milk shake ready. Needless to say, I didn't bring up the book or Rush Limbaugh.

We have also had problems with the name Hobo's.

In naming our ice cream parlor, I really wasn't trying to start a political controversy. Many people do not like hoboes, or the homeless people in America.

"If there is anybody homeless in this country, it is because they are too damn lazy to get a job. Why don't they get up off their lazy butts and open an ice cream parlor like you guys have done?"

"Oh please, please. We have all of the ice cream parlors that we need here in the county right now. What business are you in, sir?"

"I'm in the construction business."

"Well, how about if we have all of the homeless in America open up their own construction business?"

Then other people came in and before they even ordered, they started telling their life history.

"You know, there were times when me and the kids ate nothing but oat meal and turnip greens, but we always had a roof over our head, and I always had a job. And if I didn't have a job, I found one."

"Yes sir, and will that be one dip or two?"

This one guy came in and he was really angry. He came in with two other people, and he just stood there with his back to the wall and stared at me. All the while he mumbled, but I couldn't hear him. I waited on his friends and they all went into the back room and sat down. Finally the man erupts."

"Why that lyin' S.O.B. ain't never hopped a train in his darn life. He is no more hobo than my aunt Tillie."

I began to wonder, what was it with this hobo stuff? I dreaded to think what kind of people I would have attracted if I had named my place something truly controversial.

I have already decided, if Carol and I ever open a second business, I am not going to name it something controversial like Hobo's. Maybe I'll try Mom's or The Eat.

There you have it ladies and gentlemen; the story of how Carol and Dick hobo-ed around America. I hope it has lived up to all of my boasting. But if it hasn't, I would just like to remind you that this book does not come with a money back guarantee.

You know, this book is very long. Can you imagine if I had really accomplished something? God forbid that I had ever been a jet plane pilot or discovered a cure for bulimia. Did you ever read the life of Madame Cure? She never bothered to even write a small article about the whole thing.

Well, in any case, we sold Hobo's to a nice younger couple who are now in the process of reliving our experiences as aspiring entrepreneurs. As you can see, Carol and I are now in the book business. I don't know how this venture is going to turn out, but I know one thing, it has been an interesting adventure.

About the Author

Carol and I are presently living in the Florida Panhandle. I had in the past boasted to friends that we lived on a dirt road with a personal power pole in my front yard, and in a community without a single traffic light. Not too long ago, they paved the road out in front of my house and they put up a traffic light in Apalachicola. Progress and prosperity are on the way.

I continue to write more now out of habit and commitment than anything else. I am addicted.

Our Hobo-ing America lifestyle, I truly doubt, will be setting any trends for future generations. Yet the experience provided us with a most interesting life. Carol and I both hope you have enjoyed reading this book.

Made in the USA